Carol Shields

was born and raised in Chicago and has lived in Canada since 1957. She studied at Hanover College and the University of Ottawa. Author of seven novels, including *The Stone Diaries*, which was shortlisted for the 1993 Booker Prize and, most recently, *Larry's Party*, Carol Shields has also written three volumes of poetry and numerous short stories.

From the reviews of *The Republic of Love*:

'The strength of Carol Shields's exhilarating novel is that, for all her exuberant wit, she never retreats into irony . . . the novel is transformed by her poignantly precise insights into the characters and the kinds of lives that are possible in any late-twentieth-century city.'　　*Sunday Independent*

'Mythical and modern, ironic and moving, exhilarating and melancholy. A love-surveying love story that is enticingly seductive.'　　*Times Literary Supplement*

'Carol Shields's wit and sharpness keep the book lively throughout . . . there is a great deal to recognise, smile over and enjoy.'　　*New Statesman & Society*

'Shields depicts the anatomy of the human heart in a highly original and perceptive manner. This is a provocative and dangerous book. A love story which explores *all* the possibilities.'　　*Time Out*

'Shields is exceptionally intelligent, very funny and affirmative in a way far removed from the happy ever after.'　　*Financial Times*

CAROL SHIELDS

The Republic of Love

Flamingo
An Imprint of HarperCollinsPublishers

Flamingo
An Imprint of HarperCollins*Publishers,*
77–85 Fulham Palace Road,
Hammersmith, London W6 8JB

Published by Flamingo 1993
9 8 7 6

First published in Great Britain by
Fourth Estate Limited 1992

The Author asserts the moral right to
be identified as the author of this work

Author photograph by Gerry Kopelow

ISBN 0 00 654541 6

Set in Baskerville

Printed and bound in Great Britain by
Caledonian International Book Manufacturing Ltd, Glasgow

For Don

~CONTENTS~

Contents

Tom

As a baby, Tom Avery had twenty-seven mothers. So he says. That was almost forty years ago.

Ask me more, his eyes beg, ask me for details.

Well, then. At three weeks of age, there he was, this little stringy wailing thing, six and a half pounds of malleable flesh. His mother was sick, desperately sick, a kind of flu that worsened to pneumonia and then depression. In all, she was hospitalized for six months. Where was his father in all this? What father? Ha! That's another story.

A kindly social worker looked at scrawny, misshapen little Tom (rickets, one foot turning out sideways, not quite right) and said: "Leave him to me." The next day Tom was installed in the Department of Home Economics at the University of Manitoba. He was moved straight into McDougal Hall, the Home Ec's neo-Georgian practice house on the banks of the river, the wide Red, and put to sleep in a white enameled crib. Little Tom, the practice baby.

McDougal Hall was a kind of paradise, equipped with a streamlined (for its time) kitchen, built-in cupboards made of fruit-wood, a scalloped colonial cornice around the ceiling, concealed lighting, everything—even a row of clay pots on the windowsill holding geraniums, begonias, pointed spears of chives, and thyme. There was a tiled laundry room down in the basement with a mangle and a Bendix washer, and upstairs, occupying the broad landing, a linen closet with stacked sheets and pillow cases tied prettily with pink ribbons, and wonderful ironed kitchen towels that bespoke a vision of order that would first admonish and then inspire the inhabitants of this house, the fourth-year girls, twenty-seven of them, who took up residence here. A Dr. Elizabeth French, D.Sc. (1900–76), occupied the ground-floor suite. From here the daily household duties were organized, the names of those girls assigned to dusting, to silver polishing, to the turning and mending of sheets, to menu planning, soup making, table setting, flower arranging, floor waxing, spot removing—the thousand and one skills needed by young homemakers who came into being in those passionate, scented postwar years. Dr. French herself took shifts of girls out onto the second-floor balcony and demonstrated the correct method for shaking a dust mop. "We're not just here to play house, girls," she warned at the planning session that launched each new day. And there they would be, listening and nodding, the twenty-seven sweatered beauties (as Tom Avery will always imagine them) arranged like lovely statuettes in Dr. French's soft-colored sitting room, primly perched on the Duncan Phyfe sofa and side chairs or else sprawled, adorably, lusciously, on the gold-toned carpet with their full tartan skirts pulled down over rounded knees. Their gaze was tender—air and openness com-mingled—and their thoughtful chins rested on laced hands. And what hands! Some of those hands were already wearing diamond engagement rings. (These hands are now sixty years old; Tom has had occasion to meet a few of his old "mothers" around town, and he's seen, and even held, some of their hands affectionately in his own, and listened to remembrances of that charmed time.)

These were the pale pearly hands that dipped baby Tom into

his daily bath water. ("Always test the temperature with your elbow, girls.") The same hands that buttoned tiny Tom into his miniature shirts and nightgowns and tied his booties in place. ("But not too tight, girls, remember baby's circulation.") Fortunate, fortunate Tom Avery. Passed from hand to hand, rocked and tickled, fed, burped, coaxed, rewarded, exposed to the open air—if the weather was mild—and held up to the weak sunlight for five carefully regulated minutes. ("Vitamin D, girls, the sunshine vitamin.")

Sunlight and sterilized milk, strained cereal and vegetables and coddled eggs and mashed bananas and custard baked in little glass cups. Was baby wet? His diaper was checked hourly, the whitest, softest, most lovingly folded diaper imaginable. A line of these excellent flannelette diapers flapped in the clean air behind McDougal Hall, well away from the shaken dust mops, whipped by the wind and made incomparably fragrant. What went into baby was measured, and what came out as well. His miniature fingernails were trimmed, his weight recorded, his hand-eye skills observed, his small gassy noises noted. Whirled in the air, passed from lap to lap, kissed, oiled, powdered, wrapped tight, little Tom was never allowed to cry for more than a minute, never mind what Dr. French had to say about spoiling, about bad habits starting early.

The twenty-seven mothers pressed him close to their tender sweater fronts. They would have given him anything, their own breast milk had there been any to offer. With the softest of brushes they smoothed his half dozen silken hairs. Such love, such love— ah God, he'd never know love like that again. They praised his given name, Tommy, Tomikins, or else Wee Fellow or Mister Sweetmeat or Little Puff-Cheeks. They loved him just for being alive, for doing nothing to deserve their love. No wonder he thrived and babbled; his rounded boneless limbs flopped and contracted and grew strong—the cleanest, brightest, most polished, ventilated, and smiled upon infant west of the Red River, maybe in the whole world.

~ CHAPTER 1 ~

Breaking

It's Good Friday, a cold spring morning, and Fay McLeod, a woman of thirty-five, is lying in bed beside a man she no longer loves.

His name is Peter Knightly. "Happy Good Friday," he murmurs against her mussed hair, moving toward her under the blanket. He says this in his modified Midlands accent—which always sounds to Fay like someone doing an imitation of an Englishman—and at the same time he's working her thighs apart with his right hand. We can stay in bed, his right hand is saying, we can take our time, and then his thumb moves sideways, elaborately positioning itself.

Yesterday she loved him, but today she doesn't.

No, that's not quite true. She's known for a while. The knowledge has been working away at her, giving off its muted signals. For one thing, she finds that she looks in the mirror a lot lately, squinting, making rude faces, and some mornings she sits on the edge of her bed, hunched there for minutes at a time, shivering.

She has a longing to scrub herself down, cut off her hair, floss her teeth until her gums bleed, buy herself a lacy peach half-slip. She's caught herself calculating lately, with her breath drawn in sharply, the length of time she and Peter have been together: three years, one thousand days.

This morning she finds it hard to concentrate on Peter Knightly's thumb, what it's doing. Nevertheless, she registers his words— Good Friday. An official holiday. The folklore center where she and Peter both work is closed today, and somehow the next twelve hours will have to be filled.

She ponders this while Peter Knightly's thumb rotates back and forth—persistent, and very cunning, twiddling away. She's going to have to tell him, today, that it's over. Going on like this is making her sick. Her stomach, right this minute, is burning, and she knows it's not hunger or even pain, but some species of angry embarrassment. The worst of it is that all this—this predicament, this loss and damage—it's her own doing.

Now Peter's mouth has fixed itself on her left nipple, whispering and sliding, a suave licking. Oh, this is very familiar. He's learned after all this time how to please. Don't ever stop, she thinks, but knows he is about to travel over to her right nipple. Dutifully. Fairly.

Her hand comes to rest on his back, where she discovers an appalling patch of dry skin.

She tries to concentrate on the reverberations of Good Friday. The thoughts spill and roll. Does he know, she wonders, rocking him gently back and forth, that Good Friday has pagan roots? That it is the ultimate day of contradictions? Celebration mixed with gloom. Suffering with satiety. The dolorous and the delightful. Winter and spring. Cold and hot. Did he know, she silently pursues, that in certain quaint corners of England the entire population rolls a giant barrel of beer through the streets, and that this barrel has its origin in the bloodied heads of animal sacrifices?

She is a woman plagued with information, burdened with it, and always checking an impulse to pass it on to others. Is Peter Knightly, her lover of a thousand wasted days, aware that in certain

Slavic villages young men on Good Friday fashion squirt guns from reeds and spray each other with water, and that this, of course, has strong sexual implications?

What is he thinking about at this moment? Is he thinking about anything?

Does he realize the importance of Easter eggs? Could anything be more symbolically charged than an egg, a lustrous, fragile egg snatched from a hen house and piously engraved?

No, it's not just her stomach that hurts, it's her heart. It hurts for both of them, and for the passage of time. Shouldn't time add up to something?

"Well," Peter says to Fay—and his voice comes out in aggrieved gasps—"You seem a long way off this morning."

He pulls away, slides his arms from around her body, smoothing the blanket binding over her shoulder in a way that is faintly conciliatory. But his face, drained and hurt, gives him away. Why do you always have to spoil everything? his face says as he retreats to the bathroom.

IF FAY MCLEOD no longer loves Peter Knightly, there is still the question of whether she can live without him, live alone that is. She is thirty-five years old, after all, and should know something about compromise.

Toast, she says to herself, might be the test.

She is being whimsical, of course, which is one of the ways she protects herself, but she is partly serious too: can she bear to stand alone in her kitchen on a Saturday morning, or any morning, for that matter, and push down the lever of her ten-year-old General Electric black-and-chrome toaster and produce a single slice of breakfast toast? One only.

Other things she can do on her own. Traveling, for instance. Last summer, tracking down mermaid legends, she scoured half a dozen American libraries, California, Texas, Boston—three happy weeks, traveling light, one suitcase, three changes of clothes, two pairs of shoes, that was it. She relished the ease of arranging single-seat tickets and the sight every night of a neatly made-up hotel room, avoiding, if she could, those pompous doubles with their giant puffed duvets and bulging headboards. "A very small room, please," she said to a succession of hotel clerks, interchangeable behind their crisp summer haircuts and narrow shirt collars and eager looks, and they'd complied, beaming as though she'd bent forward over the desk and smoothed their faces with the flat of her hand. Occasionally, vacationing families with young children called out greetings, but mostly she sat alone by pool sides or in hotel dining rooms with a book open by her plate. People looked her way and smiled, pitying or else envious, she wasn't sure which, and it didn't matter. She finds the bewilderment of travel rousing. Next summer she'll be off again, Europe this time, her mermaids again, a second research grant, more generous than the first. She departs at the end of July and will be gone for four intense weeks. Most of the arrangements have already been made—and the thought that she will be on her own adds to, rather than subtracts from, her anticipation.

The solitude of living alone *does* worry her, a grim little visitation of concern—mostly in the late afternoons, when the day feels vacuumed out, but she's not at the point of paralysis, not yet. She's capable, for instance, of going for a walk alone. The street she lives on, Grosvenor Avenue, is old, lined with trees and with Victorian houses, now mostly converted to rental apartments, or to condominiums, like the one she shares with Peter Knightly. The snow is almost gone, the sidewalks more or less clear of ice, and she likes on Saturday afternoons to put on a pair of jeans and her suede jacket and strike off, saying to herself: I, Fay McLeod, have every right to breathe this air, to take possession of this stretch of pavement. (Occasionally during these walks, the word "single" presents itself. She makes herself sigh it out, trying hard to keep her mouth from puckering—single, singleness, singlehood, herself engaged in a single-ish stroll.) Blasts of wind smooth the sky to a glossy blue-rose, and the sun sits weak and yellow. She can set her own pace, that is her right after all, and fill up her lungs with the chilly air, stop if she likes at the Mozart Cafe for a cup of coffee, come home when she chooses. Along the way she smiles and nods at elderly couples or joggers or women dragging shopping bags, and each time this happens she feels her ties to the world yank and hold firm.

Sleeping alone is harder than going for a walk alone, oh yes, she admits it, but she's learned a few tricks of accommodation. And sex these days is everywhere, abundantly, dismayingly available.

As for the future, there will be other men. Or at least there *probably* will be others. This is one of the hopeful thoughts Fay has about herself. Before Peter Knightly, she lived for three years with a man called Nelo Merino, an investment consultant who was later transferred to Ottawa; she still feels swamped at times by her lost love for Nelo, who is married now, she's been told, and the father of three children. Before Nelo it was Willy Gifford (two years), who produced business training films and was a philosopher of sorts, a Cartesian he liked to call himself, whom she might have married if his political views had been less rigidly anchored and less tiresomely voiced. Between Willy and Nelo, and again between Nelo and Peter, there had been short periods of living on her own, and she honestly can't remember these intervals as being lonely. She has her job at the National Center for Folklore Studies, her friends, her family (mother, father, brother, sister, all of them living close by), her summer trips, and her book on mermaids that she hopes to finish sometime in the next year. She's always busy, too busy, and is always reminding herself of this fact, so that the notion of an empty apartment, even an empty bed, holds no more than a faint flush of alarm. And only when she thinks about it— those late afternoons when her blood sugar dips and the overhead lights in her office go on. She'll manage, though. She knows she will.

It comes down, then, to just one brief moment, which is interwoven in her morning routine and located in that most familiar of rooms, the kitchen. Peter Knightly, with whom she has lived for three years now, will be making coffee, stooping in the manner of tall men and registering on his long face the kind of seriousness she finds silly but endearing. A temporary hood of domesticity and sexual ease hovers over them, sending down its safe blue even heat. He grinds his special French-roast beans and measures out water, and she, standing with her back to him, is making toast, dropping the seven-grain bread into twin slots, pushing the lever down and eliciting a satisfying double click as it first strikes the bottom of its long silvery groove and then locks into place. The heat rises gradually to her face. Her image bends on the satiny chrome—a woman performing a simple but necessary task—and inside the mechanism, down there where she can't see, separate molecules of bread are transcending their paleness and drifting toward gold. She imagines a pair of scented clouds, rectangular and contained, rising up and mingling with the coffee odors. The toastness of toast, its primary grainy essence. Peter is pulling cups from a cupboard, smooth white porcelain objects out of a cartoon, and heating a little jug of milk in the microwave.

Then the toast pops. It always takes her by surprise, those two identical slices bounding upward, perfectly browned and symbolically (it seems to her) aligned, and bringing every single morning a shock of happiness.

FAY IS GREGARIOUS by nature. She's even wondered from time to time—and idly worried—about being perhaps overly sociable, too dependent on the response of others and incapable of sustaining any kind of interior life for more than a few seconds at a time. Who is she anyway but a jumble of other people's impressions? A receptor of external stimulation. A blank lake.

It's a vaguely frightening thought.

People ought to be able to appreciate a sunset, or a waterfall, or a flower, as a solitary experience; she's heard people say so a thousand times and believes it, but doubts she could pass the test. She likes sunsets but doesn't know what to do with them, doesn't distinguish much between one sunset and the next, and isn't chased by them into flights of private reverence or extrapolated awe. She'd never dream of sitting down and writing a sunset poem, for instance. What would she say? Crimson hues, orange bands. Blah, blah, blah.

When pushing up against the world, she needs companionship, someone by her side. Is it because she's the daughter of sociable parents? she wonders. She has a lot of strong curiosity about people, and often she's been praised for her ability to draw out individuals and set them at ease. People relax in her presence, grow expansive. Hannah Webb, who heads the folklore center, frequently asks her to show visitors around. She appreciates, she really does, how time can be telescoped, an hour reduced to minutes when in the presence of agreeable company. The addition of another person can lighten the most routine work and make ordinary experiences luminous—just going to a restaurant or a movie or even on a walk. When she reads about political prisoners locked up for years in solitary confinement, she marvels that they manage to hang on to their sanity. She knows she'd never survive.

Yet here she is, about to make a great change in her life, a change that frightens her with the spectre of loneliness. It's Sunday morning, and she and Peter are in their small blue Honda on their way to Fay's parents for Easter lunch. It is 12:45 by the car clock, which has yet to be reset on daylight-saving time. They are driving down a bare sunny boulevard and quarreling over the nature of time.

"It's gone," Fay is saying. "One hour just wiped out. It's like when they do those bowel operations, cut out the tumorous parts and rejoin the sections and try to fool the intestine into not noticing."

"Not really," Peter says in his adult-education voice. "The daylight-saving hour is just an illusion. It never was an hour. Nothing gets thrown away. You have to think of time as a device. An arbitrary invention, that's all. You always go and personalize things, Fay. Why are we talking about this anyway?"

"It feels like robbery, losing the hour at night when we're all asleep, that's what offends me."

"Christ. You're being whimsical again."

"You're nervous," she charges, but keeps her voice small.

"You're right." He says this acerbically, which reassures Fay.

"Just think," she says, "what you could do with that hour if you had it back." But she's having trouble keeping this going.

"What?" The edge on his voice dissolving.

"You could"—she stops to think—"you could make a sandwich. A fried-egg sandwich. With plenty of mayo and salt."

"I've never seen you eat a fried-egg sandwich, Fay. Never."

"Or you could stay in bed, then, and have an extra dream or two. A good classic REM dream, getting on the bus in just your underwear. Or finding a new room in the apartment, a whole room where you thought the closet was."

"You know what that one means."

"What?"

"That things are out of control."

"Oh."

"Look, Fay, about your parents. Do we tell them today or leave it?"

"It's Easter. Let's leave it."

"Why not get it over with?"

"The whole family'll be there, everyone. Bibbi's even coming."

"This week then. Promise me you'll phone your mother tomorrow. And I think you owe me one thing, Fay."

"What?"

"That you tell them this is your decision, not mine. You're the one that wants out."

"It's not a decision exactly."

"Then what in God's name do you call it?" His eyes are directed straight ahead, fixed on the light Sunday traffic.

"You make it sound as though all of a sudden I just clenched up my brain and decided."

"Well?"

"You said yourself you felt things were coming to an end."

"I didn't say that exactly."

"Something like that."

"Anyway, let's not drag it out. I'll see about getting a place tomorrow, a room or something. And then we'll have to think about what to do with the car."

"And the apartment."

"Right."

Fay looks sideways at Peter, who is glancing up at the telephone wires, his forehead going into lines, too. She wonders what he's thinking. What have their three years together meant, anyway? One thousand days and nights, about to be swallowed up—like last night's hypothetical hour, that lovely light-spirited hour that never was and never will be.

"OH, GOOD HEAVENS," Fay's mother said on the telephone. Chipper, breathless. But disappointed.

She was a doctor, a gynecologist with an office in a shopping mall in south Winnipeg, but Mondays she always spent domestically at home, doing the washing, tidying up after the weekend. "Well, of course I'm surprised. Daddy and I just naturally thought, well, we knew you weren't frantic for a traditional wedding and all that, but we did think when you and Peter decided to buy a condo, and that was only a year ago, a year and a half, then, that that represented something, a commitment more or less, which was how you put it at the time, remember?—something like that, anyway. I know people think of these things differently now, Fay, but do you realize that condo of yours cost more than this house, this big house? Well, that's neither here nor there. All I'm saying is that we didn't think you and Peter were just making an investment, we thought you were, well—settling down. People do settle down. They do. They don't keep moving and changing partners forever, they make commitments, not that we'd ever want you to commit yourself to somebody you weren't sure of, but you and Peter seem so, well, larky together. Sometimes things cool down between a couple, goodness, I know that, but it comes back, almost always it comes back, as long as there aren't any real irreconcilable differences. You have to anticipate certain times when things seem, well, flat. I mean, if that's all it is. But you and Peter, I always thought you two just—yesterday, when he was putting whipped cream on your pie, the way he was, you know, teasing you? And, well. We just thought that eventually you'd get the urge to start a family, you're both so crazy about kids, and you've no idea how different it is with kids of your own, you love them ten times more than you love other people's. It takes people by surprise how much love they have stored up. Young mothers are always telling me that, how they actually fall in love with their babies. Fall in love, that's how they phrase it, and I don't doubt it for a minute. I know I did, and oh, I guess I just hate you to miss out on all that, even though I know, I really do, that you have a full life. In many ways. Doing what you want, just picking up and going when the spirit moves you, but there's something to be said for having a center, for belonging to someone, your own family, not just one person living for himself or herself. Darn it all, sweetheart, I find it hard to express, but I just hope, Daddy and I hope you know what you're doing, that's all."

A FEW YEARS AGO a man called Morris Kroger gave Fay a small Inuit carving, a mermaid figure, fattish and cheerful, lying on her side propped up by her own thick muscled elbow. It is made of highly polished gray soapstone, and its rather stunted tail curls upward in an insolent flick. It weighs about half a pound and, when picked up, nicely fills a human hand. Fay keeps it on her long oak coffee table next to a stack of magazines and a flowering cactus.

Fay met Morris Kroger at a wine-and-cheese party that preceded a ballet opening. He bumped up against her, then introduced himself. A clumsy man, yet here he was at the ballet.

It was summer. They spent a week together in a tent near Clear Lake. (This was after Nelo and before Peter.) They both suffered from mosquitoes, which were especially bad that year, and Fay, with mosquito repellent in her hair and ears and all the joints of her body, felt sure at first that it was this that rendered Morris impotent. Night after night he struggled with himself on the ridged slippery air mattress. His hoarse breathing frightened her, and on their last night together he gave way to a spasm of choked sobs. Something about his parents, something psychological and hopeless had spoiled his manhood. The next day they drove back to Winnipeg in silence, four hours on the burning highway, and two weeks later he mailed her the stone mermaid. Fay remembers opening the box slowly, as though it might contain a bomb or something equally dangerous, but it was only this carved female likeness with her taunting abbreviated tail.

Impenetrable. The word rose up and socked her in the throat with its unsheathed subtlety. An accusation.

But no, she was being paranoid, it was just a present.

She found out later, much later, that the carving had been made in Cape Dorset not long after the Hollywood film *Splash!* had been shown there at the Community Hall, and this irony greatly expanded her love for it.

Its smile makes it rare. She has discovered only one other smiling mermaid, a tiny figure bobbing about in a fourteenth-century German fresco. She hopes to see it this summer when she goes to Augsburg, and photograph it for her book.

Morris Kroger is gone, having sold the family business and moved to Florida. Someone told Fay he had retired. At his age! Fay thinks of him maybe once a year. Usually when the mosquitoes come out. For about five minutes.

PETER KNIGHTLY'S FACE as it leans over his sock drawer is too elongated and bewildered for love, and also sulky, lip-drooping, not a face to live with forever. She pities him, a man of thirty-seven years, hesitating like this between black and brown. He gazes at the neat little sock balls, then stirs them with a long teacherly finger. That same finger has stirred me, thinks Fay, who is still in bed, her head turned on the pillow and her eyes wide open, mournfully watching.

In the last few days a mild dislike for him has fallen over her. The whole of his body seems a pale, elongated gland, colorless and cold and stiff with hairs. It distresses her to open her closet and see his jackets and sweaters, most of them gone nubby at the elbows, rubbing up against the smoothness of her blouses. Watching him, she feels her thoughts darken. And every time she opens her mouth, it seems, she injures his puffball innocence; she's tried, often, to locate the exact point where this weakness of his is centered—that nick, maybe, at the edge of his tucked Englishy mouth. Or the ruffled tips of his thick beige hair, like feathers, blunt and soft at the same time. Oh, why does he keep tempting her, offering up his sponge of a heart and inviting her to take a punch? She's figured it out; at last she knows. So he can blame her, so she can be sorry, so he can sulk, so she can feel guilty. This has been going on for three years now. He will say something ordinary and neutral, and the next minute she's unsnapped one of his nursery certitudes. Would she do this if she loved him? She doesn't think so.

She knows the old cliché: To fall in love is to fall out of love. Maybe that's all that's happened, something as simple and blameless as that.

LOVE IS SELFISH. Love is dangerous, impractical, wasteful. Loving, we put a pistol to our heads. It burns, it makes us into fools, always it keeps us waiting. It sickens, it makes us sick, it's the start of a serious illness, it's illness itself.

But Fay's parents are something else. They live in that big old house over on Ash Avenue and at night they read to each other in bed. Richard McLeod reads Peggy McLeod long magazine pieces about the asbestos industry, and Peggy McLeod reads Richard McLeod chunks of novels, descriptive passages out of P. D. James about Oxford or London or the Devon coast. They share a yearning for jokes and subtle proofs and oddities of language, and every single Wednesday night they sit down with their good friends John and Muriel Brewmaster, who have been married even longer than they have—for forty-three years—and the four of them play bridge. After the Brewmasters go home they discuss their hands, their good or bad luck, it doesn't matter which. They give each other gifts, admittedly only at Christmas and for birthdays, and they have a pact that these gifts must not attach in any way to the house. For example, no microwave ovens, no table saws, nothing like that. They may give articles of clothing made of knitted wool or silk. Or perfume, luggage, wrist watches, little luxuries, tickets to New York, maybe. They love to go to New York and see the latest plays and musicals. For anniversaries—they've been married thirty-nine years, forty next fall—they do not exchange gifts. They are each other's gift. Fay's mother actually said this once. Out loud. Each other's gift.

~ CHAPTER 2 ~

Beginning

FOR A MAN NURTURED BY TWENTY-SEVEN MOTHERS, TOM AVERY suf-
fers from surprising insecurities. At thirty-nine, almost forty, he
is mildly, obscurely fearful of: young children, stinging insects,
German shepherds, acupuncture, income-tax forms, street evan-
gelists, public telephones, cottage cheese, and old age.

He is acutely, palpably afraid of Friday nights, what to do with
them, those gaping, sneering, and stubbornly recurring widths of
time—how to accommodate them, fill them, use them, annihilate
them. He'd do anything to sidestep a Friday night. Friday nights
demand conviviality and expenditure. It's the time to let loose
(yeah, sure).

Well, not tonight. Tonight he sits alone in his apartment on
Grosvenor Avenue and drinks beer and reads the newspaper and
thinks dark, unkind thoughts about his life. By eleven he is in bed,
sound asleep, another Friday night erased.

WHY DO WE SEEK so strenuously, so publicly, to purify ourselves?

This is what Tom thinks as he goes for his weekly eight-kilometer run down Wellington Crescent. That crosswise slab of belly fat he's got—a disgrace. A faint hangover, too, poisonous fumes bubbling up from his intestines and pressing his lungs flat. Heated gas ripping upward and downward, shaming him, making him glad he's thumping along on his own steam. His kidneys he pictures as hard little lozenges, jelly beans in thin casings of sugar. Now that's a pretty picture.

It's Saturday morning, the last Saturday before he turns forty. On and on he tramps, past what used to be the Richardson mansion, triplexed now with a series of winking solariums shelving off at the back. Past a darkly stuccoed building with a military insignia over its door, past a stand of leafless shrubs, past the synagogue in which gatherings of men are even now praying.

It's a cold day. Damp through and through. Spring dampness. Now he's coming up toward the bridge. Dancing up and down at the curb, keeping time while he waits for a break in the traffic at Academy Road; traffic, it never lets up. It's a chance, though, to catch his breath.

He's been jogging for two years now, ever since his divorce papers came through. Ask him about it—he'll be glad to tell you. It's one of the stories he likes to pull out. Well, the papers came through, you see. It was on a Saturday morning. They were sent over by courier, Pink Lady, delivered and signed, heavy legal sheets in a strong taped envelope. Here you are, sir. A ceremonial present to start your day.

Light rejoicing seemed called for, but what? Food, drink, sex; nothing appealed, and to tell the truth, nothing was readily available. He had just moved into this rinky-dink—his mother's word—apartment on Grosvenor, no furniture, not a stick, just a shower, taps and nozzle, not even a plastic shower curtain to pull around him in the morning. The arrival of his divorce papers made him want to give himself up to the air, to get scraped down, pressed flat like an aerodynamic object. Running was all he could think of. In a cardboard carton in the corner of the living room he had the equipment, the hundred-buck shoes and the blue-and-white sweats, bought for him by Suzanne—that's the ironic bit, the kicker—their last Christmas together, and never worn. Well, he hadn't been ready then. Now he was.

That's how the Saturday-morning runs got launched.

He hates every minute of it. He stamps along saying words like "fuck," "shit," "fart," "cunt," all the sputtered grotesques of the language, and it does help, it gives him strength. It's April now, one week after Easter, and still pretty nippy. What a climate; why does he stay here? God and Jesus only know. Grit blows straight into his face, in his eyes and mouth and up his nose. A walloping old guy passes him, bald, huffing away, but with a not-bad speed on him—Christ!

Now, finally, he's got a decent pace going. Breathe in, then out, count your breaths, it makes the time turn over. And think of your feet rounding on the pavement, the heel first, bending, rolling up to the toes, keep that image in your mind.

He's grinning now, like a guy in a beer commercial. Grin, grin, grin. Transparency, bottom of the barrel. Then he's a gorilla, chump, chump, chump, arms loose and swinging. Screw that. Now he's part of a Camus fable, a lost soul, loveless. That look in his eyes, that existential light, bores right through you. Think of hot coffee, think of having it over for another week.

Now he's in the park. Just five more minutes and he can turn around and head back. What is this for, why does he care about his belly fat anyway? He's going to be forty years old in three days. Whoa there, what about that? The universe is about to shrink around him. God help him. It shames him how little he's discovered during his time in the world. This isn't where he meant to be at forty, not at all, running down a gritty sidewalk on a cold windy day with his chest burning and his rear end bouncing.

Running out the park gates now, back down Wellington Crescent, those big dopey houses, it costs a fortune to heat those houses, past the synagogue again, past the spiky hedges, past the new condos, Christ, a wall of condos, you can hardly see the river anymore, they just keep heaving them up, one after the other.

Hang a right at Grosvenor, home again, the brick building, dirty shrubbery, no leaves, no buds even, no elevator either, tiled steps streaked with wet, three small rooms on the third floor, and no one waiting for him.

TOM'S EX-WIFE, SUZANNE, recently got married again, and this marriage has released their friends from the agony of divided loyalty. Since the wedding, February 19, invitations have favored Tom, who isn't sure just why, whether old Suze has slipped sideways or upward or down on the social scale, or whether his own solitude is more clearly underlined now that she's so visibly coupled. Recoupled, that is.

Her new husband is a divorced man in his unalarming mid-fifties, and rich. His name is Gregor Heilbrun; this name strikes Tom as being phony, either too abbreviated or too ornate, too something, anyhow. Gregor's got wide, wide shoulders and soft hips and dark blue suit jackets that settle shyly around those hips of his, and he walks with a waggle. A waggle is not the same as a swagger, far from it. Tom, who was invited to attend the small wedding ceremony at Knox Church over on Broadway, a Saturday-afternoon quickie between two other full-scale weddings, had observed the waggling Heilbrun hips with triumph. And noted, too, the way Gregor's thin uncolored hair fell crudely around his ears. Some men couldn't take a haircut. Some men couldn't carry off a blue suit, no matter what it cost. Gregor teaches economics at the University of Winnipeg and has written a book on Marxist theory and the contemporary marketplace, proving that the two things are one and the same, but his driving-around money comes from the family fur business and from gambling. People say he's lucky, just two trips a year to Vegas and he comes back with his pockets full.

It used to be that Tom's old friends invited him to Saturday-night dinner parties, but lately the invitations tend to come along for Sundays, when he's fitted into family brunches, lunches, picnics, or whatever. He doesn't complain about this, but he notices. Oh boy, he notices. The other thing he's observed is that he's started buying bigger boxes of candy for his hosts and more expensive bottles of wine. He's moved up a notch in the gift department, he's not sure just when it happened. He can afford it, and again, he's not complaining, but it's as though he's now obliged to pay his way, to buy his way, even, and he tries not to think about the implications of propitiating chocolate or exotic wine. Furthermore, accepting his friends' invitations, he knows more or less what he's letting himself in for: the forlorn clutter and noise of other people's marriages, afternoons of making himself agreeable, scratching their dogs behind the ears, or a project in the yard, maybe, and almost certainly one or two dribbling babies dropped on his lap. He would like to give his heart to his friends' children, to be the sort of uncle-type guy they want their kids to have, but he can't. In fact, he can't imagine how his friends put up with the whining and the diaper smells and the out-and-out mess of it all.

Today he's on his way to the Chandlers for one of their traditional waffle lunches. One o'clock, Harvard Avenue, an easy walk, ten minutes at the most from his place on Grosvenor. Already he imagines the maple syrup running on the tablecloth, a narrow river of it, and then spreading into a lake, and then young Chrissie's fat bratty fingers poking in it, and Liz doing nothing, absolutely nothing, not jumping up for a wet cloth, but just sitting there and smiling, or maybe pressing a paper napkin down on top of it all. Gene, at the head of the table, presiding at the waffle iron, will glow with happiness. A splat of batter will decorate his shirt front. It draws attention.

Unworthy this.

Well, Tom decides early Sunday morning, he'll take them tulips. It's spring, he says, looking around. In fact, it really is a few degrees warmer today. A sweet haze hangs over the streets, and the hedges in front of his building are starting to go pea green. The caragana, they're always first. All this seems to have happened overnight.

The Safeway on the corner opens at noon on Sunday, and he'll be able to nip over there and pick up a dozen or so tulips for under ten bucks. He always buys flowers at Safeway now. (The florists downtown, they rob you blind, he's stopped going there altogether.) Even the flowers he sent Suzanne and Gregor the day they were married came out of a plastic pail at Safeway's checkout. El Cheapo, Suzanne would have said if she'd known where they'd come from, and probably she did know. He'd wrapped them loosely in paper and dropped them off early in the morning with a brief note saying: "All the best."

You sent your ex-wife flowers! he said to himself in the mirror the morning after the wedding. I don't believe it. He was shaving, paying particular attention to the tricky bit in the middle of the chin. The soap lather smelled soothing, like cantaloupe. "Is that appropriate behavior?" he said out loud. "Hey, you'd better get yourself together, you weirdo, you dumb ox, you creep."

FROM MIDNIGHT TO 4:00 a.m. Uncle Tom Avery brightens the night. Middle-class insomniacs in this city hang in with Uncle Tom, tuning in every night, and a surprising number of them call in requests. He knows what they're after. They want their edges knocked off, they want to get some sleep so they can get up in the morning and get on with their dangerous daylight hours. They're into the kind of music you pour straight from the bone marrow. Nostalgia's all the hell they care about, all they're up to. And a dose of Uncle Tom's chitchat in between, keeping it intimate, throwing in the odd chunk of fortune-cookie mysticism. Hey, you out there. Just you and me and the night, eh? Cutting the glaze of memory with an earful of Mel Tormé, folks. Mel Tormé, are you nuts, wha'd'ya take me for? Well, just a quick snort, guys and gals, a fast fix. The Velvet Fog, they used to call him. Cobweb throat. Very, very heavy back then. Still is. You mean to tell me this guy's still walking around living and breathing? Jesus Christ. Hey, hey, we're on the air. Have we got another caller there? Drunk, belligerent. Swiss-army mouth. Not him again. Insists the Velvet Fog is actually the one and only Vaughn Monroe, yeah, "Dance Ballerina Dance" and all that great stuff. You got any Vaughn Monroe? Hey, you're too young, I betcha. You gotta go back to the real mellow years, late fifties, hell, early fifties, after that everything went down the toilet, you know? Get this guy off the air, quick. The Beatles did it, did us in, they changed everything and not for the best, believe you me. They killed music, killed it dead—

Once Suzanne called in. This was when they were still married but toward the end. She didn't say who she was, but of course he knew right away. Sinatra, she said. "The Lady Is a Tramp," that one.

His scalp went tight. He felt crowded, breathless, but he managed to hold up his finger, giving Ted Woloschuk the signal to put the music on quick, and then he let Old Bag Eyes take over.

Listening to the wet-ribbony phrases slipping out on top of that absolutely solid orchestration, he marveled at the distance between them, between him and Suzanne. She'd be sitting up late, two miles away across town, the other side of the river, their place on Assiniboine Avenue, probably in her shorty nightgown, sitting on the bed with a cup of tea balanced on the sheet, orange spice, filled to the brim, about to tip over or threatening to—she wouldn't let it, though, she was too careful for messy stuff like that to happen. She had the fat plushy unmuscled love of a stuffed animal. In their four years they'd never once got close to an act of sympathy more worthy, more humanly binding, than the discussion they'd had about that bed, how she never seemed to get away from it, sitting upright on the sheets painting her toenails with Ice Glow or sprawled on her stomach reading magazines or sleeping late, then bringing plates of toast back to the warm creased bedding, burrowing down. The bed made her go lazy, she said, she didn't know why. The two of them exhausted themselves on that bed, giving it too much of their energy, lying there in the morning until the sun was high and everything seemed suddenly too much trouble, even talking. Well, that was the problem right there.

It got to the point where he was on edge all the time. He was like a coconut tree ready to be shaken. Ask me, he wanted to say to her when he got home that night. Ask me what I'm thinking, what I want, what I'm made of, why I've gone so sick and slack. Invade me, suck me dry. But don't call up the station where I work, where I earn my living, for the first time in four years and say you want to hear Frank Sinatra. Ask me something, for God's sake. Ask me anything.

In Tom Avery's refrigerator are a carton of orange juice, six bottles of beer resting on their sides, and one cracked egg stuck by a skin of burst yolk to the plastic egg tray. In a cupboard he's got a box of raisin bran but no milk to pour over it. He's got a pound of coffee in a sack but no coffee pot. He's got some glasses on a shelf, but he's become the kind of man who drinks juice straight from the container and cereal out of his hand. That's breakfast. Breakfast can be in the middle of the night or the middle of the afternoon, it all depends. Lunch and dinner he eats out, burgers, steaks. All these habits are relatively new. He hasn't even admitted to them yet. In fact, he's planning to get himself organized soon and cultivate a better set of habits. All he needs is a theory to set things in motion. He's going to start working on that.

Tom works at the radio station down on Pembina Highway every night except Fridays and Saturdays, just him and Ted Woloschuk, the technician, holding down the fort. On Friday night Lenny Dexter takes over the show. (His real name is Offenshaur, but Big Bruce, CHOL's president, says a name like Offenshaur wouldn't ripple right on the air waves.) Friday night is a western version of Tom's "Niteline," mostly blather about Hank Williams, what a great and innovative and creative and terrific genius Hank Williams really was and what a lousy deal the guy got in his short career. Friday nights get a pretty good audience, better than on week-nights, but Tom's just as glad he doesn't have to do it. Country music makes him feel ashamed of himself for some reason, the way it drags on the primal tear ducts. And then on Saturday night "Niteline" gives way to sports—hockey, football; scores and recaps all night long, with a little pop in between.

That leaves Tom Sunday, Monday, Tuesday, Wednesday, and Thursday; midnight to 4:00 a.m. Twenty hours a week, but he's paid for forty, and pretty well paid, too. He gets fan mail as well as call-ins. This week, for his fortieth birthday, he received over a hundred and sixty cards, mostly from strangers. A lot of people in this town know who Tom Avery is, and in a sense he's a sort of local celebrity, having been profiled three times in the papers. "What do you personally get out of this, Mr. Avery?" he's been asked.

It's a living, he tosses off. Really? Yeah, really. He's a night person. Hey, he feels good when he's communicating. He feels in touch with, well, with a certain segment of the population, the night segment. Not just nutsy insomniacs, hell no. All kinds of people come awake at night. The highly intelligent, the cranks, the rednecks, the lovers. Eccentrics. The unemployed. People who feel life's kicked them in the teeth. And the kickers—they're out there, too. The lazy. The hip. The drinkers. People who worry. People who don't. Old people who don't need their sleep anymore, that's a medical fact. The actively ill. The passively violent. The trapped, the unlucky, the unclaimed, the lonely. They're all graduates of Mea Culpa College. Really, they're just plain people out there, and there're a helluva lot of them. And they're real folks, Tom Avery says, every last one of us.

~ CHAPTER 3 ~

Put That on My Tombstone

"LET ME THROW YOU THIS ANALOGY," PETER KNIGHTLY WAS ALWAYS saying to Fay in a voice that went roomy and reasonable and deep in its reaches. Or "Let me try this on you," or "Let me emphasize this point."

This was his pedagogical tone, which he seemed unable to suppress. At the folklore center where he and Fay work, his official title is Co-ordinator of Education, and he's a man who's perceived generally as being good at his job, erudite but easy, a nonsmoker with a pipe lover's insouciant, reasonable air of capability, a man who likes going at questions sideways—slyly, it seems to Fay, who can't get over the way Peter's boyhood is always pushing up to the surface of his lips and eyes and urging him toward detachment. He grew up in postwar England, on the outskirts of Sheffield, the son of schoolteachers, and Fay supposes that someone or other in that suburban English house was always sitting him down and saying with softly focused sincerity, "Why don't we re-examine this issue, why don't we approach this problem from a fresh angle?"

"We should at least," he said to Fay on a Friday night in the middle of April—he hadn't yet moved out—"try to put our finger on what went wrong."

"Finger?" said Fay. The word brought a breath of disgust, and so did Peter's manner, the way it worryingly seemed to concede to her certain reserves of glacial ice and feigned boredom. Her voice rose. "Our finger!"

"Christ, what now?"

"When I think of fingers," she said after a minute, modulating carefully, "I think of the finger of blame." She set down her pencil, flat on the coffee table, put her hand on it so it wouldn't roll off, and imagined how she would replay this conversation in her head during the months ahead, shaming herself with her deliberate insensitivity. "I see a large green finger coming down from heaven. Poking out of the clouds. Bits of lightning coming off it."

"That's not what I mean, and you know it. I merely suggested that we try to sort out our feelings."

"Feelings?"

"You don't like that word, either. Fingers. Feelings."

"I just think people should spend more time feeling their feelings and less time talking about them."

"You sound like your father, saying that. Exactly. His intonation, and his substance, too."

That made her smile. Somewhat to her surprise he smiled back, and she was glad to see him turn genial. "My father, yes," she said to prolong the moment.

"It's uncanny," he observed, and reached across to pick up the pencil. "This familial distrust of feeling. The idea that feeling is junk. The soul's junk."

She could think of nothing to say. In an hour they were expected downtown at a restaurant called Act Two, dinner with old friends, Mac and Iris Jaffe, who, she supposed, would have to be told, and soon, that she and Peter were about to separate. Separate. The icy release of that word. About to go their separate ways. She felt suddenly lazy and unaccountably happy, as though she were hovering at the center of contentment, halfway between weight and weightlessness. Peter went on. "We're going to see each other every day. We should at least work out a strategy as to how we're going to handle it."

"Oh, Peter." She was careful to keep her gaze mild. "You know perfectly well what we'll do. We'll smile and nod and be polite and decent. We don't have to discuss how we're going to behave at work. Why don't we just concentrate on getting through this list?"

There was a pause, then, "Where were we?" from Peter.

She consulted the pad of paper on her lap. "CDs, Pachelbel."

"Christ."

"What now?" She said this as nicely as she could.

"This is demeaning. It's bruising—like a bloody divorce. Fritzi and I went through the same quaint theater piece. Only it wasn't compact discs. It was 45s."

"Oh." An arrow of sadness passed quickly through her. Her head ached. Even her eyelashes ached. "The air in here," she said, shaking her head. "Let's open a window."

He ignored her. "Exactly like a divorce," he said.

Then she felt herself revive. "And did you and Fritzi put your 'finger' on what went wrong?"

"You won't let it go, will you?"

She stared at him over the clutter and detected in his face a betraying trace of satisfaction. "I guess I'm tired. And hungry. And you're right, this is demeaning, splitting up objects, as if we really cared. Do we care? Why don't we call it quits for now? Before we start getting mean and shrewd."

"I'm pretty tired too, but in half an hour we could have all this sorted out. . . ."

"Okay, okay, okay." She liked his rudeness. It told her that she hadn't knocked his courage out. He could still come at her.

"Jesus, you're touchy," he accused her.

"I know."

FAY'S FATHER, who owns a chain of dry-cleaning stores ("McLeod—Soft Garments in 24 hours"), does not go at things sideways. He's famous, at least within his immediate family, for his frontal attacks.

"I'd be interested to hear," he said to Fay, "why exactly he's still there. I mean, here you are, you've declared an end to things, a separation, and he's still living with you. You're still in the same apartment. You're still—" He stopped himself.

"Still in the same bed," Fay supplied. "Well, it's true. What can I say?"

She and her father frequently meet for breakfast on Saturday mornings. At one time Fay saw these breakfasts as a chance to pull herself together, and she believed that her father, with his measured questioning and patient, listening face, would help her put her thoughts, and her routines, in order. She longs to tell him everything, but neither of them could bear it. They favor a place on Osborne Street, Mr. Donut's, where they generally pass up the donuts and order a pair of apple-bran muffins and large coffees.

"Well," she said to her father, "I have to admit it's taking longer than we thought it was going to."

"Why is that?" her father asked. Frontal, yes, but his voice traveled quietly.

"I don't know. We seem to have such a lot of stuff to sort out. I mean, just three years together, it's amazing, and we own all these things."

"I see," he said, and then a minute later, "Like what, for instance?"

"Well, we have all these spatulas."

His eyes widened; she loved that, his simplicity about domestic details. "How many?" he asked her.

"Three."

"Three." As though he weren't sure that were too many or too few.

"We also have the Joe Fafard print you and Mother gave us last Christmas."

"Ah."

"I'm keeping that."

"Good."

"The way you say that!"

"How?"

"Well, that was pretty emphatic. The way you just said 'good' like that."

"Was it? I didn't think I was being emphatic. Not at all. I'm trying, in case you didn't realize it, to be unemphatic. Neutral."

"I know."

"Ah. Well, then."

"Just tell me one thing." She made an effort to control her breathing. "Do you think I'm doing the right thing?"

"What kind of question is that?" He set an eave of muffin afloat in his coffee, then captured it on a plastic spoon. "I just told you I was intending to stay on the sidelines."

"Like an umpire, you mean?"

"Like a guy in the last row of the bleachers. Just watching and hoping for the best. You're old enough to know what you want."

"You ought to put that on my tombstone. 'She's old enough to know what she wants.' "

"All right."

"Oh, Lord, how did I ever get to be thirty-five?"

"How did I ever get to be sixty-six?"

"You must hate having such an old kid. It's obscene."

"Well, I don't really think so. Not obscene."

"I wish *I* were sixty-six. Then I wouldn't be going through this fake divorce."

It shamed her to be saying this; she didn't mean it. Being sixty-six was the worst thing she could think of, and she'd only said it to cheer her father up. She knew it did people good to be envied, even for a minute, and even when they knew it was less than authentic.

"It's never easy, Fay, these breakups. Believe me, I know. A lot turns on them. A whole life can turn on them, though I honestly don't believe it often happens that way. Most of our heavy decisions amount to nothing. Momentary thunder and then it's all over, everything back to normal."

"So, do you think I'm doing the right thing? I mean, after three years, and here I am, still not sure of this person yet. I just don't feel too much. Not enough. Not much spark. What a word, spark. Fizz is what I mean."

"Passion?"

She blinked. The word startled her, coming from her father's lips. "He's not a bad person," she said. "He's really quite a decent person, as you know. He certainly would never do anything outrageous. He's even got this wretched saintly side to him. He wouldn't ruin my life or anything. That really drives me crazy, knowing that it could just possibly be okay to go on with him. But do you think I'm doing the right thing, ending it? Just because the fizz is low. Yes or no? Be honest."

"Yes."

And then he put down his cup and said, "If it's what you really want."

FAY DIDN'T TELL her father that Peter was moving back in with his ex-wife, Fritzi. She didn't know herself until Sunday morning, when Peter broke the news. He offered it not in his usual juicy Sheffield tones, but with a truculent chop, as if he wanted to get it over with fast. "I think you should know, Fay, that I've arranged to rent a room at Fritzi's for the next couple of months." He hurried on. "They've got this room on the third floor. Don't look so stunned, Fay. They can use the cash. Sammy was telling me about the market, it's been a bit slow this year, and they've got their mortgage to meet, and for the time being this room will serve the purpose as well as help them out. I can look for an apartment in September, when a few vacancies will come up. But it's a perfectly decent room, and there's a bath . . . for Christ's sake, you look stricken, Fay. Be sensible. There's nothing untoward about it. Fritzi and I've been divorced for years, you know that, and she's happy as a hen with Sammy. Oh, I know you think he's a bit of a dolt, so do I, but she's happy. We're certainly not about to go kinky or anything, if that's what you're thinking, and even if we were, what would it matter? That is what you're thinking, isn't it? That's rubbish. It's even got a separate entrance, the room. Why in hell am I bothering to explain this, will someone please tell me? Anyway, it's a fait accompli, I'm afraid. I've already given them postdated checks for the next four months. And it's furnished, so I won't be needing the pine table, that should simplify things for you. I don't even need a bed. They've got one of those fold-out affairs. They were thinking of renting it to a student, but then I ran into Fritzi and Sammy at the Belgian Bakery when I picked up the croissants. You know, sometimes I think you're dead right about this city, that it really is a bit too small. Okay, I admit it's a somewhat eccentric arrangement. The whole world doesn't have to know, and it's just temporary, it's practical, we have to be moderately practical until we decide what we want to do with the condo. We can't afford to be unreasonable. What I mean is, we can't be foolishly extravagant and overly delicate. This opportunity has, well, presented itself, running into Fritzi and hearing about their spare room. You're not crying, Fay. Oh, for God's sake, why on earth would you cry about a thing like this? It doesn't make sense, it's ludicrous. Half the time I don't know what's going on with you, what's inside your head."

FAY LOVES HER WORK at the folklore center.

To begin with, she admires the new building of pale sandstone, the large, accommodating display area, the administrative floor with its soft green carpet and painted doors, each a different color—hers is yellow—and each opening onto a fresh cubicle of polished plaster and a trio of high slit windows like open mouths. Fay's three windows overlook a sliver of the old warehouse district and a section of disused railroad track and, beyond that, clear to the sky, the curved crust of the Red River, which is really brown, sliding its way northward.

The staff numbers forty, and there is not one among them who refers to her as Miss McLeod or even Ms. McLeod. She is Fay to Hannah Webb, the director, and Fay to Art Frayne, who does electrical work around the place and simple carpentry.

Her office is modest. One wall holds shelves of her books, and the opposite wall is covered with family snapshots—her parents, her two nephews, a blown-up photo of her sister, Bibbi, holding a hammer in her hands, one of Peter at Victoria Beach, and so on—and three large posters, all of them framed, all of them announcing special exhibitions the center has put on in recent years. At angles sit two molded chairs covered with textured blue cotton, and, behind her desk, her own shiny desk chair. The desk itself is wide and handsome, composed of some hard white unscratchable substance; no one liked these desks at first, but now everyone does. Her official title is Associate Folklorist. Sometimes she swivels sideways in her chair and looks over at her books, then her posters, then her tumbling green plants, and finally the glistening desk top, and says to herself, administering a dose of bracing tribute, I am an Associate Folklorist. The word fills her mouth with meaninglessness. She takes a shy secret pleasure in knowing she doesn't quite fulfill this role, and sometimes, thinking of it, she looks straight up at the ceiling and laughs.

At the center, each day is swallowed by the next, Monday to Friday, over and over; the pattern can be read in its tides of energy. Fay can see, but not feel, the monotony of it. In the morning she attends to the necessary administrative details, the not unpleasant meetings in the board room, then the correspondence, the memos, the conducted tours, which the staff shares, then lunch at the nearby Amigo Cafe—a bowl of soup and a carrot muffin, or else she brings a bag lunch and eats it at her desk. In the afternoons, at least for the last three years, she does her mermaids. ("I do my mermaids," she says, in the same way her father, sitting down on weekends to his balsa wood and glue, says, "I'm doing my windmills.") The mermaid hours pass quickly. Mermaid work means poring over journals and offprints, making notes, following up clues, sending out dozens of letters. Each jotted note, each new file adds to the sum of reality. One idea opens magically to ten or twelve others, and she knows by now that this is going to be a problem, that there's altogether too much twirl and spread to her inquiry and not enough in the way of tight, helpful boundaries.

Around three o'clock she wanders down to the canteen for coffee. Beverly, Anne, Hannah, Ken, Donna, Colin—her friends, her colleagues—they'll all be there. The youngishly old Beverly Miles, doyenne of popular-cultural forms and a lover of social gatherings however humble, will be there early and already digging vigorously into her cracked black purse for a paper sachet of rosehip or chamomile, an expectant convivial glow on her broad face that emends the brightness of her gray ponytail swinging and twitching and keeping time with her conversation. Anne Morris, Ken Merchant, Donna Watts, who heads the volunteer program, and Katherine Hill, secretary to the director, will wander in, talking, talking, talking—snatches of their talk float over the heads of the others—Nicaragua, strip mining, Earth Watch—and Colin King will shortly join them. If Peter is not in the field—off to Regina or Calgary or Ottawa—he may join them, too.

On Mondays everyone tends to be full of pleasant fatigue and minor grievances. By Friday the tenor of canteen talk will be up a dozen degrees. Anne Morris, who is Fay's age, will be heading up to her cottage in the Lake of the Woods with her husband, Frank, opening it up for the season and urging invitations on the others. There might be talk of a new position coming up, an assistant for Donna Watts, who any day now will be announcing her pregnancy, not that she needs to announce it. The possibility of this new appointment has been discussed on and off for the eight years Fay has worked at the center, and always it seems on the brink of fulfillment. Fay will reveal to the others the latest news from the mermaid world, real news from the Loire delta in France, where two teenage girls claim to have sighted a fishtailed woman, a *sirène*, rising from a shallow lake at dusk. Colin will snort and discredit, Anne will be analytical, and all the rest will offer up the cool glee and helpful tactics of professional scholars. "I don't know," says Hannah Webb, sliding into an empty chair and opening her carton of milk with a scarlet thumbnail. "I wouldn't discount it entirely."

Fay knows that before too many days have passed, someone will notice that she and Peter no longer sit at the same table. Anticipating the tactful, consoling questions that inevitably will be put to her, she can already feel the comedy of her tragic role. *Single again, our junior folklorist. My, my. Our education outreach man, too. Nothing lasts, it seems.*

But these laments lie in the future. As yet, nothing has changed, nothing that anyone would notice. At 5:30 Fay knocks on Peter's door, or else he knocks at hers, and the two of them go down the back stairway to the parking lot, where their Honda is parked, and then they drive home, turning right on Portage, bucking the worst traffic of the day, turning left onto Osborne, right again onto Stradbrook, as far as the second light.

This, Fay tells herself, glancing in the rearview mirror—nose shiny, hair collapsed (not that it matters if straight hair collapses)—is the only part of the day that will change, and this week is the last lap for them both. Peter intends to move out on Friday evening—he's announced this firmly—and, in a mood of recklessness, good citizenship, and guilt, she's offered to help him pack his things.

WHAT DOES IT MEAN to be a romantic in the last decade of the twentieth century? This was the question Fay put to her brother, Clyde.

"To believe anything can happen to us," he said, and gave her a look.

This conversation took place in the sunroom of the large three-story stucco house in an old residential section of Winnipeg where he lives, quite happily it seems to Fay, with his wife, Sonya, and their two small sons, Gordon and Matthew, who at this moment are asleep upstairs. The air is stuffy and dry because Clyde, an ardent conserver of energy, is reluctant to open a window so early in spring. It is nine o'clock or thereabouts on a dark, blowing April night. Sonya, as usual, is at a meeting. She is a short, spreading, humorous woman, a lawyer for a women's-rights group. People all over the country know her name, and because she's often interviewed about abortion on TV, they'll stop her on the street or in theater lobbies or at dentists' offices and say, "Don't I know you?" It scares her, she once told Fay, the sharp way these people examine her features, boldly, frowningly, without the least sug-

gestion of apology, making their calculations and private judgments. Once when she was getting into a car after a public meeting
a man threw a rag doll at her. It had been ripped open down the
belly so that the stuffing was coming out, and something red and
wet, paint, or else ketchup, had been poured over it. Several times
she's received late-night phone calls, a high, driven whine saying,
"God will punish you, God will drive a spike up your cunt." She
laughs when she talks about these things; you expect a certain
amount of craziness when you work in the abortion area, she says,
it's part of the territory. But the hard, random, assigning eyes of
strangers are more than she can deal with. Is she there or not?
Real or unreal? It makes her wonder, she says.

Fay's brother, Clyde, has his own business, McLeod Mind-
scape, designing computer software. His is an exceedingly spe-
cialized line, mathematical and painstaking, to do with knitting
machines for women's hosiery patterns, and he sometimes jokes
to friends about being in the erotic end of the electronics business—the world of ankles, knees, thighs, and lace. From infancy
he's suffered from severe stuttering, but in his particular work he
has scarcely any need to meet clients face to face, or even to speak
to them on the telephone. He's arranged his business, his whole
existence, this way. He works alone out of a cork-walled office in
his basement, which means he's available when Gordon and Matthew come home for lunch and after school.

It's always the same when Fay sees her younger brother: she
has to adjust to that jolting stutter of his, remembering to shift the
ordinary rhythms of conversation and reminding herself that
though he speaks haltingly, he takes in information at the normal
human speed. He is a sociable man who loves speculation of all
kinds, courts it in fact, and he has always been exceptionally patient
with Fay's involutions.

Tonight, though, it took him a full minute to respond to her
question about the contemporary romantic rubric, then another
minute to gather the syllables on his tongue—"To believe anything
can happen to us." (*B*'s are especially hard for him, also *p*'s.) His

consonants flop and spit, and then teeter maddeningly—almost, but not quite, locked to the roof of his mouth.

Fay sometimes tries to imagine the interior of her brother's head, and what she sees is pink crosshatching and vacuum tubes and erratically flashing lights. Stuttering, she knows, is considered a crippling affliction, yet Clyde is far from crippled. That stutter of his has saved him from critical severity, which is the wound she assigns herself. She's wondered (flinching at her own indecent curiosity) how blocked are his cries of rapture or his expressions of love, or whether he and Sonya have worked out some sort of declarative gesture that serves in place of words. His happiness seems double-distilled: at thirty-three he has achieved a kind of plant life down there in his basement, but he comes up the tiled stairs to full-blown domesticity. An urban fastness: house, garden, garage, everything wired tight and warm. Fay knows he worries about her, his big sister, that she's missing out on something essential which he lacks the arrogance to define.

To be a romantic is to believe anything can happen to us, he said, and later Fay considered how, in his metonymic way, he had summed it up exactly right, although she notices he has set himself carefully outside its gravitational force, and also ignores or rejects the retractable malice romance holds out. Romance, Fay knows, grabs on to people like a prize deformity; it keeps them on edge, taunts them, then slitheringly changes shape and withdraws. Romance—that holy thing. A cycle of rupture and reconciliation. Recently she has begun to understand it for the teasing malady it is.

FAY AND PETER worked hard all evening. She folded and packed his shirts and sweaters, and then his bunched-up socks and underwear. One summer when she was a student, she worked at a suburban shopping center in a place called Jean Junction, and there she was taught the art of precision folding. It still, after all this time, gave her pleasure to transform a jumble of clothes into neat rectangular packets, as flat, trim, and uniform as fast-food hamburger patties.

While she busied herself folding and stacking, Peter wrapped coffee mugs and plates in newspaper and lowered them into cardboard cartons. The kitchen radio was tuned to a soft-rock station, old-fashioned rock, and when the Beatles came on with "I Want to Hold Your Hand," the two of them sang along as if they were any happy couple preparing to move to a new location.

Later they went for a walk in the neighborhood. The night had turned cold, with a strong steady breeze that kept at them, and a moon that stared down hard and glassy. They walked southward first, down a street quaintly named Gertrude, and then up a parallel street called Jessie. Many of the streets in this part of the city were similarly named: Minnie, Agnes, Flora, Bella, and Lizzie, immortalizing, Fay has always supposed, the patient or demanding wives of early-twentieth-century developers, women who would feel proud to walk down streets that bore their names, or else ashamed and self-conscious, but in any case assured of their thread of connection to a place where they had, however accidentally, found themselves.

Fay is able to see more beauty in these small front yards than she used to, and this has made her feel hopeful about the future. Each yard is fenced with varied, incongruous materials, so that wire netting meets with wooden pickets, and woven metal strips with peeled poles. One house, on the corner of Adelaide and Edna, is surrounded with an odd, low mesh of plastic tubes in astringent shades of orange and yellow, an effect that is oddly cheering. The purpose of these fences must be territorial, Fay thinks, since they are far too flimsy to keep dogs in or out, and offer no protection at all to children, who can easily step over them. Two miles away on Ash Avenue, where she grew up, the front yards flow uninterruptedly in broad even waves down toward the rolled curbs, not even a sidewalk breaking the illusion of easeful neighborly trust, while here on Jessie, street sovereignty remains on guard, and sidewalks run down both sides, the cement broken by a combination of harsh winters and sprawling tree roots. Tonight, walking slowly along one of these old buckled sidewalks and turning a corner, Peter and Fay came across the chalked markings of a hopscotch game.

In the dim street light, the pattern was barely discernable. Fay supposed that the children who had made these scratchings must now be asleep in their beds.

The image of her own childhood dissolved and reformed in the remembrance of such learned street inscriptions, especially the game of hopscotch, with its magic numbered squares and its wide empty arc of heaven. Every winter the rules were forgotten, and in the spring they were relearned. As the summer wore on, the squares grew larger, the lines straighter, and the rules more stringent or fanciful. The smoothest piece of pavement would be sought out and its location memorized, and it would be remembered one day that real chalk was not needed, since a common piece of stone dug out of a garden might do almost as well. Most of Fay's notions of fairness and improvisation, she believes, were learned in the quiet streets of this city on evenings such as this, learned and relearned, rehearsed and perfected, but then, oddly, forgotten.

She can't remember at this moment exactly how the game of hopscotch progresses, what is required of a player in order to win or lose or get to heaven. The intricacies of play and penalty have eroded, forming part of a larger ebbing of memory, and that worries her. The weave of her life is growing thinner, plainer, and she sees she may be in danger of losing what she has unconsciously assembled.

At the same time, new possibilities present themselves. A month ago she might have stopped under the cone of street light and pronounced the word "hopscotch" aloud, asking Peter if he had ever played this game on the streets of Sheffield, and pressing on him—never mind his sigh of exasperation—her set of rules, her sense of the game, going on and on and demanding a corresponding account from him.

But not tonight. Tonight she says nothing, and inside her head she offers up congratulations. A certain amount of silence might be useful at this point. She hopes it will be the kind of silence that mends its own tissues, and that maybe she's learning something out of all this difficulty.

IT WAS LATE on a dark night, Thursday. Peter's mouth came down on hers awkwardly, almost missing, like a kiss in a silent movie, and she heard an eruption in his throat that might have been laughter or else surprise at his own clumsiness.

We've lost our ear for love, Fay thought sadly, our touch. But the next minute Peter was moving lightly above her, striking shocks off her slicked body. Her skin was only half dry. A damp bath towel lay under them.

After three years the absolute length of his thigh bones still came as a shock, and also those long covering stretches of surprisingly tender skin.

She shivered, reading the lower edge of his rib cage with her fingers, willing herself to be engulfed, feeling a passionate, frantic sense of loss, and wondering, a minute later, how it was possible to be so simultaneously bored and excited. Was this a trance she was entering or a period of illness? What are we doing? she imagined her own voice saying.

~ CHAPTER 4 ~

I Believe in

One Thing

———

LAST WEEK WHEN TOM WENT FOR SUNDAY LUNCH AT LIZ AND GENE Chandler's, Liz turned to him and said: "I believe in one thing, and that one thing is routine. I didn't always. I used to look at my mother with her Monday wash and her Tuesday ironing and think, Oh my God, spare me. My parents sat down to lunch every day at 12:15. They even had the same things on certain days, like lamb on Wednesday, beef-and-vegetable stew on Thursday, and so on. Imagine! I used to look at their narrow throttled lives and say, hey, is this ever pathetic. A twentieth-century form of slavery, and they don't even realize it. But do you know what? My mother and dad are in their eighties and they're in perfect health. Perfect. They live in their own house, and my father does all the gardening and repairs and my mother still does all her own housework. They're never sick. They hardly ever complain. They're happy. They're happy because of their routines. They watch the news at ten. They turn out the light at eleven and go straight to sleep, presto. It's taken me years to get a perspective on this thing, why we need certain fixed patterns in our lives. And I've figured it out. Routine is liberating, It makes you feel in control. A paradox, isn't it? You think your routines are controlling you, but in fact you're using the routine to give you power. Like, for example, we have waffles every Sunday, Gene and I, and that might sound boring to certain people, but it soothes me. I need it, dumb as it sounds. And Tom, listen, I know the last thing you need is advice, but has it occurred to you that you need, maybe, an element of routine in your life?"

Tom protests. He *does* have routines. Besides his Saturday-morning jogs he has his Friday-night meetings at the Fort Rouge Community Center, the Newly Single Club.

"Yeah, well," says Liz, who more and more assumes the right to scold and who now, sitting across the table from Tom, dramatically rolls her eyes. "But where is that getting you exactly? I mean, you're not newly single anymore, Tom, are you?" She shifts her weight. "You've been going to those meetings for two years now. Could it be you're just a bit of a newly single junkie, if you don't mind my saying so? Just where is it getting you?"

He wonders himself. The program at the Community Center rotates every six months or so, and by now he's heard all the speakers. Some of them he's heard several times. The one he's heard the most often is a woman called Jennifer Keeley Harvath from the psych department at the University of Winnipeg. Dr. Harvath has a set piece she does on Divorce Guilt. Her long Mexican earrings shake with fervor when she outlines on the blackboard the four separate stages of guilt, which are: realization, responsibility, reconciliation, and realignment. Her whole body shakes, trembling inside the strong folds of her trim professorial clothes—short skirts, long jackets, blouses that seem to spill and froth and confuse. "If you deny your guilt now," she tells the pale faces before her—faces that make Tom think of cauliflowers, so outspread and porous are they—"then you'll pay later."

Tom once invited her out to dinner. He made reservations at a new place across the river, expensive, advertised as French, thinking that if the two of them were going to get acquainted they would have to travel as far as possible from the beige and blue floor tiles and folding chairs of the Fort Rouge Community Center.

She had ordered roughly in American-accented French, though the waiter protested that he spoke no French at all, only English, Portuguese, and a few words of Filipino.

"About your divorce," she asked Tom directly over the first course, which was scallops in *beurre blanc*.

"Which one?" he said, already convinced the evening was lost.

"You've had more than one divorce?" Her head jerked forward, releasing fragrance.

"Three." He made separate syllables of it—thuh-ree-ee—made it a gift, just handed it over.

She chewed the tender fish, chewed and chewed, using her molars in long circular thoughtful grindings. Watching her, he felt his guilt turn into a spray of brilliant colors and fan out over the dull white tablecloth.

"So," she said, and at last laid down her knife and fork. "Three."

He watched her crumple. He was amazed that he had been able to bring this crumpling about so easily, by uttering a single word. The collar of her suit jacket had by now collapsed, and her blouse, too, and the tender upper parts of her mouth. It was painful to see, but it also brought him a thrill of excitement. The room felt anchored with the force of declaration. Cutlery plinked, a kind of foolish incidental music. Jennifer Harvath's long silver earrings brushed close to her plate. The part in her dark blond hair caught the light harshly.

He decided to fake a laugh. "I tell myself," he said loudly to her, to the earrings, to the wallpaper, "that I've been unlucky."

THERE IS SOMETHING, Tom knows, called learned dependency, and there's a lot of it around, more than there used to be. He hears it mentioned all the time. Its victims send out subliminal pleas for help, wringing from their family and friends advice about how to conduct their lives.

Tom's mother, Betty Avery Barbour, in Duck River telephoned recently and said: "Tom? Is that you? Well, what do you know! I didn't know if I'd find you home, on a Saturday night. Sitting at home. You watching the game? Mike's watching the game, we're just taking a breather here, I'm about to fix us a sandwich and put some coffee on and I thought I'd give you a call, see what you were up to. But I said to Mike, knowing you, you'd be out probably, out to a show, or someplace dancing. The way you used to dance. "Rock Around the Clock," that was your middle name, remember those days? You alone? Right now, I mean. I don't know for the life of me why you don't come up here for the weekend. It beats me why you want to stay in the city. On a Saturday night. That Suzanne isn't the only fish in the lake, you know, at least I hope you know. There's plenty more, all kinds. Nice gals just looking for a real man to settle down with, raise a family. Look at all those years I was on my own, footloose and fancy free. I was looking, let me tell you, I had my eyes peeled. But you're not going to find someone just sitting home moping. On your own. Oh sweetie, on a Saturday night."

THIS BUSINESS OF being a guy, it never let up. In the morning, getting out of bed, he left his pajama tops buttoned, just yanked them over his head, balled them up, rammed them under his pillow. Was that being a guy? Or did guys buy those knitted pull-over pajamas? Or sleep in their underwear like his stepfather, Mike? Or in nothing at all, damp skin, sweaty genitals, and chest hair, like Burt Reynolds?

He looked hard in the bathroom mirror and said to himself: All I have is this self. Not another thing. Just this irreducible droning self.

But a guy has to eat. Hey, protein, carbohydrates! He considered lunching on a handful of cereal, but decided instead to walk down to the A & W for a Papa Burger, maybe some fries and a milkshake. Guy food. Gut food.

The girl who plunked down his plate verged on pretty. A boil-in-a-bag kind of pretty, someone who looked like she'd just grown into her bones. He would have bet money that two years ago she was having trouble with her skin, but now she'd got it under control. Nice hair, too, clean, yellowish, long. Guys liked long hair.

Oh Christ, he was boring himself stiff.

And it was only two in the afternoon. No invitations to waffle lunches today, no phone calls either. No plans. Well, he was going to have to do something about his life. Smarten up, big fella. These loops of time had a way of widening out if you weren't careful.

"Look," the waitress said, waving at the window. "It's a parade."

Hey, that was more like it. He bolted his coffee, paid his bill (leaving a guy's kind of tip, twenty percent), and went out into the sunshine, directly into a holiday crowd strung thinly along the roadway, breathing in immaculate air.

But what was this? The parade that bumped along Osborne Street had too much sweetness and fancy to be a military parade. Its marchers were dancing and skipping on the wide cleared pavement, and singing some high light hymn with a floating descant that rose straight up on a current of air, and scattering love behind them like a kind of rarefied mulch. They carried one banner that read "Jesus Our Lord and Master" and another that said "Hope and Glory." A squadron of slender girls, so freshly skirted and sandaled and garlanded with paper flowers that they seemed like flowers themselves, circled as they moved along, and swirled over their heads long colored ribbons for Jesus. Close behind them walked a small brass band, a dozen men with bugles, trumpets, trombones, and drums. Such manly, non-guy men—Tom's breath wheezed in his chest—so closely barbered, so clean and beefy and calm and beating their drums for their Lord Jesus.

It was over almost before it had begun, and Tom, stricken by a sharp, sweet craving for godly forgetfulness and unwilling to let the paraders pass out of sight, strolled along beside them for a while as they made their way over the Osborne Bridge to the Legislative grounds. He felt his feet obeying their light drifting holy contagion of music and gaiety. Behind, around and in front of Tom, were women in summer dresses, some of them holding children by the hand. Other children ran past him shouting. The sunlight falling down around him seemed made of little grains, and the air was milder than it had been in many months, so clear and blue he wanted to blubber with the beauty of it. O spring, he thought. O longing. O love.

MONDAY NIGHT down at CHOL is survey night. Listeners call in between 1:00 and 2:00 a.m. to answer the question of the week. Tonight's question is: What do you think about when you're in the shower?

One caller says, "Well"—his voice is old, webby, androgynous—"we don't have a shower, but if you want to know what I think about in the bathtub, I'll tell you. I think about the condition of the world. The Chinese, the Russians. Even these Romanians. How all of a sudden the Russians are good guys, after all these years of being bad guys, wanting to drop bombs on us. Well, I think we had the wool pulled over our eyes. People don't change overnight, you know."

"What worries me," a woman says, "is how a shower wastes water. This really comes from when I was a kid and lived on a farm. Up near Amiota? We had a well, but not a very reliable one, and so we were darned careful about wasting water. I think of that when I'm standing in the shower, all that water just running down the drain. I'm forty-six now, and I've got my own family, with all the running water in the world, but I still think every single time I'm in the shower that I shouldn't be so wasteful, and that takes all the fun out of it."

"I feel like a jerk in the shower," a man says. He has a youthful voice with tenor margins to it. "I feel dumb or drunk or something. It's the steam. I've got this head of naturally curly hair, but in the shower it gets all slicked down so I look like a nerd. Looks are kind of like a priority, and with me, priorities come first."

Another caller says: "When I'm in the shower I get this compulsion to count. Like how many showers I've had in my life? And how many more I'm going to have, all those showers stretching out into the future, three hundred and sixty-five a year, and on and on. I try to keep my shower time down to ninety seconds."

"I find," a woman says, "that I have a very hard time getting out of the shower. I favor very hot water, probably too hot for most people, I must have some Japanese blood in me, and I keep thinking, Oh God, now I have to get out and be cold again. I'd like to stay in there, just prolong and prolong it and never get out."

"I study my shower curtains," an out-of-town caller reports. "I've got one of those map-of-the-world shower curtains and I would recommend it to any listener. It's supposed to be accurate, and I'm telling you, the stuff I've learned. South America. Africa, too."

"You want me to be honest?" a young male voice says. "Taking a shower makes me feel sexy. I think of all the great girls I've known lately. I like to take a shower with a girl. Hey, can I say this on the air? Well, it's a great way to go. And at the same time you're getting clean."

"The thing about a shower," the final caller says, "is not just getting clean. A shower takes you down memory lane. You go under the nozzle and it's like a time machine. Taking a shower, it's like being back in the ocean or back in your mother's womb. Safe and full of these far-out thoughts. When I'm in the shower I feel powerful, but also like I'm a better person."

TOM HAS TO ADMIT he was touched by all the birthday cards he got for his fortieth.

Most of them, to be sure, came from listeners, mailed in to the station on Pembina Highway, and quite a lot of them were anonymous, signed simply "from a grateful listener" or "from your late-night comrade in arms." Why would anyone go to the bother, he wonders, but his wondering is colored with gratitude. *I want to thank you folks out there for all your . . .*

And yet, here he is bundling these same cards into a green garbage bag. It's house-cleaning time, a Tuesday morning. This is a pigsty he's living in, and he's determined to do something about it, to get some order into his life. Into the garbage bag with three half-rotted apples, two empty wine bottles, the crushed cornflakes box, last week's newspapers, a ripped T-shirt, some slivers of soap, and an unidentifiable toothbrush, and all one hundred sixty birthday cards, plus a box of homemade oatmeal cookies (uneaten—why risk it? says Big Bruce) from a listener who wrote in hot-pink ink, "To the man who lights up my life and who I love most in the world after my husband. Hang in there, Tom, forty is just the beginning."

"AH, TOM," said Tom's first wife, Sheila. "How could I forget your birthday, and especially this birthday! Anyway, it all of a sudden hit me, wham, and I thought the least I could do was take you to lunch, better late than never, and I remembered you used to love coming to this place. I can remember sitting at this very table. A million years ago. You had a seafood crepe, I think. Crepes were just coming into their own, crepes, not pancakes. Why do I always remember things like that? It's insane the stuff I store in this brain of mine. Anyway, I'm glad you were free today, I know how busy you are, but listen, you look great. I'm serious, you do not look forty. Now tell me, what's new, what's happening in your life. It's been weeks since I've seen you. Where've you been hiding out?"

Almost immediately after Tom and Sheila were divorced in 1979 Sheila made two decisions, one bad, one good. The bad decision was to marry a man called Sammy Sweet, a real estate agent. The marriage lasted exactly eighteen months, and then Sammy left her, saying he had fallen desperately in love with a woman called Fritzi Knightly. Sheila went around telling people this. "He says he's 'desperately' in love and 'can't live without her,' and her name is Fritzi, if you can believe it. Fritzi!"

Her good decision was to leave her secretarial job and enter law school. She was in the middle of her second year when Sammy Sweet left her, and so busy studying and working on the Law Review and volunteering for the legal-aid program that the shock of his betrayal, she said, was like a bomb dropping in another country, though it cured her forever of the idea of marriage. "It's clear I'm lousy marriage material," she announced at the time, and since the divorce she's lived with three other women, two lawyers, one accountant, in a large modern house in a new subdivision. Tom is invited there now and then when they need an extra man for parties, and he's reasonably fond of Patricia and Sandra and Dru, though somewhat guarded, never sure how thoroughly Sheila has described their old intimacies.

It was Sheila who handled Tom's divorce from Suzanne. "A good clean divorce," she said when it was over. "No embarrassing strings hanging off it. I hope to hell you're grateful."

His other friends told him his situation was ludicrous, a first wife negotiating a divorce from a third. It was the material of soap opera, but for Tom the shame of a third-marriage breakup—and he was pierced through with shame, it lingers still—seemed softened by the fact that it was dealt with from within the family, so to speak, that its ripple of failure was laid smooth by the clean hand of a former wife for whom he still feels a shy fondness.

He loves her pressed lawyer clothes, her nifty dark suits and silk scarves, even her restive, edgy way of holding her knife and fork. "I think I loved you best of all the wives," he said today, loathing himself for yammering so cheaply—and not saying what he means, either. Light from the window fell on her mouth, her rounded cheeks, her young girl's nose. This was in the middle of a spinach-and-bacon crepe, during a lull in the conversation. He rubbed his teeth with the tip of his tongue.

She was ready for him, and fluttered a hand across the table to take his. "We liked each other a lot," she said, "but we were not, as people say, in love. Whatever the hell that means. I've never been in love. I think I do have an inkling of what people mean when they say 'in love,' and maybe you do too, but we didn't have it, you and me. I'll never have it. But Tom, you might someday. I honestly think you have the capacity. But I sure don't." She sipped a little coffee and resettled her cup on its saucer. "Love," she sniffed rudely. "Who needs it."

Tom was twenty years old, a history student at the University of Toronto, when he first heard the phrase "Who needs it." This was in 1970, a year of turmoil. He possessed at that time a thick uneven beard. His hair curled around his shoulders, chestnut hair, beautiful, but his head was befuddled. With six other students, one of them a part-time drug dealer, he lived in a small illegal basement apartment in the Riverdale area of Toronto, and throughout the long winter months he slept on a shredded mattress between unwashed sheets. Every morning he looked into a square of broken mirror and winced at the grayness of his skin. There were mice in the apartment, possibly rats. Something, anyway, that gnawed on the electric wires. He could never find his own clothes, and his one pair of shoes seemed to be continually wet. Most of the time he was wretched and cold and worried about what would happen to him next, but that odd phrase—"Who needs it"—so brilliant, defiant, and novel, so explicitly emblematic of its time—carried him through. Like a flag, he unfurled it before sleep, and again on waking, and he applied its compacted and plenteous powers particularly to the new territory of love and accomplishment. He wasn't sure what it meant—he still isn't. "Who needs it." Who needs *what*? But back in that foolish, puny time he needed a weapon he could hold next to his body, something that would make him brave, or make him appear to be brave.

CHAPTER 5

How Are You,
How Are You?

FAY PUTS DOWN THE NEWSPAPER, STARES OUT THE WINDOW AT THE budding trees, and thinks: I'm getting along fine. Peter's been gone for one week now. I've eaten seven breakfasts alone (seven single-toast breakfasts), and four dinners, and one lunch. I've slept alone for seven nights now, seven nights in that big bed.

There were only two nights when she'd slept badly, and only one when she'd curled to the edge of the bed and given way to a fit of whimpering—but that lasted for only about five minutes. Seven chaste nights punctuated by a single long engorged sexual dream that woke her suddenly with its intensity, leaving her limp, sweating—and mildly curious about who it was who entered her sleep and aroused her to such a pitch.

She's bought a new tube of toothpaste, an expensive off-brand she's never heard of. She's bought herself a new summer robe, widely yoked and prodigal with poppies. She's bought a large economy-size pack of Q-Tips—she doesn't know quite why but suspects she's preparing for a fanatical scouring and scourging of her flesh.

She thinks: It's May now, a new month.

The idea is bracing, and so is the fact that June, July, and August will follow, a series of green arches she can walk under, reassuring herself as she goes, pinching herself awake and knowing she will always, somewhere, be driven into little deceptions of happiness. She has a knack, it seems, for deception.

Peter took Fay's flowering cactus with him. She had insisted on it, an obscure gesture of good will, but now a bitter thought comes: I wish I'd kept that cactus, I was a fool to part with it.

Forget what's in the past, go back to the newspaper.

One of the headlines says, "Buddhists Go on Rampage." That makes her smile, and she's pleased that she's able to sit alone in a room and smile over a trifle. Then she reads another headline, which says, "Iowa Woman Fears Losing Looks; Drowns in Well."

She says aloud, cherishingly: "The world is full of pathos," and she is startled by the foreign quality of her voice, erupting, it seems, from some newly discovered vent in her throat, so rich with dignity, so cool and artificial it might have come out of a radio.

FAY'S BROTHER, CLYDE, and his wife, Sonya, went to Minneapolis for the weekend, and Fay offered to baby-sit.

High up in an upstairs bedroom she reads her nephews, Gordon and Matthew, a bedtime story. The three of them lie sprawled on a bed, a woolen blanket pulled up to their chins. A circle of yellow light from the small shaded Mickey Mouse lamp falls on the book's pages and across the fluffed heads of the two boys. She feels a wrenching ache of love for them both, their two small heads on her shoulders, the rounded polish of bone and flesh, and a wondrous conjunction of bath soap and soft fur. The story she reads is one of her favorites, "The Boy Who Cried Wolf."

But it is not a good choice, not at all. Gordon, who is only six, cries when she finishes and pounds her arm and says she's mean. His face twists into an ideogram of a face, and Fay, putting her head back on the soft pillows, quickly improvises a new ending. She makes the father in the story say he's sorry about the whole thing, that little boys have no business being out all night anyway. They need their sleep, and from now on the sheep are going to be put in the barn at night.

Gordon laughs loudly. His laughter is ranged along a single note like an electric mixer. He has a trick of looking grave even when he smiles.

During the night, Matthew wakes up crying. He has been dreaming about wolves. "Shhh," Fay whispers, placing her hand against his cheek. "There aren't any wolves here, I absolutely promise you. Not a single one."

She switches on a lamp, and together they inspect the closet and check under the bed, even peer into the dresser drawers and behind the curtain.

After that he falls asleep at once, but Fay lies awake on the bed beside his compact, humming little body for an hour or more, trembling at what she has almost forgotten: the rivery end of memory, wolves, bears, nakedness, falling down holes, aimless and solitary wandering—all the rain and weather, in fact, of her own scrambled dreams.

FAY'S MERMAID WORK goes back to the time when Morris Kroger presented her with the little Inuit sculpture and, unknowingly, set her on her way. She has yet to understand what mermaids mean, their place in the human imagination, but she knows how they look and behave. Hair, vegetablelike, weedy and massed. A face that is beautiful or cunning, and sometimes both. Lungs and larynx, a singing voice but without a song. Arms, usually rudimentary, but able to hold a mirror, and sometimes a comb. The torso may vary from slender to voluptuous; an earthy mermaid—is that possible? Very occasionally mermaids, as seen in art or described in legend, wear garments of some sort, or at least a piece of fine veiling or aquatic plant that flows over and partially conceals their high, hard, rounded breasts. There might also be a necklace or hair ornament.

In the matter of mermaid tails there is enormous variation.

Tails may start well above the waist, flow out of the hips, or extend in a double set from the legs themselves. They're silvery with scales or dimpled with what looks like a watery form of cellulite. A mermaid's tail can be perfunctory or hugely long and coiled, suggesting a dragon's tail, or a serpent's, or a ferocious writhing penis. These tails are packed, muscular, impenetrable, and give powerful thrust to the whole of the body. Mermaid bodies are hard, rubbery, and indestructible, whereas human bodies are as easily shattered as meringues.

The asexual morphology of mermaids is obvious, there being no feminine passage designed for ingress and egress.

The mermaid image in art is highly stylized, and Fay, responding to that stylization, and perhaps defending it, has taped over her desk a quotation from Leonardo da Vinci: "Art lives from constraints and dies from freedom."

Mermaids are the color of water and of watery vegetation—brown, blue, green, silver. Mermen are found in art and in folk tales, and even merdogs and mercats, but among mythical fishy creatures, mermaids predominate.

Some folklorists have suggested that mermaids are matter and spirit fused.

Mermaids exist in all the world's cultures and go back to the dawn of time, always gesturing, it seems, at the origin of life itself, which began in the sea.

Once someone asked Fay a surprising question: Did she ever imagine how it would feel to be a mermaid? No, she said, never.

In fact, if she ever thinks of herself as having a different shape, especially these days, it is more likely to be a sailor lost at sea.

Frequently, people greet Fay McLeod with the question: How are your mermaids coming along? Instead of asking: How are you?

"How are you, Fay?" Beverly Miles asks on Monday morning, poking her head around the doorway of Fay's office. Fay and Beverly have been good friends for about five years, ever since Beverly came to work at the center.

Today her eyes are bright with health, and her partially graying hair is skimmed back from a girlish face dabbed with bits of
color, blue on the eyelids, pink on the rather heavy lips, and pools
of deeper pink on the cheeks. She has the look of a merry, earnest,
convivial woman, which she is. At twenty she had married a man
three times her age, an Egyptologist, and had borne him three
children. By thirty she was widowed. Now, though she is just four
years older than Fay, her waist and hips are thickening, and she
still loves to wear full-skirted dresses in diminutive prints and trim
ballet slippers. She seems to possess none of the dissatisfaction
other women feel toward their bodies. "How are you, Fay?" she
asks, and in a conspiratorial tone, the skin around her eyes creas-
ing, "How is the real you?"

This is a joke between them—the real self that hides beneath
the public skin. "Fine, fine," Fay says abruptly, then tries to amend
with a softened, "Well, not bad."

"Can I come in for a sec? You got a minute?" Already Beverly
has shut the door and is easing herself into a chair and grasping
her knees in a gesture of benignity. "Is there anything," she begins,
her voice urgent and unsteady, "I can say or do?"

"I suppose everyone here knows by now."

"Well, this is a very small club."

"Maybe you'd better tell me what they're saying."

"Just that it's a rotten shame. A great pity, a waste. All the
usual clucking. And then the frivolous stuff, what a striking couple
you are, et cetera. You know, both tall and slender—"

"Like a pair of pepper mills."

"—and how they're fond of you both. All of which is true."

"Oh," Fay says. Her throat feels full of sand.

"And when I saw Peter skulking around looking so chilly and
silent, and you turning into a hermit here, I started to wonder,
well, how final all this is."

"He's moved out."

"Well, yes, but that doesn't mean it has to be final."

"There's no one else, if that's what you're wondering."

"I was wondering."

"My mother thinks I expect too much. I expect the world. Her very words. And she's right."

"I expected a lot myself at one time. Oh, you can't imagine how greedy I was. You didn't know me then. I thought I could have everything because I'd been a good girl, a nice girl, and I deserved to be happy. People do make compromises along the way. They do."

"We were just half happy. No one should settle for being half happy."

"Really?" Beverly's pink lips close over her teeth, then slowly open again in a smile. "What do you think they settle for, then?"

"You've got your kids, Bev. You've got a whole life."

"Well, part of a life, anyway."

"PEOPLE," FAY SAID to Peter, catching sight of him in the corridor, "are talking."

"I know, I know." His face was busy arranging itself in what Fay supposed was a rueful grin.

"I guess we should have expected a certain amount of talk, but I hate it."

"It'll die down. It's the topic of the week, that's all."

"I'm also getting advice. Counseling."

"Beverly?"

"Yes."

"Me too. She means well."

"I know." Fay nodded. "And Colin had a lunge at me too this afternoon."

"Really? That's interesting. What did he have to say? Or was it that same old line about what a striking couple we made?"

"How did you know?"

"He's got that kind of brain, I'm afraid. Retinal clichés."

"I found that leather case of yours. For your travel alarm clock, I think. It was under some blankets." To herself she said: A little ghost.

"I've never used it. Why not just pitch it out?"

"How's Fritzi? And Sammy?"

"Good, good, just fine."

"How's . . . the cactus?"

"Blooming."

"Really?"

"Not really, but about to. Would you like it back?"

"No thanks."

"You were right—about coexistence. It is possible." He gave his watery laugh. "We're being decent and polite and civilized, aren't we?"

"Hmmm."

"Fletcher Conrad's coming on Friday, did you know? He's supposed to be fairly sharp."

"I hope so," Fay said. "It seems I've been given the job of looking after him."

"Thanks for your bank draft."

"Thanks for yours."

WITH SURPRISINGLY little effort or discord, Fay and Peter have settled their affairs. A single trip to Fay's lawyer, Patricia Henney, and a visit to the bank were all that was required. Afterward, they shook hands like characters in a comedy act and went out for a drink. Fay, negotiating a loan from her parents, has bought Peter's half of the condominium, and Peter has bought Fay's half of the Honda.

Life without a car is somewhat awkward, but for the time being, with spring coming on steadily, the shrubs leafing out and the temperature rising, Fay's been taking the bus to and from work. This is a novelty. She welcomes it. Light breezes flutter the hem of her pale pink raincoat as she waits by the bus stop. From the bus window the streets have the gray-and-amber freshness of a foreign city, stretching purposefully toward the doors of serious institutions and office blocks where the intricacies of commerce and learning unfold. The traffic lights blink cleanly against the fleece of clouds, and Fay thinks how fortunate she is to live in a place where the air is relatively pure and where she can almost always, even during rush hour, get a seat on the bus.

She finds herself inspecting the other passengers intently, and notes with surprise—but why should she be surprised?—that those who ride the early-morning buses are mainly women, a separate caste, who seem to carry with them a suggestion of their flushed domestic chaos, the imprint of families hurriedly fed and admonished, cupboard doors left ajar, and greasy cups and plates stacked in the sink until evening. The expression on these women's faces is rushed and resigned. Boarding, they hold their breath hard in their chests, as though it were a kind of precious guarded pain, lean tensely forward in their seats, and only gradually, after two or three stops, relax, gazing around them, and quite often launching into conversation with their neighbors.

Fay closes her eyes and listens, catching dismaying scraps of talk. She supposes it is only a trick of the senses, a reflection of her own unsettled state, that she hears mainly stories of connubial disarray and impending crisis.

"A promise is a promise" comes floating toward her one morning in aggrieved tones.

"All he does is watch television," she hears. "Anything that's on."

"—and if I've said it once, I've said it a hundred times."

"—hides her birth-control pills on this little ledge—"

"—windows broken, dishes broken, pictures smashed—"

"—no sooner gets off the lung machine and he collapses a second time—"

"—a broken jaw, every tooth knocked loose—"

"—but the insurance didn't cover—"

"—doesn't grow on trees."

"—and ending up like this."

ON FRIDAY AFTERNOON, the Australian folklorist Dr. Fletcher Conrad, age fifty-five, spoke in the center's auditorium for an hour, without notes, on the survival of superstition among the aborigines.

He spoke with fluidity, lining up his points firmly, but softening them with little dashes of self-deprecation and gentle tips of the hat toward otherwise examples or extenuating circumstances. His lips were wet. He had a fine cantering laugh with elegant high notes. His anecdotes—about birds, about his wife and children, about the Australian landscape—were charmingly spaced and delivered, and he closed his lecture by praising the audience for their attention, exclaiming over the honor they had done him by inviting him to the center and placing him—and here he paused and smiled—in Ms. Fay McLeod's capable hands.

It was Fay's responsibility to take him to dinner. Hannah Webb, full of apologies about a previous commitment, lent Fay her car. "Treat him nicely," she whispered in Fay's ear.

They went to a restaurant called Dubrovnik's and, at a table overlooking the river, ate smoked-trout salad, rare roast lamb with baby green beans, and a strawberry torte, and drank a bottle of dry red wine. Just a short distance beneath their window the currents of the river shifted, and a drift of wind made it hard to know which way the river was flowing; this was a familiar optical illusion of the region, Fay pointed out to Dr. Conrad in her role as guide. Toward the end of the evening—the sky was full of flat blue light—they talked about Margaret Mead, a new biography in which her reputation had been further capsized. "Reputation," Fletcher Conrad said, quoting Balzac, "is a prostitute." "A crowned prostitute," said Fay, who remembered the quotation. They both looked pleased with themselves about this exchange. They got up to go. It was then Fay noticed that he was approximately half an inch shorter than she. She had already noticed his tiny hands, the left one curved inside the right on the tablecloth, like a captured bird.

An hour later they were in her bed, and his small pointed movie-director's beard was nudging its way, diagonally, roughly, across her belly. "Ah, dear Christ," he gasped, and Fay found herself floating between waves of appetite and a stern minor-key voice, her own, that said: You must not let this happen again.

There are certain moments in her life of which she is deeply ashamed, and this, she knew, even as she took him in her mouth, her tongue circling, was going to be one of them. There was too much carelessness here, and down in the tangle of damp limbs and body hair and hooded flesh, struggling to catch her breath, Fay was unable to remember, for the space of a minute, what this man's name was. Who was he? Who? Tiny hands, thumping knees, panicked flesh. Fletcher Conrad. Or was it Conrad Fletcher?

No, it must not happen again.

~ CHAPTER 6 ~

Love Is the Only

Enchantment

LIFE IS NOT ALWAYS FILLED TO THE BRIM. CERTAINLY NOT TONIGHT. Tonight the capricious winds of May, a bad head cold, and a dab of bird shit on the windshield of his newly washed Riviera drove Tom Avery back to a meeting of the Newly Single Club at the Fort Rouge Community Center.

Two weeks ago he'd attended a Friday-night talk there entitled "The Ghettoization of the Single in Contemporary Urban Society" and was introduced to three key coping strategies—bonding, re-bonding, and disbonding; that was the point at which he'd dozed off. There was something too droningly familiar about the way in which human behavior divided itself into categories of three, some-thing too cozy, too suspicious, too sleep-producing. Enough al-ready. He was wasting his time. Finis. So long, newly singles. He had better things to do.

But here he was again, back for an evening of tactical analysis. Patsy MacArthur, the spirited club co-ordinator, announced the evening topic: Meeting New Mates. Small squares of paper were distributed on which everyone was to write down places where a possible Significant Other might be encountered. "Take your time," Patsy called out in her high, harsh, pulsing voice. "Think outside the clichés. Think beyond singles bars and Laundromats."

Tom fished in his pocket for a pencil. He never carried a pencil, but still he fished hopefully. "Here," the woman next to him whispered, "I've got an extra."

Had he imagined it? Had she winked at him through her long dark bangs? He offered back his monkey smile. "Thanks."

All around him he heard the industrious application of pen to paper. The woman beside him—those bangs were either a fussy, self-protective ploy or an indication of monstrous neglect— scratched frantically, well down already into a list.

"Be creative," Patsy sang out, striding between the rows of chairs. "Look beyond the obvious. Forget want ads. Look past the art gallery and the zoo. Nobody ever met anybody at the zoo, except maybe a baboon."

The woman next to Tom—she looked about thirty—peered up through her stringy fringe, then sorrowfully stroked "zoo" and "art gallery" off her list. Her chin was pointed. She had the look of someone turning, about to be greeted. A dull silver brooch in the form of a musical note was pinned to her blouse.

"Hey, you're all doing great," Patsy encouraged. "I can actually feel the energy in this room building. Five more minutes, will that do you?"

More scratching, and then the pieces of paper were collected. And read aloud. And discussed item for item.

Supermarkets got poor marks. Men who attempted to strike up an acquaintance by humbly seeking the advice of women on the choosing of melons were too obvious, too sexist; jerks, in fact.

Parties given by friends? Friends invited unattractive people they felt sorry for or people getting over depressions who "needed a night out." Friends preened their own marital harmony. Friends were so hysterical about being thought matchmakers that they ended up doing nothing.

A choral group? Very, very original, said Patsy approvingly.

Yes, someone else said, but choirs are too churchy, too good. Not necessarily, you could always shop around for a singles-oriented group, it was something to keep in mind.

Aerobics classes. Too many women. The wrong kind of men. Letches. Trendy. Grunt and sweat. Temporary liaisons only. If that.

Political meetings. Wrong kind of heat. Committed people weren't out there looking for new bonding units. Too sincere, too boring, too much work—delivering leaflets, stuffing envelopes, and so on.

The library. You could sit down at the same table with, say, someone who was reading a book you'd read or a magazine you liked, it could be an indicator.

Poetry readings. Poetry readings? What?

"Hey," said Patsy, holding up a final scrap of paper and taking a jocular, accusing stance. "Here's someone who didn't write down a single thing."

Tom at that moment was busily studying the woman next to him, wondering if under her hair she might be attractive. Wondering again if she really had winked at him. Or if he was going squirrelly.

He got her name and phone number from Patsy. This effort on his part was in response not to a summons of desire, but to a summons to fill his time. Time was the gnat in his ear: no more time must be wasted, especially the open, fertile width of a Saturday night.

Elizabeth Joll. She lived in a duplex on Lanark Avenue. Turn a sharp right after the lights, she told him.

He parked beside a small lilac tree that was just coming into bloom, and it seemed to him as he walked up the porch steps (peeling paint, loose boards) that if he could only fill his lungs full enough with hypnotic lilac fragrance, it would carry him through the first hour of anxious stiffness. Valor, valor, he said to himself.

"Care for something to drink before we go?" Elizabeth Joll offered.

He was able to see more of her face tonight, since she'd fluffed her bangs slightly and tied the rest of her hair back with a piece of yellow ribbon. Lilacs, a sloping front porch, yellow ribbon in the hair; something chimed in his head, some scrap of tired music. The living room was small and very clean. He sat down on a hard plastic bitter-smelling armchair, behind which he spotted a wicker basket, neatly filled with plastic toys.

She followed his gaze. "I couldn't get a sitter," she said, "but my little boy's asleep, and the next-door neighbor said she'd check on him every half hour."

"We don't have to go to a movie," Tom said. "We could always stay here and watch TV," but even he knew this wasn't much of an offer.

"He's good as gold. He never wakes up at night."

"If you're sure."

She tiptoed into the kitchen and came back carrying a small round tray on which were balanced two glasses of wine. "I don't have any real booze, I'm afraid, just this wine."

"Great."

"Hmmm. It's not bad."

"Not too sweet."

"Don't you just hate sweet wine?" She seemed to wear about her head an aura of apprehension.

"A lot of people like it, though."

"So I've noticed." At which she laughed, rather loudly and long.

The movie was surprisingly entertaining, what the reviews had described as a comic thriller: a car-theft ring, hardened criminals all, who find themselves in possession of a hot Volvo containing a litter of purebred puppies, one of the world's rarest breeds and worth millions.

Tom, who was fond of dogs, though he'd never actually owned one, was enchanted by the puppies' antics and forgot to reach for Elizabeth Joll's hand until half the film had elapsed. The hand, when he found it, was smooth, ringless, and rather small. He squeezed, self-critically—was his squeeze a skillful squeeze? She squeezed back, and laughed her disproportionately loud laugh once again.

After the movie, heartened by the availability of her hand, he suggested going to a jazz club he knew.

"Oh, I don't know." She brushed back her hair. "My little boy—I'd better get home. Why don't you come back and I'll make us some coffee?"

The night was warm, the moon nimble and shy, and they drove along the spacious dark streets with the windows down. She was a bookkeeper for a Ford agency, she told him, shifting sideways on the upholstery. He was in communications, he said, and she bobbed her head vigorously as though this were something she already knew but was too embarrassed to discuss.

When they pulled up in front of her house, he breathed in another noseful of lilac, but the scent, instead of sharpening his longing, made him wish, suddenly, to be elsewhere, not inside the clean cramped airlessness of this house, but in some dark, starry place where he could be as still and unconscious and alone as Elizabeth Joll's sleeping child. This was all wrong. Let me out of here, his heart cried.

And then the two of them, sitting in the parked car, entered what Tom afterward remembered as a dialogue of pure pathos, the script of twin losers, a couple of chumps anxious to spare each other's feelings.

"Maybe I'd better not come in," he said. His face felt broken, weak. "I'm kind of tired. And I've got this cold."

"That's okay," she said with one final peal of her hungry laughter. "I've got my period anyway."

"Mom."

"That you, Tom? I thought it might be you phoning. I said to Mike, 'I bet that's Tom phoning.' "

"How you doing, Mom?"

"You all right? Everything okay?"

"Just phoning to say hello, Mom. See how you're doing."

"You sound kind of stuffed up."

"I've got this cold."

"It's going around. Summer colds. Could be hay fever."

"Sun shining up there?"

"Rain. Same thing every darn Sunday. It's like the weatherman's got it in for us, but good."

"Here too, it's crazy."

"You sure sound plugged up."

"I'm fine, fine. I just called because I thought you and Mike might've phoned last night. When I was out."

"We were down at the Legion. Big retirement party, a real gang."

"Great."

"Out? You were out last night?"

"Yeah. A movie."

"With a girl?"

"Well, more like a woman than a girl, I guess."

"Nice?"

"Pretty nice."

"How about you bringing her up one weekend? Mike's been talking about doing some fishing, keeps asking when you're coming up. You could bring her along, we're not shy."

"Oh, I'll be up in a couple weeks. This is kind of a busy time of year."

"Yeah, I know."

"Lots to do, this time of year."

"What's her name?"

"Whose name?"

"The new girl. The one you were out to the show with last night."

"Oh, she's just a girl."

"Yeah, well, I bet you anything she's got a name."

"Elizabeth."

"Elizabeth, eh."

"Well, I just thought I'd give you a call, Mom, in case you phoned last night and wondered where I was."

"So, you doing anything special today?"

"Nothing much. I've got some work I've got to do. Say hello to Mike."

"Gargle."

"What?"

"For that cold. Look after yourself, gargle."

"I will, I will. Take care, Mom."

"You too, kiddo."

ALL SHE WANTS for him is everything.

This is what Tom, talking about his mother, sometimes says. All she wants is his success, his health, his total happiness, but mostly she wants to see him settled.

"So you've hit some rough spots, so what. Next time you'll hit the jackpot. I've seen it happen. I never was a hundred percent sure of that Sheila of yours. She had the career-girl look in her eyes right from the start, real ambitious, I could tell. And that Clair, what a girl she was, she just had you by the short and curlies, thought she'd have herself a free ride, butter both sides of her pocket. I think you just felt sorry for her. I sure was glad when you caught on to her. I was pretty worried, let me tell you, and then out of the fire into the frying pan with your Susie-Q. Well, she sure wasn't ready to settle down. Frying an egg was too much bother. Making the bed was too much bother. But how're you supposed to know how she'd turn out, how she was going to play the queen bee all the time. There're plenty of nice girls out there ready to settle down. They'd give their heart to settle down. Nice house, couple of kids, a camper for trips. They'd give their eye-teeth. So don't let yourself get bogged down on a plateau. Be a little choosy. You had your wild oats, that's fine, but you got to be choosy when you think about really settling down. Oh boy, do you ever."

SHE HERSELF MARRIED for the first time at the age of fifty-two. The man she married was a retired barber named, appropriately, Mike Barbour. She'd known him for years, and she'd been a good friend of Cissy Barbour, too, before she died of cancer of the uterus.

Once they'd even gone on a vacation together, the three of them, driving down to Las Vegas to play the slot machines.

When Mike Barbour married again so soon after Cissy died, no one in Duck River raised so much as a squawk. Certain men can't keep house or cook a proper meal, but more than that, they need some softness in their lives to answer to their own. And Betty Avery, despite her rattletrap voice, was a softie. A hellion in her young days, though lots had been worse. She'd gone ahead and got her practical nurse's license, and when her son, Tom, was away at university she took extra shifts at the hospital, on her feet half the night, and home to that suite over the barber shop, three dinky rooms and the pullout couch she slept on until Tom went away for good, all by her lonesome up there, just her and the TV set, black-and-white, too. No one should be alone forever, people said after she and Mike Barbour tied the knot, no one.

"Don't stir yourself," Tom's mother used to say to him when he was growing up. It was one of her expressions. Don't stir yourself, I'll get your socks, your glass of milk, your book, your pencil, your pillow, your aspirin. Sit tight, don't exert yourself, let me, let me sew on your button, polish your shoes, bake your favorite dessert. Sit back, be comfy, let me do it.

What could he do but obey? She possessed a combination of good will and vulnerability that made it hard to refuse her. Why should he stir himself when this deft, energetic, wily mother of his was so insistent, and when doing things for him gave her so much pleasure—for years, her only pleasure.

"I was what you call a spoiled brat," Tom told Ted Woloschuk down at the studio five minutes before air time. In front of him on his felt-padded table was a box of Kleenex, a package of cough drops, and a tall glass filled with hot water, lemon juice, and honey. "I was spoiled on a daily basis, but when I was sick I was spoiled rotten. And this, right here in front of me, was my mother's prize cure, hot lemon and honey." He raised it to his lips. "May it work its healing magic."

It was Wednesday night, guest night, and tonight's guest, on a telephone hookup from Thunder Bay, was Helen Ryder, who had recently invited a blue-ribbon bull into a friend's china shop. It was really a charity stunt, she explained, a money raiser for multiple sclerosis, but it turned out to be a crazy kind of community extravaganza. The sidewalk outside the store was full of people peering through the window, trying to see how many teapots and plates the bull knocked off the shelves. Some of them were placing private bets as well as buying raffle tickets on a Royal Doulton cake server. Well, nothing much happened. A lot of money got raised and a lot of excitement was generated, but the bull just stood placidly in the aisle for half an hour, only once or twice sniffing a cup and saucer with his big soft nose.

"People kept asking me if we'd tranquilized him," Helen Ryder said, "but we didn't. He's just a very nice bull. He belongs to my brother who farms about thirty miles from here. His name's Bobby. The bull, that is, not my brother."

It always surpises Tom that guests are willing to come on his show in the middle of the night—the Wednesday-night guest slot is between 2:00 and 3:00 a.m.—and without getting paid a cent. Hardly anyone ever says no. He can't understand it, whether it's vanity or a yearning for a crack at show biz or maybe some naive reverence for the air waves that makes an invitation seem like a summons. He's also surprised at how chatty even the shy and nervous are at this hour. Of course, late-night radio invites intimacy; he himself finds he can ask outrageous questions. People seem to feel they can say almost anything, open up confidences they wouldn't dream of touching in the daytime.

"Let me ask you this," he said in tonight's wrapup with Helen Ryder. "You made a lot of money for M.S. and you provided some fun for Thunder Bay, but what did you, Helen Ryder, get out of it?"

There was a pause, the kind of shrewd, resonant pause that would be fatal on daytime radio, and then she said: "It's funny you should ask that. I don't usually go in for being center stage, it's not my thing. But I was having a few personal problems at the time. And, I don't know, I felt this urge to do something wild and strange. Well, I had my brother who owned this bull, and I had a girlfriend in the china business, and it just sort of fit together. It was a really great feeling. My self-esteem was zilch before, and I kept getting these colds. I thought, hey, maybe there's some connection. Speaking of colds, you sound like you've got a humdinger. What you want to do is get yourself half a dozen oranges and eat them throughout the day, all six in one twenty-four hour period. I guarantee it. I'll tune in real soon and see how you're doing, okay?"

"LOVE IS THE ONLY enchantment we know," the woman in the green blazer was saying.

She had a touch of gold on one of her front teeth. Her brown shoes were scuffed on the toes like a child's.

She was standing in a corner of the Safeway parking lot early Thursday morning when Tom walked over to buy a bag of oranges. She was talking to a rather heavy middle-aged man with a bald head and a face like a dish, and speaking in a tone so mild, speculative, and cheerful that Tom wanted to rush up to her and pay her an elaborate compliment: her eyes, her hair, her grasp of experience, the portentous beauty and simplicity of her utterance.

Later, as he was peeling oranges over a garbage bag, the phrase came to him again: Love is the only enchantment. This, he said to himself, is how a Chinese gong must feel when it's struck by a hammer in its absolute center.

~ CHAPTER 7 ~

How Fortunate

She Is

~~~~~~~~~~

FAY MCLEOD'S FOUR GRANDPARENTS ARE DEAD, BUT SHE DOES HAVE an active and official godmother, a woman of sixty-five named Onion who was present at her christening thirty-five years ago and who lives a mere two blocks away from her in a condominium on Wellington Crescent. Onion is an ungodly woman, but she takes her godmotherly bond seriously.

Rafe, the condo doorman, who greets Fay by name when she comes to visit Onion, wears a strange sky-blue uniform that makes him look like a character in a Spanish operetta. He is a compulsive chatterer but a persevering mechanic, tinkering endlessly with the fountain in the lobby, an affair of plastic and anodized copper that at least twice a week overshoots its rim and soaks the soft gray carpet. Onion Boyle lives twelve floors up in an apartment that overlooks the Assiniboine River.

Onion. She acquired her name—just how and why no one can remember—when she was in medical school, one of only three women enrolled at that time. Fay's mother, Peggy, another of the three, was called Carrot, though the name didn't stick. The third girl, known as Rhubarb Leaf, married a Baptist missionary and went with him to India, where she still lives, a passionate, pious woman who every Christmas writes a letter to her former classmates, beginning: "My dear Carrot and Onion, may the Light of Jesus direct these poor words of mine." Onion, reading these letters, gives a snort of impatience. She is known for her tart pessimism and salty tongue.

Until her retirement a year ago, she worked as a pathologist, and during most of that time—nearly forty years—she was engaged: engaged to be married, with a ring, a diamond solitaire, large and rather forlorn looking in its four platinum claws, to another pathologist, a man named Strom Symonds. Fay should know Strom well after all these years, but she doesn't. He is a thick, white-bodied, silent bachelor with hair whiskering out of his ears, a golfer, a fisherman, a lover of big-band music, a dancer of rumbas, only now he is a patient in the stroke unit at St. Boniface Hospital, speechless and paralyzed. Once, years ago, he had turned to Fay in a restaurant and said, "Without Onion there is nothing of value in this world for me, nothing."

Why have Onion and Strom never married? Fay, who drops in on Onion at least once a week, usually on Friday evenings on her way home from the Handel Chorale, has never come out and asked. Fay and Onion generally have a glass of wine together, sometimes two or three, since Onion is shyly fond of drink, and talk with easy pleasure about local politics, women's rights, nutrition, heart disease, the biography of Lucy Maude Montgomery and how that poor tortured woman suffered all her life from cystitis, the weather, the latest adventures of Rafe and the lobby fountain, and, quite often lately, as the tide drops in the wine bottle, Strom's blood count, Strom's medication, Strom's failing pulse rate—but they never touch on the reason Onion and Strom have chosen to live separately all these years. (Fay's mother believes it must be a sexual problem, a dysfunction, with one of them, or perhaps both, but Fay defends the values of the single life, vigorously or mildly, depending on how she's feeling.)

Tonight Fay tells Onion what she's told no one else—how hard it's been for her to adjust to living alone again, without Peter. The last few weeks of their parting were so senselessly drawn out, and now his absence is so—so sudden. Her evenings feel airless and unbalanced. At first there was a sense of relief, but now she wonders if she made a mistake, if she and Peter shouldn't have persevered, making the best of things, as most people seem to do. "What do you think?" Fay asks Onion.

Of all the people in the world, she can speak most directly to Onion. It's always been like this. Onion is not quite family, not quite friend, but a presence that hovers between the two. Their investment in each other's lives rests on consideration rather than instinct, on something that has been constructed out of happy accident and allowed to have its way. Fay loves her but would never formulate the thought in words, never say, I love Onion. It would embarrass them both.

At 9:30 in the evening there is still enough tattered sunlight to coat the river, a pink border meeting a band of blue and bending out of sight. Fay keeps her eyes on the large window and waits for Onion to respond with her usual snagging, ironic voice, to say something dissonant and loyal, like "I always did have my doubts about that man" or "I never thought he was good enough for you." She seems about to speak, a pulse starting behind her lips, but all she does is lean back on the headrest of her chair and close her eyes, sighing.

Fay has seen this chair a thousand times, but tonight she notices how ill-proportioned it is, one of those ubiquitous Danish designs from the late fifties. Doesn't Onion mind that aggressively grained teak and hard-souled orange upholstery? Why does she hang on to something this ugly?

She is a lean old obdurate woman with legs like sticks of chalk. Lunch for her is an apple. Dinner is a boiled egg. No scent of any kind attaches to her. To speak of devotion to the world of the senses would make her sniff. Her face is spare, clean, organized, alert, but tonight her half-closed eyes are adrift. Fay wonders if she is thinking about Strom in his hospital room across the river.

Can she be grieving as she sits there, feeling her loss, her injury, that shell of the self that breaks against another? Perhaps. Probably. Yes.

"I really came by," Fay says, "to invite you to Sunday lunch. I'm having the whole family. Even Bibbi's coming. Promise me, Onion, that you'll come."

LIKE HER MOTHER, and even her sister, Bibbi, Fay attaches importance to her immediate surroundings. She likes white walls, dark polished floors, brilliant handmade rugs, interesting furniture, comfortable chairs, good reading lamps, plenty of books and pictures, and, when she can afford it, fresh cut flowers on the coffee table. In her apartment, which has been carved out of a former house, there are nine-foot ceilings and angles of wall that darken subtly in lamplight, and here and there remnants of the original stained glass. She particularly likes the colored window in the kitchen, a design of interlocking leaves and curled yellow flowers dating from the twenties, which casts bright blobby reflections on the kitchen floor and also serves to block out the rundown brick apartment building across the street.

On Saturdays she cleans her apartment. She notices, with a measure of detachment, that she's been cleaning more thoroughly lately, since her thirty-fifth birthday, since Peter's departure, since Fletcher Conrad. With her rubber gloves, her brushes and rags and chemicals, she cleans not just avidly but furiously. Jabbing at corners. Scouring. Bashing. Today she finds a trail of black grease on the floor of the utility room and experiences a perverse shiver of satisfaction. She will annihilate it with steel wool, then buff the white tiles back to gloss and perfection.

Such triumph is obscurely worrying, but she's not yet willing to think about what it means.

Briskly she irons a red cotton tablecloth for tomorrow's lunch. She loves to see a dining table with a red cloth. Her dining room is small, really only a corner by a window, but in a pinch she can seat ten, though Matthew and Gordon, her nephews, will have to sit on the oak coffee table, raised up on cushions.

It's bourgeois, she knows, and vaguely discrediting, the gratification she gets from setting a table, the alignment of silver, the lovely rolled napkins. She'll buy white flowers in Osborne Village this afternoon, just a few, maybe lilies if they have any, and arrange them in a low frosted-glass bowl she has.

All morning there have been rain showers, but now a fan of sunlight cuts across the table, and she stops to admire the effect. How fortunate a woman she is to possess this kind of skewed double vision. To be happy. And to see herself being happy.

HERS IS NOT a reticent family. Everyone, in fact, is talking at once, talking as they cut through the tender chicken breasts and hearts of artichoke, as they reach for another spoonful of rice salad, as they pass the crusty bread, as they raise glasses of white wine to their lips, as they brush crumbs from the tablecloth or mop up a few drops of spilled milk with the corner of a napkin.

Sonya is talking about how she's getting a permanent groove in her bottom from sitting on the edge of the bathtub and coaching her two sons in the art of effective teeth brushing.

Fay's mother and father are discussing, and politely disagreeing about, the medical treatment their friend John Brewmaster is undergoing at the Mayo Clinic, and Fay's brother, Clyde, is stumbling his way toward a statement about the civil-rights aspect of fluoridated water, saying that in the end it all comes down to society's collective wish.

Yes, Bibbi says, her eyes smiling, that's all very well, but measuring the will of society has become an impossibility now that pollsters have become our generals and the media our legislators.

Onion says, sharply, hoisting an eyebrow, that something or other is perfectly self-evident, and Fay's Great-Uncle Arthur, eighty and deaf, is pointing to the example of Mackenzie King, how he wouldn't survive five minutes under the scrutiny of a television camera, and neither would Roosevelt, for that matter.

Fay is clearing the table and saying, "Now listen everyone, be sure to save room for this marvelous dessert I've toiled and slaved over," eliciting groans of pleasure around the table and an appreciation for the phrase—toiled and slaved—which is part of an ancient and complex family joke.

And six-year-old Gordon is dreaming, humming, singing over his untouched plate, the light from the window glowing on his smooth forehead, while Matthew whines and whines because his fingers are covered with butter, until Sonya turns to him and says, "Just lick them off, sweetie, we're all family here."

ON MONDAY MORNING, going to work, Fay missed her bus by seconds. It was raining, a cold rain, and though she waved frantically at the driver, he didn't see her.

"Oh, damn it, damn it," she mouthed into the wind.

A truck drew up along the curb, a small clean yellow truck; the truck's cab was like a little car. A woman with curly red hair rolled down the window and asked Fay if she'd like a lift downtown.

Between River Avenue and Market Street she told Fay her life story. As a young girl she'd worked at Eatons, the drug and cosmetic section. One day a tall American came along and asked her to dinner. He'd been watching her for days. "Here I was with my red hair and freckles, I guess he thought I was colorful if nothing else." She married him and went to live on a farm in North Dakota. They raised pigs, seven hundred at one time. It was a terrible marriage. "You're acting like your mother," he accused her all the time, but how could she help it? Her mother was inside her, as mothers are. "Our sex life was awful. He just wanted me to lie there and stare at the ceiling, not touch him at all." It was her father-in-law who urged her to think about another life. After seventeen years she left the marriage. Back in Canada, she discovered her childhood sweetheart in the middle of a divorce and custody battle. They married seven years ago. "There're lots of sevens in my story." She's never looked back. Life is bliss, sex is good. "We've got his kids and my son, he plays jazz piano at the Nostalgia Club, and in a year Jim'll retire. I give pottery lessons, I'm having a show next month. My name is Molly Beardsley."

"I KNOW MOLLY BEARDSLEY," Beverly Miles told Fay at lunch. "Jim Beardsley's first wife was my sister's best friend."

This kind of thing is always happening to Fay, circles inside circles. Last week Hannah Webb told her she'd attended an evening seminar on menopause given by a marvelous woman, a Dr. McLeod. "That's my mother," Fay said. "Peggy McLeod? That's my mother."

The population of Winnipeg is six hundred thousand, a fairly large city, with people who tend to stay put. Families overlap with families, neighborhoods with neighborhoods. You can't escape it. Generations interweave so that your mother's friends (Onion Boyle, Muriel Brewmaster, and dozens more) formed a sort of squadron of secondary aunts. You were always running into someone you'd gone to school with or someone whose uncle worked with someone's else's father. The tentacles of connection were long, complex, and full of the bitter or amusing ironies that characterize blood families.

At the same time, Fay has only a vague idea who the noisy quarreling couple on the floor above her are, and no idea at all who lives in the crumbling triplex next door, though she knows, slightly, two of the tenants in the building across the street. Her widowed Uncle Arthur lives one street over on Annette Avenue, but she knows no one else on that street. Some days she can wait anonymously in the bus shelter at River and Osborne and speak to no one, and the next day she'll run into any number of acquaintances. These surprises used to drive Peter crazy, the oppressive clannishness they implied and the embarrassments, but Fay again and again is reassured and comforted to be part of a knowable network.

When her former lover, Nelo Merino, was tranferred to Ottawa and wanted her to come with him, she had to ask herself, in the sternly analytical style she favored in those days: Do I love Nelo more than I love these hundreds, thousands of connections, faces, names, references and cross-references, biographies, scandals, coincidences, these epics, these possibilities? The answer, and it didn't take her long to make up her mind, was no.

Geography is destiny, says Fay's good friend Iris Jaffe, and Fay tends to agree.

"I FORGOT to tell you," Fay said to her mother on the telephone, "that Hannah Webb was at that seminar you gave at the Y last week."

"Hannah?"

"You know Hannah Webb. Our director."

"Really? Was she there? Well, there was such a huge turnout. I never did get a chance to look at the registration list."

"She said she found it extremely helpful."

"Oh good, I'm glad."

"And that you were a marvelous woman. How do you like that? Sympathetic, she said. But with a practical grasp."

"Heavens."

"You must have seen her there. She's got grayish-goldish hair. Sort of piled up with combs. Lovely hair. She's about five-foot, six. Probably wearing a white raincoat?"

"Oh dear, there were so many there, you'd be surprised."

"She asked you a question during the discussion, about hot flashes. What caused them."

"Oh, of course! I remember now. Well, I can't have been very helpful on that subject. I mean, we don't know for sure about hot flashes, what brings them on."

"She said you had some good ideas for handling them. She was really pleased she'd gone. She's been having a rotten time."

"Isn't that amazing."

"What?"

"I mean, that your director discusses her hot flashes with her staff."

"Well, she's very—"

"You'll never guess who else was there. Marlene Fournier."

"Marlene Fournier? Becky Scott's aunt?"

"We had a good chat afterward about Becky."

"I haven't seen Becky in years."

"She and Calvin are in Newfoundland now. Some job with the federal government, in fisheries. They love it there, the freedom. And she and Cal have just had their first baby. A boy, I think Marlene said."

"I wonder if he looks like Cal."

"Or Cal's mother. Remember her? That gorgeous Icelandic coloring. A nordic Amazon, or is that possible?"

"It's Cal's father I remember. I had him for math two years running."

"That's right, you did. A miserable man. Exceedingly dour."

"I saw him about a month ago. He remembered me, or so he said. He was part of a tour group at the center. From that Green Pillars place."

"Green Pillars? You don't mean the retirement home?"

"That place way out on west Portage."

"I didn't realize Calvin's father was as old as that."

"Time goes."

"It certainly does."

Do MERMAIDS TALK? Do they possess language? The question interests Fay, but she's found scant evidence of actual speech in mermaid lore. Even their songs are wordless. Their underwater journeys and adventures, their consuming drive to tempt and console—all remain wrapped in silence. And, disappointingly, the legends in which they figure are almost never satisfying as stories. What Fay uncovers are mostly fragments, blurred visions, partial accounts, and even these tentative offerings are underpinned by the suggestion of hard drink and the deceptive algebra of the imagination trying to make a story out of an absence of linearity.

"My life is a story," Molly Beardsley said to Fay the day she gave her a lift downtown.

But Fay knows better; however much Molly Beardsley yearns to bring narrative wholeness to her life, hers is not a complete story, and not because it isn't comic, brave, touching, and possessed of a happy ending. Her experience is too random and unreasonable, too large-scale; it has a bulging, uneven shape; there are too many pigs, too many years, and no recorded trace of reflection.

Most people's lives don't wrap up nearly as neatly as they'd like to think. Fay's sure of that. Most people's lives are a mess.

~ CHAPTER 8 ~

Running Lightly

TOM'S FACE WAS EIGHT FEET HIGH. HIS NOSE—FAIRLY STRAIGHT, decently modeled, for which he has his mother to thank—was a yard long, terminating in nostrils deep and dark as caves. The self-mocking mouth widened out gigantically, ready to eat whole sheep and goats, or children, in a single bite. The Avery eyes, famous for mischief and blueness, full of brio and fake tenderness, blinked turquoise like a pair of comic-strip lakes. Anyone driving over the Norwood Bridge in the center of town came face to face with the continent of Tom Avery's chin, the long left basin of his ear, his hugely combed strands of hair. An obscenity, this aggressive bill-board merriment. Two-dimensional flesh and print. A paper-faced ogre whose morality was clearly an invention of chance and default.

RELAX THE NIGHT AWAY
WITH TOM AVERY'S NITELINE
CHOL—MIDNIGHT TO 4:00 A.M.
"HE'S OUR BOY"

By coincidence—well, more like the right word dropped in the right ear—it was Tom's old friend Ken Baggot who had flown in from Toronto to take the photo. Back in 1970 the two of them had shared a student apartment in Toronto, where Tom was majoring in political science, having switched from history, traveling from the surreal to the superreal, as he liked to put it in those days. Ken Baggot was a skinny white-faced draft dodger from the States, enrolled in the journalism program. He talked about dying his hair and getting himself a fake ID and slipping back over the border so he could "photo-essay" the antiwar movement, his way of "paying his dues." On weekends he relaxed with a few joints, but he was clean as a monk during the week, acquiring his "tools," as he called them, so he could get back to the real struggle. The Canadians, as he saw them, were a tribe of nobodies, too bland, cool, and disengaged to claim a real existence.

At least not until the spring of 1973, when the advertising firm of Anderson & Soles offered Ken Baggot a job, and he dropped out of his course. He could make his contribution by bringing a little color to this safe, bleak, end-of-the-underground-railroad nation, and while he was at it he was going to find himself a better apartment, buy a hi-fi, and marry a girl he'd been seeing.

Last week, when Ken Baggot was in Winnipeg to take Tom's picture, the two of them went out for a fat expense-account dinner at the Winnipeg Inn. Urban males, Ken Baggot confided to Tom, have been paralyzed by Woody Allen-ism. "It's pernicious how we've let this scrawny postadolescent nerdbox screw us with guilt. We're supposed to be ashamed for driving a decent car. And having a closet full of suits. I like my closet full of suits. Back in '73 I had two pairs of jeans, you remember. I never washed them. How could I? Woody wants me to go back to wearing smelly jeans. Hey, remember how we got together in the first place? The guy you were going to share with ducked out on you and you needed someone quick to make up the rent. Seventy bucks a month. Weird. And here you are. And here I am. To take your picture, to blow you up sky high."

HE HATED IT. The size of it. The indecency. It was altogether too public. It lunged at motorists, at perfectly nice guys driving by in their cars, guys who had a right to look up and see someone maybe drinking orange juice or reaching for a tea bag. God. It was a shocking face, irresponsible, far too much protoplasm hanging on to the edges, a fake Olympian, a greaser, a hoser. (Would you buy a used crutch from this man? Are you kidding?) Tom Avery, he's our man. Yeah, yeah. Smarm. That's a leer you got, fella. It made him sick just to look at it. And there were eleven others just like it dotted across town: He wasn't even going to think about that.

And yet, on Sunday morning, waking early and pulling on a pair of jeans and a sweater, he walked over to Mr. Donut's for coffee and then found himself continuing down Stradbrook, a street overleafed by elm and ash trees, past Posters Plus and the AIDS Information Center and the Kitchen Refit place, down toward the Norwood Bridge. Ah, God! Still there—the imbecile grin, the acreage of forehead, fleshy pinks, flashy oranges, a guy drooling sunshine all over the public. Weary, bleary, arghhh, get rid of this creep. He's a menace to the environment, an insult to the calm daily river of traffic.

But today was different.

Main Street was full of commotion today. A Sunday morning, a flawless sky. People were lined up along the curbs, an air of carnival. Another parade? Unlikely.

Then he remembered. Today was Marathon Day, the fourth Sunday in May. He'd been announcing it on the air every night for a week, but he'd forgotten today was the day. A terrific day, too. A flushed, salmon-colored sky filled in the narrow spaces between stone buildings, keeping them buoyant and friendly.

"Hey, Tom. How ya doin', fella?"

It was Sammy Sweet running by, light and fresh in blue-and-white shorts and beautiful Nike Air-Max running shoes. Pale, plump Sammy, who had briefly been married to Tom's first wife, Sheila, and then married a woman called Fritzi. Tom had met

Sammy four or five times around town, a nice enough guy, but not someone he'd figured for a runner.

He was caught off guard, and as a reflex, or a gesture of apology for having misjudged Sammy, he wasn't sure which, Tom fell in with him—despite the fact that he was dressed in jeans and street shoes. The two of them ran alongside each other for a matey half mile or so.

"So," Tom breathed out, his shoes slapping the pavement, "you going the whole twenty-six?"

Sammy was in a cheery mood. "Hope so. It's my sixth year."

"Not bad, not bad," Tom said. He meant it.

"This first five miles is the easy part, though. After that I start to feel it in the old lung sacs."

Tom said to Sammy, "I guess you learn to pace yourself." This struck him as an appropriate remark between two guys running along together. Two guys who'd both been married to the same woman.

"Oh, well"—Sammy exhaled noisily, as if to demonstrate an underlying humility—"I'm one of the slow ones. Never made it under four hours yet. Probably never will. I'm not in it for the competition. I get plenty of that in my working life."

"How's the market doing, anyway?" Tom remembered now that Sammy was in real estate and that the market was slow.

"Starting to pick up."

"Great, great." He felt his pants ripple against his calves. He and Sammy were trotting past the handsome old train station now, and the crowds along the sides of the street were getting heavier.

"A perfect day," Sammy said socially. "Last year was a bummer, we had the heat and the humidity both."

A perfect day? Was it? Yes, it was. Tom looked up. The sky over the Trizec Building was hard and brilliant, like a stretch of painted scenery.

"You ever think of going for it?" Sammy asked, glancing down at Tom's shoes. "You look like you've got a great stride on you."

This tossed scrap of praise warmed Tom extravagantly. "I just might one year."

"Here's where I have to start paying attention," Sammy said. "Fritzi said she'd be in front of the Richardson Building with the kids. Waving me on."

Fritzi. Fritzi Knightly? Tom tried to remember what she looked like. Reddish hair. More blond than red. A heavy face for a woman. Big toothy smile. But sensual. He'd met her once, at a football game or something, and shaking her hand he'd thought: So this is the woman Sammy Sweet "couldn't live without." He remembered the phrase—how the force of Sammy's rumored passion (relayed to him by Sheila) had gripped and puzzled him.

"I don't see her," Sammy breathed. "Do you see her?"

"No," Tom said, looking to the right, "but there's a lot of people."

"Oh, Fritzi'll be right out in front. She's bringing a change of socks. It's worth losing a minute for fresh socks, you can make it up. That's one of the little-known truths of the marathon game. Fresh socks."

"I don't see her."

"She must've got the time wrong," Sammy said. He was panting faintly.

"Maybe she said *across* from the Richardson Building."

"No." The suggestion seemed to irritate Sammy. "She's always in *front* of the Richardson Building. With the kids."

"We must've missed her, then."

"Or else she got the time screwed up."

"That's probably it."

"But I can't figure out why—"

"Well, I'll leave you here," Tom said. "Best of British luck." And he turned off—he was beginning to feel his heart chopping away—into the quiet Sunday stillness of McDermot Avenue, leaving Sammy Sweet running northward along the roadway with his light, rhythmic, arching steps.

IDLY, LAZILY, Tom looked at the Monday paper. Sammy Sweet was not listed as a finalist. He checked again. No Sammy.

Sammy was a harmless likable guy, so why should it give Tom

a flush of warm pleasure to see he hadn't made the whole twenty-six?

He read on. The first-place winner this year was a thirty-four-year-old runner named Steve Fitzsimmons, from West Kildonan; time, two hours, ten minutes. Tom looked him up in the phone book and gave him a call.

"My name's Tom Avery," he said in his chummy radioland voice, "and I'm host of a late-night show here in Winnipeg, music, talk, guest shots, and so on, and we wondered if you'd be willing to come on the program and chat a bit about how it feels to win a marathon."

"It feels great. It feels like about time. You know how old I am? Thirty-four. On the brink of middle age. Not exactly there, but for a runner I'm brinking, let's face it. The fact is, I could be competing with the old guys with leaky hearts and varicose veins, doing fun runs, but no, I went into the marathon, with kids who're maybe nineteen, twenty, kids in their prime, and I came out on top. I've trained five, six years. Every morning before work. It's still dark, but I'm out there training. I'm an airlines reservation clerk. Mainly I just sit on my butt listening to beefs, not exactly what you'd call the world of the athlete, eh? At the end of the day I'm out there again, it's dark, cold, but I put in another few miles of the hard stuff. You know how I see this victory? I see a twofold kind of thing going on. Age is immaterial, that's the first point. Mind if I ask how old you are, sir?"

"Forty on the nose."

"Secondly, perseverance pays off."

"How about coming on the show tonight and talking about it."

"Glad to. I've done some TV around town, and the way I see it, there's a real message I can give. A, age is immaterial, and B, perseverance pays off."

"This is radio," Tom said.

"Radio?"

"Yeah. Late-night audience."

"How late're we talking about?"

"After midnight."

"I don't know. I need my sleep. I don't know if you're aware of it, but I'm going into the Boston biggie. I'm going to show those guys. Training never stops, know what I mean? You can't let up."

"Right," Tom said. "Right." And he hung up.

Prick!

SAMMY Sweet was dead. It was in the Winnipeg *Free Press*, the front page, but somehow Tom had missed it.

CITY REALTOR, 44, COLLAPSES DURING MARATHON

He had died on the north end of the Redwood Bridge, which would make it fifteen minutes, twenty at most, after Tom had turned off at the corner of McDermot and Main.

There they'd been, chugging along, shooting the breeze, the sun shining down, a nice easy May wind keeping things cool, and half an hour later, while Tom stood at the counter of the Scotsman Cafe raising a cappuccino to his lips, Sammy was stretched out in an ambulance, already dead. Dead on arrival, the report said.

The obituary read:

> Survived by his wife, Fritzi, and daughters, Heather and Elsbeth. A member of the Manitoba Club and Rotary International. Past Co-chairman of the United Way. The family requests that in lieu of flowers, donations be made to the Heart Fund.

Tom, hideously shaken, put a hand to his own chest, feeling sudden pain, constriction. He took several deep breaths—there, that was better—then replayed his last few seconds with Sammy. "Best of British luck," he'd said stupidly, meaninglessly—a phrase from his boyhood in Duck River—and what had Sammy said in reply? Nothing. Just flashed him a loopy undirected smile and pressed on his way.

Should he phone the police? The family? The hospital? Didn't he, as the last person to talk to the deceased Sammy, have some moral, or even legal, responsibility? As usual when faced with a dilemma, he asked Ted Woloschuk down at CHOL for advice.

Talking to Ted was like talking to the drywall. Ted never interrupted. He never said, "Are you sure of that?" or, "Let's go over that again." He listened, nodded, poured more cold coffee into his cup, and finally, after thirty seconds of pure silence had elapsed, said, "Forget it, Tom, it's over."

WHO KILLED SAMMY SWEET? This was a necessary question.

He killed Sammy, who else? With the guilt of the survivor, Tom accepted full responsibility. First, there was that sneering billboard, which Sammy must have seen but was too decent to mention; and then he'd poisoned Sammy in his final moments by asking him how the market was doing—an incendiary topic—and topped that off with his bland agreement about the perfection of the weather. He'd failed to look into Sammy's eyes, where he might have deteced signs of fatigue and stress. He'd raised Sammy's anxiety level simply by being there, flapping along beside him in clumsy street clothes. That light urea smell of Sammy's sweat: a warning he'd missed. The color and size of his pupils. There were questions he might have put to Sammy: Why exactly are you pushing yourself like this? What are you trying to prove? Why don't you come have a cappuccino with me, we can have a real talk for the first time in our goddamned lives. About the really important questions that face us. The fact that we've both been married to the same woman, a woman called Sheila, we loved her and left her, how about that? We could talk about love. Passion. You could tell me about some of those things.

No, it was Fritzi Sweet who killed Sammy. Why had she defaulted on the clean socks, why hadn't she been in front of the Richardson Building at the appointed time? It was for Fritzi that

Sammy was out there running. Fritzi—his sun and his moon, without whom he had not been able to live, Fritzi the culpable, the betrayer.

No, Christ, no, it was Steve Fitzsimmons, winner of this year's marathon, who had sprung forward at the starting line, ten years younger than Sammy Sweet, leaner, better muscled, more disciplined, unfettered by love (probably), by children, by the plunging real estate market. Prideful Steve Fitzsimmons, who never once looked over his shoulder at those he overtook, who slept easy in his ignorance of the delicate springs of cause and effect, happy with his terrible guilt.

STEVE FITZSIMMONS gave Tom a call at the station.

"Steve Fitzsimmons here," he said. "I'm taking off a few days from my training program and I've got a little more time than I thought, and, well, someone pointed you out to me yesterday, that humongous billboard, wow! And I hear you've got a pretty big following. So I just phoned to say that, sure, I'd be glad to come on your show, do a one-on-one interview kind of thing."

"Well, that's great," Tom said, affable, smarmy, "but the fact is, I've got this week covered, and next week, too. But I'll tell you what—give me a call after the Boston biggie, and we can rap."

"Yeah, well, I might do that. Or then again, I might not."

"Suit yourself," Tom said, and then added, trembling, "and the best of British luck."

~ CHAPTER 9 ~

The Pageant of

Romance

FAY WAS GLAD TO GET AWAY FOR A FEW DAYS, EVEN IF IT WAS ONLY to Minneapolis. She'd had enough for one week with three funerals—first her Uncle Arthur, then John Brewmaster, and then Sammy Sweet.

Uncle Arthur was really her father's uncle, a man with a heavy forward tilting belly, saturnine, monosyllabic. "We never expected he'd hang on for as long as he did after your Aunt Velma went into Eastgate Manor," Fay's father told her five minutes before the service at Westminister Church, a service attended by fewer than thirty people. "He depended on her, adored her. You wouldn't remember this, but he used to have a pet name for her. He called her Cricket. He liked to buy her jewelry, gold chains and long ropes of pearls. Once he said to me—this was just after she was diagnosed with Alzheimer's—'Your Aunt Velma has the most beautiful throat in the world.' "

Fay grew up thinking of her Aunt Velma as a lump in a corner of a sofa, tutting and wincing over inconsequential items of news, and now she's a silent lump in a ghostly hospital bed. The possibility that she might once have stirred ardor in a man, even a man like Uncle Arthur, came as a surprise to Fay, the kind of surprise that made her smile inside her head. At the same time, suspicious of condescension, she is wary of extravagant, arcane tributes, especially those that attach to something as soft-tissued and nonthreatening as a woman's throat.

Those at the funeral attributed the small turnout to the fact that Arthur McLeod had outlived most of his friends, of whom it was said he once had many. This was one more thing Fay found hard to believe. Her uncle had been taciturn and top-heavy, bending stiffly from the waist when he spoke to people, though perhaps that was because of his deafness. She thought to herself during the singing of the final hymn how kind she had been to invite him to lunch recently, how thoughtful, but in the next breath castigated herself for her smug self-approval, then lightly forgave herself before the music had altogether faded.

About eighty people gathered to mourn old John Brewmaster. He had been not quite seventy years old, but the early onset of Parkinson's disease had aged him dreadfully, and Fay always thought of him in that way—old John Brewmaster. He and his wife, Muriel, were old friends of Fay's parents. Muriel had, in fact, been matron of honor at the McLeod wedding, and John had been best man. "The first of our crowd, to go," Peggy Mcleod said to Fay, shaking tears from her eyes.

Fay had been fond of John Brewmaster but had never known what to think of him. An insurance executive, he had possessed a smooth handsome face and silky manner but was unaccountably shy with women. He laughed rarely, which was a pity, because he had a vibrant musical laugh with a peculiar patterning of high and low notes. Fay remembers that when she and Bibbi were children, they were always trying to imitate "Uncle" John's laugh. After the funeral people spoke of his ability at the bridge table, his golf scores, his generosity to charities, and how well Muriel was bearing up. This was true. Muriel was almost rosy at the reception that followed the service, pressing the hands of friends warmly. The round pink transparency of her face, which always reminded Fay of a peony, held a social glow. Would she be staying on in her Oxford Street house? friends asked. Perhaps, she twinkled, perhaps not.

Several hundred people, family and friends, attended Sammy Sweet's funeral at St. Ignatius, and many emerged from the church weeping. The sight of Sammy's young daughters, four and two, their hands joined, was poignant. Rain fell heavily on the church roof and on the sidewalks and on the small trees that lined Corydon Avenue. Fritzi was brave and handsome, stepping along in a navy silk suit that set off her hair. Peter Knightly, Fritzi's first husband, walked behind her with an umbrella, a gesture which a number of people found unusual. Fay searched his face for an expression of—what? Triumph? None was there, and she immediately felt ashamed.

"She's totally broken," Peter said to Fay the day after the funeral, his own face breaking into waves. "Devastated. It was a complete shock. Sammy was in perfect health, and then this."

Fay seldom reads the death notices in the newpaper, but when she's tired or dispirited or personally affected, as she was last week, she studies them closely. She likes the formalism of obituary language, what it suggests and conceals. Died suddenly while on vacation in Santa Fe, after a long struggle, after a difficult battle with, after a brief illness, as the result of a tragic accident, peacefully entered into sleep, into Our Maker's arms.

This week, between the notices for Arthur Rutherford McLeod, eighty (suddenly), and John Brewmaster, sixty-nine (courageously), and Samuel Patrick Sweet, forty-four (tragically), there was a brief mention of the passing of someone called Winifred Noyes, sixty-five, who had "joined her Creator" and who would be "sadly missed by a niece, Edith Noyes, of New York City." This fragment of kinship seemed to Fay to be miserably inadequate, as did the heart-cracking phrase that summed up the life of Winifred Noyes and brought the sting of tears to her eyes, tears she had not managed to produce for Uncle Arthur or old John Brewmaster or Sammy Sweet: "Miss Noyes enjoyed her collection of salt and pepper shakers and was fond of attending garage sales."

THE EARLY-MORNING flight to Minneapolis was stormy. However, breakfast was eventually served—the usual soft unmeatlike ham pressed into perfect circles and a pale rolled-up omelet. But no coffee or tea was offered; it was too rough, too dangerous for the pouring of hot liquids. People stayed in their seats and read the harsh headlines of newspapers and kept to themselves. Fay had C. F. Whitehead's *Myth and Anti-myth* in her briefcase, but didn't open it. Instead she accepted a copy of *People* magazine and read about Liz Taylor's brush with death, and a résumé of her diet and exercise program, her secret past, the burgers and fries she once wolfed in private, the bottles of wine she'd tossed down.

The plane bobbed and plunged, and ropes of lightning jerked past the windows, but to her surprise she was not in the least frightened. It seemed to her that as long as she kept her nose in *People*, she would be safe. The slick paper and the faint electrical charge that clasped one page to the next formed part of a hieratic defense, and by running her eyes along the lines of print, she was helping to keep the plane aloft.

Next to Fay, by the window, sat a woman with smoothly combed white hair and polished spectacles, the temples of which dipped stylishly. She had about her body, her hands and neck, an intimate bulk, cultivated, learned. Her broad shoulders were held erect, neat as a syllogism, and like Fay she had a briefcase at her feet, an excellent one in real leather, but rather scuffed. A pediatrician? A librarian? No. Perhaps the editor of an in-house publication, insurance or finance. Immensely valuable to her associates. Revered rather than loved. Passed over but depended upon. An aunt. Someone's older sister. A person who received boxes of bath powder at Christmas.

On another sort of morning Fay might have turned in her seat and opened a conversation. Their briefcases, their gender, their longing for something hot to drink would have been enough to set things going. What difference, really, Fay asked herself, was there between herself and her white-haired seatmate, or her sister-in-law Sonya, or Aunt Velma, or Muriel Brewmaster, or even Winifred Noyes? Weren't they all pleading for a share, a role of some kind, in the pageant of romance?

Not Onion, though; Onion was on the other side of romance, above it, perhaps, too sharp of eye or too solidly tied to her own whims.

And the flight attendants, too, seemed to Fay to stand outside the romantic iconography. They were exempt, these nerveless automatons. Fay couldn't help wondering why she, strapped in her seat, should remain vulnerable, while they, in their pumps and skirts and skinny looped scarves, were permitted to move untouched down the aisle, collecting breakfast trays and dishing out their jaunty consoling oxygen-enriched advice. They came forth in pairs or coveys—bending, reaching, adjusting, offering their balletic strategies and quick thinking.

Fay's former lover, Peter Knightly, postulated that these hostesses of the air are the mermaids of our present age. That the watery diaspora of legend has devolved to these half-women, so brilliantly smiling and unreachable, so emptied out and knowing. We get the myths we can handle, he told Fay on their last day together.

WHENEVER FAY ran into her Uncle Arthur at family gatherings or on the street, she used to shout into his ear: "How're you feeling, Uncle Arthur?" and he would grunt and clear his throat and, from deep within the arthritic rectangle of his upper body, compose a reply which was always, "Well, I suppose I'm feeling my age."

And this is what she has been feeling all spring: her age. It's not so much that she dwells on the number thirty-five, but that she feels its authority glowing incandescently over her shoulder or tapping gently on her wrist. It has a voice, too, a lightly mocking scold, somewhat humorous, but ultimately stern. When she runs for the bus at the end of the day, dodging cars, stepping around puddles, it says, "This is the way a thirty-five-year-old woman runs." When she notices one morning that a measure of buoyancy has gone out of her long dark hair, that it may not come back however much she douses it with rinses and sprays, it says, "This is what thirty-five-year-old hair is like." She examines her face and body minutely, watches for fluctuations in her periods, in her ability to concentrate, for accrued habits of manner or speech: Is this a thirty-five-year-old voice, she asks herself, so disingenuously courteous and droll on the telephone, and on occasion so sharp? In the act of love, her legs wrapped and locked around a man's back, the thought has come: Is this seemly? For a woman of my age? Isn't this maybe a touch absurd? Her arm with its gold bangles, her hand with its garnet ring—these are attached to a thirty-five-year-old person. The new dress she's bought to take to the Regional Folklore Association in Minneapolis has a fullness of skirt and boldness of color that might be just a fraction girlish for a thirty-five-year-old woman. It suits her, even flatters her; yet next year she may decide to put it at the back of her closet and buy something more appropriate for a woman of her age.

SHE LOVES CLOTHES and is superstitious about them.

She once owned a pair of white crêpe de Chine pants for which she paid ten dollars in a store called Marguerite's Nearly New Boutique. Tiny buttons, like tears, brought the material together at the ankles. In the waistband she found a concealed pocket, and in the pocket was an Irish sixpence.

When she was a graduate student at the University of Wisconsin she bought herself a short suede jacket that buttoned at the hip in a slightly military manner. She loved to run her fingers up and down the sleeves, which felt almost soapy in their smoothness. A man she was in love with then, a Renaissance scholar writing his dissertation on *Coriolanus*, told her that the jacket made her smell like a colt, and also like long wet grass.

Once, when she was driving somewhere with her father, her stocking caught and ran. "It must be terrible," her father said, "wearing those things on your legs." No, she said, it wasn't, it felt wonderful, one knee sliding over the other, a leg skimming under a skirt or pointing into a boot—but he had remained unconvinced.

She has a tightly woven flannelette nightgown—she's had it for years—with a ruffle around the hem. On extremely cold winter nights, or on nights when she feels the world is unfair or cruel, she wears this old nightgown to bed—drops it over her head, buttons it up to the chin—and sleeps soundly.

The day she met Peter Knightly she was wearing a two-piece outfit in moss-green wool. She wore that outfit for years, but last fall she put it on and it suddenly looked wrong—it looked silly; it make her look like a mother frog.

All spring she's been wearing a raincoat in a dusty-pink color, and this collarless coat with its deep dropped sleeves has carried her through the last few difficult weeks of being on her own. Every morning she slides her arms into it and feels grateful. At night she adjusts it on the hanger with a feeling of relief; she's gotten herself through another day.

You're coping, she breathes into the mirror.

And now, having checked herself into the Hotel Normandy in Minneapolis and taken a long shower, she is thinking about clothes again, a dress in rough purple cotton with a wide woven belt in purple, white, and brilliant green. She bought the dress with the idea that she would wear it when she presented her mermaid paper to the association, a paper entitled "Mermaids: A Feminist Perspective." She is uneasy about her approach and about how the paper will be received, and she hopes that the fullness of the purple dress, those yards of redundant material, will disarm her critics, or at least distract them.

She loves the way this dress dips away from her neck and the spread of its pleats beneath the belt. When she turns, even slightly, the skirt, with a small swirl of resistance, follows.

BOTH MEN AND WOMEN, but particularly men, like to look at a pretty girl. Beyond the tug of sex rides the simple wish to gaze upon what is fresh, appealing, and unself-conscious, and Fay knows that this elemental attraction must have encouraged lonely sailors to manufacture visions from sea waves and mist. This is one explanation of the mermaid myth, but it is not the one she places before the Regional Folklore Association in Minneapolis.

The mermaid, Fay says at the conclusion of her paper, touching a pensive finger to the side of her jaw, is thus, an emblem of sexual ambiguity. Traditionally, women were regarded as lesser versions of men, with abbreviated sex organs, but the mermaid preceded even that image, being a female whose development was arrested at an early stage of evolution. She is erotic but passionless, a culturally charged gender model whose seductive capacity is valued over her reproductive capacity. In her double-tailed version she may call to mind the old Celtic sheila-na-gig, or the Indian Kali, aggressively squatting and displaying her yoni. In her far more familiar single-tailed version, though, she is closer to an Eve figure overlaid with the cult of the Virgin, a sealed vessel enclosing either sexual temptation or sexual virtue, or some paradoxical and potent mixture of the two.

What's that again?

As Fay speaks, hearing her voice, traveling, plaintive and persuasive, through the microphone, rising and falling, pausing and charging, she glances up from her notes, being careful not to lose her place, and thinks: Do I believe one word of this?

"I DON'T GET IT," a man named Cliff Eggleston says to Fay over a drink. "You talk as if there really were such things as mermaids. Are you sure you haven't corporealized the myth? Overinvested? It's a temptation in our field, you know. I've been guilty of it myself. Anyway, why don't we skip tonight's banquet and go find a decent restaurant somewhere? Seafood should suit your mood. With a good bottle of briny wine. On second thought, why don't we skip dinner and go up to my room and have a nice long leisurely fuck. Hey, come on now, don't look so appalled, you're too grown-up a lady for that. You know you want it as much as I do. That purple dress, I'm sure you know damn well what purple signifies. No? It's the color of engorgement. I'm not kidding. Oh, for Christ's sake, have I said something to upset you? Oh, look, I'm terribly sorry. I didn't mean it. Oh, what the hell."

PEOPLE ARE ALWAYS looking for consolation and accepting it too readily. They find clever ways to invert their humiliations, little tricks of self-deception, a form of artistry.

Fay, lying awake in the Hotel Normandy in Minneapolis, is thinking about how she will re-create her encounter with Cliff Eggleston for the entertainment of her friends at home. She'll set the story up, give an astringent little sketch of a ruddy, alert, shrink-wrapped, denim-clad assistant professor from a third-rate Lutheran college: chin like a teacup, the ubiquitous academic hair-cut—you would think one barber serviced the entire male teaching population of North America—then the clumsy, weak, rolled-up shirt sleeves. (All this undercut by an unfocused leer; some men could not master a leer. Then the punch line: *You know damn well what purple signifies.*)

Sonya and Clyde will roar. Bibbi will be angry at first, but will end up laughing. Iris Jaffe can be counted on; Mac, too.

The coffee-break crowd at work, will she tell them? Maybe, depending on whether or not Peter is present.

Not her parents, though; she won't tell them—not because they're prudish about such things, but because she doesn't want them worrying about her, their thirty-five-year-old daughter adrift and unprotected in the world, opening herself up to injury on this scale.

~ CHAPTER 10 ~

Don't Worry About It

TOM WONDERS WHY HE STAYS HERE. THE CLIMATE GETS HIM DOWN, and so does the grid of streets, bridges, shopping centers, traffic lights, and pedestrian crossings—at times the punishing municipal familiarity of these fixtures causes him to lean forward on the steering wheel of his car and whimper. How many hundreds of times has he spun his wheels off the ramp at the St. Vital Mall and entered that hard-surfaced glaring corridor between joyless shoe stores, trust companies, fast-food counters, discount drugs, and the hollow blue interiors of video franchises, all of it pushing up against his other cravings—which are forceful and persistent, but something of a mystery to him.

Worse, the history of his failed marriages colors the various decent neighborhoods of the city. There's Sheila, his first, out there in the Linden Woods subdivision, then Clair—but he never runs into Clair—in Tuxedo Park, then Suzanne, on South Drive in Fort Garry. A three-starred constellation flung across the city; there isn't a day when he doesn't feel its configuration bearing down on him.

He's invested a lot here—left quite a few marks, sat in a fair number of bars and back yards, stamped snow off his feet on numerous front and back porches, eaten at a thousand tables. Once he started to add up the number of different apartments he's rented since he first settled here (after graduating from Toronto with a degree in sociology, having switched from the grease pit of polysci), and stopped counting at twelve. During that time he's owned six different cars—his favorite was a beige Citroën sedan—and held jobs at four different Winnipeg radio stations. Friends have entered and left his life. But he has no children, no relatives, no property, none of the blown aftermath other people attach to their arrangements.

Downtown Winnipeg has its city-share of graffiti-spattered back alleys but is mostly made up of wide formal boulevards lined with handsome stone buildings, piteously exposed despite repeated attempts at landscaping. This is a place with a short tough history and a pug-faced name. Elsewhere people blink when you say where you're from, and half the time they don't know where it is. An American woman Tom met in San Diego on his last vacation there dug her fingernails into his bare shoulder and said, "God, I don't believe it. You mean to tell me you live *north* of North Dakota!"

RIGHT NOW, early June, is the worst time of the year, worst because he forgets from summer to summer that it's really going to happen. Just when the trees have finally filled out their crowns with great glossy leaves, the cankerworms go on the march. The beetles make their way up the tree trunks, the larvae are hatched, and then the munching begins. It takes no more than two days to transform an avenue of foliage into ragged lace, and ten days to strip the trees bare. At night there's a steady drizzling rain which is not rain at all but the continuously falling excrement of billions of cankerworms, chewing and digesting. The streets and sidewalks are covered with slippery syrup. The air turns putrid; the worms, grown fat, spin themselves long stick threads, and on these they descend, like acrobats, to the ground.

To walk in the old treed areas of the city is to brush against this resiny web, to feel it break on the face and body, to catch at the eyelids, hair, and clothing, to breathe it in through the mouth and nose.

This morning, a Saturday, when Tom is paying for a box of raisin bran at the local Safeway, the cashier raises her impassive young eyes, reaches over the counter, plucks a green cankerworm from his hair, and flicks it delicately to the floor, crushing it with the toe of her rubber-soled shoe. She caps her offhand charity— dispensed without emotional waste—with a lazy, expressionless smiling curse: "Have a nice day," she says, staring numbly into the middle distance.

AND YET, three weeks later the leaves are back, thick and green, as though the trees had somehow been tricked by their old xylem hearts into performing an additional annual cycle of regeneration and doing what is expected of them, which is to flourish. To give shade. To provide nesting space and runways for small creatures. To produce the astonishing artifacts of flowers and nuts, fruit and seed, that give comfort and color to this northerly splotch on the map where by accident Tom Avery spent his infancy (that fortunate house on the river, those twenty-seven mothers) and where, for the past seventeen years, he has elected to live.

He loves this light-filled city in the same unarticulated way he loves the throwaway intimacies of Safeway cashiers, in the wordless way he expresses his most passionate and painful moments—in screeches and howls, moans and cries, the disjointed, valleyed vowel sounds of *aeiiii* and *oweeee* that mend the effects of weather and repair the damage he does to himself and to others.

AFTER THE CANKERWORM CRISIS, the mosquitoes arrive. The question to be addressed is: to spray or not to spray.

A number of "Niteline" listeners phone in and offer their opinions.

"I'm not one of your environment cranks. But I'm telling you, Tom, that last year, after they went down our street with the spray trucks, the paint peeled off the hood of my husband's truck. Now I ask you, if it does that to a vehicle, what's it going to do to your insides? Your arteries. Your stomach wall."

"Okay," another caller says, "we have to compromise with nature. We give nature some room, but we get a little room too, okay? Now, is it too much to ask to go on a picnic and enjoy yourself? How're you going to enjoy yourself if you've got an army of four-pounders swirling around the barbecue, ready to take a dent out of your arm? I say, let's be reasonable. Let's spray."

"Hey, let's think of another way to blitz the little rascals. Let's bore them to death with Michael Jackson."

"The main thing is to get rid of breeding grounds, swamps, ponds, and so on. The Chinese—"

"We're already doomed. What's a few more chemicals?"

"I say, let's put up with a few bites and scratches. This is a beautiful planet we live on, and if God made mosquitoes, she must of known what she was doing."

Dear Tom,

The children and I were deeply moved by your expression of sympathy in our time of sorrow, and for your kind and thoughtful words about Sammy. I hadn't realized you knew each other that well.

I was also touched by your extremely generous contribution to the Heart Fund in Sammy's name. Thank you.

Yours sincerely,
Fritzi Sweet

"Your heart's fine," Tom's doctor, David Neuhaus, beamed after a checkup that lasted exactly three-quarters of an hour. "Your weight's about right for someone five-foot, eleven, you could drop maybe five pounds, get down to one sixty-five, but you're not in bad shape. Plumbing's all in order, from what you tell me. Blood pressure on the high side of normal, nothing to worry about, but you want to keep an eye on it. Let's face it, you live a slightly irregular life, working all night, so naturally your diet's going to be somewhat hit-or-miss. By the way, I've been seeing your face all over town, those billboards, fantastic! Keep up with the fiber, fiber's the thing at our age. Three ounces of booze a day? I spill that much, don't worry about it. Blood's okay, you shouldn't be feeling tired. Could be the time of the year, feeling the need to get away, relax. You want to get yourself on a beach somewhere, take a girlfriend along. No, I mean it, you need to unwind. You're maybe a bit tense. Give yourself a break, some sun, a little swimming. And don't forget the girlfriend. I'm serious.''

So! It was visible. It was hanging right out there for the whole world to see. Even a white-faced eunuch like David Neuhaus had picked up on it. A little tense! Right! Blood, plumbing, unwind, fiber, working all night. So why didn't his own doctor have the guts to come right out with it instead of standing there kvelling?

Probably he should have said something himself. Maybe it was that skeleton diagram pinned to the wall, grinning away, and the greenish glow of its winged collarbone. Fairly inhibiting. But what about professional responsibility? Guys like Dave Neuhaus are pulling down maybe two hundred thou a year, and they can't get it together enough to write a prescription: get out there and get yourself good and laid.

It's been months since he's even dreamed about sex. His last erection? He wasn't one for keeping track exactly, but it was probably early March. A feeble one, too, that night he'd driven Sheila home from a party. Fade-in, fade-out.

His last real honest night of sex was in San Diego with what's-her-name with the fingernails, Tracy somebody, and that had seemed more like practicing for ecstasy than the real thing. That was—God!—that was December. This was June. He was forty years old, not eighty.

So, six months, that didn't mean he was going through the rest of his life like this, impossible. It was just some medical slippage, temporary, like a gear unwilling or unable to engage itself with his other bodily parts and needing a tuneup. Or maybe a jump start. If he owned a VCR he could rent a wringer, that would do it. Or he could go downtown and take in a blue movie, a good teenage spanker, but, God, he hated those places and the creeps who patronized them—the minute he sat down he started scratching his armpits. Well, how about a classy art-porno piece, then?

He checked the paper to see what was showing, but the only movie that seemed to qualify was a German film called *Juice of the Larger Orange*. However, it had subtitles, which always gave him a headache after half an hour. Well, he could buy a good girlie mag, a clencher. Mickey's Smoke Shop on Corydon was exactly four minutes away, and Mick had a choice selection. He'd spend the afternoon browsing through a few *Penthouse* stories, catching up with those Midwestern frat boys squirting crème de cacao up their girlfriends' twats and then going after them on all fours. One way to prime the pump.

Or why not phone Elizabeth? What was her last name? Elizabeth Joll? Dinner, a movie, drive her home, take a chance on his body, that it wouldn't let him down. He had her phone number somewhere under this pile of newspapers. Hello there. Tom Avery calling. From the Newly Single Club? We went to that movie together a few weeks back?

Sure, sure.

What was it Sheila once said to him? That any time he felt like some harmless bed-a-by (her word), she was willing to help him out, no strings, no nostalgia, just a little mutual rehabilitation, her place or his, she was a free agent. But that offer was made a good five years ago, and Sheila, he suspected, was into women nowadays.

He should have leveled with Neuhaus instead of diverting him with all that heart garbage. If you can't level with your own doctor, who can you level with? The guy had had his finger up all the orifices of his body, so why hold back out of macho pride? All he had to do was say—gritting his teeth, drumming his fingers on the table—"Ahem, Dave, you got any recipes for a weary libido?"

He could phone him right now. Reel it off fast. "Hey, Dave,

there's this one small medical problem I forgot to mention, it's this crazy sex thing. I can't seem to, well, you know, work up, ha ha, much interest these days."

Or he could corner Ted Woloschuk before they go on the air tonight. Ted and Maeve, they'd been married forever, they'd probably had the odd dry patch. "I've got this little problem, Ted, nothing serious. I know we've never talked about this kind of thing, you and I, but I was wondering, do you know anything about cancer of the prostate, the early symptoms?"

He could maybe take a run down to Fargo on the weekend, go to one of those clinics, check it out. So what if it cost a couple hundred bucks? This was his life.

No.

He'd settle for *Penthouse*, let it work its chemical poison, and while he was at it get himself good and pissed. Think about escaping the present plot of his life. Make that plotlessness. Think positive.

Or maybe he'd just opt for the latest issue of *Sports Illustrated*. Fuck the frat boys.

He ached for something, but it wasn't sex. What he wanted was something to love. Something in need of protection. Someone, some person he could love.

~ CHAPTER 11 ~

Love and the
Absence of Love

———⟡———

FAY IS A BUSY WOMAN. SHE HAS A WIDE CIRCLE OF FRIENDS. HER weekends are packed. As a matter of fact, she's out almost every night of the week.

Tonight, a Friday, she attends the end-of-season party of the Handel Chorale, hosted this year by Judy and Rory Sharpe, who live on the older end of Park Boulevard in a large mansard-roofed house made of soft-yellow brick.

The air is mild, the evening is long. "It's almost midsummer," at least three people remark to Fay as they stand sipping white wine or Perrier or Judy Sharpe's iced grapefruit-and-vodka punch on the broad flagstoned patio overlooking a thick wall of evergreens and a line of young birch trees.

Fay has been singing alto with the Handel Chorale since she was twenty-five, ten years now. Her mother had been a member, too, for some years but had found the Friday-night rehearsals inconvenient, as Fay also does on occasion. Nevertheless, and though her voice is only fair, she continues, partly because she loves the music and partly because she's fond of the thirty-odd choir members, almost all of them a few years older than she (a bit of a bonus, she thinks wryly, playing junior miss one night a week). And partly because—well, because she doesn't have to think about Friday nights, what she'll do with them, how she'll fill that end-of-the-week slot, that most harrowing chunk of time for the unattached. *Busy every night of the week.*

Tonight Andrew Ballstaeder is seated on her right, contentedly drinking a second cup of coffee and telling Fay about how the old Caruso records have been cleaned up by an extraordinary new electronic process. What a voice! Sweet, tender, supple, with a warmth of tone unmatched by anyone since. It should be bottled and pumped into the veins of the infirm or insane. It should be shipped to the Middle East, introduced into the drinking water of the world.

Across the room Mary Ballstaeder is saying to Morley Hurst in her sharp, droll, carrying voice: "Well, he was once married to Fritzi, you know. Anyway, that went sour, but after the divorce she married Sammy, who was crazy about her, and Peter got together with Fay. Well! When that went kaput this spring—didn't you know? I thought everyone knew—he rented a room at the Sweets', a kind of apartment on the third floor, and he's still there. How's that for musical chairs!"

"Sometimes," Andrew Ballstaeder is saying to Fay, "I get these attacks of insomnia. It comes in cycles, and when it comes, I know better than to stay in bed tossing and turning and disturbing Mary. So I get up, I pour myself a glass of milk, and I tune in to Tom Avery. That's where I heard these amazing Caruso recordings for the first time, on the Tom Avery show."

"Who's Tom Avery?" Fay asks.

ON SATURDAY MORNING Beverly Miles and Fay drove up to Anne Morris's cottage in Beverly's old Volkswagen, and all the way, a hundred and forty miles, they talked, as they have all spring, about love and the absence of love.

"It's a kind of perversion," Fay said, "the whole love business."

She doesn't really think anything of the kind, but she likes to toss her half-formed thoughts at Beverly, who has a talent for weighing all conjectures evenly, taking them into the neat drum of her head and abstracting the outrageous along with the rational.

"Perversion?" she said. "Pu-lease. You'd better explain that."

"Boiled down," Fay said, "isn't love just a form of vanity? You know, the wish to be adored. To be the absolute center for someone else."

"Well, why the hell not? I wouldn't mind being someone's center. Only thing is, it's not worth the hassle. There just aren't enough grownup men out there."

"Everyone's telling me that lately," Fay said.

"Look around. I'll tell you what I really think, even though it hurts my heart to say it out loud—"

"Go ahead."

"Well, I've finally figured out that being male is the same thing, more or less, as having a personality disorder."

It was a hot morning, and expected to get hotter. Beverly was wearing a long, loose, immensely ruffled sundress in corded white cotton with bands of red rickrack around the hem. Fay always wondered where she found such clothes. "So what are our options?" she asked.

"Keeping busy. Work. Kids, if you're lucky. Good women friends. Talk. Like right now."

"What about . . . ?"

"What?"

"What about loneliness? Middle-of-the-night variety of loneliness. Maybe not right now, but in the future. Waiting for us."

"Maybe it won't be all that bad. I mean, just because you sleep in a narrow little bed doesn't mean you have to live in a narrow little world. By the way, do you miss Peter?"

The question surprised Fay, and so did her response. "No," she said, wondering why she would lie to an old friend, "not in the least."

———

FRANK AND ANNE MORRIS are a hospitable couple, and Fay almost always spends two or three weekends every summer with them at the lake, sleeping rather exotically in an upper bunk, while the two Morris daughters, Jenny and Kelly, move into a tent set up on the lawn.

That phrase—"the lake"—makes Fay smile. "Lake" in this part of the world is used generically, meaning any inland body of water large or small, and the word "cottage" applies equally to a twelve-room house on the Lake of the Woods and a primitive one-room cabin without electricity or running water. The Morris's cottage is old, dark, comfortable, and smoky, an improvisation of logs and clapboards built on stilts in the late forties by Frank's father.

Fay and Beverly and Anne, who works as an ethnologist at the center, spend all Sunday morning on the cottage dock, Fay and Beverly stretched out on beach towels, and Anne, who has been in poor health recently, in a reclining canvas chair with a terry-cloth robe drawn over her shoulders. The Morris girls have gone around the Point for a sailing lesson, and Frank Morris is up in the cottage, which is perched on a height of wooded land overlooking the lake, preparing his specialty lunch, known as Frank's Fish House Salad.

He is a recovered alcoholic, or a *recovering* alcoholic, as he insists on saying, and today is his four hundredth dry day. He wakes up every morning, he says, unable to believe his good fortune, that somehow he's been given back his life. His counting of days is a form of thanksgiving, and his sobriety wakes him early for a swim, makes him whistle as he scythes down the grass behind the cottage, fills the hummingbird feeder by the door, tinkers with his outboard motor, and admires, proudly, passionately, the spread-out reds and pinks of the sun setting each night over Falcon Lake.

But it seems to Fay, lying on the warm pier and listening to the cool sulky slap of lake water beneath her, breathing in its flat fishy odor, that Frank Morris has been blinded by his dramatic renewal and doesn't even see how his wife, Anne, is slipping away.

Where will they all be in a year? It frightens her. Will Frank still be up there on his glory wagon, Anne still occupying that chair, her body chilly even at the height of summer? And Beverly? And herself, will she still be bluffing along, hearty and brave, posing questions, boarding buses, attending showers, buying hospitality gifts, writing thank-you notes, and trying not to get too mouthy and mean?

FAY'S GODMOTHER, Onion, has sprung an immense surprise: she is going to get married. The wedding is tonight, a Monday—and why not a Monday night, Onion says tartly—in a hospital room at the St. Boniface stroke unit, where over the weekend Strom Symonds has manifested several small signs of recovery. The muscles on the left side of his face have pulled back to form a leather puckering which might be a smile, or a sneer; one eye blinks and glitters; a throttled sound like a monkey's beep comes out of his corded lips; the fingers of his left hand twitch as though all his seventy-year-old volition, all his withheld eloquence, were concentrated there in a terrace of brown knuckle-bone and grained skin.

Onion is a nonbeliever, but she's phoned the office of the Unitarian Church, which has sent over a tall fat young woman named Dot, and it is she who stands at the foot of Strom's bed and reads the brief marriage ceremony. The window is wide open on this warm night, and the floor nurse, Gloria—her name in the form of a brooch is pinned to her uniform—has set up a fan in the doorway. Seated around the bed with Fay are her mother and father; her sister, Bibbi; her brother, Clyde, and his wife, Sonya; and Robin Cummerford, the young doctor who has been looking after Strom since he was brought to the hospital. Strom wears a pair of blue pajamas; everyone else is in loose summer clothes, including Onion, who appears to have dressed hurriedly, in an old denim skirt and a white blouse that is rather severely cut. She wears a yellow grin, a comical boniness of tooth and jaw that says: I have lost my wits. And Fay recalls something her mother once said about Onion, that she was a darling woman (Fay's mother called all of her friends darling women) but was possessed of a heart not easily made glad.

To Fay the wedding scene seems set into motion by the heft of accumulated postponement. Why, after all this time? Sonya has brought flowers from her back yard, phlox and daisies, and these stand in two large vases, one of them on the bed table—which also holds a water flask and what looks to Fay at first to be an interesting piece of sculpture but is, in fact, a plastic urinal. There is no wedding music, since no one could think of how to provide it without disturbing the other patients or bringing about stretches of extreme self-consciousness.

But there are, at least, wedding rings. These had been selected, rather frantically, by Fay and Onion, who had met at a jeweler's downtown at noon today. Plain gold bands were decided on; they'd guessed at Strom's ring size and, to their surprise, have got it right.

"In sickness and in health," Onion repeats dryly, affecting a wince, drawing wide the corners of her mouth and raising her eyebrows. Strom, who is supported by three large pillows, beeps back his assent, his fingers aflap and his one good eye madly dancing.

Presents are opened: a VCR from Fay's parents; two soft leather wallets made by Bibbi, a hand-woven blanket in light Icelandic wool from Clyde and Sonya, a set of high-power binoculars from Fay (who is rather proud of this inspired choice), and a pair of matching dressing gowns from Dr. Cummerford, hospital greenies. No one is sure if this is meant to be a joke, whether it is a gesture of practicality or intended to salute the curious valor and contradictions of the event; everyone stares with discomfort as the gift is unwrapped and revealed.

Then Clyde uncorks two bottles of champagne, and even Strom drinks a little, through a plastic drinking straw. Onion reaches under the bed and produces a chocolate cake, and for an hour everyone eats, drinks, brushes crumbs from the bed sheet and discusses with varying degrees of heat the situation in South

Africa—until a voice over the loudspeaker announces that visiting hours are over. Gloria hustles in with her tray of medications and apple juice, making noises. It's time for everyone to go home, and they do, except for Strom—and Onion, who elects to sit with him for a few minutes longer, until he falls asleep.

"So, HOW'RE YOUR MERMAIDS coming along?" Mac Jaffe asks Fay.

"Never mind her mermaids," Iris interrupts. "She's in the middle of telling me about Onion. And Strom Symonds. They got married. Last night. At St. Boniface Hospital. During visiting hours, yet."

"Well, well," Mac Jaffe says.

The three of them are sitting in the Jaffes' striking black-and-white kitchen in a newly converted warehouse on Ballentyne Street—or, rather, Fay is sitting. She feels lanky and powerful perched here on a bar stool, as though her bones had been whittled clean; Iris is standing at a chopping block snipping fresh dill and throwing it into a bowl of green beans, and Mac is standing in the doorway, just home from a day at his office in the Grain Exchange, where he advises, consults, whatever—Fay's never entirely understood what it is that Mac Jaffe does, except that he appears to do it well and to be amply rewarded. Condominiums in this building start at two hundred thousand dollars, and the Jaffes have bought one of the penthouses, six rooms roofed and sided with immense sheets of tinted glass. Fay's here a lot. "Hey, get yourself over here," Iris says to her at least once a week, "I need your elbows on my table."

Iris Corning Jaffe, who is the same age as Fay, divides her life down the middle. Half the time she works as an actress, picking up small parts on radio or television, doing occasional commercials, and every summer taking a part in one of the musicals at Rainbow Stage. When she isn't being an actress, she's trying to get pregnant, so far without success. What she's done to this end forms a production in itself, from sexual gymnastics to tarot cards to taking her ova to Toronto, where they were placed in a Petri dish with Mac Jaffe's sperm and encouraged to reproduce. Recently, perhaps with tongue in cheek, perhaps not, Iris drank a glass of tea made with lilac blossoms and suffered an allergic reaction so severe that her understudy at Rainbow Stage had to be summoned. A short, slight, curly headed woman with a cool oval of a face, Iris is Fay's oldest and closest friend. They've known each other since they were four, two girls growing up on the same tree-shaded block of Ash Avenue. Yaf and Siri they called each other when they were younger—their names spelled backward. Among their ancient rituals is the exchange of elaborate compliments. "Well-snipped dill," Fay will say to Iris. "Exquisitely combed hair," Iris will say to Fay, or "That lip gloss brings out your essential youness," or "Your shoulder blades are looking particularly goodish today." They love the word "goodish," as in goodish sunsets, goodish travel bargains, goodish men. Iris is a woman of emphatic gestures and a nervous resonant voice, who worries about becoming what she calls "actressy," one of those self-dramatizing dollies she despises, and occasionally resembles.

"Why oh why?" she asks Fay, wagging the kitchen shears. "Why would Onion, after all these years, go through with it?"

"Is that garlic I smell?" Mac asks. "It smells beautiful in this room."

"Have a drink, Mac," Iris commands. "Fay and I've already had two."

"No one really knows," Fay says. "It's odd, but not one of us actually asked her. You know how private Onion can be. You never want to step over that invisible line. But my mother thinks it's guilt, that Onion's always been the one to postpone marriage, not Strom, and that now she wants to make amends before it's too late. My father just thinks she's gone soggy in the head, he thinks retirement's tipped her judgment, given her too much time to regret and grieve."

"Regret and grieve," Iris picks up. "That sounds like the title of one of those murky German movies. The other night we saw—"

"Clyde thinks Onion has deluded herself into thinking that Strom will make a complete recovery, and that they'll have this lovely bit of wedded bliss together. Sonya thinks Onion has a subconscious desire to be a bourgeois housewife and that she's suppressed it all these years. I don't know. I think it's one of those necessary gestures. That she can't let go of him somehow until she's sealed their life, with a ceremony. Okay, I'm talking like a folklorist, God forbid, but I don't think she's crazy at all. I think she's listening to her instincts for once. And Bibbi more or less agrees."

"Don't tell me Bibbi was there, too?"

"Yes."

"How is Bibbi? Does she seem happy? Do you think she is? Happy, that is."

Fay shrugged. "I don't know. I haven't asked her for ages. But I'm going to see her tomorrow night. We're going out to that new Greek restaurant on Arlington. Maybe I'll ask her."

"I always loved Bibbi," Mac says. "I hate to see her wasting her life."

Fay says, "I don't know about that, Mac. I'm not sure she's wasting her life. Anyway, she's not even thirty yet."

"Almost."

"Dinner's ready." Iris says this with a mock curtsy. "You two guys ready?"

"Ready," Mac says.

"Ready," says Fay. "Where'll I sit? My usual place?"

FAY'S SISTER, BIBBI—her baby sister, she sometimes calls her—is one of only three women cobblers in Canada, one of only twenty-four in North America, of sixty-two in the English-speaking world—at least as far as anyone's counted. She learned the trade in St. John's, Newfoundland, where she found herself at the age of nineteen, having hitchhiked from Manitoba and arriving with four dollars in her pocket. She lived that winter with a young alcoholic shoe-repair man and within eight months had learned the trade. "I can make anything," she says. She repairs all manner of shoes, belts, bags, and luggage. Her shoe-repair shop is on Selkirk Avenue, in Winnipeg's North End, and for the last five years she's lived above the shop with her lover, Jake Greary, a professional communist.

Jake scorns the entrepreneurial system, and so the shop is run as a co-op, and most of Bibbi's labor is bartered for goods and services, with the result that she's almost always short of cash. Jake Greary, who has remained unmoved by the crumbling of the Eastern bloc, also disapproves of Bibbi's middle-class parents and refuses to enter their house. An austere and joylessly resolute man, he thinks Bibbi's godmother, Muriel Brewmaster, is a joke, a healthy woman who has never worked at anything in her life. He despises Bibbi's brother, Clyde, calling him a tool of the system. His hatred of Fay—they have met only twice—seems to derive from the fact that as a folklorist she accepts public money for nonproductive ends, lives in a clean apartment with attractive furniture, and insists on paying the bill when she and Bibbi go out for a meal. He works in a glove factory by day and attends meetings most nights. Wednesday night is his union meeting, and it's on Wednesday nights that Fay usually meets Bibbi.

These evenings are a little tricky, since Bibbi insists on simple food and spartan surroundings. The new Greek place, Spiro's, with its cloth napkins and subtle lighting, clearly makes her uncomfortable, but she compensates by ordering a plate of plain rice and vegetables and accepting only a single glass of chilled retsina.

She is as tall as Fay but with fuller breasts, shapely and rounded breasts, lovely even beneath the dark, stretched, slightly soiled sweatshirt she wears tonight. Her hair, unlike Fay's, is very light brown, almost blond, and she wears it in a thick loose braid that comes halfway down her back. She has a beautiful and collected face. People have always exclaimed about the glory of Bibbi's facial bones, sometimes with a hint of disbelief or regret in their voices—

this extraordinary creature, those eyes, that coloring, that natural grace, all that intelligence, too, and for what?

Her younger sister's beauty has never given Fay anything but the most intense pleasure, not that she expects anyone to believe this; it's almost more than she can believe herself.

"Tell me what's new on the mermaid front," Bibbi asks Fay, then sits back and listens with the whole of her face and body.

The two of them can talk about anything—anything, that is, but Jake Greary and whether or not Bibbi is happy.

"Are you happy, Bibbi?" Fay asks tonight, looking down at her plate, cutting her almond pastry carefully in half with the side of her fork.

Bibbi doesn't miss a beat. She reaches across for a portion and stuffs it into her beautiful mouth. "Happy enough," she says, as though the pure pleasure of eating excuses her from taking this question seriously. And then immediately she changes the subject.

Later they share a taxi, dropping Bibbi first at the shadowy doorway on Selkirk Avenue. There is a light on in the window above the repair shop: Jake must be home from his meeting, waiting for Bibbi's return, perhaps even now rising from a chair to slide back the bolt and let her in. Will he welcome her home?

The words of that welcome are unimaginable to Fay.

The lives of others baffle her, especially the lives of couples, the chancy elusive cement of their private moments. What exactly do Iris and Mac Jaffe *think* when they lie down together at night in their glittering midnight-blue bedroom? How have Onion and Strom, now husband and wife, filled up their thousands of sequestered hours—with stern conversation? With silence? And Clyde and Sonya—do they balance between them, like an extra child, an image of that amorphous thing they've brought into being, their love, their marriage? Do her own parents, after forty years of being married, still glance shyly at each other, coax from each other's bodies new expressions of tenderness or definition, and are they stricken from time to time with incomprehension:

Who is this person? Whose face is this next to mine, this flesh-not-of-my-flesh, this stranger?

PEOPLE WHO MAKE movies know less about love than people who pay good money to see them.

This is what Fay thought coming out of a movie theater with Robin Cummerford at ten-thirty on a Thursday night. There was a time when she would have voiced her skepticism aloud, but recently she's grown more cautious about opening her mouth, perhaps more kind, too. For one thing, it was Robin Cummerford who had paid for tonight's movie, and for another thing, he appeared from his post-movie demeanor to have been deeply moved by the film, a black claustrophobic import called *Juice of the Larger Orange*.

He had phoned Fay unexpectedly on the Tuesday morning after Onion's wedding, having tracked down her phone number. He apologized twice for calling her at work. He wondered if she was by any chance free one night this week. For dinner, or maybe a movie?

And there they were, on their way to have a drink at the Fort Garry Lounge, having endured an hour and a half of curiously translated subtitles in which men and women uttered breathy jealous threats or spoke in varying shades of cruelty of their mutual enthrallment and disgust. "Extremely powerful," Robin Cummerford announced, "the emotional force of love."

It surprised Fay that a man trained in science, a physician, could so readily mistake the angers of erotic transport for love. At the same time, she wondered whether there was something amiss with her own appetites. Was she shriveling up inside her jangling singleness? Or had she maybe dozed off in the middle of the film and missed something obvious?

A little later, dropping her off at her front door, lightly touching the sleeve of her pink coat, he said, "I've really enjoyed tonight. Is there any chance you're free for dinner next week? Thursday night?"

"That would be very nice," she said. *Nice!* Had she really said *nice?*

She realized, suddenly, that she was about to be pursued by this quiet, awkward, rather opaque man, that the clutter and flutter of courtship was going to sweep her up once again, and that before long there would be difficulties. *This isn't going to work out, Robin,* she imagined herself saying over a restaurant table, over the phone, over a twisted pillow. *This just isn't going anywhere.*

~ CHAPTER 12 ~

Riding High

SOMEONE SENT TOM A PRETTILY WRAPPED PACKAGE OF SHIT. So! Some goon out there in big wide radioland had it in for him, and for a man like Tom, whose chief disability—he admits it—is his wish to be liked, the gift was deeply disturbing. He ran a few possibilities through his head.

That marathon prick, what's-his-name? Steve Fitzsimmons?

Or some crank who'd called in to "Niteline" and got cut off too quickly. It happened all the time. Ted Woloschuk did his best to screen the calls, but it was really Tom who had to juggle the drunks and crazies and get them off the air fast.

And then there was Mike Healey, who emceed the all-night show on CRSM. But Mike was far too sweet a guy to think up this kind of vindictive monkey stuff. And who else? There was that hoser of a songwriter around town, Benny Kaner, a sleepy old ponytailed creep who'd been badgering Tom for a couple of years to air some of his tapes on the show.

For a day or two Tom made a point of not mentioning the

shit incident to anyone, and then suddenly he found himself telling everyone.

Big Bruce, who owned the station, said the same thing had happened to him once, only it was plastic poop, not the real thing. It's part of the game. You stick your head up out of the crowd and you get shot at.

Rosalie Summers, the receptionist at the station, told Tom about someone who'd put an underarm deodorant in her locker back when she was in high school, and attached to it had been a scribbled, unsigned note that said "A Word to the Wise." It still made her blood boil, just talking about it.

Everyone Tom talked to told him not to worry. These things happen. It was par for the course. There were a lot of nuts out there, all kinds of berries on the bush. Forget it, everyone said.

HE DID FORGET IT, or almost. He was too busy to worry, he was riding high, out almost every night.

"We've been trying to get ahold of you," his mother said when she phoned from Duck River on Saturday morning, minutes after he'd come back from his weekly run. "Night after night we've been trying and the phone just rings and rings. I guess you're pretty busy, eh, leading the gay bachelor life. Ha. But you can't say that word gay anymore. I keep forgetting. Leading the wild life, is that better? You still seeing that girl, Elizabeth? Mike and I were thinking, it might be nice if you brought her up here, had yourself a nice relaxing weekend. We've got the pullout, you know, it sleeps two, or she could sleep on the rollaway, depending. It doesn't matter one teensy bit to Mike and me, whatever you feel comfortable with. We've been freezing fish. Someone gave us a great big catch of pickerel, that Archie Frobish, you remember him, his wife passed on about a year or so back. Well, we fillet them first, or rather Mike does, and then we freeze them in milk cartons that I rinse out real well, and then we top them up with water and stick them in the deep-freeze. It works like a charm. Archie can't eat what he catches nowadays, not since he's been on his own, the poor old guy. It's no fun being on your own when you get to be that age. Any age, let's face it. Mike says he's got a dilly of a Newfie joke for you. I can't tell it on the phone, it'd turn the wires blue, but he says he'll save it up for you, you'll get a good laugh. It would do you good to have a nice couple of days, get out of the city, relax. And tell Elizabeth we've got lots of room. Tell her we don't bite."

ASKED TO NAME his ideal land form, what part of the earth's geography he would choose to be, Tom said a peninsula.

This was at a dinner party, a Sunday night, and he was praised by the others around the table for his originality. Why a peninsula? Because it was separate yet joined. Because, well, it surrendered part but not all of its independence. Because it was permitted a measure of eccentricity. Because a peninsula can be easily defended.

"You mean you want everything and nothing," Mark Klein charged, and Tom replied, well, yes, maybe that was true.

At a round painted table on the screened front porch of Jeff and Jenny Waring's house on Waterloo Avenue, along with Mark and Emma Klein, and a woman called Charlotte Downey, he ate an odd and beautiful pasta salad and took part in the discussion of geographical entities and private choices.

He was happy to be here, grateful to be remembered by old friends like the Warings, to be telephoned in advance and included in a low-key summer evening. Outside, beyond the dark screening, a low wind could be heard stirring the full trees. Inside, the only light source was a low shaded table lamp, against which a number of moths batted intermittently. He wondered if the others guessed how he relished such evenings. The faces of the Warings, of the Kleins, of Charlotte Downey, seemed to possess a golden plasticity, and the white wine, the bowls of raspberries, the coffee poured from a tall ivory-colored coffeepot brought Tom a convulsive upsurge of feeling and a doubling of consciousness, so that he was able to see the evening as it was as well as the way he might afterward remember it.

He had not met Charlotte Downey before. Her powerfully

made-up face was square-jawed but sensual, and able to shift rapidly in its expression. Her languorous quizzing eyes and her dark hair, cut short so that it bent above her ears, gave her the look of a sex-wise teenager. The inclination of her head seemed to invite his approval. She wore a dark red sundress and white sandals, and when she turned sideways in the light he could see a thin gold chain burning on her tanned neck. Of course she had been invited for him, and he for her; Tom knew this as a certainty and knew that she knew as well. "I think," she said, when her turn came, "that I'd like to be a coastal ridge. Like the Sierras, maybe, sharply defined, but at the same time not too intimidating."

Emma Klein wanted to be a river delta. An island, said Jenny Waring, who was the mother of three young children—a choice that made her husband look up, puzzled. But only in winter, she amended. In summer she preferred to be a long low valley—she gave a sexual laugh, or so it seemed to Tom—with a guaranteed abundance of rainfall.

"I suppose it would be too arrogant to want to be an ocean," Jeff Waring began—but at that moment Tom looked at his watch. It was 11:35. He had twenty minutes to get to the station. He would have liked to whisper in Charlotte Downey's ear, "I'll give you a call" or "When can we get together?" But the opportunity did not offer itself. He left quickly, hurrying down the cooled sidewalk to his car, saddened but also relieved—he admitted it—to be alone again.

AT PARTIES where there is a good deal of drinking and where a large number of people are crowded into a small space, or where the social mix is familiar and also random—at these kinds of gatherings there is often someone who, late in the evening, will make a teasing remark to Tom about his three disastrous marriages. Whatever is said will be put forward with a spirit of light good nature, something like: "Hey Tom, when's round four coming up?"

Or there will be some slipping, winking comment about alimony, about rice coming out of his ears, about going for the *Guin-*

ness Book of World Records, about getting the wedding march on a compact disc.

Men tend to make these kinds of jokes more than women, jokes that are meant to be chummy, to simulate envy.

Tom imagines that the gibes, digs, pleasantries, whatever, possess the same weight and texture as those that involve the humiliation of large noses, big feet, balding heads, and double chins.

It seems clear that a man of forty with three ex-wives is fair game. In the public domain. It seems clear, too, that Tom has become a comic figure.

How does he respond to this kind of male joshing? He feels his mouth move sideways in what he supposes is a grin. A stone enters his throat, and the skin of his face freezes over. As soon as he can, he moves away to safer territory.

ONCE A YEAR Big Bruce (Bossman Bruce) throws a barbecue for the CHOL gang out at his riverside property west of the city. He goes the whole hog: colored lights all around the grounds, an illuminated sign at the end of the driveway that says "This Way Folks," an open bar set up in a trailer, a striped canopy big enough for a small circus, and everything catered. Then fireworks, then dancing to a live trio, and around dawn a huge breakfast.

Big Bruce is *big*, two hundred and fifty pounds of resonating flesh. Sixty years old. A lawyer by training. The son of a Ukrainian farmer. He made his first big money in real estate and then bought a radio station and found his true love.

Big Bruce's wife, Erleen, makes her own sauerkraut. Otherwise she does nothing. If you ask her about her grandchildren, she'll say: "Those little bums, they're spoiled rotten." If you ask her about CHOL: "It's a hole to pour money in." About her husband, Big Bruce: "He's an old sweetie-pie."

Lenny Dexter's at the party. He arrives in denim and leather handmade boots, and a string tie. On his head is the white cowboy hat he bought at an auction for a thousand bucks—it's got the name Hank Williams sewn right into the lining. Lenny's in radio for the kicks. He gets a high from the late-night intimacy of it, the thought of his voice spilling over the city perimeter and entering the cabs of truck drivers, beautiful guys hauling their tankers to Fargo or Minneapolis or up to Thompson.

Carly Blackwood, from the wake-up show, is at the party. Through thick lenses she gives Tom a scampish wink. "If I were in TV, they'd make me get contacts. They'd want me to fix my hair into one of those gravity-defying jobs stuck back with hair spray, no thanks. I see morning radio as something that energizes people. People wake up feeling ugly and lonely and weak and they'd just as soon hide out at home, right? But all they have to do is reconnect. Get their hearts restarted. It's hard work being a person, you have to do it every single day."

Simon Birrell is also at the party. He's in charge of the noon-hour farm show, and after fifteen years in that slot he still reels with the irony of it—that he, a musician's son from New York City, should be chatting knowledgeably for fifty minutes every weekday about the fertile measurement of bulls or effective weed management or cucumber blight or crises in egg marketing. He lives with his wife, Stephanie, and four teenaged children in a large old-fashioned Roblyn Road apartment. "People are always surprised to find I don't live in a manure field," he once told Tom. It was Simon who first told Tom about the reissued Caruso records that have been such a surprise hit on "Niteline."

The old timekeeper moon shines down, nested tonight in whirling vapors of clouds. Tom keeps a careful eye on the time. Before he leaves he exchanges a few words with Maeve Woloschuk, Ted's wife. Maeve tells him about her oldest son, Patrick, who has fallen in love. "This may be just a summer romance," she says, "or it may be forever, who can tell. All we know is he's got a bad, bad case. I look at him all moony and in a trance and I want to hoot, but I don't dare. Ted says it's like a case of flu. Well, she's a nice girl. Her name's Joan, she's studying education. All of a sudden Patrick loves the whole world. He keeps giving me these big hugs and asking if there's anything he can do to help me out around the house. Oh, if he can just hold on to this! But I don't know, it might kill him, a case of love like this. I don't think anyone can survive for long at this pitch, they'd die of it after a while."

A WEEK AGO Tom got an invitation in the mail. "Drinks" the card announced in big block letters; "5:00 to 7:00 P.M." The invitation had a black-and-white line drawing of a martini glass, and in the glass was an olive with a happy face. It was from Tom's ex-wife Suzanne, wife number three, and her new husband, Gregor Heilbrun.

Tom was surprised. His sleepy Suzanne had worked up the energy to give a cocktail party. "Hope to see you" she'd written next to the martini glass in her lazy script; he'd know that sloped hand anywhere.

During their brief marriage she worked a mere eighteen hours a week in a bookstore, and when the shop offered her more hours, she refused. Why bother when she could wander all day around the apartment in her kimono with a cup of coffee and a magazine? It was a joke, at first, that it took her half an hour to floss her teeth, an hour to take a bath. It tore at him, his inability to rouse Suzanne from her torpor. He began to think her condition was hopeless and degenerative—and, even more worrying, contagious.

And now, suddenly, a few months into her second marriage, she had awakened. This was his Suzanne, this perky creature in the deep pink dress who opened the door for him when he arrived at the Heilbrun house on South Drive. Her kiss was fluttery and full of sweetness, but nonetheless a hostess kiss, one that drew him swiftly into the coolness of the house and directed him toward Gregor, who waited, solid and serene in an open-necked sports shirt, ready to put him at his ease. "Tom, Tom," he boomed. "What can I offer to quench your thirst?"

"Let me get it," Suzanne said in a voice that sounded to Tom like a chiming bell. "I know exactly what Tom likes."

"You're looking wonderful," he said to her later in the evening. Even to his own ears this sounded social and insincere, the comment of a man too wised up for love. She had a new gesture, a trim way of lifting her shoulders and signaling the start of a delicate shrug. "I mean it," Tom said into her ear, "you look wonderful." "I feel," she said, "as though my life has just begun."

IT'S POSSIBLE for a man with three ex-wives to have six ex–in-laws, and Tom is on remarkably good terms with four of his.

Sheila's mother and father, Walter and Margaret Woodlock, live for most of the year in Sarasota, Florida, but they always send him a Christmas card with a cheery note and remember him on his birthday, usually with a postcard inscribed with a comic adage— on life in general, and on getting older. They seem for some reason to have decided that Tom is a man with a jokey, comedic core who contributed, briefly, a measure of welcome bounce to their family—Tom, the good-hearted clown, the failed son-in-law.

Suzanne's parents live in Trent, Manitoba, a semi-retired farm couple, deeply, narrowly religious, and strong believers in family values. Suzanne's mother, Christa Friesen, likes to come into Winnipeg to shop now and then, and when she does she always telephones Tom for a chat. Even when she doesn't catch him on the first call, she perseveres. "Just wanted to say hello. Harvey's been pretty well all winter, back's better and so on, and I can't complain. He specially wanted me to give you a call. You know how he is, likes to keep in touch, and I feel the same."

But his second wife's parents, Foxy and Lily Howe, are another matter. They live in a large, dark, Tudor-style house in Tuxedo Park, and, since the divorce, Clair has lived there with them. Tom can imagine the poisons that have been breathed against him in that house, the accusations, the act of cruelty he's been charged with, the insensitivities rehearsed and endlessly dramatized.

He doesn't have to worry about running into Clair, since from all reports she never leaves the house. But occasionally he does run into Foxy or Lily—this is, after all, a small city—and receives, every time it happens, the full force of their hatred. It knocks him flat, as sudden and oppressive as waking up in a room that's caught fire.

Tonight, a Thursday, it happens.

He has phoned Charlotte Downey and invited her to dinner, a Vietnamese place on Sergeant Avenue. Charlotte is talkative and lively, and she seems, though he may be flattering himself, extravagantly happy to be sitting here across from him, eating stingray salad and sipping at a glass of cold beer. And then a waiter leads Foxy and Lily past their table.

Tom looks up and meets Foxy's cold eye. And wonders how he could have forgotten so quickly the box of shit that arrived for him in the mail just a few short days ago, its stench and bulk, and its power to hurt him.

~ CHAPTER 13 ~

Seduction and
Consolation

BOTH FAY MCLEOD AND HER MOTHER, PEGGY MCLEOD, ARE IN THE middle of writing books, and whenever they see each other, which is at least once a week, sometimes oftener, they compare their progress.

Fay will say: "The thing keeps getting beyond me. Either I stick to my original notion of collating mermaid legends and visual images and trying to isolate the common element, seduction or consolation or whatever, or I work the more primary grid, sorting out the primitive significance, goddess figures, the intersection with the Virgin cult, and all that stuff. It's a blessing, but a curse, too, the fact that these mermaid narratives are so tentative and that they never got pinned down and codified the way the Olympian hierarchy did. I'm just grabbing at odd straws and trying to make a basket of them. It's true I don't get myself trapped in other people's rigid interpretations, because there aren't any. I can stir and construe to my heart's content, but it's all so formless and loose. It's a little like documenting air currents."

Peggy McLeod will say, her forehead frowning into a kind of lace: "The last thing I want to produce is another self-help manual. We've got all kinds of books that reassure menopausal women but offer nothing in the way of information, what's really happening to their bodies. My head just isn't made that way. I don't want to give a pep talk to aging women, and I don't think women will swallow that kind of pious wishful thinking anymore, that rubbish about the beauty of life after sixty and liberating the mature body and so on."

Fay, who cherishes the divagations of research at the same time she curses them, and who gets lost in the dark rooty middles of her own paragraphs, will say: "If only I could stay detached. I'm always looking for some crazy twentieth-century signifier. Freudian junk, Jungian. Archetypal. Somehow I've got to try to stand back and observe. I've got to let the observations speak for themselves. The overall pattern, if I ever find it, is going to come out of the accumulated stories or visual recordings."

Peggy McLeod says: "I look at the statistics, the calculations, and think, now I've got it in focus. And then I remember my own menopause, how it coincided with that terrible time Bibbi ran away and we didn't know where she was for four months, and what that did to me, the way it tore my insides apart. I don't know. We seem to be doomed by our body's capriciousness—at least your mermaids don't bleed and then stop. And we're double-doomed by our history, where we happen to be in our lives when we hit age forty-seven or fifty."

Fay, stricken, feeling real panic, says: "Oh, God, I could be there, in just twelve years, menopause. I'll be forty-seven in twelve years. Can you believe it? I can't. What'll I do? Oh, God."

Her mother says: "In twelve years I could be dead. I'll have had my three score and ten."

"You won't," Fay says.

"I sometimes think that the best thing about your mermaids is the fact that they never age. And then I think, no, I couldn't bear that either."

THE HOUSE on Ash Avenue where Fay grew up, and where her mother and father continue to live, is filled with light and air. The pale-colored rugs in the McLeod house are sent out twice a year for cleaning, January and July. There are polished tables and soft chairs, shaded reading lamps, kitchen equipment in good repair, and a pretty garden with shrubs and pansy borders. The freezer in the basement is full. The cupboards are also full. In every room are shelves filled with books, and with magazines that are stacked neatly and chronologically arranged.

On the second floor, beyond the wide square balustraded stairway, are four bedrooms. Fay's parents, Peggy and Richard, aged sixty-two and sixty-six, respectively, occupy the large rectangular room at the front of the house. Sometime ago their old double bed was traded in for two singles. The wallpaper in this room is renewed every five or six years, and these wallpapers are always subdued, always some variation on stripes, always in a shade of blue or mauve, so as to fit in with the blue Thai silk curtains which were in place when Fay was a child and which have just now begun to rot along their seams.

Next to the front bedroom is Clyde's old boyhood room, now a study, sometimes called an office, for Fay's father. It is a small, relatively sunless room furnished with an oak table, a swivel chair, file cabinets, and more bookshelves, but, according to family legend, it has never been used; Richard McLeod says this is not true, that in fact he once sat for an hour (well, almost an hour) at the expensive oak table and riffled through a folder of tax receipts. He retired officially from his firm one week ago, but even so, he has never been a man to bring work home from his office; his time at home is spent downstairs in the sunny living room reading books about windmills or building windmill models. It has been suggested to him by friends that he write his own book on windmills now that he'll have time, but he says he has nothing new to say, and that it is quite enough anyway to have a wife and a daughter who are writing books.

Bibbi's old room is now referred to as the guest room. This

room has been redone in white, the walls, the curtains, the bed-spread, everything white except for the rug, which is a soft-edged Swedish design in shades of peach and apricot. A tiny, strictly functional bathroom has been carved out of the closet. This is the room where the McLeods' two young grandsons, Gordon and Matthew, often stay on weekends, or where Fay from time to time, too lazy to go home, or in need of family walls, spends the night.

Fay's old bedroom at the back of the house, overlooking the garden, has become a workroom for Peggy McLeod, a large organized space where for the last five years she has been assembling her menopause project.

Work on the book has cut sharply into her private time, which is why the blue silk curtains have not yet been replaced, why her two best friends, Onion Boyle and Muriel Brewmaster, have seen so little of her recently, why she dropped out of the Handel Chorale, why she is spending this summer at home instead of renting, as she and Richard usually do, a cottage on Clear Lake. "I try to visualize this book as finished," she says to Onion or Muriel or Fay or Bibbi or whoever is about, "but I can't get hold of it, I can't seem to hold it in my hand with its cover and pages all in place, like a real thing."

All her life Fay has watched how her mother takes pleasure in the small acts that order and thread the day, straightening a drawer, wiping a surface clean, folding sheets and towels. Her father's bright face expresses a similar shock of contentment, as if a light were passing over his features, every time he takes his place at the dining table. Seeing the two of them growing old in this house, Fay imagines that even the rude surprises of illness and infirmity will be lessened by the presence of familiar walls and by the fact that they have each other.

She knows they must worry about the temporary and unresolved lives of their two daughters, that she and Bibbi are not "settling down" in the usual way, marrying, producing children, and investing in property. As parents, the two of them have been both loving and broad-minded. Each of them, at different times, has expressed a belief that every life should contain a measure of anarchy. That possessions in themselves don't bring happiness. That attachments are not always their own recompense. That love is imperfect and can even be the cause of suffering, but at least it is better than ending up alone.

This last they don't actually say, but Fay believes they sense it as the ultimate horror: ending up alone.

PEGGY McCREARY, Fay's mother, became Peggy McLeod at the age of twenty-two. Hers was an afternoon wedding, a golden postwar autumn day. She was a virgin (she has confided this fact to Fay), which was not in those days the least remarkable. There was a matron of honor (Muriel Brewmaster, already four years married to young skinny-as-a-broom-handle John Brewmaster) and six bridesmaids and a reception at the Manitoba Club; before the event she had been given seven separate showers by her various friends, accumulating measuring cups, sets of towels, and egg beaters enough to last a lifetime. She and her new husband, Richard McLeod, whom she had known since the age of ten, honeymooned in Banff, and when they returned two weeks later, they moved directly into the Ash Avenue house, which was a wedding present from Richard's family; her own family provided furniture and curtains and carpets. Richard went to work the very next day for his family's dry-cleaning firm, where before long he was made a partner. Peggy stayed home for a year, "playing house," as she put it, and then matriculated in medical school—and this really did take everyone by surprise.

"I was showing off, that's what I was doing. Being flamboyant. Oh, it was a perfectly respectable thing to do, going to medical school, but still pretty rare at that time for a woman, especially a woman with a nice new husband and a nice big house. I suppose you could say I did it for attention, although I don't know why I should have been in need of attention, I'd always had my fair share. I certainly hadn't received a 'call,' as people used to say back then. I had no idea, in fact, what medicine would entail. You've heard about people who go into law because they like the look of those black courtroom gowns? Well, I think that was how I saw medicine. I think I thought I might look pretty important with a stethoscope around my neck. The standard fantasies. My father paid my tuition, not a loan but an outright gift. He and your father sat down in the living room of this house and discussed the financial arrangements, the two of them—can you imagine!—but even he seemed to think it was a sort of girlish hobby. It didn't consume me, going to medical school, not at all. We were always going to parties or dances or playing bridge or tennis, your father and I. There seemed to be time for everything, and then, before I knew it, I was interning, and just when that was halfway through, I discovered I was pregnant. It was you. 'Well,' people said, 'you certainly timed that well.' Hah! We didn't time it at all; but as soon as it happened, I knew it was what I wanted. More and more I believe people end up doing what they really want to do. It only looks like they're drifting or fumbling or wrestling with decisions or making arbitrary choices. They're really chopping their way straight through to what they want. Even people like Muriel Brewmaster who somehow end up doing nothing, well, that's what they really want to do. Nothing."

FAY SEES HER parents once or twice a week, so frequently that she's scarcely aware at all of how they've aged, the graying of their hair, the facial wrinkles, the few extra pounds they carry, their softening flesh. Recently, having lunch with her mother in a downtown restaurant, she caught a glimpse of her mother's bared elbow as she reached for her coffee cup and saw how shriveled and nut-brown it looked, like something knitted, like the elbow of a very old woman. Her father's face has lost its sharp lines; the edges of his mouth, eyes, and chin have given up their distinction, are blurred now like smudges in an old drypoint. Occasionally he is irritable.

What she has noticed are the changes in the house, chiefly the attempts to make it ever and ever lighter, so that a kind of transparency seems to have overtaken it. The house feels rinsed, cleansed, more organized, more aligned, more deliberate.

When Fay was a child, there were boxes of old clothes and

curtains in the attic, and in the basement there were cartons of glass jars, paperback novels. Fay could open an odd drawer in her mother's desk or in the kitchen and come across a stray hairpin or a wooden golf tee, a packet of bridge tallies, a book of matches, old letters, odd coins, a deck of cards, a tennis ball, a Christmas-tree bulb, a key—all the spicy decomposing miscellany that families create, the unsortable and valueless relics of happy, busy, useful people. Whenever she looked at these items or held them in her hand, she seemed to be reading something of her parents' private and obscure youth, and also something of her own future.

This is no longer the case. The attic and basement have both been cleared and swept clean. Drawers hold what they were intended to hold and nothing else. There is a place, at last, for everything. Fay, when she thinks about these changes, can't help wondering how much effort has gone into this immense reordering and what it means.

PEGGY McLEOD, writing her book on menopause and running her full-time medical practice, still has time to take care of her husband. Fay can hardly believe some of the things her mother does.

She carries, for instance, a three-by-five index card in her handbag, and on this card is printed her husband's collar size, his sleeve length, his inseam, and his preference in socks and ties, and when she happens to find herself in the men's department of a downtown store, she buys whatever is needed, underwear, suits, even overcoats.

When Richard McLeod in the long winter evenings sits working on his windmill models at a table in a corner of the living room, inevitably a drift of sawdust falls on the pale carpet and the smell of glue fills the air. Peggy McLeod never says to him, "I wish you'd work in the basement or in the garage the way other men do." It seems that it gives her pleasure to see him at the center of this contained chaos with its exotic fumes rising around him.

When he's reading, she tiptoes past his chair and keeps the radio turned low.

She and Richard play bridge every Wednesday night with John

and Muriel Brewmaster—or they did until John died in May—even though she finds bridge a slow, mindless, and dreary game.

She visits her husband's incontinent, senile Aunt Velma in a hospital on Eastgate Avenue every Saturday morning, whereas he goes only once every couple of months at the most.

She renews the fire insurance on the house.

She circles with a pencil those items in the newspaper she thinks might amuse him, but which he may overlook.

She censors her concern over Clyde's stammer, over Bibbi's eccentric choices, over Fay's recent despondency.

She restricts his salt; counts out his vitamin pills in the morning; praises him for his recent weight loss; renews his magazine subscriptions; sorts and pairs his socks; carries with her at all times an antihistamine tablet in case of bee stings. And she mails him a valentine every year—actually buys one, puts a stamp on it, and mails it to her own address, the pinkest, laciest, most sentimental valentine she can find.

AT LEAST FAY'S MOTHER, while clearing out the house, didn't throw away her old clothes. Instead she offered them, with an abject shrug, to her two daughters, who seized on the wonderful old pleated skirts in their muted tartans and the New Look blouses and the chiffon evening dresses. Bibbi claimed a pair of authentic 1940s dungarees, boxy and riveted and topstitched in red, and Fay, momentarily covetous, pounced on the broomstick skirt.

This is a skirt in flowered cotton which, after being laundered, is dipped in cold water and then tied with string in several places around a broom handle and allowed to dry in a thousand crisp irregular pleats.

She wears it tonight when she goes with Robin Cummerford to a production of Shakespeare in the Park, the third consecutive Thursday evening they've spent together. She doesn't know what to make of him, this diffident and old-fashioned man. He seems mildly embarrassed to be spreading a blanket on the grass, a blanket they will share, and embarrassed, too—but nonetheless determined—as he unpacks from a canvas bag a tube of mosquito repellent, a Pepsi bottle filled with light red wine, two plastic cups, a small cushion for her head, a well-wrapped section of brie, and a packet of rye wafers. He has not forgotten a folding knife for the cheese.

These details, these attentions, make her think of her mother.

Why is it that certain people elect this role, while others sit back and accept what is offered, grateful to be served, but never quite grateful enough?

~ CHAPTER 14 ~

Entering a Period of

Good Fortune

By accident, Tom has missed out on a number of major episodes in his own life.

On the day that Kennedy died, that gray overcast morning, he was standing with his good friend, Finn Hoag, in the principal's office at Duck River Consolidated School. Both boys were trembling, but standing their ground. Old Ash Can, as he was commonly known, wore a look of blue thunder; this was serious, but what was it? Smoking? Setting off firecrackers? Mr. Ashton's telephone rang; he bent over stiffly and picked it up, listened, made a choking sound that turned into a cough. "You may go back to class," he told the boys when he'd replaced the receiver, and afterward Tom was never able to think of Kennedy's assassination without a shudder of reprieve.

He'd missed his chance to witness the Beatles' triumphant North American TV debut on "The Ed Sullivan Show" (though later he was to see it frequently on tape). At the time of the famous tour, television reception in Duck River was at best irregular, so that the strains of "She Loves You," Tom's all-time favorite song, the one that still sways and drifts through his dreams, reached him through a snowstorm of dots.

He was eighteen years old at the time of Woodstock, but didn't know that it existed until he saw the photo spread in *Time*, nude bathing, drugs, a rainbow of colors, a realm of sweet splendor from which, through some cosmic carelessness, he had been excluded.

During the early seventies, in the days of student riots and rebellions and marching in the streets, he had gone on attending classes at the University of Toronto with fair regularity, handing in his term papers more or less on time, bending with acceptable seriousness over his examination booklets. His jeans and poncho, his beard, his shoulder-length hair—all this was a disguise; he was toeing the line, about to graduate, ready to get out there and look for a job.

HE DIDN'T HAVE to look far. A woman named Val Webber from CFRA in Toronto telephoned him one day during his final term and offered him a part-time job as disc jockey on a Saturday-afternoon show. He had been recommended, she said, by someone who'd caught him on the university station, where he sometimes filled in on a program called "Brass Alley." She liked his voice. She told him that radio voices were moving away from the old sixties gravel into seventies hip. People were relaxing, healing.

He stayed a year with CFRA and then took a better-paying job with CKND in Winnipeg. From there he moved across the street to CFWG, then down the dial to CJBR, and finally, six years ago, to CHOL's "Niteline."

In the tone-sensitive world of radio Tom has what is known as an "up" voice. It's got a bit of infrared in it, his first wife, Sheila, used to say; that's what attracted her to him. People tune in to "Niteline" and say to themselves: This is the voice of a healthy and optimistic human being who if he has dark visions keeps them to himself.

All this is partly true, since despite the moments of melancholy that nip at his heels, despite his occasional loneliness and sense of failure and his fear of aging, despite al! this he wakes up most mornings believing that he is about to enter a period of good fortune. He is making progress; he knows this because he can look back at the follies of recent years, at his terrible and fragile arrangements, and sort them into bundles, saying—to the ceiling, to the shower tile, to Ted Woloschuk, who is right this minute giving him the one-minute-to-air signal from the control room— those brave words: Never again.

NEVER AGAIN will he attend a meeting of the Newly Single Club. No matter how restless he finds himself on a Friday night, no matter how the width of a vacant evening yawns and beckons, no matter how fiercely his guilt yearns for the punishment of Patsy MacArthur's sharp, minty merriment, he will stay away.

He should have guessed that Elizabeth Joll would be there waiting for him. All during the lecture—one he'd heard before, "Hanging Out, Hanging In, Hanging On"—he felt the rage of her dark sideways stare. Afterward, on the steps outside the Community Center, she caught up with him.

"Excuse me, Tom? Can you spare a couple of minutes? There's something I want to ask you."

Her voice was moderate, polite, yet he felt he was about to be bayoneted. He resented her hand on his arm. He resented having to turn his head and acknowledge her.

"Okay," she breathed, "I'll be very, very brief. I thought of phoning you, but I held off. For days, and then weeks. And then I thought I'd maybe write you a note, but I didn't. I didn't want to intrude on your space. I mean, we only had one date, big deal, so that doesn't give me the right to ask questions, does it? Oh brother, do I ever know that. But I'm trying to make a new life for myself now that I'm on my own. I come to these Friday-night things and try to figure out what I should be doing to get on my feet again. Do you have any idea how hard it is for someone on her own to meet someone? I'm doing something wrong, I know that much, and I just want to know what. We had a nice time that night, didn't we? I mean, I'm no Linda Evans, but I'm not Count Dracula, either. Was it something I said? I don't think it could have been. I thought about it, and I don't think I said anything off-putting or dumb. What I figured out was, it was because I've got a kid, this nice little kid. Is that it? Are you scared to get involved with a woman who happens to have a kid? Is that it? Or is it something else? Something about me? I know you're this big media honcho. I mean, I see your face plastered all over town, and maybe you think I'm just not up to your level or something, not worth bothering about, but don't you think you could at least give me some kind of idea, like is it bad breath or bad vibes or what?"

Her voice cracked and closed; her face turned red and then blotchy as the blood settled. She let go of his arm, at last, and pushed past him down the stairs, but he managed to catch up with her. All the parts of her body were writhing, her mouth, her hair, but he caught her elbow and held on.

"Look," he said to her, "I'm not in very good shape at the moment." He took a breath. "This isn't easy to talk about, but I've been going through a pretty bad time. You're an attractive woman, I really enjoyed our evening together, we had a nice time."

"Yeah," Her voice was ugly. "Some nice time."

"And I've got nothing against kids. I like kids. I wish to hell I had a couple—"

"I'll just bet."

"And I wish I was in better shape."

"So what is it, then? Your big problem."

"Look, what if we went and had a cup of coffe—"

"Christ, no," she said, yanking her elbow away. For a minute he thought she was going to punch him, but all she did was shrug. A monumental, careless shrug. "Just fuck off, why don't you, just get out of my way."

NEVER AGAIN would he marry a woman who rated his sexual performance on a one-to-ten scale (Sheila) and invited him to rate hers, but sulked when he did.

Never again would he marry someone who was hooked on tranquilizers, sleeping pills, and codeine (Clair) and who bit the skin of his back during the act of love, bit it so hard she drew blood, and in the morning couldn't remember.

Never again would he marry a woman he'd known only three months (Suzanne) who thought dinner was a boiled egg or an apple salad.

Never again would he marry a woman who didn't want to have children because it would take too much time (Sheila) or because it was too heavy a responsibility (Clair) or because she didn't want to get stretch marks on her abdomen (Suzanne). He didn't know if he wanted children, never mind what he told Elizabeth Joll. Some kids he liked, others he didn't. Chrissie Chandler was a brat, everyone said as much, but Gary Waring was a great little guy with a bright contagious laugh. Anyway, whether he wanted to have children or not was beside the point; what he wanted was a wife who wanted children, even if she didn't actually have them. This was illogical and antiquated, he knew that much, but that was the way it was.

Never again would he marry a woman who didn't have the energy to take her clothes to the dry cleaner (Suzanne) or a woman who hid a bottle of brandy in the linen cupboard (Clair) or a woman (Sheila) who, for no reason he could determine, was untutored in small acts of tenderness such as smoothing his coat collar or brushing lint from his sleeve.

Never again a woman like Clair who accused him of cruelty when he insisted she see a doctor or a woman like Sheila who, though otherwise intelligent, addressed him as Baby, as in "Let's screw each other silly, Baby," or a woman like Suzanne who tweezed the hair off her legs one by one, whimpering with the pain of it, glorying in it. Never again a woman (Suzanne) who read the *National Enquirer* and believed what was in its pages, or someone (Sheila) who wanted him to take rumba lessons, or a poor lost soul (Clair) who lay awake night after night and who once struck him across the chest with a belt as he slept because a voice had directed her to do so.

NEVER AGAIN would he live the way he'd been living for the last year, surrounded by unpacked cartons, with no furniture, an empty refrigerator, and inadequate cooking equipment.

No, things were going to be different. They already *were* different. Saturday he went down to Sears and bought a decent bed, a bedside table and a lamp, a desk, two small tweedy sofas, a coffee table, a bookcase, more lamps, a rug. He wrote a check for all these items and asked for a Monday-morning delivery. It's extremely urgent, he explained. Then he went to Safeway and bought meat, cheese, butter, milk, fresh vegetables and fruit, cans of soup, a paring knife, a new Teflon frying pan, an efficient coffeepot. He bought a hammer, a screwdriver, and a small pair of pliers so he could fix the bathroom tap. He bought a plastic drinking glass for the bathroom. Never again would he stumble toward the basin in the middle of the night and slurp water out of his hands. He bought two sets of sheets and four bath towels, two kitchen towels and a pair of striped oven mitts. It was all so easy. Why hadn't he thought of it before?

He was entitled to a few comforts. There was something oxlike and docile about him, yes, but wasn't he entitled to a vision of plenitude and order, clothes freshly washed, freshly ironed? Why not? Other people had these things. He worked hard five nights a week. He earned a good salary. He had money in the bank. He'd been crazy to live the way he'd been living. It had got him down, worn him out, made him feel lonely and abandoned. Never again, Buster Blue-Eyes, never again.

AND NEVER AGAIN would he spend an ounce of his human energy on father-quest crap. What did it matter who his old man was? Whoever it was wasn't a father anyway, just a misplaced sperm on a misplaced night.

"Your dad's dead," his mother told him in the beginning, which was a nice simple slug of information for a kid until the time came when he wanted to know what the man had died of— was it a car accident or cancer or maybe killed in action? Well, his mother said after a while, he's not so much dead as disappeared. But where? he asked her—hoping for Alaska, maybe Mexico or Hollywood—and got one of his mother's burnt, bright smiles, the lips wrinkling up. "He's just disappeared, just vamoosed." But what was his name, then, what did he look like? These questions came later, when Tom was twelve, thirteen, and starting to pick up auxiliary information at school, pieces that were at odds with Betty Avery's version.

The question of who his father was began to obsess him, and there was no one else to ask. His mother had come from the tiny town of Ramston Portage, a crossroads really, raised there by a grandmother who had since died. Her history was full of unposed questions. Tom sneaked looks in her dresser drawers, hunting for letters, photographs. Somehow the time had passed when he could ask her freely for information. The space between them had grown shy and slippery. He had no sense of what he was entitled to know, or even needed to know. It may have been that the vital facts had been explained to him years before, only he had forgotten, and now the information gap would never be closed.

Eighteen years old and filling out a scholarship application for the University of Toronto, it occurred to him that he might solicit his mother's help with the personal-information sheet, that this crafty ploy would force her to declare a few of the facts he needed to know.

It was a Sunday. The two of them, he remembered, sat close together at the kitchen table, brown plastic bordered by chrome stripping. She picked up the pen he gave her, slowly and carefully filled in all the blanks—except for "father's name." Aha!

"You can't leave that blank," Tom told her triumphantly. "You've got to put something in that space. A name."

He was shaking with excitement.

She stared at the paper for a few seconds, one of her hands reaching up and rubbing the back of her tiny, tightly curled head. Then she leaned over the table, her hand cramped like a kind of shellfish, and printed, neatly, "John Smith."

John Smith? What? Who?

Her face collapsed. Her arms shot out. She'd been a crazy mixed-up kid in those days, she told her son, Tom, just sixteen, a wild one. "I had a lot of boyfriends," she sighed, dropping her eyes and doing her little trick with her mouth. "Just which one was your father, well, I never was exactly sure."

Boyfriends. He hated the word. Its trivial twang. A sour lump formed in his throat. He wanted to punch this woman, her crumpled, pleading face. Instead he squeezed his eyes shut, rolled his head back, and the moment passed.

He wasted a lot of time after that looking around Duck River for men who might have been on the scene at the time, men whose coloring and bone structure resembled his. In his daydreams he imagined a meeting with "John Smith" and what he would say to him. "Dad," he'd cry, choking up and embracing him. Or shaking hands in a husky Lorne Greene way. Or giving him a punch in the gut. Even when he went away to Toronto he examined the faces of men he saw on the street. Several times he considered reopening the question with his mother, trapping her, insisting she be more specific, that it was his right to know.

But lately he's come back to his old child's assurance, that his father is dead, dead to him, anyway, and that he's prepared to live with the mysterious wear and damage of that fact. He's going to have to accept it, and now that he's made up his mind, it seems as though he's taken a step forward. He's hanging loose, he's stopped dreaming up sly scenarios. He's wasted too much time thinking about something that doesn't amount to a hill of beans. It's over, it's done with. It's pointless torturing himself with what's dead and buried. Never again, he's decided.

NEVER AGAIN is he going to have the kind of sex he had with Charlotte Downey last night. He'd rather do without. He'd rather enter a life of celibate denial than go through the hard labor and humiliation of bringing Charlotte Downey to quality orgasm. Quality orgasms were the only kind worth having, she told him. She said this sitting on the edge of Tom's new bed. Her clothes were off. She flicked back her short hair meaningfully. Her face was vaporous, her eyes gelid.

They had been to a movie, a German soft-porn piece with the kind of subtitles that give him headaches. He had a headache now, looking into Charlotte's wide open face.

"We'd better talk about the matter of precautions first," she said. She showed him her condoms and he showed her his. "I hope you don't mind if we use mine," she said. "I'd feel better."

"You don't mind if I ask if you're a complete hetero," she said. She was beginning to sound not tough, but toughened, which was something different. "I mean, I assume you're a hetero, but I need your assurance, if I'm going to relax."

"Do you by any chance," she asked, "have a herpes history?"

"I don't have anything against oral sex," she told him, "but I prefer not to the first time with someone. I hope that's okay with you. I don't want you to think I'm against it on principle. It's just this thing I have."

"This may sound kind of weird," she said, "but could you start by rubbing the instep of my feet. Both feet. My feet have always been erogenous. Only about one percent of people have erogenous feet, at least that's what my therapist says. Also the backs of my knees and the insides of my wrists. But especially my feet. I always get there if my partner starts with my feet."

After a while she said, "That's good, that feels so good, but your elbow is putting just a bit too much pressure—there, that's better. Yes, that's a lot better. Would you mind reaching over and turning on the light. On. Thanks."

"I don't mind if you talk," she said later. "Just say anything that comes into your head. Any words you like."

"I'm starting to get there," she said. "I'll be another few minutes, though, if you can hold off. Maybe if you flick your tongue back and forth. Not like that, though, that tickles. Maybe if you tried doing it a little harder, sort of a circular movement. I think you're getting the idea."

Then, "Here I come, here I come. Keep me flying, keep me

up there. Oh, lovely, hmmm, yes, like that, heavenly, oh that was nice."

Finally: "Let's just talk now. Let's just hang on to each other and talk. Let's be, you know, spontaneous. Oh, you don't know how I've needed this. Next time we can try something else if you want. You plan the menu next time."

Never again, he said to himself. Never again.

CHAPTER 15

Something I've Been Thinking About

FAY CRIED ALL NIGHT LONG.

It was a Friday night. She had spent the evening at a baby shower for Donna Watts, who was the coordinator of the volunteer program at the folklore center. The shower was held at the house of Beverly Miles, on Smith Avenue, just off Wolsley, in an old treed part of town where individual family houses were jammed together on short busy blocks. Beverly's teenaged daughter, Lara, had decorated the screened front porch with garden flowers and candles and long swoops of ribbon. Lengths of this same ribbon had been threaded through a wicker bassinet, positioned on a card table, which was to hold the bounty of baby gifts. (For Donna's first baby, due late in September, Fay had knitted a bunting bag in fine white wool with a band of fuchsia around the hood.)

The women ate from plates which they balanced on their laps. It seemed to Fay, looking around, that the faces of these familiar women appeared softened, beautiful. Beverly said she was sorry they had to use their laps, and someone else said: "Why is it people are so nitzy about balancing plates on their laps? You'd think it took some special kind of acrobatic finesse. It's the most natural thing in the world." One of the women, Sarah Jane Brady, reminded everyone of the lap suppers that had been a part of frontier life in the west. The older Morris girl said to Fay, "I've never been to a shower before, they're really neat," and at that moment Fay cut into her cake with a fork and struck a silver dollar, which declared her the next to become pregnant. Fay looked around the darkening porch and thought how happy she was to be here. There is nowhere else I'd rather be, she said to herself, and meant it.

But the minute she opened the door of her apartment she began to cry. She set down her key ring in the flat glass dish on the hall table and then she tore off her clothes, just left them in a heap on the floor, and stepped into the shower, turning the water on so that it was as hot as she could bear. It struck her breasts and the inside of her thighs, and she made herself turn her face to take the stream full force. She opened her mouth and let loose a wavy howl of anguish. Stop it, she said, and turned the water off. A sudden silence closed around her. She wrapped herself in the largest towel she owned and made a pot of tea, then forgot to drink it. She fiddled with the television and sniffled through fifteen minutes of an old movie starring David Niven, then switched it off with a snap. "I hate your guts," she blubbered to the dead screen, to David Niven's vanished image. "I hate mustached jerks like you."

She held on to the sides of her head, pressed as hard as she could, and thought: I will not be placated, I will not be placated.

She got into bed, twisted her pillow as though it were a human neck, and cried. "Why, why," she wept. She listened to herself weeping, her torn, startled gasps, the sliding octaves which she recognized as being melodramatic. "Boo hoo," she said aloud, experimentally. She tasted her tears. Only a week ago someone at work—Colin?—had told her that the chemical makeup of sad tears was different from that of happy tears. One was saltier than the other. She blew her nose and thought about how ugly nose blowing was. If you lived alone for a long time you might get to the point of blowing your nose on your bed sheets, why not? She got out of bed and paced up and down in her dark living room. She looked out the window at the bulky buildings across the street. Not a light anywhere. This kind of loud, bleak sorrowing should be saved for sudden and tragic death—she knew that, but at the same time she didn't know how to make herself stop.

Why was it people in books threw themselves on beds to cry? Because it felt as though you were pushing up against something real, a shock of grief that became a shape. A mattress was the next best thing to a person; oh God, it was true, what a terrible thought. To weep into springs and padded cotton. She lay on her bed and sobbed for two or three minutes longer. Where did all this bodily water come from? Where was it stored up? In her sinuses? The ventricles of her heart? She got up and looked in the mirror. The wings of her nostrils were reddened and raw. "I can't bear this," she said out loud, forcing her voice up to an abrupt, dissonant pitch. She said it again, with an English accent. "I cahn't beah this." She squinted at the clock. It was 4:00 a.m.

FAY LOOKED SHYLY at her father and said, "I'm thinking of having a baby."

"Oh," he said. "A baby."

"I'm at the critical age, as they say."

"Are you sure"—he paused— "that you want a baby?"

"No."

"Oh."

"But I don't want to leave it until it's too late and then be sorry."

"You've got a little time," he said.

"It gets risky."

"I know, I know."

It was a Saturday morning, and Fay and her father were sitting across from each other at Mister Donut's, drinking coffee out of heavy mugs and eating bran muffins.

"I've been mulling it over," Fay said. She considered the rim of her cup. "I'm earning enough now to support a child. That wouldn't be a problem."

"I gather you're thinking of taking on this project alone?"

"Well, yes." She gave a minute shrug. Her mouth collapsed downward.

"I see, yes. Hmmm. And, of course, I don't have to remind you how fraught with difficulties the life of a single parent is, quite aside from money."

"I know, I know. That's one of the things I'm taking into consideration."

"You haven't made up your mind definitely, then?"

"I'm just thinking about it. Considering. And I guess I wanted to test the notion on you."

"Me?"

"You wouldn't find it too awkward to handle? This husband-less daughter of yours, producing a kid."

"Believe me, daughter mine, awkward is not a word that would occur to me. And since when, may I ask, have you felt obliged to ask for your parents' blessing?"

"I'd just like your reaction. For instance, do you think it's selfish?"

"What?"

"Plopping a child into a single-parent situation?"

"I think you want to ask yourself something, Fay. Whether you'd be doing this as a kind of insurance against loneliness."

"But I'm not lonely." She said this loudly, then lowered her voice. "At least not too often. Not really. No more than anyone else. It's just that having kids seems to be one of the big pieces we're given. You only get a few pieces and that happens to be one."

"Lots of people don't have children. They have perfectly valid lives, full lives. Look at Onion."

"I am looking at Onion. It's the part of her that seems a little—damaged."

"I don't think she'd agree. I don't think I'd agree, either."

"They're not rooted in anything, childless people."

"They're connected to love. And to work. The two good Freudian anchors."

"How did we get to Freud so fast!"

"I'm just pointing out—"

"I've got a feeling you're trying to discourage me. You're being altogether too broad-minded and tolerant. Too *fatherly*."

"I suppose I'm just trying to feel out how serious you are."

"I'm serious."

"And whether you've thought about . . . well, the logistics. Of getting pregnant, I mean."

"I'm seeing someone right now." She shrugged and felt her face go foolish. "I could keep it all reasonably simple and discreet."

"This doctor person?"

She smiled. "Yes, this doctor person."

"I take it he's not someone you'd like to carry on with."

"You mean on and on and on?"

"Yes."

"No."

"Hmmm."

"I do realize this has a predatory side," Fay said. "Helping myself to someone else's gene pool and so on. Like shoplifting."

"Well, yes, I suppose so."

"I'm just worried about time running out on me."

"Can I give you some advice?"

"I adore advice. And you never give me any anymore."

"Wait six months before you decide definitely. Oh, I know all about the biological clock ticking away, I've heard your mother talking about it, but six months won't affect things that much."

"Why six months?"

"I don't know. It's only been a short time since you and Peter went your separate ways—"

"It's been four months now. Nearly."

"That's not long. Why not make sure you're clear of all that first. Besides, anything could happen in six months."

"You're sounding awfully prophetic."

"Well, you never know what's going to happen. What's just around the corner."

Fay drank her coffee. After a minute she looked up and said, "Anyway, it's only something I'm thinking about."

She left her muffin uneaten; she was so sorry to hear herself talking the way she was. Her pronouncements, her plans, her foolishness—they filled her up with sadness so that she couldn't eat a thing.

"CHURCH BELLS!" Onion pronounced with scorn.

"Yes," Fay said. "Where is it, St. Luke's or Holy Rosary?"

"Wherever it is, it's an imposition."

"Onion! It's a lovely sound, church bells. I love it."

"Tinny."

"In a way."

"Have another glass of wine before you go."

"Just a slurp. I've still got some notes to look over for tomorrow."

"Mermaiding?"

"Yes."

"Church bells are no more tolerable than those blasts of rock music you get from car windows."

"I think it's Holy Rosary. It's coming from that direction."

"Calling the faithful to prayer."

"Have you ever said a prayer, Onion? Tell me honestly." (She was loving this, sitting in Onion's living room, letting the words drift along.)

"Not since I entered the age of reason."

"And when was that?"

"Eighteen. Or was it nineteen."

"What happened when you were eighteen? Did a light go on?"

"I saw a body."

"A body?"

"A dead person. An aunt of mine, stretched out in a coffin. She had on rouge and jewelry. She had a dressy black dress on and a string of pearls. One day she was alive and the next day she was lying there dead. I had this sudden notion that it didn't make a pinch of difference if you were one or the other."

"But of course it made a difference. To the people who loved her."

"It made a ripple. That's not a difference."

"Some people make bigger ripples than others."

"A ripple eventually subsides. What does it matter if it subsides next week or next year? That's what I thought, looking at her. It was a bitter little thought, let me tell you. And chilling."

"And were you shattered? About the revelation, not your aunt."

"Just the opposite." Onion's voice went firm. "I was relieved. I felt the mystery go out of things, whoosh, it was gone, and everything seemed a whole lot more solid as a result. I was a bundle of protoplasm and so was everyone else."

"And it never came back? The mystery?"

"There they go again, those damn bells. They're as bad as those prayers they pipe into Strom's room at the hospital. Morning and night he's got to put up with that mumbo jumbo."

"How is Strom?"

"No change." She sipped, then sighed harshly. "Well, he's a little worse. His hand, he can't move it at all anymore."

"Do you think he even hears those prayers?"

"Probably not."

"What if he does, though? What if he finds them a comfort? Not the words maybe, but the repeating of them. Something to measure off time."

"Hmmm," Onion said, closing her eyes. She looked inexpressibly tired. "Seeing my aunt lying there that time, an odd phrase jumped into my head, and I've never forgotten it. I thought, there she is, all dressed up and nowhere to go. All alone there and no one to swank for. She'd been a great one for swanking, as we used to call it. People used to laugh at her behind her back. But there she lay, this singular being. This singular, insensible being. My uncle, a terribly pious old goat, came up to me and said, 'I hope you said a prayer for Auntie.'"

"And what did you say?"

"I said yes. But my fingers were crossed. That's the way I was. A person with crossed fingers. My identity, if you like—not that I have any patience with all this search-for-identity nonsense."

Fay listened to Onion and found herself nodding. She, too, is uneasy with people perpetually searching for their identities. She's sick of her identity; in fact, she's afraid of it. She has all the identity she wants, all she can absorb. Daughter, sister, girlfriend, all her Fay-ness, and all of its tints and colors, her clothes, her bed sheets, her cups and saucers, her writing paper. This looks just like you, people tell her. This is your sort of book, your sort of movie, the kind of thing only you would say. Fay McLeod. Yammer, yammer, yammer. She's sick of the woman. Throttle her, put her on the back shelf. (Only when she's with Onion does the image retreat.)

She's learned, too, how unstable identity can be, how it can quickly drain away when brought face to face with someone else's identity. Talking to Hannah Webb, the placidly genteel Hannah, Fay feels herself coarsen; she wants to slap her knee, wave her arms boisterously, shift into an alien diction, say words like "fuck" and "lousy" and "bitched-up." With Clyde or Bibbi she becomes the calm older sister, slightly ponderous, immensely charitable. With Iris Jaffe she grows a coat of acute girlishness; with Beverly Miles she's a skeptic. With Peter Knightly she was intermittently outrageous and determined, as though she were locked into a desire to keep him off balance; she never knew why; probably she was feeding some strain of *his* identity, reflecting, deflecting, fading back, re-emerging. And with herself? A woman not even on speaking terms with her own loneliness.

Enough of this, enough.

It was exhausting, the battle to give yourself a shape. It was depressing, too, like an ugly oversized dress you had to go on wearing year after year after year.

"I suppose I should say bon voyage," Peter said to Fay, running into her one morning in the staff cafeteria.

"Oh, but I don't go for another ten days," Fay told him. "A whole week and a half."

"Lucky you to get away from this heat. It's been a pretty cool summer in Europe from all reports."

"Except in Greece. It's been terrible there, people collapsing on the streets."

"Right, I read something about it. But in England, and in Paris—"

"I'll have to take a raincoat."

"And an umbrella."

"Yes," Fay said, "there've been record rainfalls in the U.K."

To herself she said: Here we are, this man, this former lover and I, standing on a strip of beige public carpeting in front of a soft-drink machine, talking about rain and cold. The most neutral of all subjects, the most harmless.

"Quite a lot of flooding on the Saône," Peter went on. "And in the north of Italy, Tuscany. Devastating. We saw some clips on the news."

We? Of course. Peter and Fritzi.

This is the man whose mouth has read the length and width of her body.

She knows his tongue and teeth. She's acquainted with the fine tremors of his long thighs. His surprisingly silken pubic hairs. The reddened veins of his penis. And what else, what else? All those nights. She's absorbed those strange moans of his that seemed to originate not in the throat but in some primary node of memory, nothing to do with his real voice, nothing to do with *him*.

Oh, the things he's done to me, Fay thought, staring into the shaded knot of his tie. Maroon with blue flecks. Nubby. The things I've done to him, *for* him.

"Of course," Peter was saying, "the wind off the North Sea."

"Brutal."

"Never really lets up."

The death of intimacy, so this is what it means: Bodies dissolved in water. Bodies made of water. A trickle of memory left, thin as the mention of rain in a weather bulletin. The waste of it.

"How's Fritzi getting along?" she asked Peter. Her confected social voice.

"Oh, God, this has been a tough time for Fritzi."

"And the girls."

"Terrible, terrible. Heather's been having nightmares. And acting out, tantrums and so on. Fritzi's worried about her. We both are."

Both. The word hung in the air, small and subtly textured, like a tennis ball.

"I'm staying on for the moment," Peter said, as though he felt an explanation were called for. "It's not just the rent money, which does help out, God knows. It's more the emotional support. Although I suppose it's got the communal tongue wagging." At this he peered questioningly at Fay, who could think of nothing to say.

"Well," he said, moving away, "I won't say good-bye just yet. I'm sure to see you before you head off."

Familiar tucks appeared at the corners of his mouth, a retractable smile in a face composed of cartilage and muscle, of aqueous matter, social tissue, a long malleable humid face. A face that Fay has sometimes thought of as ecclesiastical.

How impervious and ongoing his life seemed at the moment: Fritzi, the girls, a household hanging together.

Protoplasm, she said to herself, and shivered with hurt.

FAY AND IRIS Jaffe had planned to go to an early movie on Tuesday night and then stop off somewhere for a pizza, but Iris phoned at the last minute to say her temperature was up and she and Mac were going to spend the evening in bed trying to make a baby.

Well, Fay thought, I'll have a "singles" evening at home—and I'm going to enjoy it, too.

I *will* enjoy it!

She would make herself a salad, she decided, but when she opened the refrigerator and looked at the drawer full of lettuce, tomatoes, radishes, and parsley, all those wet things, things that needed cutting up, she thought: Why bother.

She would boil an egg. And make some toast. And a pot of tea. An odd meal for a hot night, but less pitiable than chopping watery vegetables for a scrabby little salad she would consume in four minutes.

Boiling her egg reminded Fay of the story of the mermaid who was captured by Manx fishermen early in the eighteenth century. This creature, according to legend, had been held in a house for several days before being returned to the sea, and her only comment was that humans were so ignorant they threw away the water in which they boiled eggs. A ridiculous story. Pointless. Why was she thinking about it now?

Well, she had to think about something, didn't she?

Her "ideas," her "attitudes." They roused her deepest suspicion. Yesterday she used the word "paradigm" twice in a single conversation, and her tongue had stumbled along, unsuccessfully, in an effort to retrieve it.

She arranged the table. Forcing herself. A place mat, an egg cup, a spoon and knife, a small plate, salt and pepper. A paper napkin? Did people eating alone bother with paper napkins? She handled these objects roughly and gritted her teeth with boredom. She supposed tea really could be made of egg water, but wouldn't it taste of eggshell? Perhaps the water contained calcium. She would have to ask someone; someone would know, but who? And why bother with puzzles as pointless as this, as trivial.

She admitted it: her curiosity was at a low ebb. A dangerous sign for someone fueled by the need to know things.

She ate quickly. Cut, chew, sip. A phrase frolicked on her tongue: old-maid's fare.

Stop it.

How did she end up at loose ends like this? She supposed if she sat here long enough the mysteries of self-knowledge would be revealed to her.

What did other women do on their own? They ate out of saucepans or straight out of cans. Yes, they did. They chugged wine straight from the bottle, stuck their finger into the yogurt carton and licked it off. There might be some pleasure in this kind of private vulgarity, giving vent to it, getting away with it.

What, she wondered, was the recently widowed Muriel Brewmaster doing at this precise moment? Knitting, probably. She was always knitting. Sitting in her green-and-white living room, that round posy face of hers, with her needles going. A silent room. Click, click, click. Maybe she should phone Muriel Brewmaster. They might, for the first time in their lives, have things to say to each other.

At one time she felt she understood other people's lives, but now she doesn't.

If only Onion weren't tied to Strom's hospital bed. Onion knew how to pump courage into her. Onion would squint into the hollow of her loneliness and judge her as roughly as she deserved to be judged.

She could do some ironing. Her blouses, her summer skirts. She could even get an early start on her packing.

No, that was idiotic. No one packed a whole week before going away, not unless they were insanely compulsive.

Nothing, nothing on TV. She might telephone someone. Or what about curling up with a good novel. One of the nineteenth-century novels she loved: predicament, resolution, a happy ending, always a happy ending.

Why not? She recalled how it used to irritate her when Peter interrupted her in the middle of reading. Well, there would be no interruptions tonight. It was only seven o'clock. If she went to bed at eleven, that would leave her four hours.

Four hours!

She would open a bottle of wine.

No. This wasn't the sort of situation that floated. Well, what sort of situation is it, Ms. McLeod?

It was starting again, the tears that sprang from nowhere, the impulse to jar the room with a whimper of pain. She would have to get hold of herself. What if she became one of those people who talked to themselves or made up lists of pathetic tasks, dusting their suitcases, waxing their window sills, striking out alone for desperate walks?

There goes Fay McLeod. Such a sprightly stride on that woman. Such dignity. What a shame she never—

She knew what she wanted. She wanted to let the tears come, to let herself slide under the dangerous edge, giving way for once.

No, she said, trying for an astringent tone. Open a book this minute and start reading. Don't move until you've reached page fifty. Until you've buried your thoughts in print. Cover yourself with words. Wash yourself away. Dissolve.

TWENTY-FOUR HOURS later Fay was sitting on a lawn chair in her brother Clyde's back yard, saying, "I hereby call this meeting to order."

She and Clyde and Sonya and Bibbi had gathered for a final session of planning for their parents' fortieth wedding anniversary celebration. The party was to take place at Clyde and Sonya's house on the first Thursday in October, a month after Fay got back from Europe. Most of the details had been worked out weeks earlier, the menu planned, a few of the dishes divided among them and the rest ordered from a caterer. Bibbi was making the invitations and in a few weeks would mail them to a hundred old family friends. Fay had organized a program, arranged for music and speeches, for the presentation of gifts. There were only a few items to discuss tonight, and Fay, relishing her big-sister role, presided. She held a pen in her hand and a list on her lap. Who would pick up the wineglasses from the caterer? Also, who was going to keep track of the RSVPs? Should they have a punch bowl or not? What about flowers?

The four of them were drinking mugs of decaffeinated tea; this was the sort of abstemious household that lightly mocked its own austerity. Clyde refilled the cups and at the same time argued the merits of renting a tent—for some reason his stutter was particularly pronounced tonight. No matter how much furniture he and Sonya carried down to the basement, he said, it was still going to be crowded. A tent in the back garden would hold a hundred easily. Hmmm, Fay said, a tent might be cold. Bibbi was worried about the cost.

"We don't need a tent," Sonya said firmly. "You remember, Clyde, how we squeezed more than a hundred in for that open house we had last Christmas. People like to be crowded. Besides, tents feel too *obviously* festive."

Fay agreed. "It's probably folksier to huddle," she said, going back to her list. "Now, who did we decide was going to make the fruit trifle?"

"Me," Bibbi said.

"Do we really have to have fruit trifle?" Clyde asked. He hated shapeless food.

"Yes," said Sonya and Fay together.

Sonya leaned back in her chair, knitting steadily, a sweater for one of the boys. Her love of domesticity shamed her at times, and earlier tonight, talking about her plans for improving the garden, she had waved an arm and referred to the yard disparagingly as a curtilage, giving it its ancient legal term, making light of the ground she cherished.

Now she brought up the subject of whether or not the party should be a surprise. Some people, she said, resented being taken by surprise. A surprise can be an act of aggression. A surprise singles out the guests of honor, makes them strangers at their own celebration.

She'd raised all these arguments before.

For a minute no one said anything. The growl of a lawn mower reached them from some distant point in the neighborhood. Crickets sang. Fay and Clyde and Bibbi exchanged glances.

Sonya came from a large quarreling angry family. She was used to heading off trouble.

"I think the folks can survive a surprise," Clyde said quietly.

"They'll love it," Bibbi said.

Fay, who was sleepy, yawned and said, "If people can survive forty years of marriage, they can probably survive anything."

"Okay, okay," Sonya said. She threw up her hands. "I surrender."

"You look tired, Fay," Clyde said.

"Don't tell a woman she looks tired," Sonya scolded. "No one wants to hear that."

"Well, it's true," Fay said. "I was up till two last night reading."

"Something good?"

She looked at their faces, the three of them, and saw with surprise that they really were waiting for an answer. "Not very," she said at last. "Just something to pass the time."

FAY'S BEEN SEEING Robin Cummerford for several weeks now.

Or, as her mother would say, and, in fact, *has* said, Fay's been "dating" Robin Cummerford for several weeks.

Fay's grandmothers, maternal and paternal, who died before she was born, might have said that she was "walking out" with Robin Cummerford, extracting from that scented phrase several overlapping images of nature, of delicacy, of a determinism dappled with sunlight and forthrightness.

And her grandfathers, one a judge, the other the founder of McLeod's Dry Cleaning Establishment—and, like the grandmothers, long dead, too long dead to offer comment—might view the situation from a male perspective and say that Robin Cummerford was courting Fay McLeod.

"But are you fucking him?" Iris Jaffe wanted to know when she phoned Fay at her office on Thursday morning.

Fay and Iris have been friends for thirty years, and part of their code of friendship demands that Iris make shocking statements and that Fay feign shock. "Iris!" she said, or rather exclaimed.

"Well, are you or are you not?"

"Not."

"For heaven's sake, why not?"

"I've only know him for a few—" She stopped herself. How many weeks had it been? She'd lost track.

"Christ, he's not gay?"

"No. At least, I don't think so."

"Impotent? That's all you need at your time of life, a man who can't—"

"My time of life!" Fay laid on an extra decibel of dramatic shock. "And what exactly do you mean by that phrase, 'my time of life'?"

"So what's the matter with him, then, your Cummerford guy?"

"Well—"

"Well?"

"What can I say?"

"Exactly! What can you say."

"He's rather . . . formal. Quite formal."

"How old did you say this guy was?"

"I haven't asked him, but—"

"You must know."

"Well, from what I can piece together, from the information he's dropped, when he graduated and so on—"

"Yes? Out with it."

"Thirty-two."

"So! Not a babe in the woods."

"No."

"And he hasn't been married before?"

"He certainly hasn't said anything about . . . no, I don't think so."

"So where's he taking you tonight?"

"We're driving out to Birds Hill. The Folk Festival."

"Good, good."

"You do approve, then?" Fay put on her mock-formal tone.

"Partly. Measured approval, anyway. There's one thing that rings funny bells, though. Why is it you only see this man on Thursdays?"

Fay paused. "I'm not sure exactly. We've sort of, I don't know, fallen into this Thursday thing."

"Hmmm."

"What's that supposed to mean?"

"Isn't it faintly sinister and werewolfish? The Thursday-night man?"

"I wouldn't say sinister, exactly."

"A little overprogrammed?"

"Maybe. Look, Iris, I've got to go. We have a staff meeting in two minutes."

"What about kissing?"

"What?"

"Have you at least brushed your tender lips against his rough manly lips?"

"This is getting silly."

"Well, have you?"

"No."

"You've got to get rid of this man."

"You might be right," Fay said, then added with more despair than she felt, "but who else is there?"

~ *CHAPTER 16* ~

Fortuitous Events

TOM AVERY HAS JUST BEEN STUNG BY A WASP. SOMETHING, ANYWAY, with wings and proboscis that landed on the back of his hand while he leaned on his bathroom-window sill, breathing in the shining powdery morning air and gazing at the condominium across the street, an immense old mansion renovated two or three years ago and jumped up with skylights, stained glass, and slashes of bright hardware on its heavy, rather forbidding oak door. Only occasionally has Tom ever seen anyone coming or going through that door, and he supposes there must be another entrance at the back, next to the parking lot. He can't actually see the parking lot from his window, but he imagines it to be filled with glossy little Japanese models in bright assertive colors.

He stares at his hand, which in less than one minute has puffed up to nearly twice its usual size, a reddened, meaty paw. The pain strengthens, and seems to sing at the edge of his dissolving surprise. He strokes the swelling flesh reproachfully. Forty years old and this is the first time he's been stung.

He's read about people who've died of insect stings, and for all he knows he's one of those afflicted with the deadly allergy. He should drop everything and race over to the drop-in clinic on Osborne Street. Fortuitous. (He imagines himself telling friends at some later date how *fortuitous* it was that this clinic should have been so close at hand.) The waiting room would be full, but he could explode into that circle of arthritic ladies and pregnant women, holding up his arm and shouting, "This is an emergency!"

He feels a bubble of compacted air in his chest. His hand, this stiff red appurtenance which seems no longer a part of his body, demands that he keep his eyes on it, that he blink several times in an attempt to squeeze it into focus. Down below him on the street a young woman rides by on a bicycle. She wears red shorts and a white T-shirt. The harsh light that fills the street is softened by her bare arms, which are fetchingly free, and around her head is tied a printed scarf, knotted there, he supposes, to keep her hair from flying around her eyes. He could love a woman like that. She rides along so primly, with her back so straight and neat. Should he call down to her, ask her for help? Her legs are pale, girlish. Does he have the right to offend her with his ugly swollen flesh?

He might pound on the floor and rouse the old man who lives downstairs, a Mr. Duff, retired, a widower who rarely goes out till evening, and then only as far as the Quick-Shake for an ice-cream cone. Once, on the landing, Tom had had a brief conversation with him about fishing in the Lake of the Woods, about Mr. Duff's late wife, who suffered from hypertension, and about their son, who has moved to Los Angeles to work in the plastics industry. Mr. Duff might be immensely flattered to be asked to play a role in a medical emergency. How do we know who our rescuers will be, or when we ourselves will be called upon? Tom puts this question to himself, finding it more speculative and interesting than the issue of hypochondria, a shameful condition boiled out of ego and abetted by loneliness. But am I really lonely? he demands of the chipped paint work on the window frame.

Inhale. Exhale. The pain is beginning to withdraw, and he

examines his hand with curiosity now, this bloated fishlike thing which seems suddenly at the center of his body, as vital and solid as an organ.

It comes to him that his life has been minutely altered. Unstung five minutes ago, he has now been inducted into the territory of those who understand the injury bees do, and he feels a compulsion to announce his changed state. But to whom?

To nobody he can think of.

Perhaps he really is lonely. Undoubtedly he is. Of course he is. Why else had he been so moved last week seeing a young father in the Portage Place Mall stoop suddenly and tie his child's shoelace? The tenderness of the man's bent head had reminded him of his own solitariness, how it was possible to get used to this condition and to die of it.

He raises his hand to his lips and holds it there for a minute, pressing into the numb private flesh the imprint of a kiss.

BY THE NEXT MORNING the swelling was down, leaving a patch of itchy reddened skin with a dull button of pain at its center. "What you do is put baking soda on it," his mother instructed him over the telephone—showing how little she knows about his life, imagining his kitchen and bathroom shelves to be as fully provisioned as her own. "If that doesn't do the trick, you might give it a dab of calamine lotion. Or a little E."

"E?"

"You buy it in a tube."

"Did you get the flowers?" he prompted.

"Flowers, oh boy, did I get the flowers! I said to Mike, this must of cost him an arm and a leg, long stems and all. And that's a real cute birthday card, a hoot. I heard you interviewing that lady politician last week. Tuesday, I think it was. On the radio. What's her name again?"

"What were you doing awake at that hour?"

"Hay fever. Do I have a dose! Especially at night."

"It's all the dust in the air."

"Well, I've got my nasal spray, I've got my drops. But I'm still up sneezing my head off in the middle of the night. Mike says—"

"But you heard the show?" He tried not to sound pleased.

"Did I ever! She's one smart cookie, as I told Mike the next morning. A gift for the gab. And do you want to know something? You've got a teensy-weensy bit of it too, Mr. Blarney Stone, those snazzy words of yours. Is she good-looking?"

"What?"

"Pretty? Is she pretty?"

"Not bad."

"Married?"

"Married? I don't know. I think so. Anyway, she's old enough to be—"

"Can't hear you. Mike's got the sander going, he's taking the finish off that old spice rack of mine, he's going to do it in driftwood gray."

"I just said happy birthday."

"That's what I thought you said."

A DRY HOT WIND's been pestering the city all week long. Dust from a hundred miles away has settled on the trees that line the boulevards, and even the petunias in the beds along Wellington Crescent are coated with gray powder. When Tom opened his mouth to say good evening to Mr. Duff, he felt it fill up with dust.

The thought has come to him that he ought to be kinder to lost souls like Mr. Duff. He'll be old himself one day, old and— the image arrived like a blast of hot air—perhaps living alone. Yes. Very probably living alone, and dealing with the creak and chagrin of an old body. The days would stretch. His income would shrink. The dread he's already begun to hoard might find inappropriate outlets. An odd man, people would say, bent in his yearnings. A loner with a fatal lack of animation. His joints would stiffen. People, strangers and friends alike, would avert their glance from his watery eye-sacs, hurry past him on the stairs as though he were invisible. It wouldn't be worth their while to divert Old Man Avery ("one of your old-time radio hands") with everyday anecdotes, or even to comment on the weather.

"Well," Tom said to Mr. Duff, after running into him on the sidewalk in front of the apartment block, "we're certainly having ourselves a good hot summer." He made a special effort at eye contact.

"Little *too* hot, I'd say." Abuse or else ridicule marred Mr. Duff's tone, and a red bubbling of flesh appeared at the corner of his mouth, a kind of sore that matched the irritation in his voice. Tom tried for a pitch of jokey optimism. "I suppose we should store up some of this heat for the winter. Won't be long."

"Never minded the winters myself."

"You don't feel the cold then?" A fake chuckle rattling beneath his voice.

"I stay indoors."

Tom said, after a pause, "I got stung by a bee the other day. Just standing and looking out the bathroom window." If nothing else, his years in radio have taught him how to keep the ball up in the air. "It can be pretty dangerous, a bee sting."

A curtain dropped across Mr. Duff's face. Incomprehension or boredom, Tom wasn't sure which.

"First time in my life," Tom went on, as though this were an intimate offering between two seasoned friends.

"Excuse me," Mr. Duff said.

"Pardon?"

"Excuse me, I said. I just farted."

"Don't mention it, Mr. Duff. It happens."

Tom said this joyfully. "It happens all the time." Laughter rolled out of him. He was ready now to embrace the man, declaring him his brother. Why, this person standing before him was a spirit colliding with his own, a random particle, a face, a name, a set of testicles, a crumbling body frame, a breather of oxygen, a farter—living his life in a set of rooms suspended beneath his own, connected to him by water pipes and plasterboard and a few cubic yards of fraternal air. The differences between them were infinitesimal; they were the same flesh, neighbors, brothers. Agghh!

"LET'S HEAR THOSE telephones ringing," Tom pleaded to his "Nite-line" listeners on Monday night. "Tonight's our annual roundup of civic affirmation. It's booster night. Are you ready out there? Okay then. 'I love Winnipeg because—' "

At first the calls dribbled in.

"Well, it so happens I love Winnipeg," the first caller said, "because my roots are here." He interrupted himself with an eager piercing laugh. "This is not a city of transients. You just plain old-fashioned live here. And so does everyone you know."

"I don't love Winnipeg, I adore Winnipeg." The voice was boozy, female, full of squawks. "And I'll tell you why. I like seasons. Have you been out to the west coast? They've got one season out there, the rainy season. Gets boring. Bo-ring."

"I don't love Winnipeg at all," the third caller said. "Everyone here is trying their damndest to love it, that's the whole problem. Methinks they doth protest too much. We've got a lousy climate here; we've got to grit our teeth and put up with it. So let's can all this you-know-what about loving it here. Let's be honest for a change."

"Hey, Tom, you there? You mind if I reply to Miss Sourpuss, your previous caller? She's forgetting what this city offers. I'm talking sports, entertainment. I'm talking great movies, and the biggest shopping mall this side of Edmonton."

"Go ahead, caller," Tom said. "Are you there?"

"My permanent home is in Winnipeg at the moment, but I've got a transfer coming up and I'm going to be putting my house on the market. If anyone out there's interested in a fantastic bargain, split-level, three bedrooms—"

"Your listeners might be interested to know that there're more restaurants here per capita than any city in the world. How 'bout that?"

"I love Winnipeg because the people here are the salt of the earth. You walk down Portage and you get smiles from everyone, even the cops. I do wish they'd stop their scrapping on City Council, though. We've got some real nerds on City Council, one or two in particular, real dinosaurs. Okay if I mention their names on the air?"

"Maybe we should just leave it at that," Tom suggested, giving Ted Woloschuk the wind-up signal.

"I love Winnipeg," the final caller said, "but I'd love it more if we had a few more heated bus-shelters. It's summer, but I'm starting to dread winter already, standing out there every morning on Henderson Highway and freezing my buns off. Otherwise this is paradise. I mean it. It's heaven."

"Are you sure you don't mind, Tom?" Jenny Waring was saying on the telephone. "I mean, we could get a sitter, but the Chandlers are taking the girls to the lake with them, and that just leaves Gary. The whole thing came up so suddenly. Jeff only found out about this conference at the last minute and he thought, what a chance to get away, just the two of us, even if it is just Minneapolis."

"Hey, Minneapolis is a great—"

"If it were the weekend my mother could take him, but Thursday night's her bridge tournament, and besides, ever since her hip went she finds the kids a handful. But listen, Tom, I just hope you mean it when you say—"

"It's only two nights, Jen. And it'll be a great change for me to have a sidekick—"

"He thinks the world of you, you know, he's always asking when you're coming around—"

"You tell him I'm looking forward to it. Tell him we're going to have two whole days without vegetables. Just morning-to-night milkshakes and maybe the odd burger thrown in."

"He's going to love this. And I'll be sure to send his sleeping bag—"

"Don't worry. You haven't seen my place lately. I've got real furniture now. I'll bed him down on the couch. And I've even got sheets. I went wild. All the modern conveniences."

"But what about Thursday night? You've got the show to do on Thursday night. Is that going to be a problem?"

"I'll roll him in a blanket and take him down to the studio. Just tuck him up in the lounge, no problem. Someone'll keep an eye on him."

"He's not the best sleeper—"

"If he wakes up he can watch us do the show. I'll let him do a commercial."

"I just feel, you know, this is such an imposition—"

"I'm the godfather, remember? It's time I acted a little godly."

"I still worry—"

"It's two nights, Jenny. Relax. You'll have a great time, and it'll do me good to have company."

"I'll get Jeff to drop off his stuff, his pajamas and toothbrush and all. And if you can pick him up at this birthday party—"

"I've already written it down. Thursday afternoon, five o'clock. Yale Avenue. The McLeods, 307 Yale."

"You probably know them. Clyde and Sonya McLeod? She's the abortion lawyer. He's got this stutter—"

"I don't think so. But don't worry. It'll work out fine."

"Right. And Tom—"

"What?"

"You're a sweetheart. Really, I mean it."

"I know."

MISERY DOES NOT love company. The lonely can do very little for each other. Emptiness does not serve emptiness. The wormy black dreads (as Tom pictures them) come bubbling out of a swampish fatigue, out of the most innocent or shallow breath, the least word, the way your necktie unknots or the hair on your head sits. A gesture, a sigh, can spread contagion. Darkness rubs off. It only gets darker. It's blank, viewless.

Knowing all this—too well, too well—Tom spends all day

Wednesday in bed. Around noon he calls the station and reports in sick. Lenny Dexter can take the show for him. Lenny will jump at the chance, leaving Tom free to sweat out his hyperbolic self-pity, if that's what it is.

Here he lies, a man alone in an apartment, in the middle of the day, in the middle of the North American continent. A man who produces nothing but noise. A man attached to no one. A man sliding downhill.

These attacks have occurred two or three times before in his life, and he knows how to deal with them. He's got a method. He sleeps and reads, gives himself punishing chores, treats himself unkindly, then sleeps again. He resists the urge to whimper. He clenches his fists, trying to be hearty, rubbing his hot face. He resists the notion of a mid-afternoon Scotch. He resists phoning his mother and telling her he's feeling terrific.

The rain falls continuously in the windless air. It gathers in beads on the window screen, filling in one small square after another with a film of silver. Tom watches this progression for an hour or more. Life's offerings ought to be more vivid than this, he knows that, more ablaze with meaning and more splendid. He could put on some music, he could turn on a lamp, he could make some coffee—but he doesn't. He mutters to himself instead. He accuses himself of cultivating a sadness in order to cast it off.

And he will cast if off. He is reasonably certain that tomorrow he will undergo a mending of his fibrous tissues, climb out of this marshy place. It's possible, he knows, to win himself back. He's done it before. More than once.

Tom remembers that he woke up hungry on Thursday morning. Wake up, the sunlight said, wake up and eat.

He asked himself when he had last felt so hungry. What blew through his body was a starved clean longing for food, and this longing was accompanied by an impeccable asceticism. He ate a basic breakfast, cereal and milk, and immediately, ritualistically, washed and dried the dishes and put them away.

He took a long shower and dried himself with a clean towel.

A brand-new towel, never before used. The price tag was still stapled to the hem. "You wimp," he said to his dusky penis, but in a friendly tone. He dried carefully between his toes. It had been some time since he had regarded his toes closely. Years. He found some foot powder on the bathroom shelf and sprinkled himself lavishly. This seemed for some reason a large and noble gesture.

He put on clean pants and the least creased shirt in his closet, added a light windbreaker, and walked to the A & W for a hamburger; he remembered afterward how theatrical the sky had looked with its packed, pulsing clouds, each one outlined by a band of garish light. On the balconies of apartment buildings outdoor furniture sat suspended in exceptional stillness, the webbing and chrome chilly, bright, and mortal. Soaked leaves lay smashed on the street; some of them, though it was still July, were nut-brown.

Tom read the newspaper as he ate his burger. There was a photo on the front page that showed a young woman in a swimsuit dipping a toe into the water at Gimli Beach, and beneath it was a caption: "Making the Most of Summertime."

Summertime—what juice that word contained, what roll and pitch, what indolence and pleasure. These seasons tricked him sometimes into the belief that his life was cyclical and endlessly renewable, when all the time he was traveling, like everyone else, straight toward a famine of the senses and the dryness of his own death. Today, though, he was able to delude himself. The smell of food fattened the air. The cheeseburger he bit into was hot and moist, the fries crisp, thin, and winking with salt. He rejoiced in the twirl of pale cream in his coffee and the convivial crackle of the little sugar packet.

Afterward he shrugged off an urge to take in a movie. He said no to the idea of phoning Sheila's office and inviting her out for a friendly drink. Instead he walked along River Avenue and across the Norwood Bridge, discovering, happily, that his vast public face had been scrubbed from the billboard and replaced with a pastel invitation to take a Caribbean holiday—palm trees, blue water, muscled bodies. The start of a song twitched in his throat. He stopped at a lunch counter for a cup of coffee and—thoughtfully, taking his time—counted out the exact change, lightening his pockets of their heavy pennies. He kept on walking—through pared suburban neatness, then around the fake rural greenness of Kingston Crescent, then over the footbridge and north toward River Heights. The sun had returned, blinding; but the next minute a light drizzle began, and he welcomed its cool fine spray on his face, on his lips.

Now it was late afternoon, nearly five o'clock. A whole day obliterated. He arrived, his hair slicked with rain, at the cream stucco house on Yale Avenue. Three stories. Clumsy but comfortable. A wide porch. A shiny green door standing open. He knocked lightly and was invited in by Sonya McLeod.

She was a flushed, breathless woman. Something purple, Kool-Aid, probably, was spilled down the front of her white skirt. The party, it seemed, had been driven indoors by the rain, and half a dozen small boys were running relays in the large cluttered living room. Crepe-paper streamers gave a look of madness. "This is calm compared to an hour ago," Sonya told Tom cheerfully, and introduced him—shouting the names—to two or three other parents who had arrived to pick up their children.

Tom, bewildered, still breathing the ether of his recovery, stood in a corner of the narrow front hall, leaning against a wall. Someone handed him a glass of cold wine. His hand was shaken several times. "So you're Tom Avery, I certainly know that name."

Seven-year-old Gary Waring hurled himself at Tom's legs, rebounded, then abruptly disappeared into the kitchen. "I'm Clyde McLeod," a man said. "I'm p-p-pleased to meet you, sorry about all the chaos."

Afterward Tom remembered that a small red-headed boy, whose birthday it apparently was, flew into the hallway, shouting, "It's Aunt Fay. Here comes Aunt Fay."

Someone opened the wide screen door, and Tom saw a woman running up the sidewalk toward the house. Oh my God, he thought, and seemed to see her pinned to the air like a hologram. He had an impression of thinness, of dark hair swinging from side to side as she ran, of a wide skirt in several shades of blue. One of her hands kept her skirt in check, and with the other she held on to the strings of a dozen rainbow-colored balloons.

Someone, one of the adults standing beside Tom, exclaimed, "Why it's Fay McLeod."

~ CHAPTER 17 ~

Anything Might

Happen

FAY'S HAD REMARKABLY GOOD LUCK WITH PEOPLE SHE'S MET BY chance while traveling, particularly on long flights, overnight flights when the dimmed cabin lights, the blankets, the pillows, the compact trays of food and drink, have summoned a surge of intimacy. But tonight, traveling between Winnipeg and Amsterdam, a direct flight that arches boldly over the top of the globe, she resists the friendly overtures of her seatmate. She's polite enough. She nods and smiles (faintly) and makes appropriate replies, and even contributes, when asked, a Tylenol tablet from a bottle at the bottom of her bag. But she refuses to be drawn in.

She is suspended inside an image. Hanging there by a thread.

She resents even the necessity of looking sideways and shifting her body. What she focuses on is a pressing incantation, a chant. It thrums inside her throat, adheres like silver plate to the rise and hollow of her breath. It seems to her that this is all she requires to keep her alive and steady in the long blue tunnel of Atlantic air. Just two words: Tom Avery.

AMSTERDAM IS COLD and damp, but the small hotel where Fay is staying has a thick comforter on the bed. Not a new light-weight duvet, but a heavy old-fashioned wool-filled cover with a warm lumpy substantiality that mimics the feel of a human presence. Travel and its disorderly aftermath, taxis, trains, the clink of unfamiliar coinage, have left her with a longing for sobriety. In a thin cotton nightgown she surrenders to the comforter's intimate, uneven pressure. She badly needs sleep but finds herself lying at attention between the starched sheets, unwilling to give up the stream of lighted images that rolls beneath her eyelids.

Tom Avery. She pronounces the syllables in her head and readies herself for a re-enactment.

"How do you do," she'd said when they were introduced at the birthday party, and her first thought was that she would like to reach up and press the back of her hand against his cheek.

The smooth-shaven face and the bulk of his body unsettled her. And the way he was looking at her, with a question shaping itself behind his eyes.

"You look very familiar," she said. The two of them were squashed in a corner of Clyde and Sonya's front hall, which was really just a narrow passage.

She rested one arm along a cool shelf of gumwood paneling, steadying herself. The big, normally airy house was suffocatingly humid. Outside, a summer rain was battering the grass and the flower borders.

"Do I?" he asked.

"Pardon?" She needed time to think.

"Look familiar. You said I looked familiar."

"Yes. We must have met somewhere or other."

He shook his head slowly.

He had untidy hair, uncombed, medium brown—hair that was thinning. She wondered how she knew this.

"No," he said, leaning toward her. He had the teasing look of someone holding flowers behind his back.

"At school maybe?" she tried. "Or a party? Or maybe here. Clyde's my brother."

"I don't know Clyde. Or at least I didn't until a few minutes ago."

"At the folklore center, maybe?" She was watching his mouth. "I work there."

"Oh, I don't think so," he said in the tone of a man who had never thought of going to such a place.

"A restaurant?" Why was she pursuing this? "Or maybe just on the street."

"Well, I've lived here for seventeen years," he contributed. "In Winnipeg."

"Pardon?" She saw his lips move but couldn't hear a word.

The little boys were running in the living room, shrieking and thumping on the floor. Some incomprehensible activity was taking place, chanting, singing. Their shirts made wild blocks of color against the white walls. Fay began to wonder which of these children belonged to Tom Avery, who was staring at her, staring hard.

"I said, I've lived here for seventeen years," Tom said. Then, "Noisy, aren't they?"

"I've lived here all my life." Was she boasting? "Except for intervals now and then."

"A native daughter."

"Pardon?" The noise was overwhelming.

He leaned down, and she felt the roundness of his warm breath on her face, as though he had reached out and touched her with his hand.

"Maybe it's your name that's familiar," she said.

"Maybe. You don't by any chance listen to late-night radio?"

"Radio? Not very often, I'm afraid. How late?"

"I do a radio show. 'Niteline.' CHOL. You might have heard my name in connection with—"

"What time is this show?"

"Midnight to four."

"The middle of the night!"

"Yes." He was smiling.

A warm fold of moisture formed on her brain. It was his smile that caused it, a smile that held a normal proportion of teeth and gum, but an angle of good humor that was slightly mocking.

"I have to confess," she said, shaking her head, "that it never occurs to me to turn on the radio at that hour."

"You're probably asleep."

"Well"—this, too, seemed a confession—"I guess I am usually."

"Lucky you."

"Lucky?"

"It's a program for insomniacs mostly. The night folk. They're a different breed. You wouldn't want to be one, believe me."

"But you're one."

"A charter member."

Fay looked sideways. Her brother, Clyde, was handing Oh! Henry bars to three little boys who had finished first in the straw race. Sonya was bending from the waist, wiping a spill from the green carpet. "This is a fairly wild scene," Fay said, raising her voice.

"How old are your kids?" he was asking.

"I don't have any, I'm afraid. I'm just the aunt." She said this with a ripple of emphasis, putting a set of feathery quotation marks around the word "aunt."

One of the parents, a man standing next to her, was saying something about voter apathy, about an article he'd read in the *Atlantic* on the conscience of the electorate.

"I would have remembered if I'd met you," Tom Avery was saying to Fay. His voice was touchingly persuasive and so close to her ear she could feel its vibrations.

"The public is drugged by information overload," someone standing next to Fay said.

She put her feet together and made herself concentrate on what Tom Avery was saying. He had a mouth that moved carefully, the way a mouth does when someone is about to begin an elaborate joke. She wondered how it would feel to kiss that mouth. Tender. Slow-motion. She wondered if he could be thinking the same thing.

She felt perilously close to the toe edge of incomprehension. The heat, the noise, the thunder outside, his face. "I can't hear you," she said finally, lifting her arms in a broad shrug.

He leaned toward her, and again she felt the touch of his breath on her neck. "I just said," he shouted, "I just said, I don't have any kids, either."

FAY HAS BEEN in Amsterdam for forty-eight hours and hasn't seen a thing. She hasn't read any of the papers or journals she's brought along with her, nor has she visited the State Museum of Folklore, where there is a celebrated collection of mermaid lore. She's wasting Amsterdam, wasting her time, wasting her grant money, wasting herself.

Sailors, in ancient times, stuffed their ears with beeswax to keep themselves from succumbing to the sirens' song, fearing the power of distraction, how it could initiate acts of carelessness and cast mortal souls into a state of thralldom.

Fay knows she must somehow recapture her concentration. She is a woman who is writing a serious book. She's waited three years to make this trip. She holds a travel grant funded by a public institution, and she went to a good deal of trouble to secure this money. She's made promises and committed herself to deadlines. There is so much to uncover and analyze, so many strands of myth and legend and art and theory to bind together.

But so far she's done nothing but walk down chilly stone streets, gaze into canal water and shop windows, and buy a few postcards. She chose these cards with sacerdotal reverence and paid for them with carefully counted guilders, but they're still in their plastic envelope, not yet written upon or stamped. She's spent considerable time lying on her sagging bed in the hotel, flat on her back with her eyes open, observing a splash of weak sunlight on the wall and on the slightly soiled ceiling. She's taken in the voluptuous broken curve of the plaster cornice and sniffed the cooking smells from the ground floor, meat roasting or burned milk. She wills her mouth to go slack. Her hands curl against her thighs. Between her body and what she is thinking is a smiling, devouring complicity. Gleeful. Precious. Inside her head she pronounces Tom Avery's name and waits for his face to come into focus.

"I'll drive you home," Tom Avery had offered.

The other parents had picked up their children and departed. Only Gordon, Matthew, and little Gary Waring were left, the three of them sprawled in a corner of the living room watching TV while Sonya and Clyde busied themselves making coffee for Fay and for Tom Avery.

"God," Sonya sighed happily, looking around, "this place looks like a combat zone."

Paper plates and cups littered the living room, dining room, and kitchen. Gift wrap lay curled in the corners. Shreds of balloon were scattered on the rug, and other balloons, still intact, bobbed weakly against the ceiling.

"I'd appreciate a ride, yes," Fay said to Tom when he offered to drive her home. "But I really could walk. It's only twenty minutes or so from here."

"Have some coffee first," Clyde said. He had cleared off the kitchen table and set out four pottery mugs. "We d-d-deserve a little caffeine shootup after that circus."

"Well, it went pretty well," Sonya said. Her arms were folded flat across her front.

Fay said, "I should really be on my way. I've still got some packing to do."

"Fay leaves at midnight," Sonya explained to Tom. "Four weeks tramping around Europe. Our hearts bleed for her, don't they, Clyde?"

"P-p-p-profusely," Clyde said. He and Sonya had not met Tom Avery before, though Sonya announced that she'd sometimes listened to his show when she was driving late at night, coming home from out-of-town meetings.

"It's more work than vacation," Fay told Tom. "I wouldn't want anyone here to think I was actually going just to enjoy myself."

"God forbid," Sonya said, and handed around the filled cups. She was flushed with postparty satisfaction, smiling across the kitchen at Clyde and saying, "It's a good thing, love, that we only have to go through this punishment twice a year."

Occasionally, seeing her brother and his wife together like this, in a scene fragrant with earned exhaustion and with the mild, disordered pains of domesticity, Fay has felt herself suddenly starved of oxygen. Jealousy, or else panic, grips her at such moments. Will she ever own even a portion of what they so effortlessly possess? The question strikes like a blow and never fails to leave a trace of shame.

But tonight she regards the two of them almost with pity, a pair of oversized children swept away on their own forward current. They'll drink their coffee, clean up, make a panful of scrambled eggs, put the boys to bed, watch the late-night news, and then go to bed themselves. Probably they'll make love—up there on the third floor in their big cool water bed with the windows open to the familiar dampish night air. They must know already, the two of them, as they drink their coffee from heavy blue mugs, precisely what the rest of the day will offer.

Whereas she is about to be driven home by someone she's never met before.

This simple premise magisterially suggests something grandly unsettling—that anything can happen.

FAY HAS AN appointment with Maja van Ginkel at ten o'clock on the other side of Amsterdam. She rises early and dresses herself in extraordinary clothes—extraordinary, that is, for a late-summer morning: a wool skirt, a sweater, stockings, a jacket of fine-woven wool.

The clay-colored sky is overcast. Downstairs in the hotel she sits in a low-ceilinged room with a dozen other hotel guests and is served thick milky coffee and slices of bread and cheese. The cheese comes in transparent sheets and tastes sour. Fay, imagining Maja van Ginkel, her rank and reputation among folklorists, supplies her with a wide shy eager face and fleshy chin. Dr. van Ginkel has published a paper in which the mermaid trope is identified with the sexual subconscious, with a primitive fear of castration and an urge to return to the watery womb.

The double spine of this theory is a little flat-footed for Fay, who hopes to question Dr. van Ginkel closely. Are human beings really so locked into their own cherished anxieties that the only vibrations they feel are solitary and private? Aren't people capable of more than this? Please, please—don't they sometimes commit acts of abandonment, calling out to each other, demanding to be buried in each other's mortal or immortal flesh?

THE COMBED YELLOW HAIR of Maja van Ginkel was unyielding, the rectangularity of her eye sockets fixed. English words burst from her throat with a puncturing explosive rattle. She was beautiful, and her particular kind of waxy beauty made her opaque. After their meeting Fay was struck with the shocking thought that this woman was probably two or three years younger than she herself was.

That night she dreamed about her. The two of them were perched on the ridgepole of a small dwelling, making polite conversation, and behind them, lost in a mottled sky, were the eyes, mouth, and hairline of Tom Avery.

The next morning, her fifth in the hotel, Fay looked into the bathroom mirror, puzzling over the disguise of her body. She was still there, her long dark straight hair cut with bangs across her forehead, a decent-looking woman whose smooth skin concealed her body's other secrets, its leakages and cracks. Who was it, she asked herself; who was the woman Tom Avery had offered to drive home?

A dozen harmless vanities keep her balanced. A man once said to her—and she remembers exactly who he was and all the details of their meeting—that she had lovely earlobes. A manicurist, years ago, had commented passingly on the length of her nailbeds. (She hadn't even known the word "nailbed" but was grateful nevertheless for this minor tribute.) Her sister, Bibbi, confided once, "You have the kind of face that doesn't have to smile all the time. You can just go around with your face as it is, not having to try too hard." All of these casually offered comments have been stored carefully at the back of her brain.

Earlier in the day Dr. van Ginkel, with her beautiful solid Dutch mouth, had delivered a nervous creed. "Our bodies are inescapable," she said to Fay. "They are the only bodies we can ever know."

And Fay, who cannot now recall what Tom Avery looks like, had nodded in agreement.

~ CHAPTER 18 ~

What I'd
Really Like

IN THE LAST FEW DAYS, SINCE HIS MEETING WITH FAY McLEOD, Tom's been living the mechanical glassy life of a sleepwalker. A segment of his conscious existence has been dislodged and assigned to automatic pilot.

So this is how a robot functions, he thinks, coming and going as through various humid dreams and wakenings, eating hamburgers and donuts, driving to the station shortly before midnight and home again after his four-hour shift, gunning the car down the dark narrow streets, breaking through the nightly quiet with spurts of gas, a foot on the pedal pushing the gray-colored air ahead of him. That's all he does: eats and sleeps and attends to the continuous, unfolding surface of his day and night routines, always surprised that his arrangements can be managed this mindlessly.

But inside his head he's cooking up a stew of audacious fantasies, midnight strategies of stealth, flash, and perversity which he recognizes, but only in his calmer moments, as being insane.

A fertile, lucid happiness has taken charge of him, made him exaggerated and crazy about what he should do next, what is required of him. This feeling, though unfocused, cannot be put down, cannot be cleared out of his mind.

His first thought was to get on a plane and go to Europe, where he would intercept Fay McLeod. He's never been to Europe; nothing there has ever seemed compelling enough to compensate for what he imagines to be an assault of massive stone monuments and continuous drenching rain. He fears, more than damp feet, the narrow Continental streets full of toxic haze, and unreadable European maps whose rivers, roads, railway lines, and national boundaries wrinkle and shrink the eyesight of travelers and strip them clean of volition, of identity. Europe with its sneering face. Europe the mercenary uncle.

But now? He could surprise her, arriving suddenly and presenting himself, his bones, his wayward, undisguised self. Tonight she'll be arriving in Paris after a week in Amsterdam and Copenhagen, and he's succeeded, with only minimum difficulty, in tracking down where she's staying: the hôtel de l'Avenir, on the rue du Cherche-Midi. (*L'avenir?* He remembers from his high-school French what the word means: it means future; he embraces this pellet of knowledge, this omen.)

First he had phoned the switchboard at the National Center for Folklore Studies, where Fay worked, and asked, with cautious, underheated guile, for her forwarding address. ("I'm trying to reach . . .") He put his question quickly, drawing in his breath and managing to suggest that a small but urgent crisis required that he get in touch with Ms. McLeod immediately. *Ms. McLeod;* he'd stretched out that murmury syllable *Ms.*, layering it with solicitude.

He was firmly refused. "I'm afraid we cannot give out that kind of information," the shocked, reproving switchboard operator told him, in a voice that was, at the same time, oddly drenched with sweetness.

Fay existed, at least. That much was confirmed, and he longed suddenly for the outside world to keep on confirming it.

Next he phoned Sonya. "Would you happen to know," he

began, suspecting he sounded solemn and bogus, "where Fay is staying in Paris?" "Hang on a sec," she'd said, cheerful, offhand, phlegmatic, as though there were nothing untoward or desperate about this request of his. "Lemme ask Clyde, he's got Fay's itinerary around here somewhere. Oh, here it is, right on the bulletin board. Hôtel de l'Avenir, rue du Cherche-Midi, number fourteen."

If he really intended to go to Europe he'd have to approach Big Bruce, and quick, about getting time off. He'd have to pitch his plea a grain huskier than usual. "Look, Bruce, I've got to get away. I'm close to exhaustion, that's the truth of it. These late nights, it's crazy, and I've been going at it hard for three years straight. The ratings are right up there at the moment. Plus, summer's slow anyway, with everyone at the lake. Plus, Dexter'd kill for a chance to take over for a couple of weeks. Right now—this is just between you and me—right now I feel like I'll maybe crack up if I don't get away, and I mean really away. I was thinking of, well, maybe going to Europe. . . ."

No, no, no, no. What kind of presumptuous nut case was he. Think it through, buddy.

He decided he would phone her instead. He'd sit down and figure out the time difference, catch her early in the morning before she left the hotel. Hello. (Reminding himself not to yell.) It's Tom Avery. From Winnipeg? We met last week? At your brother's. I walked you home, remember? Well, I just wanted to . . .

To touch base? To connect? To hear your voice? To remind you of mine? To see how you're making out over there? So, how's the weather? (Keeping his voice up, keeping his throat full of jolly sparkles.) When you get back, I was thinking we could maybe . . . Yeah, right!

She'd flip. She'd run. At the very least she'd be confused, alarmed. Is anything the matter? she'd probably ask. Or, after a smarting, doubting silence, deliver her own cold inquiry: Why exactly are you phoning? What is it you want?

No. A phone call was madness. And to think he'd got as far as looking up the international dialing code.

He'd read somewhere, a novel, maybe, about a man who'd

sent a woman a bunch of flowers every hour for twenty-four hours. The flamboyance of this gesture had impressed him at the time, also the foolishness of it. It was a folly, one he could suddenly understand but knew himself incapable of. And the expense of an act like that might, well, convince her of his utter fecklessness.

Or else remind her of a novel *she'd* once read in which a man had sent . . . Oh God!

He'd write her a letter instead.

If he mails it to the hôtel de l'Avenir today she'll have it in ten days, or so he was told at the post office when he went to buy an air letter. (An air letter seemed jauntier than plain paper and an envelope, and more innocently motivated.) Ten days. The thought of the time gap is crushing, but he sees its usefulness. Ten days to cool and objectify the words on the page.

But what *will* he say?

He has the thudding sensation of new spaces entered and instantly lost, but he latches on to one nuggety word: now. He cradles that word close to his body.

Now. This minute. Before it disappears. Now or never.

He spreads the blue tissuey aerogram on his kitchen table, which he has first washed and carefully dried. The paper lies flat like a lake, empty and blue, its glued edges slightly curled, offering up to him a spacious, clean, formal permission. For this sheet of paper he feels an excruciating tenderness.

"Friday morning," he writes in the upper-right-hand corner, then shuts his eyes and allows an image of Fay's intricate mouth and eyes to form and dissolve, her oval face, her chin, her neck, her long supple arms swinging, a dozen balloons floating above her.

The white plastic pen he holds in his hand has the words "Imperial Bank of Commerce" on it. Its ink is vivid blue. This ink will be the vector of his pleading, he will trust it absolutely.

"Dear Fay," he writes carefully.

"Can I drive you home?" he'd said to her that night. Or maybe— he can't remember the exact words—"Would you like a lift?"

She had turned toward him, pausing. "It's only a twenty-minute walk," she'd said, or something to that effect, smiling all the while with that large mobile mouth of hers, the lipstick eaten away. "I don't want to take you out of your way."

"No trouble at all." Where had that wheeze come from? Shameful, like an old man. He cleared his throat ostentatiously, observing her lower lip and imagining how it would feel to draw his tongue along its length, a pencil feeling out a line. "I'm not in any special hurry."

"Well . . ." Biting down on her lower lip, considering. A light at the back of her eyes sizing him up.

"I'd be glad to give you a lift."

"If you're sure."

"Clyde could easily run you home, Fay," Sonya offered.

"Sure," from Clyde, who was yawning, who had slipped off his shoes.

"No, really," Tom said too loudly, setting down his coffee cup, giddy. "I'll be happy to. I've got Gary with me, but there's plenty of room in the car."

"Well . . ." She was still doubtful, or was this a brand of politeness he hadn't encountered before? Or did it hold a measure of suspicion? Or judgment? "I live just over on Grosvenor Avenue."

"Grosvenor? So do I."

"Where on Grosvenor?" Her eyes opened wide, her mouth moved up. Brown eyes. Eyebrows faint. That mouth. He searched her features for some fault that might reassure him.

"Between Stafford and Wellington. Closer to Stafford."

"You do? So do I. What number?"

"Near the corner, eight-forty-eight."

"That's amazing. I'm at eight-forty-seven. The condo conversion. I've been there two years."

"With the wood door? The flowers? I'm right across the street."

"The red brick?"

"Third floor."

"We're neighbors."

Had he said that, or had she?

"Neighbors," Sonya repeated. She was standing by the sink, briskly wrapping up a wedge of birthday cake for Gary. She said it again, preoccupied, neutral. "Neighbors."

TOM STOOD BY THE CURB. Next to him was Fay McLeod, and holding on to Fay's hand was seven-year-old Gary Waring, solidly gripping in his other hand a plastic bag of birthday cake and candy. Overhead a double row of elms met, their full crowns nodding with rainwater. The air was cool, damp, the pressed wet unfocused air of early evening. Eight o'clock. In the western sky a column of peach-colored cloud spiraled upward. Yale Avenue at this hour was tranquil. And empty.

"Hey." Gary was yelling in high, childish pips of relish. "Hey, Tom, I don't see any car."

WHEN JENNY WARING had phoned to ask if he would look after Gary for a couple of days, Tom had been taken by surprise. Jenny had never before asked him to do anything of the kind, and it had never occurred to him to offer, though he could see, when he considered, how it might do her good to get away for a change. On the telephone she had been breathless, excited, but he heard apology in her voice, too, and when he at once agreed to look after Gary she had seemed almost cravenly grateful.

He had had to assure her that he was overjoyed at the idea of taking care of a small boy, that the two of them, child and man, would abandon themselves to a disordered male reign of junk food and bacchic license.

In fact, Tom was nervous about how exactly the two of them would get along. Ages seven and forty thrust together. The substance of a sentimental film, maybe, but the reality made him itch; it was not what he would have chosen. He liked Gary, who was a sturdy child, dark haired, watchful, his mouth perpetually hanging open a thoughtful quarter inch, but how do you keep a kid amused for two days? What would they talk about? He imagined long silences, uneasiness, false enthusiasm.

Children baffle Tom. He hardly knows any. Children are unpredictable, the way they behave and the way they turn out. It strikes him that a good many of his friends are frightened of their own children, that the little ruins and ironies of married life were furiously multiplied by their presence. Noise, mess, complication, dangers to watch out for. Children go crazy at times, seized by bizarre, primitive notions. Tom knows all this; he even remembers at times something of what it was like being a child, the precise sensations. The hands of children are sticky. They wet their pants, stick out their tongues. That people love them seems amazing to him, heartening, too, even miraculous.

And they do. Once people have produced a baby, their world softens up and becomes a baby world of pink toweling, tiny teeth, diapers, highchairs, scrubbable plastic toys that nevertheless acquire the fetid sweetness of the babies themselves. The funny or outrageous misdeeds of their progeny were recounted again and again, with wily dejection, as though to confirm membership in the rueful, sober, laconic confederacy of parenthood.

Nevertheless, it was where Tom's friends wanted to be, the only place—this is what he's concluded. Even Nathan and Judy Kappel's little Melody, who hits her head against the wall and who once bit Tom's wrist, even Kelly Waterford, who throws himself down in supermarket aisles screaming, even Trevor Masterson, with crossed eyes and curious webs of flesh between his thumb and forefinger, even these damaged, difficult offspring consume their parents' love.

Tom, invited to houses where children are present, does his best; he does what he thinks is expected of him, pats bellies and diapered bottoms, brings gifts, comments on the agreeable shapes of baby heads—always a safe topic—or the presence of baby hair, baby resemblances, baby cleverness, the promise of widely spaced eyes or a muscular grip. He knows what to do, more or less, and he likes to think he does it with sincerity, but he knows better. Children are not much fun. They're not—for some reason this is a well-guarded secret—they're not particularly interesting. And so Tom knows there's something here he doesn't understand. Some joyful, consuming secret.

And he'd been touched when the Warings some years ago asked him to be Gary's godfather. At that time he had been between marriages; it may have been that they felt sorry for him—oddly, this occurs to him today for the first time. Gary was a lump of baby tissue packed into a blanket. He smelled of urea and baby powder (that dense blocked odor) and soap and milky vomit. His bundled arms and lolling head appeared boneless and only tentatively connected to his swollen trunk. His features were small, snaillike, closed, and when he was placed, compacted and warm and surprisingly robust, in Tom's arms during the christening ceremony in the Warings' living room, he opened his eyes briefly, rolled his eyeballs upward as if catching the tail end of a milky dream, then fell once again into baby unconsciousness.

That's when you really love your kids, people tell Tom, when you come across them sleeping with their limbs outflung on the bed sheet, or else curled up tight like a squirrel or some other burrowing creature. The sleeping faces of children are their real faces. They're weighted with heat, painted pink by the glow of a night-light. Their skin is perfect, translucent, newly made, the visible sign of incalculable trust—the face it would gladden us to go back to and claim.

"I DON'T SEE any car."

The words came toward Tom slowly, as though from a great distance. The cloudy pillar billowing up over the trees, the concrete curb where he and Fay McLeod balanced, the pale side-parting of her dark hair—all this had pitched him into dizzy confusion.

Why exactly was Gary yelling his head off? The car, where

was it? It must be around the corner. Stolen? Had he left the key in the ignition? He knew there was something he wasn't remembering, but what?

He reached into his jacket pocket, touched the leather tag of his key ring, and remembered.

"Is something wrong?" Fay asked in a low voice.

"Where is it?" Gary was pounding on Tom's leg. "Where is it?"

"It's not here." He was groaning. "It's all right, but it's not here. I forgot. I don't know how I could forget. I walked over here. I don't have it, my car—it's at home. In the parking lot. Parked there."

The confession came running out of his mouth in the usual way of confessions, unsorted, discontinuous, but at the same time the flip side of his brain was coolly reading the screen of Fay's expression. It was lovely to see. He thought it a perfect moment. What she registered were images of bewilderment, attention, comprehension, relief, surprise, laughter, and then—and this he found loveliest of all—a brisk realignment. "Well, then," she said, looking first at Gary and then at him, "why don't we start walking?"

THEY WALKED SLOWLY. Here and there were puddles of greenish rainwater, and in the puddles floated small twigs and leaves. Overhead the branches of the separate trees gathered together, oak, elm, ash, poplar—city trees with black tarry rings painted around their trunks, put there to discourage the cankerworm larvae. The uniformity of these dark markings turned them into a tree army, marching straight up to a point of perspective.

River Heights was an old part of town. It occurred to Tom for the first time that someone had sat down and planned these streets, inked them on a master plan and given them names— Harvard, Yale, Kingsway, Oxford—suggestive of older, more settled, more easterly territory. Sixty or seventy years earlier, someone, thinking of families and the needs of small children had picked up a ruler and marked off lot sizes, making them generous, allowing for garages and back lanes and for space where raspberries might be grown and front yards that were broad enough to give the houses a touch of dignity, of unassuming definition.

It seemed to Tom, recalling this walk later, that he and Fay had strolled past these houses at a kind of princely pace. Their strides were those of the long-limbed, the unhurried. He must have shortened his steps to match hers, or else she had stretched hers to meet his. It would have been a minuscule adjustment. She was perhaps two inches shorter than he was, which would make her about five feet, nine inches. A tall girl. No, not a girl, certainly not a girl. How old? Thirty, he guessed. And married? If he got a chance he'd check her left hand for a ring, not that that meant anything these days. He would pay attention, listen for the plural pronoun, the attached woman's "we" or "us" or "ours."

Gary Waring did not walk at a princely pace. He had immediately slipped his hand loose from Fay's, running ahead of them or falling behind, zigzagging back and forth across the sidewalk, doubling the distance they covered, stopping to pick up a worm from a sidewalk crack, running the palms of his hands flat along the caragana hedges and transferring the glistening rainwater to his mouth. As though driven by a rubber-band motor he circled trees and poles, scooted pebbles along with the side of his foot, kicking at cracked cement, at fences, knocking experimentally against the side of a mailbox, even putting his ear up to its slot, listening. Turning the corner onto Stafford Avenue, he drummed on the glass window of Murray's Bookstore, humming to himself all the while, chanting some uninhibited breathy tune, bobbing his head up and down extravagantly, and reminding Tom of what he had not thought of in years: the curious and brave efforts of children to charge their immediate world with brilliance, making it glow with color as they move among common objects, bringing those objects alive with incantatory music, alive with texture and outline, alive with life.

HE COULDNT REMEMBER afterward what he and she had talked about, and this seemed strange to him, as though the act of walking, of rhythmically placing one foot before the other, had absorbed and determined the nature of what they said. He knows that they traded lists of current information, that she was thinking of buying a car but hadn't had time to shop around, that he was thinking of investing in a Macintosh computer but couldn't imagine what he would do with it. That she sang in the Handel Chorale, that he jogged in the park on Saturday mornings. That besides her brother, Clyde, she had one sister, named Bibbi, which was short for Beatrix. That "Niteline" was in its sixth year. That she was writing a book on mermaids—"Yes, mermaids!"—as seen from a feminist perspective but was beginning to think she would never get her various theories glued together. That he was continually surprised, and sometimes shocked, by the candor of the people who phoned in to his show, that he believed people were rendered defenseless in the middle of the night, pouring out more than they really wanted to, their loneliness, chiefly. Maybe it does them good, Fay told him; it may be that they don't regret it the next morning at all, but feel better for it, relieved in some way, better able to cope with—loneliness. If that's what it is.

They agreed, walking along, that it was surprising how quiet it was at this hour, only a single car passing, its tires hissing on the damp asphalt. The air was cooler than it had been in weeks, but this hint of fall was false; there would be plenty of hot weather yet.

He looked down at the top of her head rather than into her face. He would have liked to reach out and touch her hair. Her bare arms swung at her sides. He could see the weave of her blouse, the way it sat on her shoulders, and the shoulders themselves, the curving arc of bone and smoothed skin. He felt that if he wanted to, he could see straight into her head. He wondered if she was cold. They crossed Stafford at the light and turned into Grosvenor Avenue. Gary danced beside them as they crossed, and Fay reached out and put a hand on the middle of his back, lightly. Tom, observing the particularity of her touch, felt something like enchantment.

Someone had once told him that Grosvenor, directly translated, meant gross way, or broadway, and he wondered if she knew this; it seemed like something she might like to know.

He asked her how long she planned to be in Europe.

Four weeks, she said. That was long enough when you were traveling alone.

He almost stumbled with happiness. The word struck him full force—"alone." He posed a casual question. "You're not married?"

"No." Lightly. And then, "Are you?" So lightly he could tell she had not been deceived by his nonchalance.

"Divorced," he said to the top of her head. He'd long ago learned to keep things simple.

"Ah."

They'd come to a stop now, standing in front of her building, and she turned directly toward him. "Nice to discover who lives in your own neighborhood." She said this socially.

Struck with inspiration, he asked her how she was getting to the airport, and she said her parents were going to take her, that they lived close by on Ash Avenue, that they'd be coming for her—she checked her watch—in just one hour.

"I suppose I should say bon voyage," Tom said. Out of the corner of his eye he saw Gary pick up a stick and test it rhythmically against the tub of flowers by the door.

What had she said next? Thank you?

They stood, half smiling, divided, it seemed to him, by her fine dark hair and the soft air of congeniality. Motionless. Something holding them there.

"I'll probably," he said, looking at her with amazement, "be running into you when you get back."

She smiled. "Probably." She seemed to be waiting, as though there were one more thing to be said.

"What I'd really like . . ." he began, then stopped himself.

Her smile dimmed, but it was still there. Still there. *"What* would you like?" she asked. The sky behind her head was colored a rainy iridescence.

"I have to put Gary to bed," he said. "And you have to finish packing."

"Yes?"

"What I'd really like is to put my arms around you for a minute."

~ CHAPTER 19 ~

The Sacred and
the Profane

EVERYWHERE FAY LOOKS SHE SEES MEN AND WOMEN EMBRACING: IN Amsterdam, in Copenhagen, and now in Paris. Does this go on all year round? she asks herself. This open abandonment? This ardent, pressing, fleshly extravagance of arms and lips?

In Dutch railway stations, in the lobby of a movie theater, in the narrow streets of the old Jewish quarter—in all these places she's seen how a simple handshake can unfold into something more lingering and sensual, transformed into an intimacy of limbs that yearns for and suggests a deeper convergence. In Denmark, where Fay spent two days attending the European Folkloric Congress, she observed an exchange of greetings between colleagues, what started simply as the wave of a hand across a meeting room, then expanded slowly until it was two circling arms uplifted like bees' wings, indicating surprise, affection, invitation, friendship, and even—yes!--erotic rapture. People hand each other books, papers, glasses of water, and these small formalities imply a longing to become part of one vast undulation. Bodies of the old and young

curl toward each other, speaking of commonplace things but signaling desire—she's sure of it. It comes sighing through the si-
multaneous-translation system. She herself was kissed a dozen
times, the two-cheek European buzz that can mean nothing or
everything. Dr. Kottenheim from Hamburg, younger than she'd
expected from his monograph on angels, hairy as a wrestler, ripely
physical with a melancholy nose and smelling of starch and figs,
had gathered her two hands in his, cradled them there like nesting
swallows, rubbed her wrist with his thumbs, beamed viscerally—
"Ah, my dear, my dear, at last we meet." *Take me, ravish me.*

And here in Paris there is an epidemic of embracing lovers
putting on their showy performances everywhere, in the Métro,
in the student cafeterias bordering the Boulevard Montparnesse,
on gravel paths in the Luxembourg Gardens, at the Louvre waiting
in line for tour tickets, in the middle of the rue du Cherche-Midi
with traffic rushing past, and even, astonishingly, in the luridly lit,
massively furnished foyer of Fay's hotel, where the desk clerk, slim,
sweating Monsieur Martineau, stares candidly down her blouse
front while she registers and twists his face into a little sexual pout.

Public and private acts overlap in this city and no one blinks.
It must be that this is the season of ardor. The weather's warmed
up. In fact, it's steaming hot. The arms of women are suddenly
bare, and this bareness seems always to be begging to be taken
in an embrace. Touch me, touch me, is the cry Fay imagines
hearing in all the corners of Paris. Today she saw a bare-chested
man, hair wild and black, mouth open, running across the Pont
des Arts with his arms outstretched, and running toward him with
little scissor steps was a woman in a tight white dress whose sandals
clicked against the pavement as she ran.

Enough!

The linking of arms, the pressing of bodies, the touching of
fingertips over tiny cups of coffee—all this makes Fay want to
weep. It interferes with her concentration and keeps her awake
through the long nights at the hôtel de l'Avenir. She sits on the
edge of her bed gripping her forearms, rocking herself back and
forth, trying to revive the cooler parts of herself. In the mirror

she sees the face of a wary woman who's tired of being wary, sick of it. She gulps air. Touch me, she says to herself, to the medallion-printed wallpaper of her sixth-floor room, to the wobbly square of light that falls across the floor, bringing a glut of memory with it. *Embrace me.*

"I'd like to put my arms around you," Tom Avery had said to her the night she left home.

SHE CAN'T REMEMBER the tone of his voice when he pronounced this aberrant thing. Whether it was deferential or offhand, aggressive or halting, whether it leapt at her or fell through the air like a kind of powder. Why can't she remember? Was he asking permission or drawing on some artfully phrased macho privilege? She remembers his face turning toward hers, puzzled, something in it anxious to explain. Was he laughing at her? No, she didn't think so. It must have been that he spoke in exceptionally low tones, because young Gary Waring, ten feet away, banging with a stick on a tub of begonias by her front door, seemed not to have heard. The air was heavy and sweet smelling, for summer a dark evening, and cool after the rain. Grosvenor Avenue's slick asphalt was streaked with weak, greenish, beautiful light.

What a bizarre thing for a man to say, especially a man she hardly knew, had only just met. "I'd like to put my arms around you." Why, then, hadn't she been alarmed? Why hadn't she even been surprised?

What if she'd blinked and backed away from him?

A man had walked her home from a children's birthday party, that was all, and now he was about to take her in his arms. What if she had stopped and thought about what she was doing? What if she had resisted?

But she hadn't. She'd moved toward him through air that felt thin and neutral and had buried her face in the creases of his neck, smelling sweat at the border of his hairline and feeling its crisp tapered edge on her cheek. Her arms reached around him and she spread her hands flat against the damp tight weave of his windbreaker. Was that poplin, that closely woven cloth? His arms tightened around her, and Fay remembers that they stood together like this on the street for at least a minute.

That incongruous embrace—what had it meant? His body, a stranger's body, had fastened itself to hers in a manner that seemed unconnected with the arrows of ordinary appetite.

She told herself later, trying to make sense of it, that the two of them held on to each other in a way that was urgent rather than convincing. Weather and opportunity had supported them. Her throat had closed. Her lips were licked clean. "Oh," she said aloud, and he held her even tighter.

AT LAST she's taken hold of herself. She's given herself a talking to. Four weeks in Europe is all she has. Each remaining day can be filled with accomplishment if only she puts her mind to it, but she will have to work hard to make up for lost time.

Onward!

She's been sifting through references at the Bibliothèque Nationale, translating texts, making notes. If, after an hour or two, her back begins to ache, she hurries out for a cup of coffee, then rushes back to her assigned table in the reading room, to her stacks of books and note cards. Once or twice every day she lifts up her head and asks herself: What am I doing here? What is all this *for*?

She's spent an hour with the elderly, passionate French folklorist Hélène Givière, discussing the possible authenticity of the Amboina mermaid, captured off the coast of Borneo in the early eighteenth century. The creature, a full fifty-nine inches long, was kept alive in a barrel for four days and seven hours, and during that time it refused to eat. Naturally she (it?) died, and later, excreta like that of a cat was found in the barrel. Madame Givière, whose graying hair is exquisitely unkempt, has examined the original source document and also a drawing by Samuel Fallours, who was the official artist in the Dutch East India Company, and she has concluded, sadly, that the animal was probably an eel.

Another French scholar, Gabrielle Favian Grobet, a chignon pulling tight her elastic features, gave Fay an entire afternoon. It was Madame Grobet, in her bold imaginative article "Sirène: Les tentations sans amour," who first broke down the archetype of the sea temptress, the wicked voluptuary propelled by forces outside her consciousness. "The siren," the heavily perfumed Madame Grobet told Fay, "has been thought of as part of nature. She has been denied her volition, her soul. She has been thought of as something driven, something culpable, the embodiment of eros but without a body. A nice irony, no?"

Well, maybe. Maybe not.

Besides these visits, Fay has been three times to the Louvre, where she has examined tiny Egyptian mercreatures formed from clay, miniature mermen, merwomen, a merdog, even a mercat, and she has made arrangements in her imperfect French to have each of these artifacts photographed, and further arrangements to have the photographs converted into slides.

She splurged one day on an expensive lunch at the Station Buffet at the Gare de Lyon, where the walls are covered with immense painted mermaids voluptuously wagging their full breasts and rounded bottoms, one of them wearing her hair in an endearing Gibson Girl mop.

She has visited a private collector (pouchy, wizened) in his apartment in the Fifteenth Arrondissement, and there, seated on a carved pink-and-silver sofa and drinking iced Scotch, feeling lopsided and provincial, she listened as he bitterly excoriated all feminist scholars, particularly those from North America, and allowed her to gaze at a Phoenician coin stamped with the image of Atergatis, the feminine counterpart of Oannes, the Babylonian fish god.

She has gone to the marble foyer of the École des Ponts et Chaussées, climbed halfway up a stairway, leaned backward over the banister, and photographed a wan sculpted mermaid entangled in twisted marble foliage, its long tail rather ugly and reptilian. (It pleased her to see the mermaid of myth flourishing here among engineers and technicians!) She has taken the Métro to Trocadero, walked two streets over to the rue Longchamps, and found, after only a minute or two, the extraordinary Belle Époque building (number 12) whose ornate front door is surrounded by two ecstatic double-tailed sirens, diving down toward a bouquet composed of an anchor, rope, and swirling waves, their faces masked by sexual desire and numbed by their enforced solitude. This, Fay decides—and she stops in the street to make a note—is the mer-condition: solitary longing that is always being thwarted. No, not thwarted—denied. (She had observed, one week earlier, the same chilly denial, only more prim and simpering, on the face of the Copenhagen mermaid.)

SHE HAPPENS TO SEE one morning, while sitting and writing postcards in a cafe on the Avenue du Maine, a parade of pilgrims who are walking to Chartres, forty miles away. A thousand pilgrims filling the broad street.

At the table next to her sits a heavy, purple-faced, talkative woman in a dirty raincoat who is drinking, though it is only ten o'clock in the morning, a glass of dark beer. It is she who tells Fay—mumbling, hissing into the beer foam—about the annual pilgrimage from Paris to Chartres, about the magic number one thousand, and the fact that the walkers traditionally begin their trek with a mass at Notre Dame.

They are coming from that mass now, still bathed in a coating of holy spirit—or so Fay thinks, watching them file past. *"Ils sont fous,"* the purplish woman concludes, blowing into her glass and licking the thick rim.

But Fay is enchanted by the procession, which bears lightly along on its wisps of hymn song a bearable, sentient faith. The love for God, God's love. She wonders, a little enviously, what it feels like to be part of that holy contract. These pilgrims are of all ages and include a great many sturdily shod children whose composed, steady eyes seem to gesture toward a world in which responsibility, for the most part, prevails. (Seeing them, she thinks of her nephews, Matthew and Gordon, their hard, perfect young legs and arms.) Elderly women, both angular and ample, are present, and also numbers of very young women, fine-featured, pale of skin, some of them beautiful, and a scattering of priests, mostly middle-aged, who are not leading their charges but mingling in a way which Fay supposes must manifest the newer, more democratic Catholic Church. What she finds most startling, though, is a handful of marching friars—if that is what they are still called—robed in coarse brown cloth, their absurd tonsures shining in the bright sunlight. They look like extras on a film set, moving foward with clumsy, sacred assurance. What sort of man these days, in the last years of the twentieth century, chooses rough hooded garments and cruel barbering?

One of the brown-clad friars abruptly leaves his place in the procession and makes a dash for the cafe where Fay is sitting. His face is boyish, rounded in its features and pinkened by the morning heat. He glances her way, blinking at the cafe's dim entrance, and then, with a look of swooming deliverance, catches sight of a door marked *"Toilette."*

In a minute he is out again (Fay feels the enacted comedy of his lifted robe, the collision with stained porcelain). He stumbles slightly at the exit of the cafe, made dizzy by sunlight, then dodges the crowds of people who have gathered along the street and runs forward awkwardly, his skirt hiked up in one hand, hurrying to rejoin his companions.

"Fou," growls Fay's neighbor. Her glass is empty. Her tone is both harsh and elegiac. *"Complètement fou."*

At which Fay smiles and shrugs. She finds herself unexpectedly affected by the young friar's clumsiness and the beauty of his sandaled feet, feet that will carry him to the outskirts of this immense, puzzling city, and beyond. His maladroit body, its shaved modest head, stirs in her a kind of love and cracks open seams of sentimentality she would have thought beneath her. Well, I love him, she says to herself, I love him.

Fou says a contradictory voice inside her head.

She loves, too, the raddled, rude face of the crooning woman next to her, and the waiter who is leaning over her table, picking coins off a saucer. And the dull brown plastic of the cafe table, she loves that as well, and the way her felt-tip pen fits in her hand, a part of her body, dispensing freely its inked loops and dashes and points of serious emphasis. "Paris is heavenly," she writes to

Onion, to Strom, to Iris Jaffe, to her sister, Bibbi, to Clyde and Sonya, to her mother and father, to Simon and Stephanie Birrell, to Robin Cummerford, to the staff at the folklore center, "but I can't wait to get home."

THE VILLAGE CHURCH in Marigny, in the east of France, dates from the sixteenth century, but the small stone cross that stands outside its door is much older—twelfth century, or perhaps even earlier. Its general configuration is rudimentary, and the carving, with its look of compaction and pitted antiquity, is exuberantly primitive. A square-faced angel with blunt spread wings—a male angel, certainly—is fixed to its center, staring expressionlessly, endlessly, down into the eyes of a muscular mermaid whose magnificent tail is wrapped three times around the base. Her hands, their tiny roughened fingers, cling to the vertical axis as though it represented the only refuge in the world. Her face is a veil of rapture, her neck luxuriantly long, her breasts eroded ovals, rather widely spaced, and where the nipples once stood there is today only a pair of twin depressions filled with calcified stone, faintly green in the late-afternoon light.

Fay has traveled three hours by train and another hour by taxi in order to photograph this wonder. Its location, not just its corruption of Christian symbol, makes it rare. Marigny is far from any seacoast and has neither river nor lake, not even a spring. No one knows where the stone cross came from, but according to the village people—Fay has spoken in her slow, inaccurate French to a number of them—the Marigny mermaid has always stood on this spot.

The stone is soft. She knows from her reading it was probably carved in a day or two by an illiterate mason, an aesthetic transaction so brief and so small when poised against the grid of history that its perfection must be put down to a random accident. Like the elegant unicorn, the audacious griffin, the fleet centaur, those legendary creatures bubbling out of a dark age—not really dark at all, but stained with oddly slanted light—the medieval merfolk exploded from stone or wood to express a twisted, fey longing for the inexpressible. They never existed, and, what is more, no one ever believed they did.

Fay has a certain respect for the medieval mind, for the attention it paid, on the one hand, to a straw-and-turnip economy, and to the playful imagination, on the other hand, that shaped its bestiary. Magical creatures were a kind of shared joke or mad desire. No one believed in such beasts, not even children, not even sailors sodden with rum. Never mind the thousands of mermaid sightings, sightings which occurred as late as the eighteenth century—none of it meant a thing.

Once Fay thought otherwise, but now she more and more imagines that these mermaid testimonies were delivered with a wink of the eye or its psychic equivalent. People are, after all, sensible; people are practical and realistic; and though they create for their diversion a realm of wonder, they remain solidly embedded in what their eyes and ears tell them. The glorious mermaid of Marigny was animated out of whim, out of the moment, and nothing more. And today, stroking the lovely sinuous mermaid tail—the village priest stands a few feet away smoking a cigarette—Fay thinks of Tom Avery, how the two of them had held each other in a long impromptu embrace, a pair of random creatures assigned to a random world.

EARLY ON A Wednesday morning, a cool and overcast day, Fay took the train to the city of Nantes, and from there she drove in a rented car to the village of St. Pierre, on the shore of the Lac du Grand-Lieu.

It is a curious lake—hardly a lake at all, but rather an immense reed-filled marsh that in summer shrinks to a shallow saucer swimming with eels and coated with algae. The water looks dead, but, in fact, it is richly alive—with herons, ducks, muskrats, dragonflies, and many varieties of fish. In this water, eighteen months ago, a mermaid rose suddenly from the lake bottom with mud in her hair and a basket of small fish hooked over one arm. The phenomenon was witnessed by two teenaged girls and reported in the local tabloid, *Ouest-France*. From there it was picked up by the

Herald Tribune, and then by the international wire services. At least half a dozen of Fay's friends and colleagues had clipped the item and sent it to her.

Fay has contacted the families of the two girls and has written ahead to arrange a meeting—at noon, in the municipal office, the *mairie,* of St. Pierre. The girls are named Michelène Payot and Sophie Jaud, aged fourteen and fifteen, respectively. Michelène has a smooth, pretty, empty face atop a small, sharp, angular body. She seems suspicious of, or else frightened by, Fay's list of questions, and soon falls silent. Sophie, on the other hand, is a full-lipped, vivacious girl who can't stop talking. She wears a blue-checked smock over a pair of red jeans. Her breasts are amazing for a girl of this age, abundant, like a woman's, but when she talks it is in a jeering, bright, unstoppable, girlish flow.

Fay proposes that the three of them adjourn to a cafe across the small village square where pizza is served. Michelène's eyes brighten; so do Sophie's.

"*Voilà,*" Fay says when they are seated at a table, "tell me about your siren. Start at the beginning, and please, speak very slowly so that I will understand every word."

Sophie takes a gulp of air and begins. The *sirène,* she tells Fay, came swimming toward them as they sat, she and Michelène, on a small wooden boat dock.

Why had they gone to the dock? Fay asks, trying hard to sound matter-of-fact, and keeping her smile bright.

The two girls exchange looks. Well, Sophie says, it happened that they sometimes went to this place to smoke cigarettes after school. Their mothers and fathers would murder them if they knew they did such a thing.

Trust me, Fay says with an upraised hand.

Sophie swallows. On this particular day—it was winter and bitterly cold—they'd been there only a few minutes when they saw the lake waters part, a spot of swirling foam, and then what looked at first like a net full of eels emerged. They observed that it had a sort of face. Silvery looking. Like a cooking pot, *une casserole,* shining. The sun was on it. They thought it might be some giant fish, but then a long pale arm, like a woman's, reached up with a basket of fish. The other arm was waving. At them.

"Waving?"

Beckoning. *Appelant de la main.* Urging them to come into the water.

And had they been tempted, despite the cold?

No, no, they were too frightened. They could scarcely move, scarcely breathe.

And then what?

Then the *sirène* began to sing.

She sang? What was she singing? Was there a melody, were there words? (Fay has read about the singing in the newspaper reports, but she feels she must test these two directly.)

Non. Oui. Peut-être. She sang the same thing over and over. The tone, it was high-pitched, it hurt their ears. At first they thought she was singing *Bonne journée, bonne journée,* but afterward they decided she had been saying to them *mangez, mangez,* eat, eat.

And after that?

Then she dived down into the water. As though she were vexed with them for not responding. Exasperated. She made a great splashing sound, and it was then they saw her long silver tail. A fish's tail. It had whipped the cold air, a hard smack. (Sophie demonstrates with her fork.)

And that was all?

Oui. She disappeared. All they could see were some bubbles where she had been. And a little hole, *un trou,* on the surface of the water.

Have either of you ever, Fay asks carefully, seen pictures of sirens?

They look once again at each other and nod, *oui.*

And did this *sirène* that you saw, did she look like the ones in the pictures?

Yes, Sophie says after a minute, only she was smaller.

And beautiful? Was she beautiful?

She wasn't beautiful, no, but she wasn't ugly, either. She was nothing. Just this silver thing. And with her basket of fish.

What kind of basket?

Just a basket, *un panier*. Like this one here that rests on the table, full of bread.

Do you think that when she said *mangez* she was offering you the fish to eat?

Sophie shrugs, and Michelène, like a shadow figure, shrugs too. They don't know. Perhaps. They think so.

How did you feel when she disappeared?

Afraid. Perplexed. But mostly afraid.

What did you do then? Did you go home and tell your parents what you'd seen?

No. Not right away.

Why not?

We didn't think they would believe us.

When did you tell them, then?

A few days later. Maybe a week.

And what did they say?

Michelène speaks at last. Her father was soon telling everyone about it. All the neighbors. Everyone.

But you never saw the siren again?

No, only the one time.

Did you go to the lake again to look for her?

Our parents forbade it.

Why?

They were worried, they thought it might be dangerous.

So you never returned?

Well. Perhaps once or twice.

Do you believe she'll come back again, *la sirène*?

Non. Michelène giggles at this and looks down at her lap. *Non, non, non.*

Jamais, says Sophie.

FAY DOESN'T TAKE any of this seriously.

She is not so old yet that she can't remember the dimensions of the adolescent imagination, how she and Iris Corning and others of their friends, at fifteen years, sixteen, fantasized endlessly about chance meetings with Robert Redford, how he would happen to be in Winnipeg for a few days, never mind how or why, scouting for new talent, looking around for a young fresh-faced unspoiled star for his latest film. He would be in disguise, of course, wearing a wig over his beautiful reddish hair and dressed in overalls. There he was, staked out at Polo Park Shopping Mall, pretending to repair a light fixture, when who should walk by but . . . or perhaps it would be Neil Young. Neil Young, after all, had actually attended Kelvin High School at one time, the same school Fay and Iris attended. What if Neil Young decided suddenly to return, to make a sort of sentimental journey? He would be weary, jaded—it was understandable—and disenchanted with the plastic world of Hollywood, and looking for . . .

Fay knows what adolescence is. It is a time of intense concentrated boredom, it is never-ending in its sameness. People like to speak of the violent mood swings teenagers experience, but in fact most of adolescence is a killing procession of tedious days and numbing nights that must somehow, by imagination or a shared dramatic gesture, be kicked alive. Anything is better than nothing, monsters, virgins, wild animals, film stars, rock singers, mermaids—whatever can be prised out of the available culture and given a transitory shape. (And does it really end, this kind of fantasy? Hasn't she every single night since leaving home reached out across the sheets in her various hotel rooms, in Amsterdam, in Copenhagen, in Paris, and conjured the back of Tom Avery's poplin windbreaker?)

Before leaving St. Pierre, Fay takes a snapshot of Michelène Payot and Sophie Jaud standing in front of the cafe, smiling and looking pleased with themselves, and after that she drives out to the lake and takes another photo of its green, insect-buzzing surface. What she'll do with all this she has no idea.

But she knows there's no point in staying any longer. She might as well drive into Nantes, return her rental car, and catch the late-afternoon train back to Paris. But first she will telephone the hôtel de l'Avenir on the rue du Cherche-Midi to let them know she will be returning tonight instead of tomorrow.

She finds a telephone booth next to the post office in the tiny village of Passey, and a minute later she is speaking to Monsieur Martineau at the hotel desk.

"There is a letter here for you, Madame McLeod," he says in his best school English, all the vowels propped open. "And it is marked urgent."

Her heart squeezes. Illness. An accident. Her parents. Bibbi. Matthew or Gordon. Catastrophe.

"Perhaps you will be kind enough to open it for me," she says into the receiver, then thinks to add, trembling, *"s'il vous plaît."*

"But, Madame, if you have the intention to return tonight—"

"Can you at least tell me who it is from?"

"I am sorry. I do not understand."

"The return address. Is there a name on it, or an address, maybe?"

"It has, I believe—yes, it is a Canadian aerogram."

"But is there a name? In the corner, maybe, the left-hand corner? *A la gauche de la*—or perhaps on the back of the envelope? *L'autre côté de*—"

"Ah, oui, il y a le nom de l'expéditeur—"

"What is it?" Can she really be shouting? "Who?"

"It is not so easy to read, I am afraid—"

"Please try, please try to read it, Monsieur."

"It appears to be . . . Tome." He pronounces it so that it rhymes with loam.

"Tom?"

"And something else, but I cannot—"

"Avery? Tom Avery?"

"Yes, that is it. Tome Avery."

"Monsieur Martineau, please, I must ask you to open the letter. Right away. And read it to me over the telephone."

"But I cannot—"

"You did say it was marked urgent."

"Just one minute please. I have misplaced my *petit canif*—"

"Just tear it open, it's all right."

"One minute, *ne quittez pas*. Are you there, Madame McLeod?"

"I'm here. I'm listening."

"It says." He pauses.

"Yes? What does it say?"

" 'Deee-err Fay.' "

"And then?"

"It says—are you sure you wish, Madame, for me to read this very private letter?"

"Yes, I wish it. Please go on."

" 'I love you.' "

"I didn't hear you." But she did hear.

"In the letter there are written those words. 'I love you, I love you, I love you.' *Trois fois,* I love you. Do you prefer that I continue, Madame?"

"Yes," Fay says, "yes. Please. Please read all of it, Monsieur Martineau, every word. I'm listening."

~ *CHAPTER 20* ~

I Love You

"DEAR FAY," TOM HAD WRITTEN. "I LOVE YOU. I LOVE YOU, I love you. I don't know what else to say to you or why I'm saying it, but I have to tell you. Something is making me. I love you. I'm not a dangerous or crazy person, although I wouldn't blame you for thinking so. I loved you the minute I saw you coming up the sidewalk carrying that bunch of balloons. I loved the parting in your hair and the shape of your mouth. I loved the way you stood still and put your arms around me—that was later. I think of it every day, a hundred times, or rather I think of it continually, exactly how your hands felt pressing against my back and how it was to hold you, your wonderful thinness. I can't seem to think of anything outside that minute when we were standing together by your front door. I just love you. I love you plain and simple. I love you. Tom Avery."

WELL, HE WAS A FOOL. He was a nut case, tetched in the head, as his mother would say—bonkers, balmy. Not because he'd gone silly with love—love was unaccountable, he knew that much just from looking around, just from being alive. No, he was a loony because he'd gone and written that foaming-at-the-mouth letter to Fay McLeod, and not just written it but mailed it. (Christ!) He knows the woman for half an hour and he sends her a letter full of garbage. (What had he written, anyway? He can't remember the words, only that it was the letter of a man possessed.)

What in sweet Jesus' name had come over him. He was a mature man, forty years old, for God's sake, reasonably steady in his habits, reasonably normal. Well, except for those three marriages, that indissoluble number three. And except for the offbeat hours he kept, and his somewhat eccentric job. Normal, yes, except for his zero of a father. Except for these recent months of, well, mild depression. Impotence? (Don't say that word, don't even think it.) Maybe he really did have a screw loose. He should see someone, a shrink, tomorrow, get a referral from Dave Neuhaus. The hell he would. And don't forget his mother, she's part of his history. You can't just go and wipe that off the record, how she'd been hospitalized after his birth, for several weeks—no, several months. Well, it was all a little vague. Postpartum depression, they would have called it these days, and perfectly understandable given the circumstances. Her breakdown, or nervous collapse, whatever the hell it was, it pointed straight toward—what? Erratic behavior? And then there was the other side of his parentage. God only knows what psychotic, riotous blood pours from that unknown font.

Anyway, it was too late. He'd done something dark and dangerous, writing a letter like that. He'd committed a rash act he hoped he'd never have to account for, but knew he would. Jesus. Buying that aerogram and then filling it up with his blustering frenzy, letting it have its way, then actually sealing it, for God's sake, his tongue traveling along its glued edges. He recalls the gummy taste now with a fresh wave of sorrow, and how he had afterward walked to the corner and dropped it—irretrievable—into the mailbox on River Avenue. Farewell. So be it. Godspeed. Launched like a message in a bottle. Like a bomb.

People get arrested for this kind of thing—harassment. Every night, home from his shift at CHOL, Tom falls asleep sick with the shame of what he's done, what he's set into motion, what he's risked.

But each morning, and it's been almost two weeks now, he wakes up refreshed and hopeful. "Fay," he says to his new shower curtain and to the damp folds of his bath towel, and then he smiles into the mirror. Hello, hello. He almost, but not quite, winks; who is that overgrown boy, shaving his cheeks and chin and looking so genial? Why, it's Tom Avery, you've seen that mug plastered all over town, and he's got his mind wrapped around and around a woman named Fay McLeod. He's waking up after a long sleep, he's starting to come alive.

He trusts her. This trust of his is based on—instinct? Her hands on his back, pressing; those hands were about to solve and satisfy something in him. (Had he imagined that her fingers opened, spread themselves?) Her warm, even bodily pressure moving against him. He hadn't imagined that.

So he trusts her, yes, and—an ancillary happiness—he trusts himself, too, knowing that when he sat down twelve days ago at his kitchen table, pen in hand, scattering words over the pale blue paper—foolish words, crazy words—that he was as deeply, rationally sane as he'd ever been in his life.

"WELL, YES, I suppose I could say I know Fay McLeod," Liz Chandler told Tom. "Here, have another waffle. Not that I know her well. We say hello if we run into each other, that kind of thing. She was a couple of years behind me in high school, and you know what it's like when you're in high school, a couple of years makes an enormous difference. Actually, Fay McLeod's a good friend of Iris Jaffe's, Iris used to be a Corning, her mother was Winnie Corning, she was a friend of my mother's, they used to play tennis together, mixed doubles, back in the dark ages. She used to go with someone called Willy Gifford—Fay, I'm talking about, not Winnie Corning, for heaven's sake. Did you know Willy Gifford? He was in advertising or films or something, he was gorgeous.

Women fell at his feet. He and Fay McLeod went together for ages, and if I'm not mistaken they were even engaged for a while, but I guess it didn't pan out, anyway, he's out on the west coast somewhere, I think. Or the east coast. Gene, that waffle's about done, I think, it's going to burn. No, she's never been married, I'd know something like that, not that she hasn't had plenty of friends, *good* friends, shall we say. She was living with Peter what's-his-name, that long humongous guy, you know, who used to be married to Fritzi Sweet? Yes, Fritzi. Didn't you know she'd been married before? In fact, I think they're back together again. Fritzi and this Peter person. Poor Sammy, a sweet guy, talk about untimely—yes, I do remember Sammy was married to your Sheila. That sure was a quickie. What was it—two years? Well, that's the way it goes, a merry-go-round. Well, I'm not sure, but I could figure it out—I'm thirty-seven, so Fay McLeod must be thirty-five or thereabouts, but, then, she hasn't had any kids, so no stretch marks, no agony lines, et cetera. Chrissie, will you shut up for one minute, I'm getting you another glass of milk, give Mommy half a sec. Now listen, Tom, you've hardly eaten a thing. Well, I'm not sure why they split up. I mean, she probably met someone else, it wasn't as though they were married, and she is a fairly attractive woman. Well, okay, very attractive. Anyway, what's up? Why so interested in Fay McLeod all of a sudden?"

"YES, INDEED," said Simon Birrell, who does the noon-hour farm report for CHOL. "I've known Fay for years. Stephanie and I are both fond of her, and so are the kids—she loves kids, it's a shame she hasn't had half a dozen of her own. I'm surprised, Tom, that you've never run into her at our place. We see quite a bit of her. She's in the Handel Chorale, has been for ages, second alto, not a great voice, not a solo voice, that is, but a decent voice. Well, yes, that's true, she was living with Peter Knightly. Do you know Peter? A decent guy, English background. I don't know what happened. The usual thing, I guess, it just ran its course. She may have said something to Stephanie about it, but not to me, and I certainly wouldn't have asked. I think, perhaps, she's just one of these women who can't settle down. It happens. It's sad to see. My heart goes out to people who're on their own, who make that choice. But maybe it happens because they want it to happen, who knows?"

"WHY HELLO, TOM," Sonya said on the telephone. "Of course, it's no bother. Fay's address? You mean in Paris? But I thought I gave you her address—sure, I'd be glad to check it again. I've got it right here somewhere on a little bitty piece of paper. Good Lord, I've got so many bits and scraps floating around. Here it is. Number fourteen, rue du Cherche-Midi, Paris six, that's the Sixth Arrondissement. Is that the same address I gave you before? Anyway, her time in Paris is just about up, I think she's off to Germany next, and then she's got this little chunk of Italy, kind of a circuit, then she's on her way home, what a whirlwind tour! Well, we've had a couple of postcards, yes, and she says everything's going just swimmingly."

"GOOD AFTERNOON, ladies and gentlemen. Welcome to the National Center for Folklore Studies. My name is Beverly Miles and I'm your guide today. We'll begin our tour in just a couple of minutes. Excuse me, I hope you don't mind my asking, but you look very, very familiar, are you by any chance Tom Avery? I thought so. Well, I'm one of your fans. Really! No, I mean it! I listen to 'Niteline' every night, the first hour, anyway, and then I'm afraid I drift off. I loved your Bob Dylan special last week. Maybe you'll give the center a mention on the air sometime. We have conducted tours Tuesday through Saturday, every hour on the half hour. Well, it's time we began, I think. If you'll follow me, ladies and gentlemen, we'll start with the Great Plains room, where we'll stop and look at some interesting artifacts from our aboriginal peoples. Please just follow me and feel free to ask questions. That's what we're here for."

"HEY, TOM," cried Rosalie Summers, the CHOL receptionist, "a fax came for you about an hour ago, and here it is. And listen, you'd better put on your asbestos gloves, Romeo, this one's a sizzler."

Tom opened it, held it up to the light, and read:

I love you too. Returning home Aug. 31, 10:15 A.M., Air Canada, flight 192. I love you too.

Fay

~ CHAPTER 21 ~

I Love You Too

FIFTEEN YEARS AGO, WHEN FAY WAS A GIRL OF TWENTY, SHE WENT away to the University of Wisconsin in Madison in order to study that unstable art or science, whichever it is, that goes by the name of folklore.

Folk Studies. She liked the sound of it. It felt roughly formed and accessible, tactile and breathing. It opened doors in the corporeal world that were logical, quirky, arcane, and sometimes whimsical. Sex and economics lay at the bottom of it, and also the collapsing edge of elaborate religious observance. Folklore seemed to her a kind of poetry, a way of guessing at the links between language and behavior, and, furthermore, no one else she knew was doing it.

During her two years in Madison she had three love affairs, one of them serious, or so it seemed while it was happening. Also during that period she lived alone for the first time, a frightening but joyous experiment, in a cramped apartment on a short dark street near the main campus, and learned how it was possible to stretch a small sum of money—the Quiller Foundation Fellowship, as it was called—over the exigencies of rent, food, clothes, books, and movies (at this period of her life she found herself several afternoons a week seated in dark boxlike theaters where she drank in the dappled images and subtitles and nuanced exhortations of foreign-film makers, always, afterward, re-entering the clean sun-specked streets of Madison full of cheerful skepticism and surprise at where destiny had thus far delivered her.)

She took up cycling and then fencing, gave up red meat, smoked small amounts of hash with a wide spectrum of friends, a few of whom she is still in touch with, and once or twice became dismayingly, bone-shakingly drunk on cheap wine. She was cheerful more often than she was sad, and was prideful about her discovery that happiness was a kind of by-product of existence and not an end in itself. Wearing jeans and a coarse-knit Brittany sweater, she sat in various Madison coffee bars talking and being talked at and laying to rest such issues as the evils of imperialism, the menace of nuclear arms, the weight of the patriarchy, the insularity of the Western tradition, and the old unchartable persistence of spiritual belief. She learned, sitting cross-legged on her bed, to play a few chords on a guitar and to sing mournfully to herself, relishing this self-image above all others. And at the end of her fellowship, a few weeks after her twenty-second birthday, she was awarded a master's degree in Folklore Studies.

Working under the direction of Hector Lownsbrough, that wattled, decent, fussy septuagenarian, Fay examined the conjugal arrangements in five widely differing societies—Uganda, France, Mexico, Japan, and Albania. Ring around the rosy, ring around the world. She concluded that the marriage ceremony itself constituted a mere rubber-stamping of a more significant, though far less codified, premarriage agreement—which was the exchange of sentiments between a woman and a man that declared their hearts to be open to one another. (Not that she used the word "heart" in her thesis, and not that she risked, except within the boundaries of crisply set quotation marks, the word "love.")

She wrote instead of the ritualized exchange of gifts—rings, money, cattle, carved spoons, flowers, vials of tears, pierced seashells, bracelets of human hair, or offerings of costly fruit, all of which were portents of larger, final gifts to come.

She catalogued the traditional methods by which the couple's private pledge was broadcast to the wider community. The publication of banns. The wearing of scarlet cloth or a lace headdress. The visitation of one family upon the other, during which certain sweet cakes were eaten or a ceremonial brew drunk.

Her final chapter, and the most original—"This *is* the thesis," insisted Dr. Lownsbrough—analyzed the formal phrase, or speech tag, that attaches to a declaration of affection.

These linguistic units, in all societies—or, at least, in all those Fay examined—tend to be both ancient and economical, and their word pattern fairly rigidly ordered—a subject and object balanced like a teeter-totter over a verb, or else, as in the French *je t'aime*, the object cradled in the arms of the vital sentiment. The distribution of syllables in such phrases is close to perfect. Vowel sounds predominate, and such consonants as exist lie soft on the tongue. In even the most conservative communities the utterance is oddly ungendered, though it is generally spoken first by the male and echoed by the female. It wraps itself around a resolution that cannot readily be expressed in words of similar weight. Its currency is hard, unqualified, and almost shocking in its directness. Its subsequent disavowal is difficult to establish without guilt or loss of face. It is so deeply embedded in the culture that it is not easily dislodged by fashion, and generally it holds on to its potency despite the corruption of popular songs, cheap slogans, greeting-card verses, and the like. In most languages its music is sonorous and rhythmic—I love you, I love you. A miniature poem that fills the mouth, yet it is uttered often with curious difficulty, almost reluctance.

"I love you," Fay had faxed to Tom Avery in Winnipeg.

She had pronounced the words. Her brain felt washed, cool. At rest.

LIVING OUT OF A suitcase all these weeks has made her dizzy. Too many hotels, too many strange beds, bad beds, generally, damp and unmercifully flat and topped by a long hard sluglike roll instead of a pillow. What was inside those unyielding sausages, anyway? Compacted corn husks? Wet cotton? No wonder the French were an irascible people—they must all suffer from sore neck disease.

Now, however, in Germany, in the old city of Trier, her bed is soft, white, and generous. But still she's unable to sleep. It's three o'clock in the morning—the church bell chimes every quarter hour—and she turns and grasps a handful of smooth sheeting, wrings it unsparingly and thinks of the faxed message she's sent to Tom Avery. What, oh, what has she done!

The mermaids have affected her equilibrium. She's seen too many of them (the museum in Trier is particularly rich) and she's filled up so many note cards that she's been forced to buy a new satchel to hold them all. She's sick of mermaids. Their writhing bodies. Their empty unblinking faces shrieking for love. (She's taken over a hundred photographs herself and arranged for a further forty to be professionally done.) Not one of the mermaids she's seen has had a whit of intelligence about her. The tiny annular mouths are greedy. Love, love, love is all they can dream up down there in their underwater homes. They're starved and vapid and stupid as fish. They're impoverished by love, maddened by love, they're crazy as . . . as crazy as Fay is herself.

SHE'S NOTICED something odd: that the mermaid likenesses found close to the sea are coarse in their configuration and animalistic, while those found farther inland are finer, more ethereal, more womanly. In the German city of Augsburg, for instance, the mermaids possess an enchanting rococo pink-and-whiteness, like cherubs who have sprouted fins and tails instead of wings. Insipid, perhaps, but she likes them. And in Augsburg she had the good fortune to see, as part of a traveling exhibition from the Vatican,

Konrad von Megenberg's charming, gamboling *Meerwundern,* dating from 1475.

Oh, Tom, Tom.

The sun is shining. She is drinking tea from a large white porcelain cup, which sits on a circle of lacy paper, which sits in turn on a saucer, which sits on a second circle of lace. The air she breathes is layered with the smell of flowers and mild soap and green leaves washed with oxygen. The clock in the town square chimes.

In five days she'll be home.

"I LOVE YOU," Fay had said to Willy Gifford after she had known him for a year. They were driving down Portage Avenue in Willy's old Dodge. It must have been late winter, probably March. She remembers that the snow was falling so heavily that it was piling up in clumps under the blades of the windshield wipers. Every few blocks Willy had to stop the car, get out, and knock the packed snow loose with the butt end of a whisk broom. The wonder was that he did it uncomplainingly. Every time it happened, he broke off his monologue about—but Fay can't remember what it was about, something political, probably, his usual sunny, roaring rhetoric. He swept away the snow, climbed back into the car, and picked up at the point where he'd left off. His face shone. He was a handsome man, almost pretty. "Did I hear right?" he asked suddenly, turning to Fay. "Did you just say what I think you said? You love me? Christ, woman, I thought you'd never say it. I'd convinced myself you didn't know the words."

"I love you," Fay had told Nelo Merino one week after she met him. She was on her back. Nelo was on top of her. His legs were covered with thick fur, as was his back, his chest, and his rather heavy, childish arms. A kind of Caliban was how she thought of him, rough but enchanted with the refined. She sighed the words out, I love you, rather than speaking them, and heard herself say them again and again in a doused voice like someone drugged.

"Yes, of course I love you," she told Peter Knightly. She said it blithely. He had caught her by surprise. She was sitting across a table from him, a table covered with the debris of a meal he had himself cooked, chicken bones, scrapings of curried rice, a smeared jar of mango chutney, all of it brought brightly forward for her, for her alone, and his hand was seeking her hand, moving across the back of her wrist. "I do," she said, "yes, I do love you."

But this is different, saying "I love you" to Tom Avery; this is of a different order. (But people always say that, don't they? This time it's different.)

"I love you" is what her parents must say up there in their wallpapered bedroom in their house on Ash Avenue, a thousand times, a hundred thousand times.

And what her stammering brother, Clyde, must whisper to his dear rounded ebullient Sonya, struggling to concentrate, getting the words to come out straight.

And it could be that even Jake Greary barks it into Bibbi's ear, a harsh, compromised, Marxist version—I love you. Yes.

And Onion and Strom? It is hard for Fay to imagine, but not impossible. Across the white sheet in that hospital room? Surely mysteries have been exchanged there between the two of them. Almost everyone gets a chance to say it—I love you. And to hear it said to them. Love is, after all, a republic, not a kingdom.

"I think I love you," Robin Cummerford said to Fay a few days before she left for Amsterdam. "Believe it or not, this hasn't happened to me before. I find that I'm always thinking about you, even when I'm doing my rounds on the ward. We seem to appreciate the same things. I wonder if you think it would be a good idea if we went away for a weekend. When you get back from Europe, I mean. The two of us. To see, you know, how it goes. How can anyone really know? But I do feel that I'm, as it were, in love with you."

To which Fay, being kind, being tired, too, said: "Well, there's no hurry, is there?"

Though love is not necessarily patient. She knows that. Nor kind.

———

HER TRAVEL grant is down to its last few scurrying dollars, but there's enough to take her by train to Turin, in the north of Italy, to photograph the medieval merfolk on the old church wall.

At last! These paint-daubed creatures are joyous acrobats— oddly, whitely fleshed and wonderfully endearing. One round face in particular, with its steamy secret smile, speaks of perfect composure, of mer-ness accommodated to the last eighth of an inch. For this sight Fay has sacrificed Norwich Cathedral, with its mermaid suckling a lion, and Ripon Cathedral, with its carved choir mermaid, and also the island of Iona, where Saint Patrick in the fifth century is said to have banished old pagan women and turned them into mermaids. According to legend, one of them wept so copiously that her tears formed the strangely shaped pebbles that litter the island.

A handful of these lovely pebbles was given to Fay by Hannah Webb after she visited Iona two years ago. Fay keeps them in an old glass jar on her coffee table, where they are exclaimed over by friends, or lined up in rows and counted and recounted by her young nephews. There are forty-four in all.

She's brought one of these stones along with her to Europe, loose in her change purse, rubbing up against Dutch guilders, French francs, and German marks. It's not for luck that she's brought it—she doesn't believe in that kind of talisman any longer. She doesn't know what it's for, but every time she touches it with her fingers, its smoothness feeds her courage and reminds her of her fundamental and obstinate sanity.

If she were really insane, she tells herself, she would have torn up her excursion ticket days ago and bought a one-way ticket home, home to Tom, straight into the embrace of love.

WEDNESDAY NIGHT. Another city, another civic clock chiming the night hours. In her dream she is swimming. Her long skirt is entangled in her legs and she unable to kick herself free. Her arms, too, are caught in a kind of webbing, which she divines, finally, is her own hair, grown impossibly long. Air, air, she struggles for a mouthful of air. And wakes suddenly, gasping.

TONIGHT, in a spartan hotel room near the Amsterdam airport, she has the same dream again, her hair, her trapped arms and legs, her stuck breath, and this time she decides to turn on her bedside lamp and read for a while.

But the moment she pushes the switch, the light bulb burns out. There is a blue burst, a crisp little smacking sound like an electric kiss, then a scratched red line in space. Tiny explosive particles travel up her arm, or seem to, and carry a wave of weak guilty shock. If only she hadn't turned it on so brutally, she thinks, but this thought is exceedingly brief, hardly a thought at all, more like a leaf falling or a flash of heat that buzzes on the outside edge of her consciousness.

Oh, God.

Now she is fully awake, lying on her side facing her dead lamp. Its base is glazed ceramic, cheap, anonymous, but nicely rounded, pleasing to her fingertips.

Her alarm clocks says 5:00 a.m. The room is filling up with a wash of snagged light that creeps around the curtain, top and bottom, gray upon gray, and its polished fullness is as empty of shadows as the lamp base or her own blown-out breath. The room's high dusky ceiling seems to be emptiness itself, hovering over her and offering certain rewards.

But this is not happiness she's feeling; it's too dry, too shallowly drawn. This is what precedes happiness: lightheadedness, pangs of hunger, the ballooning sensation of being intensely alive.

In an hour she must get up, wash her hair, and dress. In three hours her plane will take off. In ten hours she will be home, standing in an airport with her arms around Tom Avery and his around her. Beyond that moment her imagination will not travel.

~ CHAPTER 22 ~

Everything They
Say Is True

"SO WHAT'S GOT INTO YOU?" TED WOLOSCHUK ASKED TOM AVERY. "I mean, you're like a new man for crying out loud, not that I'm going to start squawking. You come into the studio sort of almost dancing-like. Up on the air. Whistling! I didn't know you knew how to whistle. Even the music you've been choosing for the show. We've been getting calls. I guess maybe Bruce told you. People like it. Starting Monday night they've been phoning in. It's good to see you looking up. I don't give a damn about the ratings, you know me better than that, but it's sure a lot more cheerful around here all of a sudden. So what's up? Did'ya win a lottery or what? Why've you all of a sudden got that crazy big grin all over your puss?"

"WELL, FOR PETE'S SAKE," Tom's mother yelled happily into the phone. "Will wonders never cease. I've been wondering, and Mike, too, when you were going to get yourself up here for a weekend. You know how long it's been? Weeks. The weather's gorgeous, and the sunsets! Of course, we've had a couple real hard frosts, I've brought my tomatoes in, didn't want to take a chance, but it warms up real nice in the daytime. Oh boy, you should see the colors. The poplars. Real September weather. A girl? You're thinking of bringing a girl along? Is this the same one that—her name is what? Fay? I'll get Mike to barbecue some pickerel, fresh out of the lake, I'll bet she's never had fish fresh out of the lake. We've got this new gismo for barbecuing fish, a special rack thing. Two beds or one? Ha. Just thought I'd ask. All the more room to roll around, eh? Fay, you said her name was? F-a-y? Rhymes with bay. Well, you know something? You sound full of beans."

"WHY, TOM AVERY, you look like the cat that ate the cream," Jenny Waring told Tom, running into him in the Safeway. She peered into his shopping cart. "Kiwi fruit? Strawberries? Well. You look like you've lost weight. Or put some on, something anyway. You look kind of—blissed out. Have you been away, or what? You know, Gary's still talking about those great couple of days he had with you when we were in Minneapolis, and I don't have to tell you what a lift it gave me, getting away. We had lousy weather, rain, but every minute was pure joy. I needed it! I guess I was feeling kind of down, but I came back full of energy. I've enrolled in two night courses, bread making and Greek mythology. It's amazing, a couple of days away from the kids and I felt restored. That's how *you* look, Tom. Restored."

"YOU'RE IN EXCELLENT SHAPE," David Neuhaus informed Tom. "All the tests came back negative. We could do a stress test, but what the hell, you're looking great. Compared to last spring, Jesus! Still running? Keep it up. Fiber, too. Just as well you've given up the vasectomy idea, you're still young, forty is young these days. You're probably in better shape than you were at twenty-five. It wouldn't surprise me a bit."

TOM's ex-wife Sheila phoned and said, "My God, what's got into you, sending me flowers out of the blue, and what flowers! You're

a sweetie. And not even my birthday or anything. It's not like you
to do something that spontaneous, or maybe it is like you and I
never knew it. And that note, I'll treasure that note, you big softie.
Well, listen, I wish you all kinds of happiness, too."

Dear Tom,

Gregor and I were super-surprised when the florist rolled
up with that great big basket of mums, and you even remembered yellow is my absolutely favorite color. We both want to
say thank you. We're enjoying them muchly. And thanks for
the sweet note, too. It brought tears to my eyes.

Yours,
Suzanne

Dear Tom Avery,

Just want to send a big fat hug from the night staff here
at Minnedosa Community Hospital. Don't know how we'd
while away the hours without "Niteline." (We've got twenty
beds but only eight patients at the moment, knock wood.)
Sunday's show was the greatest, and Monday even better.
You're in top form!

All the best from four loyal and grateful fans,
Janice, Charmion, Marg, and Wayne

~ CHAPTER 23 ~

So This Is How

It Feels

THEY SAY LOVE MAKES ANGELS OF THE WICKED. THAT PEOPLE IN LOVE are kinder in their ways, stronger in their resolve and lit from within by an incandescence so generous, impulsive, and willing, so mild, too, and almost innocent, that other people, observing them, are reminded of young children—the good, stalwart, focused children of fairy tales.

They say love affects the blood-sugar level and that, all other things being equal, lovers will win Olympic medals, score higher on examinations, donate more generously to charities, ward off the most potent flu germs, and kindle the kind of rare happiness that deflects the envy of others.

They say love distorts judgment, so that the most morally robust can drift into evil, and the evil into goodness.

Another thing people say is that love quickens the sensory organs. Fingertips grow more sensitive and more eager. Hearing becomes acute, sometimes painfully so. The olfactory organs crackle and swell and make themselves known. And vision grows more precise, more penetrating—although Fay, arriving at the Winnipeg airport at 10:15 in the morning, was so dazed by noise and the press of other passengers that she didn't even see Tom Avery until the moment his arms were around her, the moment she discovered the side of her face resting against the hairy weave of his jacket. (The ribbed cloth, surprisingly, held an aura of chill. Why should that be? she remembers thinking. But, of course, it was the end of summer, the last day of August; it was fall.) She held on tighter, cherishing the abrasiveness, and wondered what she might say.

"You're home," he said, rocking her back and forth.

"Yes."

SHE KNOWS HOW she must have looked. People getting off international flights are so desperately tired they often look ill. Their clothes are creased, and their hair sprouts wildly in clumps or else lies too flat against the head.

"You look beautiful," Tom Avery said into the crown of her hair.

"My parents," Fay said, "I think I should tell you that they might be here to meet me."

"I phoned them. I got their number from Sonya. I told them I'd meet you."

She looked up. His face seemed a long way away, like a diagram of a face, and she realized she had no access to his thoughts. "Did you really? You did all that?"

"I explained I was a friend of yours."

She felt her mouth smiling. "What did they say?"

"Their exact words?"

"Yes."

"They said to give you a hug and kiss from them."

"That sounds exactly like what they'd say."

He moved forward to touch his lips to hers, and she remembers thinking: What will this feel like? What will it mean?

HE ARRANGED her two suitcases in the trunk of his car, and then he turned to her and asked, "Is it all right if we go to my place? Or would you like to go straight home?"

"Your place is fine." This wasn't what she had imagined, but, then, she hadn't imagined anything, only tentative shapes, colors, a shadow on the wall.

The sun was blinding along Wellington Crescent, and the tall trees seemed knitted together, tobacco colored, squashed gold, swinging their branches in long easy arcs. As he drove, Tom recited what seemed to Fay a kind of meteorological report, as though she were a stranger in this city, an exalted visitor, and he had been appointed to ease her entry with a battery of relevant facts. "The nights have been getting steadily cooler," he announced, "but by ten or eleven in the morning, it's blazing. Today, though, you can feel fall in the air. It's been dry, so the mosquitoes have kept themselves manageable, but there're forest fires in the Thompson area. Just look how green the lawns are." (He said this with pride, as though he'd been waiting to show her this greenness.) "Around eight, nine in the evening the breezes come up. We haven't had any frost yet, though, but up in Duck River they've already had a couple of freeze-ups."

"Duck River?" She tested the sound of this.

"Have you ever been up there?"

"No."

"That's where I was born, where I grew up. My mother still lives there."

"You grew up in Duck River?"

"Yes."

"That's wonderful, oh that's wonderful."

"Why?" He said it slowly, drawling it out like an old joke.

"I don't know." She meant it, she didn't know. But the naming of this place sounded to her like the opening line of a very long story that she would soon be hearing, that she would be learning by heart, and that would become before long a part of her own story, a story that will contravene and replace the abstract narratives she has been constructing for herself these last weeks. "Duck River," she said to the passing trees, to the traffic light on the corner of Wellington and Grosvenor, and at that moment they drove up beside her front door.

SHE LOOKED ACROSS the street at his building. Red brick, three stories, cheaply built, probably in the early sixties, that unlovely period. She'd never really looked closely at it before.

"What about your suitcases?" Tom Avery asked. (She couldn't yet think of him except by his complete name.) His car keys were in his hand, hooked there.

"Why don't I"—she paused—"why don't I leave them for now?"

The foyer of his apartment building was small and dusty, with a rubber mat on the floor. There were six mailboxes mounted on the left-hand wall, and Fay could see that the top one bore the name T. Avery, a smudged, hand-printed label, stuck on with a strip of Scotch tape. She had an impulse to touch it, and was just lifting her arm when an elderly man entered from the street.

The gray wings of his hair flew out sideways. His breath was coming hard, chuffing in an old-man way, and he held his head down, about to brush past them, when Tom stopped him with a hand on his shoulder. "Mr. Duff," he said quickly. "There's someone I'd like you to meet. This is Fay McLeod. Fay, this is one of my neighbors, Mr. Duff."

Mr. Duff blinked. Dull light snagged on the gold of a back tooth. He looked puzzled, and then alarmed, as though he would like to escape—but nevertheless he put out his hand for Fay to shake and mumbled something that sounded approximately like how-do-you-do.

It occurred to Fay that this was an occasion, a ceremony with something particularly spacious and kind about it. "I'm very happy to meet you," she said, and smiled at Mr. Duff, who looked stunned, off balance, his mouthful of ivory teeth catching the light so that the moment became radiant.

THERE WAS A KITCHEN, a living room, a bathroom, and a bedroom. Everything was clean. The smell of Lemon Pledge pierced her to the heart. From the bedroom window she could look out and see the front door of her condominium, the tub of begonias to one side and high above it the small stained-glass window that was her kitchen. Her watch was still on Paris time, but she calculated that it must be about noon. Noon—the thought of this unlikely hour wrung from her an involuntary cry. Down below, on what looked suddenly like a foreign street, a young woman was pushing a stroller, and Fay could see the pale blue roundness of the child's bonnet and hear the wheels, in need of oil, squeaking faintly at every revolution. She could hear birds singing, too, or rather crying out their longings, and, from somewhere not far away, a truck shifting gears.

HE TOOK OFF all her clothes, slowly, taking his time, not saying a word. First her hopelessly crushed linen jacket, with an ivory cameo pinned to its collar, next her blouse, then her skirt, with its side opening, then her underthings, one at a time, and folded all these clothes carefully and placed them on a small straight-backed chair that stood against the wall. It surprised Fay, thinking about it later, how passive she'd been, like a large solemn child, and how her whole body seemed to be smiling at this absurdity.

He took his own clothes off next, and then they lay down together on the bedspread, which was not really a bedspread but a kind of light summer blanket in a dark shade of blue.

So THIS IS what it feels like. To be coming awake. To be burning, her skin, her mouth, his hand against her burning back, trembling slightly, but a fine tremor that seemed almost electric. And grazing her knees and thighs. Come, come, she wanted to cry, meaning—come closer, closer.

She placed her hands at the back of his head, then drew them down along his shoulders, reading him as though she were sightless, memorizing his skin, with its alternate regions of texture and tenderness, his sides, sloping smoothly around the cushioned ribs—she fixed everything in her mind. Her breath rose and fell. So this was what it was like. To open her body completely and to feel another's opening in response. She felt all his loneliness coming toward her. This was how it happened.

For once, to lay ourselves bare.

She heard him moaning her name over and over, and heard herself, too, trying out his, gathering in the resonance of that single syllable. Tom. It formed a portion of her exhaled breath and like a word in a classical language grew instantly solid and unbreakable and seemed to cantilever at the top of her consciousness. Her arms, her legs, felt transparent, fluid.

She did not say at that moment, "I love you."

It was true she had spelled it out on a French fax machine a few days earlier and rehearsed it inside her head a hundred times, but this was different. It seemed to her that to pronounce the word "love" aloud would mean the beginning of the need to earn it.

CHAPTER 24

Stardust

"WE'RE ALL SEXUAL CREATURES, EVERY LAST ONE OF US," SAID PATSY MacArthur some months ago, leading a workshop called Sex for Singles at the Fort Rouge Center, "and our sexual appetites need to be listened to if good mental health is to be maintained. Keep your condoms handy, by all means, but be ready when opportunity knocks. And remember, failing opportunity, there's always masturbation. Which I'll be talking about in depth next week. Plus other alternatives." Tom had listened, but he knew there was nothing sadder or more saddening on earth than the spectre of loveless sex.

This was not a fashionable belief—he could imagine Patsy snorting out her scorn—and not even a popular belief, yet he knows it's true. He's known for—how long?—eight, nine months, ever since his Club Excelsior holiday in San Diego last December, a time of excess and failure, of unrestrained sweats and grunts with (one night) an Oregon secretary (no names exchanged on either side) who barked harsh words of self-hatred into his ears and then asked him to perform a bizarre act with a toothbrush, saying it was the only thing that turned her on. And another woman, what was her name? She had possessed a flat nasal sporty little laugh. She said she thought Winnipeg sounded like the name of a board game, thought being a disc jockey must be a gas, and told Tom there were more cards in the deck than he seemed willing to shuffle—this last she did not explain but attempted to demonstrate while sitting astride his chest.

After that there had been at least two (three?) other moments of brief hectic release followed by hours of recovery, of blisters on the inside of his mouth (frightening), dry-tongued confusion, and the intermittent terror of having forgotten his own name. Love on the loose, on the lam, the horny, porny love of the dead.

At the end of ten days he had jammed his things into his sports bag—balled-up cotton shirts, a swimsuit still damp from a post-coital dip, and a jumble of brightly colored Jockey shorts, purchased back home in frozen Winnipeg with seduction in mind and now soiled with his own body juices—and grabbed a taxi out to the airport.

He sat panting in the back seat, looking out at the vast sunless city streets. An immense disappointment seemed to be waiting for him, and heartbreak.

The taxi driver had a fat, breadlike back of the neck and was full of chat. About a son just starting out in the construction business. A daughter at Berkeley ("one of your brainy types"). And a wife who taught yoga three days a week at the Y and had the figure of a twenty-year-old. He spoke of them proudly, with ease. He was, Tom saw clearly, a man who lived simply, who kept a clean smoke-free cab and brought home the bacon and was met at the door by the wife with the body of a twenty-year-old girl who pressed ravishing kisses on his thick white neck and who, in the jagged peaks of her ever-renewable ecstasy, cried out his given name, which was . . . what?

Tom leaned forward in the cab and peered at the driver's identification card, at the small darkishly ruddy head-and-shoulders photo, and read the words: Leroy Gower. It entered his brain with a quick little sorrowful arrow, Leroy Gower, and stayed there. Leroy Gower, Leroy Gower. The name of a happy man.

HE AND FAY that first day lay down together on his bed, on the cool clean blue blanket, lying on their sides facing each other. He took her face in his hands. It was a hot day. A fly buzzed against the wall. It was around noon, he guessed. The window was open, and the greenness of trees cut by slivers of sun filled up the frame. He became aware of the scent of her skin, which was mild, faintly dusty. His fingers reached out and touched the contour of her hips, the lovely long trench of her spine, apprehended the oval concave dip at the small of her back. Her face was pale—her last week in Europe, she had explained in a rushing voice, had been filled with rainy days—and across this paleness was spread a sheet of straight dark hair, a strand of which he wrapped around his finger and tasted on his tongue. "You're home," he said to her at the airport, and now, feeling shy and happy, he said it again— "You're home"—and again heard her muffled yes, and felt her mouth opening on his.

Once, years ago, in the first flush of his first marriage, Sheila had locked her legs around him, her short muscular volleyball-player's legs encircling his naked body, and he had felt one of his ribs give way. The pain had been sudden and hideous. He had gone the next day to the Winnipeg clinic to be X-rayed and was told he had a hairline fracture. Nothing much could be done. He was given a packet of painkillers and told to take it easy for a few weeks. The rib cage was exceedingly fragile, the X-ray technician said—you could break a rib just coughing or laughing too hard.

Sheila had not reacted with commiseration or guilt, not Sheila. No, she had crowed in a kind of mirthful triumph, had bitten her lower lip, teased him, made sly jokes about Adam's rib, about the general frailty of men. He had held himself carefully away from her, feeling himself grow stiff and vulnerable. It had lasted for days, months. It became a habit.

"Our bodies are made of stardust," said Tom's good friend Jeff Waring, who is a physicist by profession. This was at a dinner party a year or so ago at the Warings' long polished table, lit on this particular night by a circle of thick blue candles. The assembled guests had been charmed but skeptical. "It's true," Jeff persisted. "Our atoms are part of the Big Bang, our blood, our bones, all of us, just cosmic matter. Stardust."

"Fay, Fay," Tom said into the darkness of Fay McLeod's hair, and felt his head fill up with images of shooting meteors and white light.

THAT FIRST DAY they slept and woke. Toward the end of the afternoon he got out of bed and walked barefoot into the kitchen, bringing back twin glasses of orange juice and handing one to her with both his hands.

"This is," she said, lying back on the pillow and sipping, "all very strange."

Strange, yes. He felt filled to the brim, yet starved.

He loved her long thin flexed arms, their rangy look of bareness against the blue blanket, but still he searched her body, wanting to guard some of his early apprehension, wanting to hoard it. Why? As a reference point or because he needed to store it up against some future disappointment? He sat down on the side of the bed as if to displace the strangeness with the volume of his body. "Maybe we should do something ordinary," he said.

She smiled. The smile was tender, shy, full of trust. "What do you ordinarily do about this time of day?" she asked.

"Usually," he told her, "I have a shower and then I walk over to the A & W on Osborne and have a burger."

"Let's go, then," she said, but continued to lie in bed watching him.

"Or we could go somewhere more . . . more"—he tried to find the right word—"more celebratory."

"The A & W sounds just right. I mean, it's your place, after all."

"I'm afraid it is." Stop staring, he said to himself.

"Then that's where we'll go."

"I'm happy," he said. The words fell out of his mouth. "I'm

completely happy from head to foot. Even my toenails are happy."

"I don't even know what your feet look like," Fay said in a tone of wonderment. "Or if you smoke or not."

He held up a foot for inspection. "And I had my last cigarette in 1979."

"When do you go to work? At the radio station."

"Midnight."

"Do you have to go tonight?"

"I'm off Fridays and Saturdays. I don't have to be there till midnight Sunday."

"Amazing."

"What's amazing?"

"The way your life is arranged. Upside down."

"In a way."

"And now it's . . . ?"

"Four o'clock. In the afternoon. A beautiful Friday afternoon."

"I'm still confused with time. The time change, and"—she gestured with her arm, taking in the bed, the room—"all this."

"I know," he said.

"What are we going to do?"

"You mean right now? This minute?"

"No, I mean, what are we going to do?"

"I want"—he hesitated and forced himself to put both feet squarely on the floor—"I want to spend the rest of my life with you."

The balance of air in the room seemed monumentally disturbed, as though he had driven it out with the wedge of his voice. A fly buzzed, surely not the same fly he had heard earlier, though perhaps it was. He stared away from her, at the half-open window, the shady blue rectangle of light, and waited, suddenly fearful.

"That's what I want, too," Fay said.

"THREE!" FAY SAID, exclaimed, cried. Her eyes were wild.

"I knew it would be a shock."

"Three." She said it again, slowly, and lowered her hamburger to her plate. Her hand groped for her glass of root beer. "Three."

"I thought it over carefully," Tom said, "and I felt it was better if I told you before anyone else did. Because lots of people know. I mean, I haven't made a secret of it, not that I could in a city this size, even if I'd wanted to—"

"I'm just so . . ." She stared at him intently across the table.

"I know, I know."

"It's such a lot to take in. A lot. Three!"

"There're times when I can hardly believe it myself," Tom said. "I look in the mirror and think, How did it happen?"

"How *did* it happen?"

"I don't know." He wondered how much to say. That there was something in him not understood. Should he bring up the twenty-seven mothers? A marriage counselor had once suggested his troubles dated from that time, that some kind of psychic confusion concerning women had been engendered. "When I want to be especially kind to myself," he told Fay, "I say I've had a string of bad luck."

"How long"—she paused for an instant, her expression rapt—"did these marriages last?"

"Four years the first time." He paused and drew a deep breath. "Then two years. Then four years again."

"Oh." She said this with a little cry.

"I wish to hell I didn't have to tell you all this. I'm not proud of it, God knows."

"It's all right, you have to tell me. I mean, I have to know."

"What I mean is, I wish I didn't have to tell you today, right away like this."

"I have to know."

"You look—stricken. Christ, I don't blame you."

"Two would be almost easy, but three—"

"I know, I know. What can I do?"

"Just let me sit here and grieve for a minute."

"I'm forty years old," Tom said, and reached for her hand. "You must have known I'd have some history."

"Of course, of course." She was moaning faintly. "Of course I knew that."

"I've told you the worst."

She looked up, bending her straw in half. "Are there any children?"

"No."

"I don't know what to say." She said this with a sob, her voice bending against itself.

"For what it's worth," Tom told her carefully, "I was always faithful. While I was married, I mean. One hundred percent faithful. And I didn't . . ."

"What? You didn't what? Tell me."

He was overcome by the crimped angles of her face. "I didn't . . . go in for wife beating or verbal abuse or anything like that."

"What was it, then?" She grasped the edge of the table. "What happened?"

He picked his words carefully. "I'm not especially good at psyching these things out, but I think that for some reason, I was always meeting unhappy women. Maybe I was even drawn to them."

She thought about this for what seemed like several minutes, and he began to think the silence would never end. But then she sat back suddenly in the chair, as though accommodating her body to its molded form, took a deep breath, and asked, "What were their names?"

"Sheila. Clair. And Suzanne." Like stones dropped from a great height.

"In that order?"

"Yes."

She nodded, absorbing, taking it in. The space between them seemed distorted by wave on wave of shy courtesy. "I suppose," she asked at last, "that you must have loved them?"

He had feared this question. "I did," he said, "yes."

"Do you still see them?"

"Not Clair, but the others occasionally."

"I see." Then, again, "I see." That clamoring *I see*.

A phrase flew into his head, a phrase he had never heard spoken aloud. *Abide with me, abide with me*. Where had it come from, this biblical imprecation? No, it was a hymn.

"Can I get you anything else?" the waitress asked them, leaning over their table. "Coffee?"

"Yes," Tom said.

He felt Fay's fingers tap a message on his wrist, and then she spoke it aloud. "I'll never leave you," she said.

LATER SHE SAID: "I have my history, too."

It shocked him, how unprepared he was for this. "Of course," he managed to say.

"There have been," she told him, "a few serious love affairs."

He said nothing, nothing.

"About half a dozen in all."

If only he could put a finger to her lips.

She went on, fully articulating, as though she were reciting a piece she had learned from memory. "I've lived with three different men. For quite long periods of time."

He wondered what his face looked like.

"Twice," she said, "it came fairly close to marriage."

"But didn't."

"No."

"What happened? Not that I've any right to—"

"But you do," she said. "You have every right. I'm not sure, though, what happened. My brother, Clyde, says I'm afraid of committing myself. That's his theory, anyway."

He leaned over and smoothed her hair, and then the side of her face.

"Or else," she went on, "it's the curse of our generation, our needy, greedy independence. But probably—this is *my* theory—it's because of my parents."

He felt his eyebrows go up. Why?

"Their—what do you call it?—their example. They've been married, happily married, for forty years. Next month is their fortieth wedding anniversary. When I think of it, forty years! We're having a big surprise party for them. You're invited. I invite you."

"I accept."

"You'd think, growing up in a family like that, I'd be filled with confidence, you'd think I'd be willing to gamble on the idea of marriage. But it hasn't worked out that way. It's made me, I don't know, just terribly, terribly careful. It's like—"

"Like what?"

"Like a spell. It's cast a kind of paralyzing spell over me."

"And now?"

"And now," she said solemnly—how he loved her for her solemnity, her mouth going into a straight thoughtful line—"now, suddenly, the spell is broken."

TOM LOVES RADIO, its buoyancy, its immediacy and verve, but he wonders sometimes, and worries, what it's done to his brain cells. All those years of radioland patter and chatter. Shooting from the lip instead of the cortex. Inanity. The fear of dead air. Microphones make people cocky, and even the mellowness that comes on late in the night is probably just one more form of brain death. Whatever comes out of those deep-night, annular, cooing mouths is mellifluous. Spin it out, pour it, spill it, give us that old sweet back-of-the-throat butterscotch, coming on cool, sweet, and clear. Fill us up, empty us out, lay it on us.

And years of pop music. Hey baby. I wanna hold your haaaand. You set me on fire, on fi-yah.

But that's how he feels. Oh, Christ, will he really go down to death with a few measures of Mellencamp crooning in his ears? Maybe, maybe he will. And maybe this is the ultimate truth. Because he *is* on fire. On fi-yah! He's over the rainbow. On top of the world. He's rockin' along. Burning, burning in a sea of love. Burning up with love.

"I LOVE YOU, FAY."

He says this to her every day, several times a day. When he wakes up in the morning, before he goes off to the studio at night.

He says it on the phone. He says it with his hand, his body. He says it with flowers (twice). He says it over tables, over coffee cups and dishes of ice cream, over glasses of wine, over the bed sheets, between their kisses, over her naked body, her breasts, her long curved hips, into her ear, into the warm, starry September night he says, "I love you, Fay."

~ CHAPTER 25 ~

#

"I LOVE HIM," FAY CONFIDES TO HER MOTHER AND FATHER A FEW days after getting home. "I really do love him."

The three of them are sitting on the screened porch at the side of the Ash Avenue house, drinking iced tea and cooling off after a record hot day.

"I didn't expect this to happen," Fay tells them. "I'm really surprised, to tell the truth. But this is it. *It*. What people mean, I suppose, when they say *it*. Oh, I know what you're thinking—here she goes again, another major fling. But it's not that. Well, it is, and it isn't. I can't tell you how idiotic I feel, a great big overgrown schoolgirl talking about being in love. Limp with love. I have to laugh at myself. Oh, I'm perfectly sane and healthy, but it's, well, affecting me. I'm jittery, just look at my hand shaking. I've lost three pounds. I seem to be hyper and at the same time peaceful, almost sleepy. I went to work today and just sat in my office and looked at the walls. Dreaming. I haven't even opened my mail. Or my slides, the ones I brought back from Europe. Onion thinks I have a case of extended jet lag, she's advised me not to do anything rash until I've got myself under control, whatever that means. Honestly, I'm a goof. And the funny part is, I have no idea why, what exactly it is about him. About Tom. But I knew right away. Well, almost right away. He's . . . he's—I trust him, that's part of it. When you know him better, when you know what he's like, you'll understand. Oh, I don't know what to say, I'm just happy, happy."

"How on earth did you and Tom Avery get together?" is the question people ask Fay.

She's obliged to produce the low-art time capsule in which she arrived some weeks ago at her nephew's birthday party, balloons, cake, and ice cream, the whole thing, and how Tom Avery happened to be there to pick up his godchild, Gary Waring, yes, Gary Waring, Jenny Waring's little boy, and, well, after the party was over, he offered her a lift home, only he didn't have a car, it was like a musical comedy in a way, and so they walked home, he actually lives right across the street, yes, an apartment on Grosvenor, he's lived there about two years, only for some crazy reason they've never bumped into each other before, and now—

She loves to lie next to him with her hand reading the back of his head, his heavy, sleepy, substantial head, pushing her palm against the taper of his hair. Her own hands at these moments seem detached from her body, not Fay McLeod's hands at all, but hands belonging to a woman in love, any woman. They might be any couple, too, any lucky couple who happened to come together and now hold a privileged but hackneyed citizenship in each other's lives.

She loves to see him captured in the midst of his own pursuits, his habits, his pocket diary inked in with appointments—and his possessions, his toothbrush, his springy shoelaces and the zipper of his jacket. The spaces of his profoundly personal moments offer themselves up, and all these unguarded offerings are rounded and roughened by love.

But Fay's noticed something she's never noticed before. That love is not, anywhere, taken seriously. It's not respected. It's the one thing in the world everyone wants—she's convinced of that—but for some reason people are obliged to pretend that love is trifling and foolish.

Work is important. Living arrangements are important. Wars and good sex and race relations and the environment are important, and so are health and illness. Even minor shifts of faith or political intention are given a weight that is not accorded love. We turn our heads and pretend it's not there, the thunderous passions that enter a life and alter its course. Love belongs in an amateur operetta, on the inside of a jokey greeting card, or in the annals of an old-fashioned poetry society. Moon and June and spoon and soon. September and remember. Lord Byron, Edna St. Vincent Millay. It's womanish, it's embarrassing, something to jeer at, something for jerks. Just a love story, people say about a book they happen to be reading, to be caught reading. They smirk or roll their eyes at the mention of love. They wink and nudge. Lovebirds. Lovesick. Lovey-dovey. They think of it as something childish and temporary, and its furniture—its language, its kisses, its fevers and transports—are evidence of a profound frivolity. It's possible to speak ironically about romance, but no adult with any sense talks about love's richness and transcendence, that it actually happens, that it's happening right now, in the last years of our long, hard, lean, bitter, and promiscuous century. Even *here* it's happening, in this flat, midcontinental city with its half million people and its traffic and weather and asphalt parking lots and languishing flower borders and yellow-leafed trees—right here, the miracle of it.

"My God," Iris Jaffe marvels, laughing her rich nutty laugh, "love at first sight, it's hard to believe. Remember, Fay, how we used to have those long moony discussions, the two of us flipped out in your bedroom—is there really such a thing as love at first sight? Infatuation or crushes, maybe, but love, that was something else. We were a couple of very, very conservative kids, now that I think about it. But I'm more and more convinced it's a matter of fit.

Things fit or they don't fit, and I'm not talking about cocks and vaginas, either, although that's a consideration, God knows. I'm talking about, you know, fitting together. I knew right away when I met Mac that we fit. And I was only nineteen, as you know, and so was he, for that matter. Well, everyone said I was too young, and he was Jewish, it was a whole different culture, all that bullshit about his family and my family raising a royal ruckus, *oy*, but I knew it would be okay because we just, well, fit. It'd be nice, of course if we could make babies, that would confirm what I knew right from the beginning, that we belonged together. It was predetermined. In the stars. That's another thing we used to talk about, remember? Destiny. Oh, my God. Anyway, when're you going to bring him over? I'm dying to meet him. Mac and I actually stayed up last night and listened to his show, part of it, anyway, till we fell asleep, it's kind of late for old married folks like us, but look, what about bringing him for lunch on Sunday? Just tell him we want to check him out, we want to give him the old once-over, see how he does on page turning—remember how you told me once you wouldn't marry a man who couldn't turn the page of a book *mannishly*. You're going *where* for the weekend? *Duck River?*"

THERE'S PLENTY going on at the National Center for Folklore Studies: The new exhibition of Ukrainian toys. The display of early-twentieth-century postcards. Fay's mermaid colloquium is coming up soon. And there's lots of buzzing during the coffee breaks, too. Donna Watts, head of the volunteer program, has had her baby, a seven-pound son, Steven Andrew. Hannah Webb has been invited to accept an honorary degree from St. Olaf College in Minnesota. Anne Morris is on dialysis and waiting for a kidney, and her husband, Frank, has started drinking again, has been on a month-long bender, in fact. Peter Knightly continues to rent a room in the house of his former wife, Fritzi Sweet, who was tragically widowed last spring, and Fay McLeod is having a torrid love affair with the host of a radio show, a man named Tom Avery.

"I am not having an affair," Fay told Beverly Miles over coffee, after the others had gone back to their offices. Love affairs were what movie stars have, or members of the royal family. Love affairs were trashy and temporary. "I'm having," said Fay, "I'm having . . . I don't know what I'm having. A romance, I suppose. What a word! Do you know what my sister-in-law, Sonya, calls romance? She calls it 'the love that dares not speak its name.' Romance fiction, those doctor-and-nurse things. It's lost its meaning, romance—if it ever had any. The romance of history, the romance of travel, the medieval romance, Ottoline Morrell tarting herself up for Bertie Russell. It kills me what people have done to the word 'romance.' Because that's what I'm having. A romance. A fine romance. Why are you laughing, Bev? Surely you believe in the wonder of romance."

"I think," Beverly says, "that you're far too intelligent a woman to be having a romance. Only deeply fluffy people have romances. Besides, wasn't it you who told me that it was impossible to speak of love in the twentieth century except ironically?"

"Me? Did I say that?"

"You said romantic love was invented in the Middle Ages, and that it was a mere literary device—"

"I don't think I actually—"

"—and that it would end with our millennium."

"But I was speaking—"

"In the abstract. Why not call what you're having a love affair and be done with it?"

Is it possible to have an intelligent love affair? Fay asks herself the question, not sternly but seriously. She thinks of Peter, of Nelo, of beautiful, distant Willy Gifford. Had she loved them with intelligence?

No, not with intelligence at all, but with blind intuition. She has—she confesses to herself, and with a shameful twinge of sensual pride—only managed in her life to be intelligent about love affairs after they ended.

To ROBIN CUMMERFORD, Fay says, "Oh, Robin, I'm sorry, I'm terribly sorry. I certainly didn't mean to—I didn't realize you felt so—I know what you said before I went away, yes, I remember, but—I really am sorry. I've been terribly insensitive, I'm afraid—forgive me. I would never have—this is just something that happened, I didn't plan it, it's one of those things. But it *is* serious, it certainly is. I think that's a little unfair of you, Robin. I think you're being more than a little judgmental. I never once, it never occurred to me that—oh, for heaven's sake, no. No, I don't think it would be a good idea, we'd just be embarrassed and awkward and mean-hearted and, and I can't honestly think of anything more I can say on the subject, I'm sorry."

TOM AVERY'S MOTHER, dressed in a pink-and-white checked pant-suit with a cardigan thrown over the shoulder to ward off the morning chill, says to Fay, "Now you be sure to come again, you don't have to let us know ahead of time or anything like that, just come. It's been a real ball all weekend, I just wish you kids didn't have to hit the road so soon, but I know how it is. It's a treat seeing Tom looking so—well, it's funny, but I always knew he'd find the right girl. Look at me, it took me till I was fifty-two years of age to settle down. To find the right person, Mike. There's someone cut out for everyone, a Mr. Right. Or a Ms. Right, ha. Oh, he's had his ups and downs, Tom, but I guess you know all about that—haven't we all? I always knew he'd find the right—and I was saying to him just now, when he was drying the breakfast dishes, I said, 'Listen, honey, this girl's a real sweetheart, don't let this one get away on you.' "

~ CHAPTER 26 ~

Happy Days

Tom has moved in with Fay.

He sleeps now on the right side of her queen-sized bed (in the same space where Peter Knightly once slept, but he tries to block out this thought) on sheets of ivory-colored cotton. His dozen shirts and half-dozen jackets hang in the left side of Fay's double closet, his socks are bunched in the bottom drawer of an old oak dresser that Fay bought, she tells him, at a garage sale ten years ago, when she was twenty-five, when she was strapped for cash, in need of furniture, and ready to tackle with sandpaper and varnish whatever she could salvage. (Fay at twenty-five; his breath hardens in his windpipe when he thinks of it.)

They are living together, yes, but she has her routines and he has his. She wakes at 6:45, shutting off her alarm clock, one arm reaching out blindly, quickly so as not to wake him, but he insists on getting up anyway, pouring orange juice, making coffee, and watching from the doorway as she dresses. As she brushes her hair. As she drops slices of bread into the toaster. As she holds a cup up to her lips. He doesn't want to waste any of this.

After she leaves for work he can sleep for another four or five hours, and by 5:30 she'll be home again, coming through the door with a bag of groceries and something of the day's accumulated industry and hum about her. He loves this buzz. He even loves the groceries she brings, fragrant bread, cartons of eggs, milk, vegetables in primary colors and shapes, rounded and firm under their skins. A red pepper. A head of cauliflower. Stooping, bending at the knee, she stows them quickly away in that lower drawer of the refrigerator, the crisper. She understands about crispers, she understands groceries; this knowledge seems wonderful to Tom.

The next few hours are the hours they live. They have until 11:30, which is when Tom leaves for CHOL. After that Fay goes to sleep, or tries to. Shortly after 4:00 a.m., he's home again, lying beside her in the dark, his legs sliding against hers.

He thinks about what a strange shuttle of hours they inhabit and cancel, and how the whole construct of day and night feels newly made, its edges and corners sharpened and its wide white livable space reorganized and made porous. He prizes it, every minute, including the opaque intensities of their late-night conversations, which he spends his days retracing. He's waited all his life for time like this.

Now and then he glances across the street at his old apartment building, whose textured brick cornice and blindly curtained windows tell him to get busy—to give notice, cancel his lease, or, at the very least, clear out his cupboards and closets. But the days go by, light as helium. It's a beautiful golden dusty September.

TOM DESCRIBES for Fay's amusement—and so she will comprehend something of his efforts to save himself—his long desperate immersion in the Newly Single Club. He does a merciless imitation of Patsy MacArthur, limns the club's varied membership (not excluding the piteous, stricken Elizabeth Joll), and elucidates the many "workshops" and "strategies" he has undergone. At last, at last, he tells Fay, he feels liberated from the panic and capsized faith of the single life and the ghastly penance of those Friday nights.

Fay, in turn, explains about *her* Friday nights, about the Handel Chorale rehearsals that occupy the hours between seven and nine. "We actually need baritones," she tells him. "Why don't you audition?"

"Me? I can't sing a note."

She refuses to believe this. "That's impossible. I mean, you're in the music business. I'm sure you can sing a little."

Touched, he says, "Completely tone deaf."

"Sing me something. Sing 'God Save the Queen.' "

"You don't want to hear it."

"I do, go ahead."

He tries a few bars, then stops. "See what I mean?"

"Mmm, yes."

He tells her about his Saturday-morning runs and offers to buy her a pair of Nike Air-Strides and give her a few pointers.

"I hate to run," she says. "I can't think when I run, with my head bobbing up and down."

"Do you have to think all the time?"

"Yes."

"Every single minute? Don't you ever give your brain a vacation?"

"Never." Then she stops and thinks, smiling, "Well, almost never."

"You're sure you don't want to try just once?"

"I'm sure. And besides, I usually meet my father on Saturday morning. At Mr. Donut's. Why don't you come, too? After your run, I mean."

"I don't want to intrude."

"Oh, Tom, it's not like that. He's my father. You've got to get to know him."

"So I can ask him for his daughter's hand?" He says this with elaborate nonchalance, but watches her face.

"Yes." Laughing a little.

"What if he says no way? What if he thinks a three-times-divorced disc jockey is a pretty bad bargain? Or does he already know? About the divorces, I mean."

"I thought I'd better tell them right away. So I did."

"A good idea." He watches the way her hair picks up spots of light.

"Anyway," Fay says, "he's exceedingly tolerant. And he's a true believer."

"In what?"

"In love. He believes in love. More than my mother, in a way. At least, I've always thought so."

"Let's make it soon, then. Let's get married and start being real people."

"Real people?"

"I've waited all these years, and I don't want to spend any more time waiting for you."

"But we are together."

"I want to stand up in a church and say the words: I, Tom, take thee, Fay."

"How soon?"

"How about next week?"

"Next week is my parents' fortieth anniversary, the big party."

"We could always make it a double ceremony."

"Be serious."

"What about November? Not that I've ever heard of anyone getting married in November."

"When were"—she pauses—"your others?" The lightly stressed *others* is something he will have to get used to.

"Do you really want to know stuff like that?"

"I don't want to, not at all. But I think I ought to."

"June, the first time around. Then April. Then, let's see . . . January."

"And you think November might be lucky?"

"I do."

"Then I do, too."

"I can't live without you, Fay. I want to marry you. I'm asking. Will you marry me?"

"Yes."

WHAT A BROAD and bountiful thing it is to be happy, thinks Tom.

Jogging in the park on Saturday morning, he seems to hold his happiness in his mouth like a lozenge. He knows himself to be favored. The banked chevron-shaped clouds in the east and the blown brown leaves are auspicious signs. His feet land lightly on the path, are nearly noiseless, in fact, and each breath he draws is exactly the right size, filling his chest perfectly, then escaping in blurred, bobbing, vaporous ovals that print themselves on the crackling air. For once nothing seems wasted; his blood sings with the optimum level of oxygen, and the linkages of his body stretch and flex. He thinks of how it felt to run across a field of grass when he was a young boy and, remembering, breaks into a fresh gait.

He imagines, or hears, the words "Tom and Fay" emblazoned on the air, on envelopes, in the mouths of friends, a single word, "Tom-and-Fay," "Fay-and-Tom."

He is driven these days to commit extravagant gestures. To each of his three ex-wives he has sent a lavish arrangement of flowers, though he had the sense, in Clair's case, to make the gift anonymous. He wrote a hearty note of congratulations to Mike Healey, of "The Healey Beat" on CRSM, who is moving to Toronto to host a major network show, and presented his godson, Gary Waring, with an elegant dragon-shaped kite, then took him to Peanut Park for an afternoon of kite flying. He has surrendered at last to the pleadings of a slightly insane local songwriter, Benny Kaner, and agreed to play one of his puzzling, scatological tapes on "Niteline." For Rosalie Summers, the receptionist at CHOL, he bought a new chemical spray (wrapped and tied with a ribbon) that's guaranteed to keep the spider mites off her fig tree. He gave Big Bruce a rough, unprecedented half-hug when he bumped into him at the coffee machine. And he's bought Fay McLeod an antique opal ring, an engagement ring, a beauty, with a strangely worked filigree setting in pale yellow gold.

His generosity grows prodigal late at night on the air, when he praises his loyal listeners. Where on the face of this earth is there a comparable audience, so lively, so intelligent, so open and faithful. He loves them all. He wants to stretch his arms out in the darkness and embrace them, he wants to share his good fortune, let them in on his concert of longing and behaving. Send me your requests, he says. This is your show, too. Keep those letters coming, keep those phones ringing, keep listening, and we'll all travel through the night together.

IT'S MONDAY NIGHT AT CHOL. It's phone-in night. "What was the happiest moment of your life?" Tom asks his listeners. "The phones are open. Let's hear from you."

The first caller is a woman who says: "My happiest moment was just last year. It was February, and did I ever have the February blahs. Remember last February? Minus thirty-five degrees and wind-chill factors like you never heard of. Well, my husband and I had ourselves a week in Coral Gables, Florida. I'll tell you, the sensation of stepping off the plane into sunshine and heat was just unbelievable. Like someone had waved a wand. I could hardly believe I was standing on the same planet. I turned to my husband and I said, 'This is it, this is the happiest moment I've ever experienced.' "

"I'd like to share something with you, Tom, and all you 'Niteline' listeners out there," comes a croaky young man's voice. "I've just come through a pretty scary time. About six months ago I started getting a few lesions on my body, and right away I got worried. I've got good friends dying of AIDS. Even so, it took me a few days to get myself down to the clinic and get tested. And I tested negative. Meaning I was clear. At first I thought I'd heard wrong. I was so sure it was going to be bad news. I felt like I'd been reborn."

"This is going to sound a bit daft," a woman begins, "but years ago I was in London and found out just by chance that Margot Fonteyn was going to be performing at Covent Garden. I could hardly believe it when they said there was one ticket left. Exactly one. It was as though I was fated to see Fonteyn dance. I went. It was heaven. She was amazing. On the way back to the hotel I was kind of like dancing myself. That's what it felt like."

"I've had lots of happy moments," says a bright male voice. "I've been lucky. But I always think the happiest moment hasn't happened yet. I'm talking about the queen of happy moments. The biggie. The unfathomable. The epitome of happiness. The only thing is, I worry that when it comes along I won't recognize it. It'll be flashing away there at the edge of my vision and I'll be looking so hard that I'll just let it float right by."

TOM AND FAY, lying in bed, exchanged the curiosities and gaps in their family trees.

The mysteries came not in a roar but in sharply defined droplets, like rainwater. Fay told Tom about her young sister, Bibbi, about her turbulent adolescence, how she ran away to Newfoundland and lived for a year in a sort of New Age haze with an alcoholic cobbler who, when she decided to leave him to return home, committed suicide, hanging himself with a leather belt Bibbi herself had made for him. Pinned to his shirt was a bitter, blaming note, the contents of which Bibbi has confided to Fay and to no one else. Now she lives with a thirty-eight-year-old labor organizer named Jake Greary, an acrimonious bully, a monster of social-democratic rectitude who, nevertheless, seems to have mesmerized her. "We keep hoping she'll leave him," Fay said to Tom, "but after what happened in Newfoundland, she's probably afraid to."

All this was surprising to Tom, who by now had met Bibbi two or three times and been struck by her look of composure, her ease and candor. To Tom she had not seemed in any way oppressed or reduced to subjugation. (It was true she was beautiful, though not as beautiful as Fay believed her to be.)

Tom told Fay about his twenty-seven mothers at the University of Manitoba, and then about his real mother, who had found herself pregnant at the age of sixteen.

"I wonder if she ever thought about having an abortion," Fay said.

Tom didn't know. There was a good deal he didn't know, including who exactly his father was. But he'd long ago laid that question to rest.

"Good," Fay said approvingly.

"She's happy," Tom said about his mother. "She and Mike. Her life seems to have worked out."

"Do you think of him as a stepfather?" Fay asked.

"Well, no, more of a friend, I guess."

"It's funny," Fay said. "When I first saw him, I was struck by—" She stopped herself.

"What?"

"How much alike you looked."

"Us? You mean Mike and me?"

"Your chin. Your eyes. Even some of your mannerisms."

"Really?" Tom said, and resettled himself on the mattress, stroking the back of her hand.

"Or else I imagined it," Fay said.

TOM'S FRIENDS REJOICE for him, and so do Fay's. They say such things as: "He's perfect for you" and "She's exactly the sort of steadying personality you need," or sometimes, enigmatically, "Opposites attract."

Ted Woloschuk tells Tom shyly, "I've prayed for you. Maeve, too." Iris Jaffe kisses Tom on both cheeks, and Beverly Miles says, "Onward!" and Peter Knightly tapes a fond note on the door of Fay's office: "Delighted to hear of your good news." Jenny Waring tells Tom that she's planning an engagement party: "I'm thinking along the lines of twenty, maybe thirty people, just close friends. A buffet, is that okay? And I want to have a few of Fay's friends, too, and some of her family. Do you think you could get a list to me by next week?"

Fay has a theory about the general rejoicing. She seems to have a theory about everything. "It's because people had given up on us," she tells Tom. "Here we were, headed up the solitary path, and suddenly we're walking hand in hand on the golden road."

She's noticed, she says, from her reading of fairy tales and myths, and also the inside pages of newspapers, that the greatest rejoicing occurs for those who have been elevated from the deepest ignominy, those who are abruptly, randomly saved and rewarded. Cinderella among her ashes, and the next moment she is claimed by her prince. The youngest son, deprived of his birthright, gaining a kingdom in the end. The unemployed car salesman winning the sweepstakes, the dried-out drunk writing a perfect poem, the ancient barren women of the Scriptures giving birth to prophets. For some reason people feel a need to honor those who have risen spectacularly. And they share, Fay thinks, an unconscious belief that they themselves have contributed to the rescue.

Only Fay's godmother, Onion, reserves judgment. Shaking Tom's hand for the first time, she said sharply, "I've seen you, of course, on those billboards"—an acknowledgment that brought him a stunning clout of shame. To Fay she said, her face wrinkling into a cartoon grimace, "Well, I suppose you're old enough to know your own mind."

THE PARTY at 307 Yale begins at seven o'clock, although the guests of honor, Richard and Peggy McLeod, will not arrive until a quarter to eight. Everything is planned. More than a hundred guests stream through the front door, and most of them exclaim over the beauty of the invitations, each of which has been hand-made by Bibbi to resemble a miniature photo album framed in soft leather and containing two photographs: on the left are Richard and Peggy McLeod as they looked on their wedding day forty years ago, all veiling and smiles backed by thin tree branches, and on the right is a recent snapshot taken by Clyde in their own back yard—their twin thatches of white hair giving them the look more of brother and sister than husband and wife. They both appear remarkably youthful. Peggy McLeod is leaning toward Richard with one hand resting flat on his knee and the other lifted in a gesture of airy emphasis. Typically Peg, everyone says, just like her. The invitation reads:

Clyde, Sonya, Fay, and Bibbi McLeod
invite you to a celebration of
their parents' 40th wedding anniversary
October 4 ~ 7:00 P.M.
307 Yale Avenue

No gifts please; just a single long-stemmed flower.
Shhhhh! This is a surprise.
Please park cars on adjoining streets.
RSVP Sonya or Clyde: 747-6290

SONYA, BRIGHT-FACED, ebullient, exuberantly hostessy in a dress of blue silk banded with green, opens the door to arriving guests. This is a role she loves, standing in the lit doorway of her own cherished house, welcoming group after group of friends. Clyde stands nearby taking coats—the evening is cool—and ferrying them to the bedrooms on the second floor. The house fills quickly with celebratory noise, with color, a happy convivial murmur. Fay and Bibbi take turns leading guests through the hallway, into the living room, the dining room, the sunroom beyond, then out through the sliding doors to the glassed-in porch.

One month ago Tom Avery was a stranger to the McLeod family, yet here he is tonight pressed into service—in fact, given a privileged role. It is his job to present guests with a welcoming glass of wine as they enter the dining room and, at the same time, keep an eye on the sound system he has spent the afternoon installing. Fay's nephews, Matthew and Gordon, by turns solemn and reckless, pass dishes of smoked pecans and black olives, and allow themselves to be patted on the head and even kissed.

The house, with its lit candles, its flowers, and its aggregation of social warmth, has grown rosy with heat. Tom keeps the background music mellow, some Sinatra to start with, a little Aretha Franklin. He has never attended a party like this, and now and then he stands back, observes, and feels the strangeness of it pour through him.

Onion is helping in the kitchen, making sure the caterer finds what he needs, keeping track of food and drink, and inspecting the buffet table set up in the dining room. Earlier there had been a crisis (only dimly perceived by Tom), when Onion suddenly announced she would not be attending the party, that she would be spending the evening at the hospital with Strom. It was Fay who finally persuaded her that she was needed and that Strom would be perfectly all right for a few hours on his own. Next to Muriel Brewmaster, Onion was her mother's oldest friend. Her presence was crucial. "I don't know what's come over her," Fay told Tom. "She's been so odd these last few days."

Everything else goes perfectly. Sonya is a born organizer, as everyone keeps saying. At precisely ten minutes to eight Richard and Peggy McLeod, believing that they have been invited by their son and daughter-in-law for a family dinner, drive up and park their car in front of the house. "Shhhhh," Fay tells everyone in the living room, "they're here."

Sonya opens the front door. "Why you look all dressed up," Peggy McLeod says.

In the other rooms there is silence, heat, anticipation. Then, from somewhere, a whistle blows: the signal. Tom puts "When the Saints Come Marching In" on the tape deck, and a minute later Richard and Peggy McLeod are standing at the entrance to the living room. "Surprise," the assembled guests shout, sing, yell, and Tom sees Richard McLeod pass a hand over his face.

The evening ripens and swells. The lights are kept low, and the walls rise into darkness and acquire a look of watered silk. Tom is astonished at all the white heads and eager thirst. He is grateful to be kept busy, pouring wine and providing music. He plays a flutter of 1950s songs, borrowed from the CHOL archives and from Big Bruce's private collection, music so quirky and crimped, so full of the swells and concavities of sentimental yearning, that it seems designed for exactly this: an evening of nostalgia in an unimaginable future. A suburban house. An October night. A graceful assembly of friends.

Fay and Bibbi, passing trays of food, seem to Tom like beings from the planet of youth. Girlish, lithe. They ought to be barefoot, he thinks, and decked with flowers and amulets. "How're you doing?" Fay says into his ear at one point in the evening. Later she says, placing the flat of her hand between his shoulder blades, "You're doing fine." Later still she asks, and now there is a rise of concern in her voice, "Have you seen my father? Clyde wants to start the speeches in a few minutes."

Tom juggles his assigned duties, sips a glass of Burgundy, and keeps a close watch on the time. He's expected at the station no later than 11:50, and meanwhile he's been introduced to the Swedborgs, the Cornings, the Scotts, the Rumfords, the Lambdas, the Skochucks, and more and more—people that Richard and Peggy McLeod have known for years, some of them all their lives. There're Caroline somebody-or-other, Muriel Brewmaster in dusty-pink velvet, Abby Aldrich, Deborah Goldsmith in a wheelchair, Alma and Edward Hicks, Lewin and May Gables and Marianne Gables, Mark Whischer, Dr. Hazel Moore, Charles and Simmie Fair. There're Tim Hale, the McBriens, the Lloyds, David Chin, Eric and Emily Haigh, Jim and Hjordis Lake, the Jaffes, Carl Peggs, Alison Konkol, Andrew and Mary Ballstaeder, the Levys, the Hollinghursts, Simon and Stephanie Birrell, Julie Freemantle, and on and on and on. Over a hundred names were on the guest list, says Sonya, and almost everyone was able to come. It was a good idea, after all, to hold the party on a Thursday night, since some people were still going to the lake on the weekends. Yes, Clyde says, but they would have come back anyway for an occasion like this. Ben Katz, after all, an usher at the wedding forty years ago, has come all the way from Montreal.

In addition, a few old friends have cabled their good wishes—

from France, from Hawaii, from India. Glasses are lifted. "Happy days," a voice calls out.

Someone puts a hand on Tom's shoulder and says, "Tom, I'd like you to meet Foxy Howe. Foxy, this is Tom Avery."

Tom spins around and stares into the face of his ex—father-in-law.

"We've met," says Foxy Howe. He does not put out his hand to be shaken, nor does he flinch or recoil. He stands solidly in place and registers across his broad, beefy, implacable face a look of hatred.

~ CHAPTER 27 ~

I Want

"I WANT TO HAVE A CHILD," FAY TOLD TOM.

"What about two?" he said.

"Yes, two."

"I want us to put one of those engagement announcements in the newspaper," Tom said.

"Really? You do? Why?"

"I want everyone to know."

"Did you ever—before? In the newspaper, I mean? The other times? With your other—"

"Never. It never came up. I can't remember why not."

"I want to give you a wedding ring. How do you feel about wedding bands?"

"Yes, a wedding ring."

"Something very plain," Fay said.

"I want you to sit down and tell me everything there is to know about mermaids," Tom said.

"You do? Everything?"

"Well, maybe not everything. But something."

"I want you to stay the way you are."

"The way I am?"

"Well, all the strange parts about you."

"Strange?"

"Like the way you come and go in the night."

"You mean," he said, making a face, "that's not normal behavior?"

"Not just that."

"What else?"

"Hmmm. I'd have to think."

"Think."

"Well, the way you duck your head in the shower, that's one thing, and scratch your scalp, hard. Why do you do that? Like you're reminding your brain of something important. And I like that you come from Duck River. Duck River! I like to say to people, 'He's from Duck River, you know.' And—now, I admit this is a bit hard to describe, but I like the way your skin stretches across your back."

"Go on."

"Well, I love the things you do. What you do to me."

"I want you."

"I want you, too."

"That's all I want. You."

SOMETIMES FAY lies in bed in the dark and listens to "Niteline."

"Hello out there," she hears. "This is Tom Avery and this (pause) is 'Niteline.' A good, good end of the evening to listeners old and new. I'll be here to keep you company for the next four hours—a little music and a little talk, and we've got a great interview coming up in an hour or so with hometown songwriter Benny Kaner, one of our own, who's going to bring us up to the minute on what's humming in the avant-garde pop scene. So stay tuned. And now, how about some Bruce Cockburn to get us into the mood."

The show picks up a glow, a buzz. Fay, drifting toward sleep on her bunched pillows, feels the music merge with Tom's voice, a voice that surprises her by becoming a slidy tenor with pliant honeyed bands of laughter. His loose tensionless melody seems after a while to form a long seamless wall she's feeling her way along. She melts in and out of consciousness, shifts on her pillows to find a cooler spot. She's come to understand love's crippling inability to look at itself but knows with certainty that Tom Avery is her star-spangled man.

"And this, listeners, (pause) is your own Tom Avery, signing off for another session of (pause, voice lowered) 'Niteline.'"

A matter of minutes and he'll be here. Twenty minutes at the most. Tiptoeing into the dark bedroom. His bare arm folding back the sheet. His body sliding into bed, next to her, moving his chest up to fit against her back. His breath on her shoulder, light and alert. Oh, she loves it, this having, this being, coming closer and closer now, turning her body to face him. Her rounded-out fullness. Her lover. Tom Avery. Her love.

IT IS IMPOSSIBLE for us to live outside the culture we're born into. Our communities claim us from the start, extending a thousand tentacles of possession, and Fay, a reasonable, intelligent woman, has long recognized that reverence for individualism is one of the prime perversions of contemporary society. It is illogical and foolish. Oh, yes. We are bound to each other biologically and socially, intellectually and spiritually, and to abrogate our supporting network is to destroy ourselves.

Yet it troubles her now and then that she is connected, albeit tenuously, with all three of Tom's ex-wives. Something tribal and primitive about these human links threatens her, offends her sensibility. She wants to weep, thinking of it. She suspects herself of harboring an exaggerated fastidiousness and entertains brief, private fantasies in which she and Tom move to another city, perhaps even another country, where she will not be required, ever, to plan, to adjust, to avoid, to accommodate, to explain, and, worse, much worse, to be endlessly aware of Clair, Suzanne, Sheila.

Clair, Suzanne, Sheila. The wives.

Clair. Clair Howe is the only child of Foxy and Lily Howe, who are old friends of her parents. They are a fat, sweet, sorrowing couple. Lily drinks far too much, as everyone knows, and sinks on social evenings into a dull, kindly, embarrassing reverie. Foxy is clever and has done well in real estate and land development, and they live, along with their crazy daughter, in a large tree-shaded Tudor-style house in Tuxedo Park. Crazy Clair. An apartment has been made for her over the garage. Fay remembers Clair as a child, turning up at birthday parties, a heavy, silent little girl. It was said that something was amiss. She was sent to a school in Toronto for emotionally disturbed children and came home thin. Her parents rarely mention her name, but Fay has always been aware, distantly, vaguely, of intermittent hospitalization, and later a term or two at the University of Winnipeg, where she disrupted classes by shouting. For a time she did volunteer work at the Art Gallery, and people spoke of the wonder of the new stabilizing drugs. There was a brief, unsuccessful marriage. (Ah, yes, now she remembers, yes, of course.) A rumor of shock treatments and their terrible failure. Something about a suicide attempt, perhaps several attempts—Fay has forgotten the details if she ever knew them. She hasn't seen Clair Howe in years. She hasn't even thought about her, but now she must.

Suzanne. Sue? Fay never did know her last name. But she recalls the slow-moving girl/woman who stood, or rather lounged, behind the counter at Chimes Bookstore on Osborne Street—thin face, long blond hair hooked behind childish ears, wide waxy hands, a lascivious mouth, greedy, blurred. Yes, you could say she was pretty. This was the person who accepted Fay's money, placed it in the drawer of the cash register, and, ditheringly, extracted change. The same person who dropped Fay's purchases, making no comment on what they might be, into one of the slippery, bright Chimes bags—and who at that very moment was married to Tom Avery, well-known radio host, well known at least to a sector of the community, the night people, but certainly not to Fay. Now Suzanne has disappeared from the bookstore. She has remarried, it seems. To someone rich. Someone called Gregor Heilbrun. The name rings a bell in Fay's head. Of course! Gregor Heilbrun's first wife was Lee Heilbrun. Who sings with the Handel Chorale. Or used to, before she moved to Vancouver last year. On and on it goes.

Sheila. Sheila Woodlock. Of course she knows Sheila Woodlock. Sheila is known to a lot of people. A smart woman. Attractive. A tough nut, some say. Possibly a lesbian. She lives with three other women in a house in Linden Woods, and one of these women, Patricia Henney, is Fay's lawyer, the one who acted on Fay's behalf when she and Peter Knightly bought their condo on Grosvenor Avenue and who did the paperwork when Fay bought out Peter's share some months ago. All this is bad enough, but there's more, much more. Sheila Woodlock, after she stopped being Sheila Avery, married Sammy Sweet, who later married Fritzi Knightly, who was formerly married to Peter Knightly, with whom Fay lived for three years and whose body she knows intimately, every inch, every crease.

This Tom-Sheila-Sammy-Fritzi-Peter-Fay merry-go-round dismays her when she stops to think about it, these unspooled connections. And she can't help thinking about it. She contrasts the tidy faithfulness of her parents' lives with her own disordered history, which is coated with an impure sheen, which is obscene and, yes, incestuous. A malevolent circle with an oily scent of the profane.

What had Tom's three marriages meant? Did they represent a helpless reaching out for happiness, or an aptitude for error? (Sloppiness?) From the corner of her eye she glimpses danger, some connection between herself and Tom momentarily loosened.

But this is nonsense, and she knows it. She's lived in this city all her life and is part of the human weave. What does she expect? To remain untouched? What childishness. What arrogance!

There's even something faintly comic about the situation. It all depends on the angle of vision. She ought to laugh or recycle Tom's marital history into a droll story. Shrugging her shoulders, holding up her hands—*c'est la vie*. Marveling at modern life's lumpish, grumpish ironies, the way they reach out and touch every last one of us.

FAY FINDS HERSELF waiting for her mother to say something about Tom. Such as: What an interesting man he is! Aren't you glad you waited? His sense of humor is delicious. And he's attractive, but it's not the kind of attractiveness that goes soft and sick, the kind that invites trouble. He's basically kindhearted. He has a sense of ease about him. Openness. Maturity. Warmth. *I adore him. I can see exactly why you love him.*

She says none of these things, and Fay can't bring herself to ask her what she does think.

Of course, Peggy McLeod is very busy. All summer she's been working on the final chapters of her book on menopause. Now she's fretting about titles. She has come up with *The Pause That Puzzles,* which delights her, but which everyone else, her husband, her children, find impossible. "I just can't think of anything else," she tells Fay, patting her white hair flat.

Until she was sixty she kept her hair dyed a warm chestnut. The shock of her pure-white head still catches Fay by surprise, though it is beautiful hair, thinly scattered but nevertheless healthy. Today, late on a Monday afternoon, Fay drops in on her way home from work and finds her mother sitting at her desk in the back bedroom that she uses for a study. The day is cool, and she wears a cardigan over her light wool dress, an expensive white cotton cardigan that has perhaps been washed once too often, so that it drags down a fatal quarter inch at the back. She has combed her hair hurriedly today, or perhaps not at all, and a similarly fatal patch of pink scalp shows through at the back. The weak light from the window cruelly outlines the formless knob of her chin. She looks old. She looks tired. Fay wonders if she is happy, but wouldn't dream of asking.

Just as her mother would never dream of asking her.

———

HER FATHER was more open.

"You seem," he told her, "like another person."

"How?" she asked, knowing she was being childishly greedy for attention, but not caring, "Tell me what you think."

"Well, it's clear you're happy. You radiate with happiness. This room, any room you happen to be in, is full of it."

Touched but impatient, she said, "What about Tom? What do you think about Tom?"

"I've only met him a few times. . . ."

"Come on."

"He's . . . what can I say? He's a man in love."

"What an expression—'in love.' "

"People these days like to pretend that being in love is a virus."

"I've noticed, especially at our age."

"Your age? What do you mean, your age?"

" 'In love' is high-school stuff."

"You want me to quarrel with that notion?"

"Yes."

"I don't think it's a matter of age at all. I've never thought that. Your Uncle Arthur. Your Aunt Velma."

"I can never believe—"

"You can't believe it because you never knew them when their bodies weren't withered and old."

"I can't imagine them—"

"—rapturously joined?"

"Well, no." She felt unaccountably embarrassed.

"I'm not sure that was part of it. It was something else. A sort of ongoing courtship. Something edgy and polite about the way they treated each other, as though they were only pretending to be normal so the rest of us wouldn't be too uncomfortable. Or too envious. As a young boy I used to find myself staring at them. You know, for all we talk and sing and carry on about being in love, I think it's a rather rare condition."

"How rare?" she heard herself asking. What was it she wanted him to say?

"Rare," was what he answered, "extremely rare," and she felt he had reached out and blessed her.

AN ANONYMOUS DONOR has presented the National Center for Folklore Studies with a small bus which will be used to transport schoolchildren and senior citizens and other interested groups to and from exhibitions, and one bright cold Wednesday morning Fay attended a bus-blessing ceremony. A priest, a rabbi, and a United Church minister were present, along with the staff of the center, the members of its board, and a few representatives from the press. Hannah Webb, the sleeves of her Burberry flapping in a stiff wind, made a short, graceful speech in which she explained how vehicles such as ships and trains are traditionally launched with praise and invocation. Why not a bus? Why not indeed! Blessings were then distributed: to the generous donor, to the appointed driver (Art Frayne), to the prospective passengers and their bodily safety, to the tires, engine, and frame of the cheeky little blue bus itself—blessings, acknowledgment, approbation, sanction.

Blessing, Fay thought later, is what she would like from Onion. From Onion, of all people. Her family will always embrace her choices, and her friends will credit her with good sense, even when she hasn't earned it. But Onion—out of a different kind of love, a love made of sinew and resolve—will guard her against true harm; Fay's always known that. *Tell me it's all right,* she wants to say to Onion.

It's not approval she wants; the wish for approval strikes her as inappropriate. She wants only Onion's blessing.

She's tried to broach the subject from a number of different directions. She's been bold about it, stopping herself just short of a direct plea for—for what? For consent? For permission? For recognition, at the very least. A word or two.

Never mind about Onion, her father told her. Onion has her own concerns these days.

That much was true. Onion spends almost all her time at Strom's bedside. She sits erect in the slippery vinyl visitor's chair, a book open on her lap, reading or not reading, or helping with

Strom's medication, with his meals. She adjusts his earphones so that his favorite recorded music flows through to him hour after hour. She watches his face for a flicker of an eyelid, for any minute sign of recognition. Often she spends the night with him, too, settling herself stiffly on a portable bed next to his.

"I won't be able to make it," she announced to Fay the day before the fortieth-anniversary party. Her voice was abrupt, short. "I can't possibly leave Strom for that long."

Fay had been dumbfounded. And injured. "You have to come, Onion. You're one of Mother's oldest friends. Just think of all you've been through together, all those years. Strom can spare you for a few hours, you know he can. Please reconsider. At a time like this, we really do need you as much as he does. You're family. You're part of us."

Speaking in this way, Fay had felt a dismaying loss of control. Her pitched pleas seemed to come from a part of her body she only dimly recognized. *Please, please, please come.*

Moved at last, Onion had agreed. She would attend the party, she said, but would leave early.

THE EVENING WAS COOL. The sky, Fay noted, was clear. A clear starry night.

And everything else went well, too. The food. The cake. The cases of wine delivered to the house. The tables. The lighting. Bibbi's beautiful invitations. And the flowers—she and Clyde and Bibbi had ordered an immense engraved pottery vase, and into this vase each arriving guest placed a single flower—beautiful. At her suggestion, Tom had installed a sound system and agreed to look after the taped music. Just seeing him, his earnest attentions, enormously enlarged her love for him. She was unprepared for it. "Tom," she said, pausing in the middle of the long noisy evening and placing a hand on his back, "you're doing fine."

Her mother's face when she entered the house at the beginning of the evening had registered shock. A hand had flown to the throat of her rather ordinary cream blouse, and her face had folded into a perplexed, obedient frown, then shifted to dazed realization, then became a mask of happiness—her friends, her family, this joyful, radiant celebration.

The noise level grew—music, voices, shrieks of laughter, the wind rounding the corners of the glassed-in porch, wineglasses clinking. The Jaffes, the Sharpes, the Lavanders. Wonderful old Hazel Moore. Helena Ruislip, all the way from San Francisco.

And Sonya. From across the dining room, Fay regarded her sister-in-law with admiration. This was the sort of occasion Sonya loved—loved to organize, loved to preside over. Except now Sonya's face was wrinkled with concern. She was looking at her watch and gesturing to Clyde; a minute later, she was working her way across to where Fay stood.

"Fay," she said, "we're looking for your father. We think we should start the toasts."

"I haven't seen him," Fay said. "At least not for the last half hour or so. Maybe he stepped out for a breath of—but I haven't seen him."

"Neither has Clyde."

"Did you ask Bibbi?"

"Yes. And Onion. They haven't seen him, either."

"Maybe—"

"Clyde's already checked the bathrooms."

"He might have gone out for some air."

"Do you think so?"

"Tom," Fay said, "have you seen my father? Clyde wants to start the speeches in a few minutes."

"Maybe he went out for a breath of fresh air."

"Everyone keeps saying that."

"I'll keep my eyes open. I'll tell him you—"

Fay stepped outside the back door, listening hard, trying to see in the darkness. The dark vault of the sky seemed depthless. The wind had risen. She walked a few yards into the garden, then turned and peered back into the lighted house. The windows were golden with light. Every room was filled. The kitchen, with its clutter of silver and china. The living room, the dining room overflowing with people. Bouquets of flowers stood on every table.

She let herself in and walked through the narrow hallway and up the carpeted stairs. Pale carpeting, a mushroom beige. A series of pen-and-ink drawings on the wall. Architectural drawings that Clyde has been collecting. The stairs creaked pleasingly underfoot.

She checked Matthew's bedroom, then Gordon's. Their beds were piled high with coats. She climbed the slightly narrower, more claustrophobic stairs to the third floor, to Clyde and Sonya's dimly lit bedroom.

The room lay before her. The wide bed was covered with Sonya's treasured quilt, a pattern of blue and green squares. In a corner by the curtained window was a small blue rather feminine-looking armchair, and seated in that chair was the shadowy neat upright figure of Richard McLeod.

Fay stared at him a moment over the glowing quilt and saw him look up. Their eyes locked. His were bright with tears.

CHAPTER 28

Moving Right Along

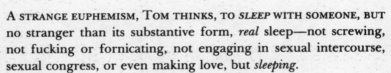

A STRANGE EUPHEMISM, TOM THINKS, TO *SLEEP* WITH SOMEONE, BUT no stranger than its substantive form, *real* sleep—not screwing, not fucking or fornicating, not engaging in sexual intercourse, sexual congress, or even making love, but *sleeping*.

He prizes it. Actual sleep, that is.

The intimacy of sleep, of falling into unconsciousness, locked body-to-body with another person, a stranger, someone not of one's own blood, the skin-on-skin unlikelihood of it. What a bonus it is that the palpable world can be left behind and the dark cave of sleep trustingly entered. All those hours pressed together in twinned silence—how does it happen? What are those hours made of? Oxygen? Ether? How can the breathing of two people be this effortless? So synchronized that it seems a single lung is blowing up with air and deflating with its long slow rhythmic release.

From time to time during the long nights he feels his limbs

shift, as though they were made of some plantlike substance, moving sideways on the bed of their own accord, swimming away from him and touching another's sleeping body. Fay's body.

She's almost as tall as he is, but thin—especially her upper body, her rib cage, her long arms. Her slenderness is her one vanity. He teases her about the bag lunches she takes to work, her clear plastic containers of cottage cheese, her carrot sticks, her yogurt, her apple, her Swedish whole-grain wafers. "I don't mind getting old," she tells him, "but not old and fat." (This is not quite true. She *does* mind getting old; in February she'll turn thirty-six; she can't believe this, she tells Tom.)

By next February—and this is astonishing to Tom—the two of them will have been married for three months. A couple. Husband and wife. They've set a date, the third Saturday in November. A simple ceremony in the chapel of All Saints Church, the same church where Fay's parents were married forty years ago. The wedding will be at four o'clock. Just family and close friends, about eighty guests in all. Ian Innes, an old family friend of the McLeods, will officiate. Stephanie Birrell and her cello will provide the music. A traditional ceremony, yes, but with a few differences. Fay doesn't want to walk down the aisle, she says; she'd feel silly. And she doesn't want a long white bridey dress. She doesn't yet know what she wants; she's planning to start looking around for something simple, something halfway between formal and informal, something marvelous.

Whenever Tom tries to focus his mind on these plans, he's overcome with confusion. A train of images moves into view: himself swaying on the red church carpet, the weave of his dark suit fragmenting into its separate threads, the swelling whiteness of his shirt collar, his knotted tie dissolving, and Ted Woloschuk standing somewhere nearby, just slightly out of focus. And then there's the blur of faces out there watching, those attentive numbered faces, eighty of them, tipped forward and lit by the midafternoon light that falls through the colored west windows—winter light, opalescent, full of trickery and wrinkles of perception. And the unthinkable moment when he will pull a ring from his pocket and place it on Fay's finger. A wedding ring, a solid but slippery thing; he has an image of her fingers drifting toward him in a miasma of grayed dots like those on the edge of a photograph.

But no, this is real. Sleeping beside her tonight, and waking drowsily at dawn, he feels an exhausted, drunken greed for each moment that holds them. Sleep presses inward, soft edged, delicately colored, burgeoning with new possibility. Now. Today. The two of them, he and Fay, lying side by side beneath the warmth of Fay's electric blanket, which is set this freezing autumn night at medium. This is really happening. It has already, in fact, happened. Love and its transforming power have laid out a far more generous future than the one he had been willing to settle for. He is soon to be married to the woman who sleeps beside him. Fay McLeod. There will be not only a marriage ceremony but annual celebrations of that marriage, the date circled each year on the calendar. The day will bring gifts and reminiscences, how they met, the special circumstances, what happened next, what was said, the retelling of that particular narrative which married people uniquely cherish. Our story. Our marriage. November, that unlikely month.

He turns on his side so he can watch her face.

Glimpsed like this, still sleeping, shadowed, her features composed, she seems not only his lover but his gallant and wistful friend. One of her arms is flung toward him on the pillow, the smooth thin girlish hand curved inward. He could if he liked, and without waking her, make a circle of his thumb and middle finger and wrap it like a bracelet around her wrist.

HE AND SHEILA had been married in June of 1975.

A hot day. Sheila had worn a backless sundress made of pink cotton and a pair of soiled, cottony Roman sandals that laced halfway up her legs and left diamond-shaped welts on her hard young calves. They'd been living together for close to a year in a third-floor apartment on Lilac Avenue, locked into what Tom always thought of as a rude, talky conviviality, not a love affair at all. Theirs was an old cheap apartment block with ill-fitting windows, and all winter they'd quarreled about an army blanket Tom had nailed across the bedroom window. It kept out the worst of the drafts, yes, but living in the perpetual brownish dark had gotten Sheila down. It got so she hated going into that bedroom. Tom told her it was not uncommon in places like Duck River for people to cover their windows in winter with blankets or with sheets of aluminum foil or plastic film. This isn't Duck River, Sheila said, this isn't the back of beyond, and she didn't want to live that way, like a mole in an underground burrow.

The snow lasted right into May, a record. On Mother's Day there was a storm, real drifts piled like meringues around the trees and shrubs. A week later they found themselves in the midst of a heat wave.

The sudden softening of the air, the humid, spongy nights, the bursting greenness along the city thoroughfares convinced them that they loved each other after all, that they would love each other forever. Tom, one morning, took down the blanket. He made a ritual of it. *Ladies and gentlemen, I am about to reveal* . . . The small square bedroom became, instantly, a golden cube, and the bed a design of furrowed light. Sheila, twenty-three years old, spread naked on the sheets, naked and also watchful, seemed to him to be aglow with vitality, her shoulders, her full hips so cheerful and shameless. There was something birdlike and beseeching about the ginger tuft that sprang from her pubis. "Why don't we get married," he said in a roughened voice, moving toward her, and three days later they were standing in line at the Law Courts, perspiring, waiting their turn, hanging on quietly to each other's hand.

Clair had worn black. A black sweater, a black corduroy skirt reaching to her ankles, flat black shoes. A single earring of blackened silver, heavy. It was the middle of a rainy April. He'd known her for two weeks. Her face had a stillness about it that he loved. He could talk and talk and her eyes never changed. He felt he could pour himself into her with a kind of retro-exploitative hunger. This concentrated calm was what he required, what he'd been looking for, that's what he told himself. When he put his arms around her he felt her shudder—a shudder that traveled the length of her body, and his too—and also the simultaneous force and blessing of her silence.

He went to Toronto to audition for a job and talked her into going with him. They stayed a week in a room at the Royal York Hotel, and in the middle of that week they walked down the street and got married. It was two o'clock in the afternoon. The rounded soot-colored Toronto clouds pressed down on them. This was his second city-hall special (that should have been a warning). Afterward he phoned the news to his mother, who shrieked out her good wishes, frightening Clair with her long-distance exuberance. ("All the best, honey.") He persuaded Clair to telephone her parents in Winnipeg, whom he had not yet met. "Who?" Foxy Howe had shouted over the phone. "Tom who?" "You've known him how long? Two weeks?" "Well, you're twenty-eight years old, what can we say?"

Tom, hovering by the telephone, had been taken aback. Clair had told him she was twenty-five. He worried about the birth date on the marriage papers. He wondered, in fact, if they were legally married. Clair, hanging up abruptly, began to cry. She wept hysterically for over an hour, beating his chest, and then took a sleeping pill, several of them, in fact, and slept for twelve hours. When she woke up her eyes seemed to Tom to be fixed dully in her face like a pair of glazed pebbles. She looked older.

He and Suzanne were married on a bitterly cold day in January. He had met her three months earlier at the Chandlers' Halloween party (she dressed as Little Red Riding Hood, he as a cowboy), and a week later he moved in with her. They had lain lightly on her narrow bed; the lightness bore down on him, and also the obliquely delivered knowledge that this love of theirs held only a minor cargo.

Suzanne's parents—meek, puzzled country people with pink

plumped skin—drove into Winnipeg for the wedding, which was held in a private room at the Northstar Hotel. (It was Tom who paid for the rental of the room and for the supper that followed.) Tom's mother was there, too, having traveled down from Duck River on a Grey Goose bus. A Lutheran clergyman presided, and a dozen friends (the Chandlers, Jeff and Jenny Waring, and so on) gathered to witness and celebrate the event. Tom had been proud to produce these solidly married friends. He was, in those days, enchanted by their marriages, their temporary apartments and cheerful makeshift arrangements. Suzanne carried pink roses against her white wool dress. She whispered her wedding vows while looking up into Tom's face. Shyly, it seemd to him. Flirtatiously. The chandeliers were blinding and so was the white cloth on the buffet table. He remembers that the smell of salmon salad was strong in the room. Salmon and pink roses. And Suzanne's favorite perfume, Ma Griffe. For a minute he had felt ill. That was all he needed, to be sick on the swirled red carpet. What was the matter with him? The charged air? Or had it been nervousness? *To have and to hold from this day forward.* That waterfall of words drifting past his ears.

These three weddings lie strewn around him. Quickies. But they are surprisingly vivid still and seem to gesture toward something essentially frivolous in his nature. He's grateful Fay hasn't pressed him for details.

McLeod/Avery
Fay Elizabeth McLeod, daughter of Richard and Peggy McLeod, of Winnipeg, and Thomas Avery, son of Betty Avery Barbour of Duck River, are happy to announce their forthcoming marriage. A November wedding is planned.

Tom is amazed at the number of things Fay owns. She has a set of china, matching china, enough for eight people. She has several extra blankets folded on a shelf, extra pillows, sheets, a stack of kitchen towels, all that stuff.

She has a toaster, for God's sake. ("Everyone has a toaster," Fay tells him peacefully. "A toaster is a basic.")

She owns a set of matching cookware, a microwave oven, a washer and dryer, and a red plastic laundry basket. Also a file cabinet (alphabetized, orderly) and paid-up subscriptions to four different magazines. She keeps a whole range of vases on hand, large, small, tall, squat, all of them lined up neatly on a high shelf in her kitchen. ("They've just somehow accumulated," she explains, puzzled.) There is an address book by the telephone, a legible, up-to-date address book with postal codes and phone numbers inked in. She has spare light bulbs stacked in a cupboard, each in its own crisp corrugated paper casing. In the corner of her desk is a pretty pottery mug full of pens and pencils, also a hollowed-out cube of glass holding paper clips. She has skirt hangers, plastic garment bags, shoe polish, a clothes brush, a sewing basket. Everything.

All these possessions, Tom sees, are emblems of her well-stocked, stable life, yet she wakes up each morning to the clanging of an old-fashioned, loudly ticking, inaccurately functioning, badly chipped and tarnished wind-up alarm clock. Unbelievable. Why does she put up with it?

He carries his own clock radio across the street one day and presents it to her. Its sleek sides wrap around to a glistening digital display and now she wakes up to weather, music, and tossed dreamy scraps of local news—about church bazaars, school-board elections, flu epidemics, inner-city housing, recreational outings for the aged. It's like a toy. She loves it, especially the "dream bar" on top, which when pressed will allow her ten extra minutes of sleep. The music comes on in midphrase, and when she hears it she stretches an arm across his chest, tucks her head under his chin; he can feel her body curling back into sleep.

Lately, though, in the days following the anniversary party, she's been waking early, and instead of fitting her body to his, she lies stiffly beside him. Light leaks in through the blinds; the clocks have been turned back an hour, bringing lighter mornings. He hates dark mornings—they seem an injustice when the year is at its thinnest—and he hates even more the breaking of the darkness, the green luminous digits of the clock radio at 6:45, the harsh bedside lamp switched on.

This morning he wakes to the sober news of a radio commentator, the Middle East again, the release of political prisoners, uneasiness, and behind the cool analytical male voice he hears the sound of Fay sighing. A sharp sigh that narrows down to a kind of whimper.

"What's wrong?" he asks her, without turning, without opening his eyes. "Tell me."

"I don't know," she says.

He wonders if she is thinking about the marriage license they applied for the day before. They had gone together to the Office of Vital Statistics in the Law Courts Building and there had filled out the necessary papers and paid the obligatory fee. "Have either of you been married before?" the pretty young clerk asked, and Tom had reached into his breast pocket for his papers, his three divorce decrees. The clerk had riffled through them, her face expressionless. "It's only the most recent we require," she told Tom. During this exchange Fay had resolutely studied her hands.

"You're worried," he says to her this morning.

"Yes."

"About us, our wedding?"

"No."

"About your father?"

"Yes."

HE HAD FOUND it unsettling going back to his apartment, to get the clock radio. Putting the key in the lock made him feel like a burglar. Stealthy.

The neatness of his living room surprised him, or rather its austerity. This wasn't how he remembered it, the new furniture and its minimal comfort, everything swept bare. If he were to clap his hands he imagined he would hear an echo. The settled still quality of the air struck him as distinctly unwelcoming; who had been the occupant of this apartment, anyway? Someone large and gloomy, a pale unhealthy balloon of a man who crashed on that bedroom mattress and banged with thick hands on those kitchen cupboards. Over there was the table where he'd sat one day and composed a letter to Fay. Pouring out his heart. Love, love.

Only a few weeks had passed since then. Unbelievable.

He opened the refrigerator. Three bottles of beer lay angled on the silvery shelf, a bag of apples, and a piece of orange cheese that had gone hard and cracked. He really should sort through this stuff, salvage what hadn't spoiled and throw out the rest. Tom Avery's leftovers. Tom who?

He let the door swing shut.

And heard at the same moment the sound of banging down below. And loud quarreling voices, male voices. Mr. Duff? Impossible; Mr. Duff came and went without a sound.

He disconnected the clock radio quickly and tucked it under his arm, locked the apartment, and went down a flight of stairs to knock on Mr. Duff's door. He noticed the stair carpet smelled musty. He noticed, too, that the overhead light was burned out.

A thick-torsoed man came to the door. He was about forty, Tom guessed. His hairline sloped sharply back from a peeled impassive face, and he wore a down vest over his wrinkled denim shirt.

"Yeah?" he said to Tom. In one of his hands he balanced a videocassette.

"I'm looking for Mr. Duff," Tom said.

"He's moved out."

"Moved?" He took a breath. "When?"

"Yesterday."

"You don't happen to know where he's gone, do you?"

"Not a clue, sorry. Didn't know the guy."

"He wasn't sick or anything?"

"Dunno."

"Someone must have a forwarding address."

"Not me."

"Maybe he went to California. He's got a son there who—"

"Yeah, well."

"Sorry to bother you."

"Hey no problem, no problem."

"No problem." Tom mouthed back the words. He felt momentarily weakened, as though he had suddenly been reminded of all kinds of important matters he had forgotten: that there was a hole now in the earth's oxygen layer, that the atoms of his own body were sloughing off, that important papers had been misfiled or lost.

THURSDAY NIGHTS on CHOL Tom likes to play a little reggae. Already it's gotten to be kind of a tradition. If he misses a reggae night he starts getting calls. "What gives?" his callers ask.

There're a whole lot of reggae fans out there.

Reggae suits his mood tonight. The compelling beat and the lightly dragging rhythm buzz his brain. It's husky, it's sweet. Marley and his pals. Yellowman. He'll do a straight hour tonight, 3:00 to 4:00 a.m., never mind Ted grimacing away in the control room. Dope music, Ted calls it. He says reggae gives him a case of the bends.

"Hey," Ted had said to him earlier, "we saw your announcement in the paper. Your wedding announcement. Maeve's cut it out. She's got it stuck on the fridge."

"Really?" Tom said, absurdly pleased and wondering if his pleasure showed on his face.

"She's going out shopping this weekend. For a new dress for the wedding, she says. She's going to blow the bank."

"Well!"

"Well, why not? That's what I said."

"Great."

"Seeing it in the paper," Ted went on, "sort of makes it official. I guess you're busy making plans."

"It's moving right along," Tom said, and in the back of his head a mechanical arm picked up the phrase and set it to music, wrapped it tight in a cool black hopeful beat—it's moving right along, yeah, it's moving right along—movin' riiight alooong.

~ CHAPTER 29 ~

Keeping the

Faith

"CERTAIN PARTS OF THE EARTH'S GEOGRAPHY," FAY BEGINS, "SEEM particularly hospitable to the incursions of legend and to certain emblems that become rooted in the culture."

It is four o'clock on a cloudy Friday afternoon, and she is standing at a lectern in the auditorium of the National Center for Folklore Studies addressing her colleagues, as well as various interested members of the public, on the subject "Mermaids and the Mythic Imagination."

"At first glance," she continues, "the Loire delta in France might seem an unlikely repository for folk beliefs. This is not the far more familiar Château section of the Loire, but the region lying to the west of Nantes. The countryside is generally flat and open and rather dull, and the villages, which are very close together, have almost nothing about them that can be described as picturesque."

From her position on the podium Fay can see that Hannah Webb, in the second row, is beginning to nod off, and who can blame her, although it was Hannah who invited Fay to present a colloquium in the first place. Fay had suggested something more informal, a slide presentation in the staff room, for instance, but Hannah felt strongly that the center should open its programs to the "wider community," as she liked to call it.

Anne Morris, in the third row, is leaning forward, taking notes, and so is Ken Merchant, who will be giving next month's colloquium (a summary of his work, thus far, on penitentiary rituals). Colin is sitting next to Ken and looking particularly attentive and thoughtful. And who else? Peter Knightly has taken a seat in the back row and arranged his lanky body in a deep slouch, corduroy pants, corduroy jacket, a corduroy composition, all angles and corded shadows; Fay predicts that he'll slip out the minute she begins showing her slides. It is Friday after all, the tail end of a cold rainy week.

"In fact"—her voice rises and swings into what she fears is a tiresome preacherly rhythm—"the Loire area is extremely *rich* in folk legend. We might look, for instance, at the interesting village of St. Philbert, which is the site of a beautiful ninth-century church. In the church crypt lies a roughly hewn stone coffin that is believed by pilgrims to be so holy that just to touch its surface is to bring good fortune and fertility."

Why is she so jittery today? There are perhaps sixty people in the audience, thirty of whom she knows well and many whom she loves, or at least admires. To give herself courage she jams her hands in the pockets of her new gray pleated skirt. She remembers to hold her head straight and not to let it go into a weak sideways tilt—it was Iris Jaffe who told her this trick.

"Not far from St. Philbert," she continues, "is the market town of Machecoul, an exceedingly unprepossessing and dusty place, yet known to be the ancient center of the Bluebeard legend."

She pauses, shuffles her notes, adjusts the height of the microphone, and takes a deep breath.

"And nearby, at the bottom of the Lac du Grand-Lieu itself, there is believed to be an ancient drowned village from which church bells are said to toll on Christmas Eve. While I was in the region I spoke to a number of people who claim to have heard these bells."

She gives the signal to Art Frayne at the back of the room; the lights dim and the first slide comes on—a view of the lake, which is wide and grassy and surrounded by low-lying fields. (Is it possible she was standing on the shore of that swampy lake just a few weeks earlier?)

"It was here," Fay says, taking up her pointer, "just to the right of this small wooden dock, where last year two local teenaged girls claim to have seen a mermaid, the first reported sighting in over a hundred years."

Hannah is asleep. Definitely asleep, her head sunk on her chest. And Peter's chair at the back of the auditorium is empty.

She swallows, turns to the next page, and continues. "The sighting at the Lac du Grand-Lieu was widely reported in the press, and these reports, in a sense, have validated the vision. The families of the two girls and the inhabitants of St. Pierre may be skeptical, but few of them are openly dismissive. Those I talked to were not unwilling to entertain the notion that a mermaid might actually have made an appearance. As with the inhabitants of the Loch Ness area, there seems to be a strong wish to be persuaded."

But who is that coming in late and settling herself into an aisle seat? Why, it's Iris! How wonderful of Iris to come.

She looks hard at her notes. She must concentrate. She's just getting to the important part of her thesis, so why is her voice threatening to close down? And why are her thoughts drifting to her father at this moment, to the image of him sitting in a chair in Sonya and Clyde's bedroom, on the other side of the wide quilt-covered water bed, his eyes bright with tears? "It seems clear," she goes on, "that immersion in a rich folk tradition facilitates the continuation of that tradition. Legend, then, can be thought of as cumulative, feeding on other legends and attaching itself to those societies that already have a well-established history of mythical and mystical associations."

Ve-ry pro-found.

"We know how visions of the Holy Virgin are multiplied and

reinforced by the blessed communities. In a hundred years the people of the Loire delta may still be speaking of the mermaid who surfaced in the Lac du Grand-Lieu, and the story, originating with a casual sighting by two girls of impressionable age, will be not only entrenched but expanded."

Someone sneezes. Someone else struggles to remove a jacket. The room is terribly hot.

"In other words," Fay says, signaling to Art Frayne for the next set of slides (the gorgeous Danish and German and Italian mermaids), "in other words, folk credulity may well be a conditioned response. A society that is open to symbolic forms continues to welcome and embrace whatever mysteries are offered."

She has convinced herself that this is true.

"Believers," she says in a voice which has now steadied itself, "develop an aptitude for belief, a willed innocence which becomes part and parcel of the folk system. Whereas disbelievers"—and she raises an arm in a broad gesture that encircles the audience and includes herself—"disbelievers, those without a mythic tradition, are unable to abandon rationality. They demand evidence. They expect their proofs to accord with the contemporary notion of reality, and when this test fails, as it will inevitably fail, they are rendered utterly incapable of an act of belief."

"Who exactly attends these Friday-afternoon lectures?" Tom had asked her. He was standing in Fay's kitchen, pulling the tab on a can of frozen orange juice.

"Well, the staff goes, of course. They're more or less expected to be there. And theoretically the talks are open to the public."

"Theoretically?"

"There's usually a little notice in the paper. But, in fact, only a handful of people ever show up. The subjects are usually pretty esoteric."

"But anyone can come?"

"Well, yes."

"Maybe I should come. To listen to your lecture, I mean. I'm not doing anything Friday afternoon."

She could hear him straining for nonchalance. "Oh, you'd hate it, Tom." She handed him a jug for the juice.

"Would I?"

"It'll be awfully dry."

"Really? I might learn something."

"You'd be bored to death. Believe me."

Gently, calmly, she had discouraged him from coming. For one thing—and she finds this difficult to formulate, even to herself—it worries her that he should feel an obligation to penetrate the narrowness of her world. It was distressing to her, the thought of him consigned to the edge of all that arcane folklore vocabulary and theoretical morass, most of it incomprehensible. It comforts her, on the other hand, to see him captured by his own pursuits. He has his solidly assimilated world, after all—music, radio, that wide-flung audience—and she loves to think of him standing at its center, sure of where he is.

But there's something else, too, that worries her—which is the thought that she might be put in the position of having to introduce him to Peter Knightly. She admitted to herself that she wasn't quite ready for that yet.

NEVERTHELESS it happened, as it was bound to happen.

It happened at seven o'clock on a cold windless Sunday evening when Fay and Tom were standing on Notre Dame Avenue, lining up for tickets for the new Woody Allen movie. Directly ahead of them in line were Peter Knightly and Fritzi Sweet.

"Why, Fay," Peter said by way of greeting.

"Peter," she said. "And Fritzi. How nice to see you again." Then, "Peter, I don't think you know Tom Avery."

"How do you do," Tom said. His upbeat radio voice. Chocolatey. The two men shook hands, and it maddened Fay that Peter should extend his arm in such a lean and rangy and proprietorial manner, as if he were the elected chairman of a hastily assembled committee, though she knew, in fact, that he was innocent of any such notion.

"And this is Fritzi Sweet," Peter said.

"We've met," said Tom. "Two or three times."

"Hello," said Fritzi, smiling widely at both Fay and Tom. "Nice to run into you." Her large happy teeth gleamed in the blue light. Her hand was tucked into Peter's overcoat pocket.

The movie was only mildly funny. Tom, who normally loved Woody Allen, sat silent through most of it, and Fay noticed that for the first three-quarters of the film he leaned stiffly away from her.

At last she could bear it no longer. She turned in the dark and put her hand up to his cheek. Uttering an abrupt breathy sound and shifting his body, he grasped her fingers and moved them quickly to his lips, touching them with the imprint of a kiss. Then he took her middle finger and placed it between his front teeth, biting down gently on it. Gently.

A FEW DAYS AGO Fay's mother, Peggy McLeod, phoned and invited Fay and Tom for dinner on Monday might. "Just leftovers," she said. "Potluck. Monday-night fare. But do come. We haven't seen you since the party. It'll be just the four of us. We'll have a chance to catch up on your wedding plans."

But late on Monday afternoon she phoned Fay at work and said, "Listen, dear, I'm afraid it's not going to work out tonight. For dinner, I mean. I'm so sorry, Fay. Something's come up. I hope you'll explain to Tom. Oh, no, nothing serious, just one of those things. Look, we'll make it another time. That's a promise. No, nothing's the matter. It's just—well, you know how things get. It's nothing."

"I CAN'T HELP IT," Fay said to Tom the next morning. "I'm worried about them."

"It's probably nothing," Tom said. "A headache. A cold. Or maybe she was just feeling too tired to knock a meal together."

They were lying together in bed, side by side, facing each other. It was seven o'clock. Tom reached out and touched her hair, then moved his lips down between her breasts.

"You don't realize," she said carefully, talking into the crown of his head, "how unlike my mother it is to cancel anything."

"No, I don't realize." His voice was muffled. His soft lips buzzed her sternum. She felt the warm tip of his tongue.

Had she hurt him, she wondered, reminding him how recently he had entered her life and how much he had yet to learn? She put her arms around him and said, "It's heaven to wake up next to you this way. I want to go on waking up like this forever."

"We'll have white hair." He raised himself on his elbows and looked at her. "Or maybe no hair. And our bones will creak."

"I won't mind if you don't mind."

"We'll be on salt-free diets."

"And vitamin-B injections," Fay said. "Oh Lord."

"But we'll still—" He was fitting himself between her legs.

She moved in closer. Her body felt bent into the shape of a smile.

"And, who knows," he said, "maybe our children will decide to throw us a big surprise party."

Why had he said that? Why? She rocked him in her arms, forcing herself against his body, trying to push away whatever it was that was nudging at her thoughts and interfering with her happiness.

"DADDY," SHE HAD SAID, seeing her father across Sonya and Clyde's blue-and-green quilt.

She hadn't called him that for years. Probably not since she was twelve years old.

He had looked into her eyes, and a wavelet of thought struck her—that a man discovered weeping in the corner of a bedroom ought, out of shame or embarrassment, to turn his head aside, or at least cover his face. But he wasn't doing either of those things.

The table lamp picked up the rounded shine of his tears. Tears—they stood out like tears in a wood engraving. And he looked smaller than he really was, shrunken against the upholstery of the armchair, against the pale striping of the curtains.

"What is it?" Her voice wobbled. She felt sick. She glanced at the flat field of the water bed and experienced a strong desire to lie down on top of all that softness, to close her eyes and drift into sleep.

Then he did something that tore her heart. He lifted his two hands, lifted them tentatively into the air, and gestured blindly in the direction of his eyes. He gave his head a single violent shake and drew in his breath sharply. In that sudden gasp she read the sum of his bewilderment.

So. Sonya had been right, after all. The shock of surprise had been too much. She remembered Sonya's exact words. That surprise can be an act of aggression. They should have listened to her, wise Sonya.

She approached him cautiously, saying to herself: I must be careful. She sat on the edge of the bed, just inches away from him, and then he did finally turn away, covering his face with his hands. She heard him gasp again, but this time it was more of a sob. He squeezed his eyes shut and groped in his pocket for a handkerchief.

A fresh linen handkerchief. It was an eccentricity in this day and age for a man to carry a linen handkerchief, but he preferred them. Every day he took a fresh handkerchief from his bureau drawer, a handkerchief ironed and folded flat by his wife of forty years.

"We should have told you," Fay said. She reached for his hand but felt suddenly afraid, as though his flesh might explode or disintegrate at her touch. "We shouldn't have surprised you like this."

He held the handkerchief over his eyes and forehead, pressing.

"Are you feeling sick?" Fay asked after a while, and he shook his head emphatically, a wide arc of denial, no, no. Not sick.

If only he'd look at her. "What, then?" she asked at last.

It took him another minute to compose himself, but even then the words came out brokenly. "I can't," he said, "I can't go on."

BUT HE had gone on.

He shook himself to attention, shoulders back, head up, then blew his nose loudly, that familiar, fatherly sound. He stood abruptly, ran his hands quickly down the sides of his suit jacket, smoothing the cloth. His hair he smoothed, too, rubbing his palms twice across the back of his scalp. He bent over to meet his body in the bedroom mirror and pulled his tie straight.

"Ready?" he said to Fay. The firmness of his tone, and the iciness, stunned her into silence.

She led the way, down both flights of stairs, then through the narrow hallway and into the living room, where they were instantly engulfed by the sound of recorded music—a full orchestra booming away, something from *The King and I*. A hundred people were talking all at once and swaying, circling, in the soft light. And Peggy McLeod was coming toward them, looking lovely, looking almost youthful, with a brilliant smile of greeting on her lips, slipping her arm through her husband's, saying, "We've been looking for you everywhere, Richard. I'm not going to let go of you again."

~ CHAPTER 30 ~

What Has

Befallen Him

"CONGRATULATIONS," EVERYONE SAYS TO TOM ABOUT HIS FORTHCOM-ing marriage to Fay McLeod.

These glad shouts fall like showers of soft rain. "Terrific news, Tom," or "All the best to you both." He's been warmed through and through by the numbers of well-wishers, surprised that so many people in this city seem happy to acknowledge what has befallen him.

But there are a few—maybe half a dozen, all of them men, mostly men of the crony sort, old radio acquaintances, late-night comrades, drinking buddies, Judd Hollander, Russ Conte, Louis Breuer—who make such deeply disturbing comments as, "So, Tom, you're off for another ride around the track, are you?" Gesturing at his unstable history. Implying that he, Tom Avery, is a trifler, a lightweight in the matter of love, a less-than-serious man. That he's moving along aboard a sharply drawn arrow, straight into an area of fresh wreckage. Again. Another fuckup. Another failure.

This time, though, it's going to be different. That's what he longs to tell Russ and Judd and Louis and the rest of the tribe—but doesn't. (For one thing, he's wary of mouthing clichés; for another, he knows his credibility is on the minus side of zero.)

But this time it *is* different. All around him are providential signs, and like an accountant he's been keeping track.

The engagement announcement in the newspaper, for example. God, but he loves that square inch of print (loves it more even than the beautifully printed wedding invitations). On the day the announcement came out he walked over to Mickey's Smoke Shop and bought several copies and clipped the item carefully with Fay's sewing shears. (He's a man who's about to marry a woman who owns a pair of sewing shears.) Two copies of the announcement he sent to his mother in Duck River. Another he mailed to an old school friend, Finn Hoag, who now works for the police force up in Whitehorse; still another went to Ken Baggot in Toronto, who has himself married disastrously, and more than once. He's even, feeling only moderately foolish, pinned up a copy on the notice board next to the coffee machine down at CHOL. (Have his fellow staff members guessed it was he and not the sentimental Rosalie Summers who put it there? Probably not.) Three additional copies he's put away for safekeeping in an envelope marked "Engagement Announcement," and this envelope he's placed in a leather folio, which also contains his life-insurance policy. One copy he's had laminated in a print shop down on Vaughan Avenue, and he carries it in his wallet. (One morning not long ago, he opened his wallet and showed it to Fay, who smiled her surprise, and also her somewhat puzzled approval. "Why, Tom," she said after a pause, the corners of her mouth rising, and then she seemed lost for words.)

Sentimental, yes, he admits it, but there's more to it than that. The announcement of his and Fay's forthcoming marriage in a public newspaper seems to him to certify his connection to his fellow citizens. He is no longer the careless blunderer he was. He's grown up. He's a thoughtful and prudent human being who takes the ceremonies of his society seriously and demonstrates his seriousness by adhering to certain primary conventions. Yes, absolutely! He is responsible, mature, and committed (Patsy MacArthur's awful C-word, but never mind). Committed for life.

He loves, too, the wording of the newspaper text, so brief and official in its syntax, yet so resonant with tribal connection. It has the feel of a poem. He knows it by heart, and occasionally these days, when caught off balance or plunged into some small and momentary condition of uncertainty or injury, he feels it thumping at the back of his head like a secondary pulse. "Fay Elizabeth McLeod, daughter of . . . , and Tom Avery . . ." He sees these shapely words as evidence of a new rationality.

Before his fellows he's declared his sober intent. Made a sacred pledge.

TOM HAS BEEN introduced to Peter Knightly. It's happened; the two men have met each other formally and shaken hands.

He hadn't even known how much he'd dreaded this meeting, yet when it actually occurred he had surprised himself by remaining cool. A part of his brain had stirred itself to attention and sized up the situation: Peter Knightly: a couple of inches taller than he was himself, thinner in the headbone, bloodless, something knobbly, too, about his upper face, and an inclination to swing his head sideways when he spoke—deferential, or else condescending. "How d'you do," he'd said to Tom in a genial enough tone. One of those Englishy voices. Soft bushings in the throat.

Two days later Tom ran into him in the Belgian Bakery on Corydon Avenue, buying a loaf of Hovis bread. "Hullo again," Peter Knightly neighed, and a strained conversation followed, an absurd, hearty discussion about bran muffins, whether they should or should not contain raisins.

A day or two after that Tom was driving down Memorial Avenue and stopped suddenly at a crosswalk. At least twelve cars had jammed on their brakes for a single pedestrian, a long-legged guy in a flapping overcoat. Not Peter Knightly again! Christ! Don't let him see me, Tom prayed to the windshield, and at that moment

Peter Knightly looked up, recognized him, smiled (wanly), and offered a limp salute.

And now—a Saturday morning—again!

There was Tom, in the middle of his weekly run, bumping along eastward across Assiniboine Park, a scarf wrapped loosely over his mouth, and keeping a sharp lookout for the treacherous black ice that forms on the path this time of year. One false step and he'd be down. A lot of joggers quit toward the middle of October because of this ice, taking up indoor pursuits instead, stationary bicycles or rowing machines. The ranks were definitely thinning, the wimps and the stalwarts parting company. Uh-huh! But who was this sprinting toward him this bright morning in the red-and-white Gore-Tex job? God, no. Picking up his feet like a pro. Rhythmic and easy. A natural. Coming closer and closer. Coming into focus.

"Morning, Tom," Peter Knightly said as he brushed lightly by.

"Morning," Tom breathed back. It came out a whisper.

Two minutes later, turning onto Wellington Crescent, his brain awash with obscene images, he slipped and fell.

"A BAD SPRAIN," Dave Neuhaus said. "You want to apply an ice pack periodically to fight the swelling, use an elastic bandage for the first week at least, and keep that ankle elevated every chance you get."

Ah, but this is heaven, Tom thinks. A Sunday afternoon that stretches endlessly forward and backward.

Dull winter light plays on the window. Outside the snow is drifting down in soft flakes, the first snow of the year, and inside the warm apartment he and Fay are sitting side by side on her corduroy couch, his foot resting comfortably on a pair of pillows that Fay has positioned for him on the coffee table. He feels peaceful. He feels married. Intimacy—Patsy MacArthur's I-word. So this is intimacy. Good old intimacy.

They've been drinking coffee and listening to the radio, a

regular Sunday-afternoon music show with a New Age theme, and Tom is attempting to explain to Fay what a vibraphone is. "You know what a marimba is?" he asks her.

"Yes."

"Well, a vibraphone is a lot like a marimba, only it resonates differently. The valves are motorized, and that's what gives it its particular buzzy sound."

"But how big is it? What does it look like?" Her face is decorated by a blaze of late sun that cuts through the window.

He picks up a pencil and draws in the margin of a magazine. She watches closely.

"So that's a vibraphone?" She pronounces the word slowly, and he can tell she's committing it to memory. "Vi-bra-phone."

They live inside different vocabularies, the two of them. This is something he thinks about quite a lot. It's true their bodies and their temperaments rhyme; witness this Sunday-afternoon peace, this quiet room, music, snow falling outside, warmth within. But the words that come out of their mouths are wildly dissimilar.

Just last week, in casual conversation, he'd heard Fay pronounce the word "encomium." She was saying something about Hannah Webb, the director of the folklore center, who was soon to receive an honorary degree. Encomium. It dropped off her tongue, fell off like any other word, like "mosquito" or "wallpaper" or "hangnail," purposeful syllables socketed into an ordinary sentence. Encomium. It sounded vaguely familiar, but what exactly did it mean? He should have asked her. The other day he overheard her talking on the phone to Beverly Miles. "It's really the elementary rubric that's so often misunderstood," she said. Rubric. Would Peter Knightly be able to define the word "rubric"? Without a doubt.

A week ago she gave a Friday-afternoon colloquium on mermaid lore to her colleagues at the center. Colloquium. Uh-huh.

Tom had suggested—keeping it casual, keeping it very, very laid back—that he might come and hear her speak. "Well," he said, "what do you think?"

She'd put her arms around him. "You'd be bored to death,"

she'd said, or something to that effect. She'd pressed a kiss against his neck.

Warning him, he supposed, that he ran the risk of finding himself adrift in an arcane vocabulary. Hers. Which was different from his. Separate planets.

He isn't sure how he should respond to these differences. Whether or not they pose a threat. Whether he should rejoice or worry.

DUCK RIVER, where Tom grew up, is a pulp-mill town, two hundred and fifty miles straight north, a five-hour drive. The air over Duck River smells bitterly of sulphur. A chain of lakes surrounds it, and in summer the excellent fishing brings tourists from as far away as Duluth and Minneapolis, but in winter it lies buried in snow, and the highway is frequently shut down. Tom has grown to hate that long monotonous drive.

As a result he makes the trip only three or four times a year, and this means that he has, to a great extent, separated himself from the town and from the life his mother leads. He talks to her almost every week on the telephone, her nickel or else his, but, in fact, he has only a minimal notion of her day-to-day life, and he imagines that she has just as little understanding of his.

Fay's relationship with her family is entirely different. Her parents, her sister, Bibbi; her brother, Clyde, and his family, Sonya and their two small boys—she talks to one or the other of them almost every day on the telephone and sees them at least once a week. Tom is astonished and also humbled by all this family involvement. "It's like living in a saga," he told her one day. "More like a soap opera," she said.

Recently Matthew and Gordon have been down with prolonged stomach flu, and this has meant extra visits, extra treats wrapped and delivered.

On Wednesday nights Fay meets Bibbi in a restaurant for dinner. This arrangement, Tom is given to understand, is inviolable. "It's the only chance I really get to see her," Fay explains.

Then there are her regular Saturday-morning breakfasts with

her father at Mister Donut's. Last Saturday, though, and the one before, she hadn't gone. Both times her father had called at the last minute to say he was unable to come. He hadn't explained why—just that he would be unable to meet her as usual.

TOM CAN'T UNDERSTAND why Fay's suddenly so worried about her parents.

Of course, he doesn't yet know them very well. On the few occasions when they've all been together, he's felt awkward, wondering if they were still looking him over, turning over in their minds what they know about him, what exactly he represented, and whether he would bring danger into their daughter's life, interfere with her happiness. Fay's mother turns her full attention to Tom and inquires brightly, winningly, about the business of broadcasting, what are its tensions, its rewards, what is his audience profile like, how does he handle obstreperous callers, does he plan to stay in broadcasting permanently? Richard McLeod, on the other hand, is quieter, more watchful, and Tom finds himself wondering whether Peter Knightly had been subjected to the same studious paternal appraisal.

Fay claims that she had never seen her father cry before the night of the party.

"A few tears in his eyes," Tom reminds her. "That's not really crying."

"I saw him," Fay maintains. "I was standing right there. He was crying. He was in some kind of pain."

"You said yourself it was probably just the shock."

"I said that then. Now I'm not so sure."

"Or overwhelmed by the emotional—"

"I don't think so."

"I thought it was supposed to be okay now for men to express their—"

"You don't know my father."

"No."

"Maybe I don't, either."

"And afterward, when he came downstairs, he was fine, wasn't he?"

"I'm not sure."

"He made that terrific speech. He toasted all his friends. He drank some champagne. He was smiling, laughing even. Dancing. He cut the cake, he ate a big chunk of it. Remember the pictures we took? He was fine."

"I wish I could believe that," Fay says, shaking her head, "but I just don't."

EVERY TIME Tom comes into the kitchen he sees the list that Fay has stuck on the refrigerator door: a prewedding list of details to arrange, events to attend, items to buy. There's the phone number of the woman who is looking after the wedding cake. Under that is the word "flowers" (but that item has now been checked off). A lingerie shower next Thursday (women only) at Iris Jaffe's. A buffet supper next week at Jeff and Jenny Waring's (twice postponed, once because Gary Waring was down with stomach flu and once because Jeff was called out of town). Photographer (also checked off).

At the bottom of the list is the word "DRESS."

Fay's been spending all her lunch hours dashing from store to store in search of a dress. Twice she's brought home dresses, beautiful dresses, it seemed to Tom, and both times she's returned them. One had a yellowish cast, she said, when held up to natural light, and the other had "pompous" sleeves.

"Why don't you try on my wedding dress?" Peggy McLeod suggested.

"It wouldn't begin to fit," said Fay, who is five inches taller than her mother.

But it *had* fit, almost perfectly, though the hem, instead of falling to the floor, struck Fay at midcalf. It was more ivory colored than white, and simply made for a dress of its period, a smooth silk bodice with a skirt that draped rather than billowed. The material, after so many years, was fragile, and the alterations to the sleeves (a row of gathers removed to yield an extra half-inch) had been done with great care.

Now there's an exuberant checkmark after the word "DRESS."

In the last few days Tom's been feeling uneasy for some reason, but whenever he pauses and looks at Fay's list, he's reassured. Each check mark moves him closer to his wedding day and reminds him that his life has turned lucky.

HALLOWEEN NIGHT. And down at CHOL, Tom's been celebrating.

Between midnight and 1:00 a.m. he played his favorite spook tunes. Creep and plunge. Squeak and groan. Witchy stuff full of wind and wolf cries.

Between 1:00 and 2:00 a.m. he interviewed seventy-year-old Cecily Holmfield, who is a self-proclaimed local witch, and between 2:00 and 3:00 he took a dozen calls on the subject of Halloween vandalism. Kids have to act out *once* a year, the first caller said; so what if a few porch lights get smashed, big deal. Yeah, someone else said, but what about those razor blades stuck in apples or popcorn balls? Listen, a final caller said, it so happens that putting on a funny costume and being greedy is one of the few authentic folk traditions we bequeath our children, so let's not get all holy about Halloween, let's enjoy it for the crazy mixed blessing it is.

Hey, that's enough Halloween. It's 3:00 a.m., it's reggae time. Let's go with it. How 'bout it, Yellowman. Boot it, Black Uhuru. Give us some shaky snakey ups and doodles, keep it dark and curvy—a little wailing and thrashing and hitting the high notes.

He loves it.

Then wrapping up, closing time, turning the studio over to the graveyard gang, saying good night to Ted Woloschuk. Hey, Ted, have a great weekend. Have a good one yourself.

Home to Fay. Driving down Pembina Highway, then the welter of dark empty side streets. Snow flurries spinning in the headlights. Should he run that red light at Lilac and Corydon? It's four in the morning, the town's dead, of course he's going to run that red light.

Then parking the car in the lot, unlocking the shadowy back

door and climbing the stairs slowly, remembering to go easy on his bad ankle, then groping for his key and letting himself in.

Usually Fay leaves the hall light burning, but not tonight. He stops in the bathroom, brushes his teeth, drops his clothes, splashes water on his face, then tiptoes into the bedroom, feeling his way in the darkness, rounding the end of the bed, pulling back the blanket edge. Pale street light leaks around the edges of the window, so that all the tones and tints in the room become grayed velvet. He swears he can smell her sweetness mingled with the smooth sheets. He thinks of a rose, its centered calyx, cup-shaped. Fay. He reaches out to her.

His arm travels through a furrow of sheeting and straight into a void. The bed is flat, empty. Fay?

"Fay?" he says out loud, and reaches over to switch on the lamp.

~ CHAPTER 31 ~

Black Holes

FAY HAD LEFT TOM A NOTE. SHE'D WRITTEN IT QUICKLY ON THE BACK of an envelope and attached it with a little mermaid magnet to the refrigerator door.

> Tom—something's come up. I'm staying at my mother's to-night. I'll phone in the morning.
>
> > Love,
> > Fay

But the tiny rubberized magnet must have been too weak to hold the envelope in place (she should have known better), and sometime during the night the note had fallen to the floor. Tom, coming home, had picked it up—a return envelope, rather creased, from the Cancer Society—but he'd neglected to turn it over and read the message.

When Fay phoned him at eight o'clock on Friday morning to

tell him the news, he reacted wildly. Where had she been? he shouted into the telephone. Why hadn't she left a message? He was in a rage.

She found herself staring at the receiver, those tiny weak perforations. She'd never heard him in a fit of fury. She had not even imagined it. Tom Avery was a gentle, patient, and quiet-voiced man. Whenever her thoughts strayed to his three bad marriages she pictured them disintegrating softly, pulling apart like fibers of wool. She had not entertained the possibility of arguments or accusations. Or fury.

All night long, he told her, he had been out of his mind with worry. He hadn't known where to call, what to do. He had envisioned a hundred different scenarios, he had—

He had what?

He had thought something really serious might have happened.

She cut him off. "Tom," she said, "listen. Something serious *has* happened. I still can't believe it, but it's true. My father has left my mother."

"Left your mother? Your father's left your—what do you mean, your father's left your mother?"

"Just that," she said, or rather shouted. "He's left her."

IT WAS CLYDE who phoned Fay on Halloween night with the news. The bedside clock said 12:30. She had been asleep for only a few minutes, a deep sleep. The telephone rang and rang, blowing through her head and mixing with her dreams. She had felt heavy-bodied and stupid groping for the receiver and pressing it up against her ear. With one hand she rubbed her head, pushing her hair aside. Who on earth could be calling at this hour?

Clyde.

His stammer was terrible. He sounded insane. Their father had left their mother. Left her.

She remembers that her hands were very cold. She felt an

urge to blow on them with her warm breath, but she would have to put the telephone down, and how could she do that while Clyde was talking? He talked and talked. A picture came to her of her brother on the other end of the line, a blocky woodcut, highly stylized. Wide front sections of his pale colored hair would have fallen over his right eye. His boyish excited look. Feverish. But what *was* this he was talking about? All her senses felt muffled. There was something here she wasn't understanding. And something, too—the thought came later—something she instantly understood, a skewer driven straight to her brain. She hung on to the telephone, swallowing, wishing she had a glass of water. A sliver of absurdity had lodged itself inside her throat. "What?" she said, and reached for the lamp switch. "What did you say, Clyde?"

"You'd better c-c-c-come over right away," he said. "Can you g-g-g-get a c-cab?"

FAY'S BEEN SLEEPING in Bibbi's old bedroom in the Ash Avenue house. She sleeps with the door open so she can hear her mother if she calls out during the night.

In the morning Bibbi or else Clyde will come to spend a few hours so that Fay can go to work. She plans to talk to Hannah Webb about taking some vacation time. A couple of weeks, maybe more. The doctor—old Dr. Plette—has told them that their mother cannot under any circumstances be left alone.

Of course, she's heavily tranquilized. "I don't like these damn drugs," Dr. Plette explained, "and I'll keep a careful eye on the dosage, but she's got to have something to get her through this. At least until she adjusts."

Adjusts! Fay can't believe he's actually pronounced such a word. She wants to strike Dr. Plette in the middle of his rounded foolish piggy belly. What a ridiculous man. Can he really have lived to the age of sixty-five believing that someone like her mother was going to adjust? Who would expect her to adjust? Her heart's been cut out of her body. Look at her. There's nothing left of her but soft, weeping flesh. Her bones have been extracted, and with one hand she picks at the skin of the other. Overnight these hands have acquired a plucked, leathery, spotted look to them. Her eyelids have purpled, and the eyes themselves are dull and childish. Her mouth sags. Her chin hangs on her chest. She refuses to dress herself. Fay has to remind her to brush her teeth. Nevertheless, her breath is rank. She pushes her food away. Despite the drugs, she can't sleep more than a few minutes at a time. Submissive, she hangs on to Fay's hand hour after hour. "Let me brush your hair," Fay pleaded with her this morning, but she shook her head; her scalp is so tender, she couldn't bear the thought of a hairbrush or even a comb.

A number of things have to be dealt with immediately. Fay sits down with Clyde and Bibbi at her mother's dining-room table—already she is thinking of it as her mother's table, not her father's—and together they make a list.

First, there is the question of Peggy McLeod's gynecological practice. What should they do? Her receptionist, Melanie Letkemann, will have to be told. Patients who have appointments during the next month must be phoned and given referrals. "Will that be enough time?" Bibbi asks in her soft, bewildered voice. "A month?"

They consider. A month is as far ahead as any of them can think.

The three of them stare down at the walnut dining table. Clyde taps the figured surface with a thumbnail. An heirloom from—but Fay can't remember which side of the family it comes from. Once, she knew. Probably it is a hundred years old. Substantial, highly polished, the grain unusual and for that reason prized. Most of the evening meals of her childhood took place at this table. Christmas dinners, birthdays, celebrations. At one end their father, irreducible, uxorious, sat and carved. At the other end their mother served mounded vegetables, divided pies and cakes, smiled, presided.

They will need a lawyer. Clearly Hank Lerner, the McLeods'

family lawyer, won't do. Like Dr. Plette he is too old, too entrenched, too familiar, too thick. Fay mentions Patricia Henney, the lawyer who oversaw her condo purchase. Clyde says he will ask Sonya for some names. As soon as they have decided definitely on someone, Fay says, they can set up a meeting and discuss what should be done. If anything. What can be salvaged.

The word "salvage" seems to clatter on the tabletop. Why has she said it? Bibbi looks up, frightened. Clyde sets his jaw. Fay puts her hands over her face.

One of them will have to talk to their father. Not today, not tomorrow, but soon. Both Fay and Bibbi look at Clyde.

"M-m-maybe we should all g-g-g-go to see him," Clyde says. "Together."

"No," Bibbi says, "no." She folds her hands tightly on the table. Her eyes are filmed with tears. "We can't do that. We can't confront him like that, not all three of us."

"No," Clyde agrees. "We can't."

This is a bad dream, Fay thinks. She stares for several seconds over the top of Clyde's head, straight into the fanciful carving of the walnut buffet, another heirloom, and then up at an old giltframed watercolor of pale green poplars against a yellow sky. Her parents have owned this painting forever. She's grown up with those splotched poplars without ever really seeing them—the daubed leaves and unspecified background. Anonymous. Bibbi is biting her nails, and Fay wonders if she is thinking about Jake Greary, wanting to get on a bus this very minute and hurry home to him, to their three shared rooms over the shoe-repair shop in the North End; Fay wonders, too, about Jake Greary. How will he regard this sudden rupture in his lover's family? With cold triumph? A bourgeois black hole?

Clyde is glancing at his watch, a quick, furtive look, and Fay understands that he's anxious to be on his way, home to Sonya and his children, his stronghold, away from this nightmare.

"Well," Fay says at last, "maybe I should go to see him."

She cringes, hearing her big-sister voice, her vowels full of deadened authority. She looks at her brother and sister, who continue to study the tabletop and say nothing. "But I haven't the faintest idea what I can say to him."

"How is she?" Tom asked. He had stopped in at the Ash Avenue house to deliver a suitcase of Fay's clothes.

"Terrible. She's asleep at the moment, but she didn't sleep at all last night."

"I miss you terribly."

"I miss you, too."

"Do you?"

"You know I do." She put her arms around him. In his heavy wool overcoat his body held the freshness of nourishing reality. And he wore a brown cloth cap she had never seen before, which made him seem like a visitor from an old-fashioned world of simplicity and privilege. "You're cold," she said. She was moved to do something kind for him but couldn't think what. "Your face is freezing."

"You're warm." He rubbed her upper arms with his hands. "You feel wonderful."

She held on to him. "It's been a misery, sleeping alone up there in that little twin bed. I feel so—" She stopped, shook her head.

"How?"

"I don't know. Maidenly and responsible. It's all so heavy. And I can hear her crying. Hour after hour."

"Ah, Fay." He held her close.

"Do you know what I did last night?" she said.

"What?"

"It was strange. In the middle of the night I had this terrible longing to hear your voice. I was all of a sudden dying for it. And then I remembered that I *could*. I could just switch you on. With a flick of the dial I could have what I wanted."

"And?"

"I kept it on low. You were doing your Paul Anka shtik. Oh, you were lovely. Corny but lovely."

"Look, are you sure you don't want me to stay here, too? Just temporarily. I could easily—"

"It would be wonderful. But she can't bear to have anyone in the house who isn't family. Not yet, anyway. She's got this idea—"

"What?"

"That she doesn't want anyone to know."

"That he's left?"

"She's made us all promise not to tell a soul. She's even sworn Dr. Plette to secrecy. Not that we trust him for five minutes."

"People are bound to know sooner or later." He bit his lower lip. "In a city this size."

"If they don't already."

He paused. "It really isn't reasonable."

"I know, I know. But *she's* not reasonable. Not rational, I mean. She's suffering. If you saw her, Tom—it's heartbreaking."

"Does she think he might come back?"

"She doesn't say so in so many words."

"What do you think?"

"I think she's expecting him to come home any minute. Every time the phone rings she freezes. She thinks he's calling to say it was all a misunderstanding. Or temporary insanity or something."

"It is possible, isn't it? Temporary insanity? Maybe he's having some kind of breakdown? In the first year of retirement people often do."

"She never dreamed anything like this could happen. Well, none of us did. I guess we're all still in shock."

"Is there anything I can do?"

"There is one thing, Tom."

"What?"

"I wonder if you'd phone Iris Jaffe for me. About the shower she's giving for me Thursday night."

"What about the shower?"

"Can you make some excuse, say I'm terribly sick or something. Maybe she can postpone it."

"Are you sure you want to do that?"

"I couldn't face it. All those old friends. All that joviality."

"What I meant was, don't you think you ought to take Iris into your confidence? She won't believe me for a minute, that you're sick, I mean."

"Maybe you can think of something else."

"I don't know, Fay. It would be a whole lot simpler if you just told her what's happened."

She stared at him. His expression seemed for a moment closed, not unkind but carrying a kind of willed incomprehension. "Tom, I just can't bring myself to talk about it yet. I can hardly talk about it even to Bibbi or Clyde. Iris will ask me why."

"Why he's left?"

"I keep thinking there's a missing piece here. Something we're not taking into consideration."

"But what did he say to your mother when he left?"

"She doesn't know, she's terribly confused about it. He felt crowded, she says, he couldn't breathe. Something like that."

"But couldn't you—ask him?"

"I don't know."

"I gather you haven't talked to him yet?"

"No."

"Not even on the phone?"

"No, not yet."

"What about Clyde? Or Bibbi?"

"They haven't talked him, either. We're just trying to—"

"What?"

"Catch our breath, I guess. And figure out our strategy."

He picked up her hand in both of his and stared at it for a minute. "When are you planning to see him?"

She opened her mouth. What came out was a shameful whimper of sound.

"When, Fay?"

"Tomorrow. Tomorrow for sure."

IN MOMENTS of great or sudden emotion people utter strange words.

"Daughter," Richard McLeod said to Fay when he opened the door and saw her standing there. It was three o'clock on a Wednesday afternoon. Six days since he'd left home.

He'd rarely addressed her in this formal way. *Daughter*, like a tag of dialogue out of an Elizabethan play. His tone was mild, deliberately so, it seemed to Fay.

"Won't you come in?" he said, and opened the door wider.

He had found himself a small furnished apartment on the top floor of a building in the west side of the city, a flat-roofed, ugly low-rise block put up in the fifties or sixties.

The afternoon sky was brushed with pink and purple. Clumps of gray snow clung to the misshapen shrubbery that flanked the entrance, and wet tracked slush made the floor of the small lobby dangerous. The walls were painted a shiny tan. Fay had never seen this building before, had never, in fact, driven down this particular street. One of the doorbells was marked "R. McLeod." She rang, and a buzzer let her in. Her own father, R. McLeod, lived in this bland brick building; the realization made her stumble slightly on the slippery tile, and she was assailed by a potent mix of belief and disbelief. R. McLeod of Ash Avenue, retired dry-cleaning executive, husband of Peggy McLeod, father of Fay, Clyde, and Bibbi McLeod, this man now occupied an apartment in an anonymous flat-roofed building off Berry Road, out by the airport; he *resided* here, was *domiciled* here.

The tiny elevator, bewilderingly lined on three sides with mirrored squares, swayed slightly as it ascended, and the single-panel door opened with a jerk. Gravy smells pervaded the long hallway, and a different smell, a sharp chemical odor, emanated from the hard, tufted, fire-resistant carpet and from the hardware on the apartment doors. Number 510 was at the far end. Her father stood there waiting, the door partly open.

What struck Fay most forcibly was the fact that he looked exactly as he always did.

Her father. She observed him as she might a stranger: an elderly, slightly stooped gentleman in a green buttoned cardigan and soft gray trousers. His white hair sat lazily on his head. He looked comfortable, amiable, self-possessed, mildly paternal; he looked, to her surprise, sane. His eyes blinked once or twice seeing her, but with his usual lively and familiar blue-toned sanity.

"I suppose," his fatherly voice was saying, "that you've come to save me from myself."

Fay considered. Those were not the words she had planned to use. She glanced at the miniature hallway, just big enough to swing a cat—as her mother always described such mean spaces. "Well, yes," she said finally.

"Then you've come in vain, I'm afraid." He spoke sadly.

"Look can't we go somewhere and talk?"

He paused for a second. "Why not right here?"

A quaver in his voice, yes, definitely a quaver, and Fay took this as a hopeful sign. "All right," she said.

He led her into a dimly lit living room.

What made it so dark? She looked around and observed that everything in the room—the chairs, the curtains, the carpets—was some shade of brown. Even the view from the ugly double window was brown, a brown sky, the color of cocoa, midafternoon on a dark November day. She saw a newspaper spread on a beige chair. Her father's reading glasses were folded on a rather spindly lamp table. Those two artifacts, his glasses, his newspaper, seemed to her to be ringed with dull light.

"Your coat," he said, remembering himself. "Can I take your coat?"

"I think I'll leave it on." She said this primly, surprised at herself.

"Sit down, at least."

"Just for a minute."

He lowered himself into a chair. "I suppose you think I've taken leave of my senses."

She settled herself on the edge of an ottoman which was

mouse-colored, rough-textured, not particularly clean. "Yes," she said at last, repeating his words and even catching his tone. "We think you've taken leave of your senses."

He sighed loudly, so loudly that she suspected him of being deliberately dramatic. "I suppose in a way I have."

"In a way!" Fay exclaimed, unable to help herself.

"I only wish it were possible to take leave of my senses without causing everyone so much pain. This is terribly awkward for you in particular, Fay, I know that, just before your own marriage, yours and Tom's. I thought I would be able to hold on a little longer, but—well, I can't tell you how much I regret causing so much anguish. Especially to your mother."

She gave a low moan. "Then why are you doing this to her?" A long weak breath rose up from her chest. "And to us?"

"It was something that happened." He laced his fingers together and leaned forward. "I didn't will it."

"When I think how her whole heart's been devoted to you, everything she cares about. You do know that?"

"Yes, I do know that."

"You've met someone else. You've fallen in love with someone else."

"No."

"Oh." For the first time she felt she might cry.

"Your mother must have told you."

"She's tried. She's not at all coherent, as you can imagine. And we didn't—"

"Didn't what?"

"We didn't believe her."

"I tried and tried to make her understand. It isn't easy."

"You felt smothered. That's what she said."

"Yes."

"What exactly is that supposed to mean?"

"Just—smothered. There wasn't any air."

"Smothered with what? Love?"

"I couldn't breathe."

"And now?" She gestured at the walls, the oppressively ugly ceiling tile, the pair of dreary windows with their stiff synthetic curtains "Now you can breathe?"

"Fay. Look at me. We've always been able to talk to each other. When I think of all the things we've talked about."

"It seems as though—" But the noise of a plane flying overhead drowned her out.

"As though what?"

"As though we never talked about *you*. We only talked about me, about my life, the things I needed."

"I thought perhaps you might have some inkling of . . . of how things were. I thought that you, more than anyone else, might understand."

"Couldn't you have just—I don't know—just gone off for a holiday or something. To think things through. This is all so . . . so—"

"Drastic. Yes, I know, I know."

She sat up straight. "I think you should see a doctor."

"Because you think I'm sick, is that it? In fact, I have seen a doctor. I, too, thought I must be sick."

"And?"

"It turns out I'm in acceptable health. For my age."

"I meant a shrink. A psychiatrist."

"That's what I meant, too."

For a minute they sat in silence. Fay could hear the wind gnawing at the window frame and, far below, the murmurous river of traffic. A second plane passed overhead, so noisy she shuddered. These cheap buildings had next to no insulation. She wondered how on earth he'd chosen such a terrible place, and if there'd been a measure of penance involved. "Do you mean to tell me," she said finally, "that a man of sixty-six who leaves his wife after forty years of marriage is mentally balanced?"

He lifted his hands helplessly, shaping them around a circle of air, and she was struck by the frailty of the gesture.

"Don't you feel anything for her at all? After all the years you've spent together?"

"Of course I do. Your mother is an astonishing woman, a warm, loving woman. I got *lost*, that's all, in all that warmth and loving. It's—"

"What?"

"Complicated. For all concerned."

"Are you living here"—Fay gestured again at the beige wall-paper—"alone?"

"Yes." And then he added, "completely alone."

"I see," she said. The room was unbearably hot, but she felt, for some reason, determined to keep her coat buttoned up to the chin. The mocking tone of her voice surprised her. "So suddenly, after all these years, you've decided you want to live in a little furnished apartment all by yourself."

He waved his wrists again, making irresolute arcs with his hands, and gazed at the window. A mottled light settled on his face. "It wasn't really sudden."

"Not"—she paused—"sudden?"

"No."

"I see." But she didn't see.

"No, not at all sudden. I've thought about it for a long time."

"There must be more to it than that."

He lifted his hands again, feebly, and shook his head.

They fell then into a short silence, broken only when Fay reached out abruptly and took his hand. "Problems between peo-ple," she began, her voice shaking with what she recognized as self-disgust, "can be resolved, you know that as well as I do. Even problems of long standing. It happens every day. Peo-ple . . . people make new kinds of arrangements. They, well, they renegotiate."

"Oh, yes, I know."

"But you're not willing to, is that it?"

"I wish," he said, "I wish it didn't have to be like this." He withdrew his hand. "I want you to understand that I just couldn't go on any longer."

"Mother thinks . . ." The word "mother" caught in her throat and stopped her.

"Your mother thinks what?" he asked quietly.

"She thinks . . . you'll be coming back. That this is some crazy phase or something you're going through. She thinks you'll change your mind, that whatever it is will blow over and you'll be coming back to her."

"Oh, Fay."

"What?" She was crying openly now, rocking back and forth, holding on to the points of her elbows.

"I won't be coming back. I can't go back."

She leaned toward him, feeling a racketing pity for him, and pity for herself, too. "Why not? Why?"

"Because there's nothing left."

"What do you mean, nothing?"

"Love. There isn't any love left."

LOVE.

Sometimes, lying in bed, resting her face against the hollow in Tom's chest, Fay feels trapped in the shallow rhetoric of Hollywood or of pop music. Everything she pronounces or thinks seems to come winking off a set of diluted song lyrics. *I wanna hold you round the clock. Love is a merry-go-round.* She feels the vapor of stale breath on her throat. *I love you. Baby, baby.* A numbing self-consciousness has made her doubt every word that leaps off her tongue. Not to mention every word that enters her ear. Love, love, how can we possibly speak of love in the last decade of the twentieth century, a century that is, in any case, in tatters?

And hearing her father utter the word "love" was something else, something far worse. What he seemed to gesture toward when he said "love" was a metaphysical ruin. Something laughable and shaggy like the American buffalo, something antique and embarrassing and touching upon a kind of huffing greed. A selfish whim. Something he has no right to say. No right to expect at an age when he can make do perfectly well, as others do, with an ordering of dignity and comfort and the warm bath of memory. Lips, hands, genitals, feet, all fallen. Eyes grown opaque with disenchantment. What does he want, what does anyone want? Love in the wrong place, love at the wrong time. Excess. Wreckage. A black hole. Nothing there.

Save me, she wants to cry out to Tom, save me from all this.

CHAPTER 32

It Groweth Cold

IT'S FRIDAY MORNING, AND HERE SPRAWLS TOM AT FAY'S KITCHEN table, shoveling in the Cheerios, honking down the java. Yup. He's reading the newspaper and trying to get his heart glad on sports scores. He's all alone. Being alone is a big pain, that's what he's thinking, and inside the big pain crouches another, smaller, crescent-shaped pain. It's fastened on to him, it's taken hold. He's trying to dissolve it with rinse after rinse of hot coffee, but it hangs in there, its little teeth brightened with caffeine, biting down mercilessly.

Tonight was supposed to be the night of Jeff and Jenny Waring's buffet supper in honor of his and Fay's forthcoming marriage. Jenny Waring's been cooking up a storm for days, weeks. She's made her famous Chicken Marbella. Forty guests or thereabouts have been invited—his friends, Fay's friends. A coming together. Two rivers meeting, a symbolically charged wha'd'ya-call it?—a confluence. He'd been looking forward to it; it shames him how much he'd been looking forward to it, and now the whole party's been scuppered.

It couldn't be helped, given the situation, but he's grieving, *grieving*.

"Of course I understand," Jenny had said to him when he'd phoned last Tuesday night. "Really, I mean it. What I mean is, things do come up, things happen. Believe me, I know that. Do I ever! I'll get busy right away and phone everyone and explain. And, listen, Tom, I've got all this Chicken Marbella in the freezer, ditto the chocolate torte, I'll just keep it socked away and we'll make it a postwedding bash, okay? Instead of a prewedding thing. When you get back from your honeymoon, you and Fay—South Carolina, isn't it? We can talk about it later. Really, I do understand, honestly. I just hope, well, I just hope it isn't anything serious, that's all."

LOUISE OF GRESHAN'S TRAVEL was nowhere near as understanding as Jenny Waring. "I'm sorry, Mr. Avery, but I did tell you when you first booked that your tickets were final. You remember me saying that, I'm sure you do. Excursion tickets are *final*. I always make that *absolutely* clear to my clients, because we *have* had trouble in the past, people don't understand what cancellation insurance is *for*. I can understand how you feel. If your fiancée was actually sick, if she had a doctor's certificate, we might be able to do something for you, but this is different, this is a contingency of a different color, someone who's used up her vacation time. I hate to say this, Mr. Avery, but she should have checked first. I'm afraid I don't know what to suggest. You're absolutely sure she can't arrange to get more vacation time? I mean, if she explained to her employer? Yes, I remember booking you to San Diego last winter, I've got your file right here in front of me, we do try to look after our regulars, but Mr. Avery, we can't take a loss every time one of our—. Yes, I know this is a honeymoon we're talking about, you told me that. I understand that. No, of course I wouldn't want you to go on your honeymoon alone, that is *not* what I was suggesting, that would be perfectly ridiculous. Look, Mr. Avery.

Please, allow me to make my point. I'm *trying* to explain. Well, I'm doing my best. I *did* speak to the manager about this. I'm sorry. There is nothing we can do. That happens to be our policy, that's all I can say, my hands are tied."

TOM'S MOTHER was on the line, buoyant, breathless. Bright little sparks seemed to fly out of the telephone straight into Tom's ear: "Tom? How're you doing? Pretty busy time right now, I bet, you're right down to the wire practically, just two weeks to go. Whew. The big day. We've got the calendar circled in red. Mike's had the car checked over top to bottom, and guess what? He's got himself two brand-new snow tires. Say we get a great big storm, and there's Mike and me stuck on the highway somewhere, just when they start playing 'Here Comes the Bride' at the church. Every time I think of Fay all got up in her mother's bride dress I get sort of, you know, teary-eyed. I guess I'm getting soft in the noggin, it's my old age or something. Who'd of thunk it!"

TOM CHERISHES his connections in radioland, otherwise he would have quit years ago. The spreading circles of listeners out there in the darkness intrude on his most private affections, and he feels especially warm toward those who phone in to the show, plucking out their own hearts and going at them with a wire brush. The faces may be blank and the voices often deceptively stripped of particularity, but he loves their eager innocence and the way in which they overlap in a kind of black festival heat, letting go for a few minutes of the tight knit of their own lives. He loves them all.

But none of this shared radiance consoles the solitary body, *his* body, alone in a bed, alone at a table, alone in the rubbish heap of his unarticulated thoughts.

Fay is half a mile away, in another bed, part of another household, a household ruptured and sorrowing. He is longing for her, day and night. He's never felt love this close up and he fears its loss. The organs of his body are swollen and dangerous with apprehension, and his throat, too, seems plugged with unspoken words. You are first in my heart, he wants to tell her, but can't.

The phrase feels dated, scented, genteel, sentimental, false, and yet it embraces the whole of his desire. You are first in my heart; now tell me I'm first in yours.

So this is where the years of maturity deliver us—to this needy, selfish, unwieldy wish to be somebody else's first and primal other.

Once—a long time ago, so remote a time, in fact, that the truth of it can be glimpsed only through cracked snapshots or accidents of peripheral vision—he had been first in the heart of a woman, a girl, really, sixteen years old, called Betty Avery. Yes, most assuredly first. But now a man named Mike Barbour is her number one, and no wishing it were otherwise, either.

But what, Tom wonders, becomes of the race of people who fail to achieve this modest human need to be first in someone's heart? Clearly they are a marked breed, a lesser breed. Something serious and damaging happens to them, so that they are irrevocably set apart from the fortunate others, the one who is the first one turned to, thought of, considered, hovered over, cherished, protected, honored. Loved before all others.

Notice me, people cry out, touch me, care for me, think of me, keep a place set for me at the edge of your consciousness, let me be first—is that too much to ask?

> O love is warm
> When it is new
> And love is sweet
> When it is true
> But when it's old
> It groweth cold
> And fades away
> Like the dum dum de dum.

How does that last line go? Tom can't remember. It's driving him crazy. When he gets to the studio tonight he'll check it out. Dum dum de dum?

It's not a song people sing anymore. A sixties song, maybe early seventies—he can't remember—based probably on some ancient ballad, it has that feel to it. It was always rather dolefully sung, he recalls, by male folkies of the Murray McLauchlan stripe, or else in the ripply water tones of people like Joan Baez or Joni Mitchell.

Come to think of it, he's not sure of the first two lines, either; maybe it goes: Love is *sweet,* instead of *warm.* And the second two lines—it might be: Love is *strong* when it is *true.* It's been a good ten years since he's heard it sung. No, Christ, more like fifteen. Maybe even twenty. Twenty years! Twenty years ago he was a kid.

But he's sure of the middle part:

> But when it's old
> It groweth cold

How could anyone forget that pair of benighted lines.

The first time he heard them sung they fell like freezing rain on his ears. A north wind came straight at him. He thought at first he must have misunderstood—for how could a pleasant, slightly schmaltzy folk ballad like this get spiked with blasphemy? *It groweth cold.* The words seemed out of joint not just with the song but with the granola optimism of the times, the way the sense of them butted against the kitschy gold of eternal love, love that swelled, endured, grew richer with the years. *When love is old.*

And yet there was something about those words that drilled straight through to him. They were chilly and strange and darkly, smoochily romantic, but they carried with them—he acknowledged it—the melodic and woeful and ultimately persuasive heft of truth.

WILD NOTIONS come to Tom these days. One of these notions is that he will make an appointment to call on Fay's father, that the two of them will sit down together, two sensible men, and discuss the wreckage that has occurred. He imagines he will be able to pierce to the heart of the calamity, which is something that Fay has not been able to manage. Why are you doing this? he hears himself asking the silver-haired Richard McLeod. What went wrong? What do you want? And then, sternly but kindly: Do you have any idea of the extent of the damage you've done?

He imagines, too, a scene in which he will say to Fay: "Come home. I need you more than your parents do right now." Or, "You have your life and they have theirs, let them work this out." Or, "It's not fair the way you're letting this get in the way of everything else."

He doesn't do any of these things. Instead, while unopened wedding gifts mount up in a corner of the bedroom, he's been living from day to day, every morning and evening phoning Fay and asking how "things" are going.

Things are not going well. She sounds tired and sad, and he pictures her standing by the telephone table in her parents' kitchen, leaning up against the yellow checked wallpaper, bracing herself. One hand will be curled into a fist, and that fist will be pressed to her forehead. She moans and shivers as she talks. Her slenderness of body, which he loves so dearly, translates itself into a thinness of voice, an agitated whisper, in fact, and a deeply distracted manner. Melancholy has eaten away her mouth, and she speaks quickly, as though in a great rush, and covertly, as though she fears being overheard. She reports to Tom her continuing discussions with her father—fruitless. With her mother—confused. With Bibbi and Clyde—conspiratorial. With the lawyer, Patricia Henney—frustrating. With the family doctor—disquieting.

And every day now for the last week and a half—he's been keeping track—she's been fretfully but systematically dismantling that *thing*, that megachip he's come to think of as his happiness, *their* happiness. This steady erosion has taken the form of living under separate roofs and sleeping in separate beds, of hurried, hushed telephone conversations, of canceled parties, a revamped marriage service, a drastic scaling down of the wedding reception, a postponement of the honeymoon. And today, Fay's decision to abandon the wearing of her mother's bridal dress. "It's suddenly occurred to me that I can't possibly wear it," she tells Tom, and it seems to him he can feel the heat of her breath over the wires. "It's not a question of superstition, it's just a question of . . . I don't know. Prancing into a church in that dress, that beautiful unlucky doomed dress, I couldn't bear it, I couldn't risk it, I'll think of something else, just give me time, let me think."

~CHAPTER 33~

Putting Asunder

EVERY MORNING TOM STOPS BY TO DROP OFF MAIL OR WEDDING PRESENTS for Fay. He stays a scant five minutes, the two of them whispering at the doorway as though this house had been transformed into a convalescent home of some kind.

On Thursday he handed over to Fay a number of lavishly wrapped gifts, including a small square package which she opened after he had gone. It was strongly done up in brown paper and bore a local postmark. Her name and address were neatly printed in blue ink, but there was no return address. Inside was a cardboard box, with no note attached, and inside the box, cushioned in tissue paper, was an entrancing little bottle.

She thought at first it was some kind of exotic liqueur, which seemed to her an odd choice for a wedding gift, but a change from the piles of linens, china, and French cookware that had been arriving in recent days. The container was of frosted glass, elegantly shaped, but without a label. The pretty glass stopper had been taped in place. With her thumbnail Fay removed it and sniffed.

The odor sprang out at her, a shouting reek of ammonia that made her wince and draw back. What? What was this! She examined the bottle carefully for a minute, and again put it to her nose. Be calm, be calm, she said to herself. There was something familiar about its awful stink, but what? She held it up to the light and observed the muted transparency of yellowish-green liquid. It was, she thought, rather beautiful; she was reminded of the top layer of lake water seen in a late-afternoon light.

Then comprehension swamped her: the little glass bottle was filled with urine.

Cat urine, dog urine, human urine—which? Not that it mattered. Someone, some person in this city, a city where she had lived all her life, and where her parents and grandparents had also lived, had sent her a bottle of urine. A little gift bottle. Carefully wrapped and consigned. Addressed and stamped. Who? It was midmorning; she was alone in her mother's living room, sitting on the center cushion of her mother's pretty yellow-and-white flowered sofa with a bottle of piss on her lap. She seemed to hear pulsing waves of blood pouring through her heart's valves.

Sun rebounded on the snow outside and streamed into the quiet room through the big southerly window, coating the flat waxed tabletops and lighting upon neat piles of books and magazines. A mantel clock ticked. Heat puffed generously through the brass-grilled registers. One of her father's windmill models sat half finished on a corner table, and upstairs her mother, a little calmer today, was moving about, going through some papers, straightening a drawer.

Her hands gripped the bottle. She was acutely aware of her unsteady body, and she perceived, rather disinterestedly, the cold lumpish entities that were her hands and feet. A bottle of urine had been mailed to her address.

She sat absolutely still, thinking. Who? Why?

Some penalty was being exacted, some bold repayment of pain

for pain, and her first thought, flashing across her mind like a blade of light through a narrow window, was that she must deserve this offering and that some righteous balance was being addressed. People are called upon to accept such judgments, she knew that perfectly well, just as they accept the slippery, dangerous notion that they are owed love.

The sun spread a layer of warmth on her shoulders; the first half of November had been gray, overcast, and now at last there was a flood of wintry yellow. This weak sun seemed to shine in her behalf, but it was not enough, not nearly enough.

After a few minutes other thoughts began to intrude, and dully she welcomed them. She felt, first, a kind of shameful relief that she was alone.

And then came the sly knowledge that she could dispose of this object swiftly and secretly. She would wrap it in several layers of newspaper and carry it straight outside and deposit it in the large plastic garbage container by the back door, making sure it was buried beneath other debris. In a day or two one of the city trucks would arrive and carry it away, and then she would be able to put all her efforts into forgetting its existence, and also what it might mean.

BELIEF, FAY KNOWS, is sometimes perverse. Black represents evil in most of the world's societies, but in a few, a rare half-dozen, black is thought to be the essence of joy.

A rainbow almost everywhere is welcomed as a good omen, but there are groups of people, more sophisticated, perhaps, or more intuitive or cunning, for whom the rainbow represents false redemption, a sneering, overdressed whore.

It once was that mothers and fathers who lost their sons at sea took comfort in the ancient mermaid myth, believing, or pretending to believe, that a form of womanly consolation would reach out from the watery depths and envelop their lost children. But weren't these same mermaids, with their wild greedy wooing, the *cause* of death, tempting the helpless with their hypnotic song? What was to be made of this doubleness, of temptation and its reverse side, which was supreme consolation? Was it possible that the two aspects could be conflated?

Asked to name a magic number, many people will give the number seven. Seven deadly sins. Seven virtues. Seven curses or blessings. Seven stars in a beaming or hostile universe. The seventh son of a seventh son, possessed of psychic powers. The seven sorrows of the Virgin Mother. Seven, that oddly numbered assembly, lucky seven, unlucky seven.

It is late on a Saturday afternoon, the second Saturday in November, and just seven days before Fay and Tom's wedding day. The year is unfolding, coming to an end, in fact, and so, Fay suddenly divines, is her good luck.

The clues lie all around her, masked by an early twilight, but sharp with logic—desertion, disruption, and a storm of foreboding that has been augmented in recent days by the trapped fetid threat of bodily harm, that bottle of urine she will never be able to forget or speak of, but which she divines is wrapped up in the darkness of Tom Avery's history, one of those wives.

The thought of this secret knowledge, how she will have to carry it all her life, frightens her. She will not be able to speak of it to anybody, she realizes, not even to Tom—something will prevent her, some inviolable notion she has constructed of herself, nice Fay McLeod, her niceness grown over her like a deadly coat of lacquer.

She remembers suddenly what she has forgotten, or perhaps brushed aside, how in Mexico women who have survived three husbands are called man-eaters. They are avoided, shunned, regarded by everyone as unlucky, and yet they exert a kind of hypnotic power.

Her own body frightens her, too, the way it feels stretched thinly from point to point so that it has no substance of its own. Her brain is tired, it wants to rest, to lie down. Everywhere she looks she is pierced with the fragility of human arrangements, and she finds that she is continuously on the point of weeping.

No, no, she suddenly sees; she cannot open her body to such harm.

Out of love people make absurd, misguided choices. Love has a way of attaching to unlucky objects and pinning its faith on a curtain of air. Out of love, or its punishing absence, her drugged mother is slumped today before a television set, watching a game show. Her father, who has survived on love's diminishing curve all these years, or so he tells her, has exiled himself to a dark brown solitary cave. And Tom Avery, that altogether shadowy presence, that dangerous stranger, is waiting, right now, right this minute, for her telephone call—she's promised to phone him at seven o'clock and deliver a bulletin on the state of affairs.

"Tom," she finds herself stammering into the receiver. "Listen, Tom, I'm so sorry, I don't know what to say, I'm so sorry, but this just isn't going to work out."

ONE DAY, a year ago, Fay was crossing Osborne Street where it meets River Avenue, and a heavy truck rounded the corner and missed her by half an inch. She was struck on her thinly covered legs by the full, breathy, immediate terror of displaced air; the truck, in fact, had passed so close to her that its swaying bulk had buzzed the hem of her coat.

She remembers that she stood swaying for a moment on the curb, too shocked and bewildered to react. The huge truck thundered on its way, dissolving into traffic and leaving her overwhelmed by a drenching sensation of weakness. The air around her felt watery and wasteful, though she took great gulps of it into her mouth. "That was a close call," someone nearby said, and someone else said, "I sure hope you got that fellow's license number."

Dazed, she shook her head, recognizing, finally, that the thudding presence in her chest was her own heart, whose violent rocking rose up and flooded the cavities behind her ears. For a moment she was convinced she was about to drown.

And then confusion receded. She found herself paralyzed with terror, but also wonder. She was alive. Oxygen flowed through the gills of her body. The relief of it, to be standing on her own feet, alive.

This sensation was close to what she experienced immediately after telling Tom Avery that it was impossible for them to go on. That it was over. That it wasn't going to work out. A sense of salvation was what she felt. Profound relief. A narrow escape.

THE PROBLEM with stories of romance is that lovers are always shown in isolation: two individuals made suddenly mythic by the size of their ardor, an ardor that is declared to be secretive or else incomprehensible to the rest of the wide buzzing world. And the moment love is seized upon and named, the lovers are magically released from a need for dentists, for tax advisers, for shoe salesmen, for anyone who stands outside their immediate sphere of passion.

Perhaps it is even a subtle form of ostracism. Fay has noticed how love in old-fashioned novels and modern films tends to be shown as a rarefied blessing, accompanied usually by perfect health, full employment, closets full of clothes, and, most particularly, a conspicuous absence of other people. She wonders why it is that lovers in books are cast adrift—at candlelit tables set for two, in the streets of alien cities, wandering hand-in-hand on abandoned beaches—where they are free to stew in their unnatural seclusion, removed from human interference or even human needs. Their families, their friends, even their work and their separate histories pale beside their rapture, which lies outside of life, not within it. The pains and contrivances of fictitious lovers belong only to themselves, an enclosed circle, a symmetry of limbs and matched yearning, a snug, rounded universe with its own laws.

But none of this is true. The world does not retreat. It presses even closer, offering relics of failure, pointing to omens, making dire predictions, whispering warnings. Which was why Fay said what she did to Tom Avery on the telephone: that things weren't going to work out after all.

FAY HAS SEEN people at funeral receptions throw back their heads and laugh. At one time she found this kind of behavior shocking, but no longer. The wiring of a human brain is, after all, complex. There's no telling how people will react to the unexpected.

When she told her brother, Clyde, that she and Tom Avery were not going to be married, that the wedding was canceled, he said: "Jesus Christ!" He was breathing hard. "You can't d-d-d-o this, Fay. P-p-postponing is one thing, but c-c-c-canceling! You just can't. Whose idea is this, anyway, yours or his?" He knocked a fist against his forehead. His face was red and ridged. "Oh, my g-g-good God, it's what I've always said, you're afraid to t-t-take a chance. We all t-t-take a chance. That's what it means, getting m-m-married. I only knew Sonya s-s-six months. I don't know how I'm going to t-t-tell her—Sonya, I mean. She'll go c-c-crazy when she hears about this."

"Listen, Fay," Sonya said. "If you've really got serious doubts about this man, now's the time to call a halt. Right now. Not that we don't all have doubts. I remember the day before Clyde and I got married, I looked in my bedroom mirror and I said, 'Holy matrimony, I'm about to give myself in holy matrimony.' Just those two words, they scared me to death. It's true you haven't known Tom that long. I liked him, though, right from that first day at the birthday party. But it's you, you're the one, you've got to trust him completely, and I mean completely. This is your life, and don't let Clyde get to you."

"Oh, Fay," Bibbi said. Her beautiful soft mouth was wide open. "Are you sure this is what you want? You've been right in the middle of all this—all this awful sadness. But it doesn't have to be that way with you and Tom—what I mean is, everyone makes their own arrangements, and we can't know how other people make theirs tick along, if you see what I mean. We can't see into their lives, into their heads. I wish I could see into your head. I wish I could help you."

"What a mess," Iris said. "Christ. A lot of mess and fuss and embarrassment and grief, but don't worry. You know how you feel and that's what matters. Let me know what I can do. Where's the guest list? I'll start phoning. And I'd better get to the caterer's fast."

"Oh, boy," Beverly Miles said, "this is bad, bad news. But you know what I honestly think? I think you've got a major case of the wedding jitters, so, listen, why don't you just give Tom a call and tell him you need to talk this over, tell him you got scared, it happens, but now it's okay."

"Hmmm," Muriel Brewmaster said, "I guess I did have some doubts right from the first. Maybe I shouldn't be saying this, but I wondered if you weren't rushing things a bit, and I kept thinking to myself, a disc jockey, Fay's going to marry a disc jockey. I couldn't get over it. Not that there's anything wrong with being a disc jockey, but. And his track record, marriagewise, that's another thing."

"Oh, Fay," Hannah Webb said. "I can't bear this, I think I'm going to cry, everything seemed so perfect, you were glowing, just glowing. We were going to have the loveliest little champagne reception for the two of you, the whole staff, and the board, too, a surprise, it was all planned, and now—"

"Oh, my dear," Richard McLeod said over the telephone. "I think you need to give yourself some time. Go away for a couple of days and give yourself a break, the two of you. These last few weeks—you can't possibly be thinking straight. Of course, I hold myself responsible, how can I not? My dear, dear child. No, I haven't forgotten about his three unfortunate marriages, but I thought you had accepted that as a given, that you'd reached some kind of an accommodation. You were certain. 'This is it,' you said. Do you remember? We were sitting on the porch drinking iced tea. Oh, it seems a million years ago, but I remember how happy you looked, radiant."

"This is a terribly serious decision," Peggy McLeod said, rising and putting her arms around Fay, who was astonished to see her mother so composed, "but only you can know what's right." Her voice was unexpectedly firm.

Fay allowed her own rangy body to be enclosed by her mother's neat little arms. "It's bound to be hurtful for you both," she went on, "but it's not the first time it's happened in the history of the world, and people do recover. They go on. There, there, love, cry your heart out if you want to, and then we'll sit down and make a list of what needs doing."

"I saw this coming," Tom said to her over the telephone, coldly, dully, from a great distance. "I knew it was coming."

"I'M SO SORRY," she'd said into the silence. "I'm so sorry."

The echo drummed in her head for days. A woman being sorry. A sorry woman. What does it mean to be sorry? Is being sorry a kind of pocket in which a hollow promise is placed, a promise to make amends, to imagine that some sort of brutal realignment might take place?

"I'll look after everything," she told him, and even to her ears this sounded like a dishonorable offering.

And there *were* things to be done. The undoing of arrangements, the phone calls to be made, the notes to be written, the explanations, the confessions of failure and doubt, the unknotting of recent time—all this busyness kept her breathing, and she was grateful, particularly after her first dazed sensation of relief left her.

She was astonished at what there was to do, so many details, so many chiming voices to be listened to and answered. The rhythms of the house rolled over like a kind of weather. Attention had to be paid to practical hour-by-hour demands, twenty-four hours a day, every day a matter of schedules and priorities, every night a sorry box where she lies down and grieves.

It's at night that she thinks about Tom. He seems at times to be in the bedroom with her, upstairs in the guest bedroom of her mother's house, pushing away the darkness with his body. An archaic phrase from the wedding service comes to her: *with my body I thee worship.* It is a phrase that has gone out of fashion; she hasn't heard it for years, but now it presses close against her, brushing her lips, disturbing, but also comforting.

"WELL, THAT'S IT, I think," Peggy McLeod said. "I think we've contacted everyone."

"What about Onion?" Fay asked. "We still haven't heard from Onion."

"I left two or three messages at the hospital. I'm sure they've been passed on to her."

"It seems funny she hasn't phoned."

"She's distracted, poor lamb, you know that." She said this in a mild shrugging manner that Fay found startling.

She looked up. "Lamb?" she said. "I never think of Onion as a lamb."

"Oh, but that's just what she is."

It was true, Fay thought—Onion, who loved her so sternly, so singularly, asked nothing of her beyond the most simple attachment. Love without indulgence, that rare thing, and her mother had recognized it. A lamb, yes.

In the last few days her mother has regathered some of her old strength. She is sleeping better and eating normally, and is on the phone daily to Muriel Brewmaster and her other friends; yesterday she slipped out for an hour to go to the hairdresser's, driving herself there in her Fiesta, and when she came home she wrote a reminder to herself to have the left-rear tire checked.

Furthermore, she has taken on herself the awkward and tedious job of returning Fay and Tom's wedding gifts, a task that she performs with the unstudied competence that has made her famous among her friends—even though the rituals of dismantling a marriage ceremony are new to her.

All this surprises Fay. She hadn't expected anything like this. And certainly not so soon.

~ CHAPTER 34 ~

Practicing
to Die

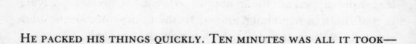

He packed his things quickly. Ten minutes was all it took— shirts, sweaters, socks, underwear, shoes.

All these things made a very small pile. His suitcase was in Fay's hall closet, parked there. He opened it brutally on the bedroom floor and filled it. Belts, ties, jackets, his razor. He reminded himself to keep breathing, to draw out each separate exhalation as long as possible, so that the air in his chest burned and blew as though there were a separate creature trapped there. This rough breathy music drove a wedge through his bewilderment. His head felt torn with fever; he imagined a spray of cartoon lightning bolts breaking through his hair and entering the stratosphere.

What else? He glanced around the bedroom and saw the clock radio. Yes or no? He touched it with the flat of his hand and remembered Fay's arm in the early morning, reaching out blindly for the dream bar, an extra ten minutes of sleep. The thought made the pulse in his throat jump like a gun. No. He'd leave the clock radio where it was. Its luminous digital mechanism sickened him, that terrible greenish grin turning over minute by minute.

He stripped the bed. He did this to hurt her, yanking back the blankets, ripping off the sheets and carrying them into the little laundry room, where he squashed them into the washer and banged down the lid.

He left a lamp burning in the bedroom. Its yellow glare fell across the wide bare mattress.

Then he picked up his suitcase and left, twisting the key from his ring and pushing it under the door.

He crossed the street, kicking through lightly falling snow. In the distance he could hear the whooping of an ambulance and the other city sounds of traffic and channeled wind. The door of his old apartment building opened easily into a cubicle of dusty warmth, and he remembered that the winter before there'd been a problem about winos sleeping in the foyer on cold nights. Well, why not? What was the harm? A refuge. He found his key in his pocket, and the thought came to him: so this is why I kept the lease up, for this.

His old rooms were silent, comfortless, chilly. Maybe they had always been chilly, he couldn't remember. He turned up the thermostat and ducked his head into the kitchen, not sure what he expected to find there. It was odorless, spruce. For at least a minute he stood in the half-dark living room, observing the shadowy arrangement of furniture. His new furniture—he could smell the newness emanating from the twin sofas, the only fragrance in the room, glue and sizing. Its richness disgusted him as much as its cheapness. At last he went into the bedroom, where he put down his suitcase, and then, with his heavy winter coat still buttoned across his chest, he lay down on the bed and closed his eyes.

"Tom?" she had said on the telephone. "Don't hang up. Are you still there?"

"Yes."

"You aren't saying anything."

"What would you like me to say?" Politely.

"I don't know. Something."

"I saw this coming. I could have bet money on it."

"We should . . ." There was a silence from her end, and then a choking sound.

"We should what?" he asked, bearing down.

"We should at least get together and talk about this. We need to talk this over."

"Why?"

"Because . . . we . . ."

He waited patiently. "Because why?"

"Because . . . we owe it to each other."

"I don't think so."

"Just for a few minutes. We'd feel better, both of us."

"I wouldn't."

"Please, Tom. I could come over right now. We could sit down and—"

"No."

"I'm so sorry. I can't tell you how sorry I am."

"I'm going to hang up now, Fay."

"Tom, wait—"

"Right now."

"I just want you to understand—"

"Good-bye."

"Look, Tom," Ted Woloschuk said on Sunday night, or rather four o'clock on Monday morning, after "Niteline" went off the air. "How 'bout giving me a minute or two before you head off home. I just want to say I appreciate you telling me what you did before airtime, for letting me know what's happened and all. It's plain as anything that you're going through a real bad time. I don't know how you did it tonight, carrying on with the show. You did great. It was a great show. This is just, just a terrible thing. All your plans, everything, down the drain. Ahhhh! I always try to be the optimist, sometimes it's hard, but I try, and what I want to say is—I've been turning this over in my head all night long—I want to say to you that maybe it's for the best. Who knows, maybe some things aren't meant to be, maybe they aren't supposed to work out, if you know what I mean. Better to find out now than, say, two, three years down the road, eh? You know what folks say about rushing into things, it's easy enough tying the knot but not so easy getting it untied. Well, you know that. But listen, Tom, you can't let this get to you. Because it can. It can get a person depressed. People can stew about things and get themselves into real trouble. Maeve and me, we're worried sick right now about our boy Patrick, he's been going out with a particular girl, all last spring and summer, right up to the end of October, and all of a sudden it comes to nothing, we don't know the whole scoop, he won't say much, he's always been a quiet kind of kid, but ever since it happened he comes home for supper and just lays around the house like he's sick. It's like he hasn't got any energy in him anymore, and here's a bright young kid with his whole future ahead of him. We don't know what to do. Maeve wanted to phone up this girl, her name is Joan, she's a real nice girl, and smart as a whip. Maeve thought she could maybe talk to her, try to tell her how serious and bad this is for Patrick, but we can't do that, that would be like stepping in where we've got no business, it's like our hands are tied. We even thought of maybe phoning one of those crisis lines. Maeve's going crazy with worry. Patrick just lays there on the couch, not saying a word to anyone, just staring at the TV but not seeing a thing. It's like he's practicing to die, Maeve says."

IT'S SAID THAT dreams come out of a darker, windier place than we like to acknowledge.

One night, soon after Fay's phone call, Tom dreams he's in a strange pink room with soft fleshlike walls. There are no windows or doors, just four pale trembling walls that heave in and out, mimicking his own breathing body. After a while the floor, too, begins to soften and heave, and he tries hard to keep his balance, but can't. He scrambles like a soft-shoe artist to stay upright, to avoid having to touch the undulating surfaces. As if to explain his clumsiness, he points to his bare feet—for some reason he has

misplaced his shoes and socks—and insists, in a stagy, grossly am-
plified radio voice, that none of this is his fault, that he didn't come
here by choice.

In the morning he wakes late with a dry mouth. He stumbles
into the bathroom and stands before the mirror, speaking to his
dwindled self. So, he says in a rough voice, what did you expect?

His face looks like a chestnut's split casing. Avid. Unhealthy.

The stickiness of pop lyrics has led him astray. Falling in love.
Falling. Fallen. (Grow up.)

He thinks about going for a walk and glances out the bathroom
window. The morning is beautiful, cold, still. Snow covers Grosvenor Avenue, a perfect fresh wafer of white extending as far as
he can see, wonderfully masking the neighborhood trees and
hedges and roofs. Overhead the sky is a hard flat blue. He remembers a local artist he interviewed on the show a couple of years
back who complained that she had a tough time selling her prairie
landscapes. It seemed people wanted a few fluffy clouds in their
skies. They wanted gradations of color, subtlety. They thought she
was faking it with her clear hard-blue paint.

He wonders whatever happened to his downstairs neighbor,
Mr. Duff—Mr. Duff with his soft meaty gums and his chestful of
phlegm.

He decides, finally, against going for a walk. He remembers
that he's left his good outdoor boots in Fay's apartment; he has
another, older pair, but he's not sure where they are—probably
in the back of his hall closet covered with dust balls. He'll creep
back into bed instead, pull up the covers.

But he's frightened of falling back into his dream again, those
pink pulsing corrosive walls.

JEFF WARING phones Tom and says in a voice that is stiff with
kindness and tact: "Tom? Jeff here. Just wanted to touch base. We
also wanted to let you know we were, uh, notified. About your
plans. The *change* of plans, I should say. Fay's sister phoned us, at
least I think it was her sister. Jen and I got to thinking, well, we
just hope things work out. One way or another. Not a bad idea,

rethinking the situation. More people should do it, that's what Jen says, before they rush into things. Jen says to tell you she'll give you a call in a couple of days, see if we can get together, maybe take in a hockey game on the weekend. How does that sound?"

Rethinking the situation. A useful phrase. A saving phrase, and he's someone who needs saving.

He adopts it as his own. "We're rethinking the situation," he tells the people who phone, the people at work, the people he runs into. He even says it to himself, eyeballing himself in the mirror. *Hi there, buddy, I understand you're rethinking the situation.*

Right.

Big Bruce says: "Take a vacation. You ever been across the pond? Now's the time. The French franc's weak right now, sterling too. I'd rather head off for the Caribbean myself, one goddamned cathedral's just like the next one as far as I'm concerned, but it'd do you good to get away, and I mean *away*. Take a couple of weeks, three weeks, recharge the batteries. Lenny'll come in and do the show for us, give yourself a break. You're doing a great job, the ratings are terrific, but this is just a radio show, fella, you don't have to nail yourself to the cross."

"Are you okay, Tom?" Liz Chandler asks. "Listen, I don't want to interfere or anything, there's nothing worse than someone jumping into someone else's private matters, but, well, I guess just about everybody knows that the McLeods have split up, Fay's parents I'm talking about. Marriage! God, it's scary. Gene and I've been married eight years now, and there've been plenty of scary times, especially right after Chrissie was born. It was rocky for a while there, maybe you noticed, I felt I was being pulled in three different directions. And listen, don't worry about the wedding present—it's a waffle iron, why don't you just keep it, it might come in useful. I just hope you're okay, we both do."

"We were very sorry to hear the news," said Simon Birrell, and then he said, "These things happen and they seem pretty catastrophic at the time, and then they blow over before you know it."

Betty Avery phoned and said, "You could have knocked me for a loop. Mike, too, we're just stumbling around here like a couple a zombies. But then, as I said to Mike, people get cold feet, I know that, and I don't blame you for a minute, wanting to be careful. I mean, you've had some bad luck and you want to be sure what you're diving into. Give it a few months, take your time. Maybe it'll work out and maybe it won't, but just you remember there're plenty of other gals out there who're dying to settle down and start a family. How about coming home for a few days, the highway's pretty good right now, the plows went right through after that snowfall we had. You've got some vacation time coming, you could stay right through Christmas, lots of your old friends'll be back, a few of them, anyways. At least think about it. And listen, don't waste your time being gloomy, that's one thing I've learned, life's too darned short to sit around being gloomy and glum."

Sheila (formerly Sheila Avery, then Sheila Sweet, now back to being Sheila Woodlock) said: "Christ, Tom, you must be rock bottom. Oh, Christ, I know what you're going through. When Sammy left me for Fritzi I thought I'd—forget it, I didn't phone to dump a bunch of ancient history on your head, and besides, poor old Sammy's gone to his reward, anyway. I phoned because I've been thinking about you all day, having to go through this . . . this anguish, not to mention plain old-fashioned embarrassment. You don't deserve this. You were ripe for things to work out for a change. Maybe they still will, who knows. I gather the McLeods are in a family mess. Well, who isn't. Would you like me to come by? We could sit and talk. To be honest, I don't think you should be alone. I mean that. I remember when Sammy left, I needed someone to hang on to. We could sort of hang on to each other, Tom, we're old hands at that. Anyway, if you change your mind, give me a call. You know me, I'll do whatever I can."

Fay said (at the end of a long letter): "I want you to remember, darling Tom, that none of this has anything to do with you—you're a fine, wonderful, loving man who has given me more happiness than my heart can hold. The problem is with me. I love you dearly—I think you know that—but I can't make this next step.

Other people seem able to do it, but I can't. I can't make promises, and for some reason which I don't understand, I can't bring myself to accept them, either. Please forgive me and please try to understand."

DOES HE WANT to understand her? What does it mean to be understood, anyway? To be eaten alive? He remembers a marriage counselor he and Suzanne once visited in their last desperate days, a sharp-jawed, unsmiling woman who laid the blame for his chaotic marital life squarely on his twenty-seven mothers. (His prized infancy, shot down by "understanding.")

He doesn't want to walk around for the rest of his life with a damaged air, with parts of him missing or mutilated. On the whole, he thinks, understanding has been highly overrated. He'd rather hang in there with his terrible, fumbled incomprehension.

This is what he thinks as he goes about his Christmas shopping. The downtown stores are filled with bustling, frowning, preoccupied shoppers. They push against him with their shoulders and wrapped parcels, knowing nothing about him, who he is, what he's feeling. Carols boom through overhead speakers. *Joy to the World.* A temporary anesthetic. He has a gift list in his hand. He spends lavishly this year, his mother, Mike, his friends, the gang down at the station. He has no idea why. He doesn't understand himself, he doesn't understand anything. Understanding is the last thing on his mind.

~ CHAPTER 35 ~

Important

Announcements

"I'M THINKING," PEGGY MCLEOD SAID TO HER DAUGHTER FAY OVER breakfast, "of maybe going back to work after the weekend."

"To work? To your office?"

"Yes."

"Are you sure you're ready for that?" Fay asked carefully.

Her mother was sipping orange juice and staring into her glass as if mesmerized by its floating particles of pulp. "I phoned in yesterday. The backlog's already enormous."

"But Dr. Suzlov was going to look after your patients for the time being."

"I know, I know, and she's been wonderful, but there are some cases you can't hand over to someone else."

"Do you really think—"

"I think I might be a lot better off if I got out of this house every day and filled up my hours with something useful. With something."

"Well . . ." Fay felt her voice falling down a steep slope.

"And I think you should go back, Fay. You've been home from the center for almost a month, since the first of November. You can't know how I've appreciated having you here. What a pair we've made, a couple of ghosts propping each other up. But your poor mermaids will think you've forgotten them."

Was that a note of merriment she heard in her mother's voice?

"Your mother's a regular dynamo," Muriel Brewmaster had told Fay a few days earlier. "She'll bounce back."

A dynamo? Fay had scowled, doubtful. But she's seen in the last few days how a subtle reordering of strength has taken place, an unconscious, saving shift in the household balance. The chemistry, the mechanics of the conversion elude her, and she senses that these proofs of perception will remain mysterious, despite the fact that they are always on view, part of the domestic scenery; they're too simple and too obvious to be acknowledged, like certain free-floating truths that are given substance only in emblematic acts or images. Lately her mother's been going through cupboards, through a new book by P. D. James, through a parcel of legal documents. (A week ago Fay sat in this kitchen and watched her write the words "Have left-rear tire checked" on a scrap of paper, a reminder to herself.)

Small acts, promptings, scratchings at the future—Fay had been startled, but recognized it for what it was: a sign of recovery, the kind of blind step forward that she herself is going to have to make.

"How ARE YOU doing, Fay?" her friends ask her.

"Okay," she says, or "Fine," or "Not bad."

To herself she announces, I can't bear this.

On Saturday evening she got into a taxi with a suitcase of clothes and moved back into her Grosvenor Avenue apartment. (It's time, she said to herself, making a face and feeling a stitch in her throat.) A pile of mail awaited her. A light was burning in the bedroom—she almost jumped at the sight of it. The bed was stripped clean, the curtains pulled shut. She opened the drawers where Tom's things had been stored and found them bare. His clothes were gone from his half of the closet, leaving a numbing expanse of whiteness filled with wire hangers. She struck these hangers between her hands like cymbals, setting off a weak jangling crash of music. ("I'll get used to this," she announced under her breath.) She thought suddenly of one of his shirts, a finely checked shirt in soft cotton, and the undertow of memory was so strong she had to sit down for a minute on the edge of the bed. If she had that shirt in her hand right now she would press her face into its folds and kiss it.

She became aware that the bedroom was overheated and airless, but it was too cold a night to open a window.

She remembered a nature program she'd seen recently on TV in which the life cycle of a lungfish had been described. The lungfish was a miracle of adaptation, an ugly earth-colored creature capable of surviving long periods of drought. During times when there was no water to be had, it buried itself in mud and slept, sometimes for as long as two years. By lowering its heart rate and blood pressure, it managed to stay alive but to feel nothing.

She lay back stiffly on the bare mattress and wondered if it was too early to go to bed and whether she would be able to sleep.

She wished she could run through the dark streets crying, doing nothing to hold back her spilling tears. But the streets were choked with deep rutted snow tonight, and the wind was excruciatingly cold.

She wondered if Tom was at home—across the street, the third floor, right this minute. Sitting in a room, the kitchen, perhaps, or the bedroom—reading a newspaper, watching television, making himself some kind of meal.

"I can't bear this," she said, bringing her hands up to her mouth like a kind of cup.

ALMOST EVERY DAY she's spoken to her father. They talk on the telephone, or else Fay takes a bus or a taxi to his furnished apartment. It seems to her that if she can only keep talking to him she will be able to bring about some kind of reversal.

Surprisingly, she's grown accustomed to the sight of the dim little living room and the brown lumpish furniture, and accustomed to the sight of her father, too, relaxed in an armchair, one leg crossed over the other, his spectacles balanced in his hand.

They both try hard to discuss normal things. Today, a Sunday afternoon, they talk about the weather forecast—a week of bitter cold—and the fact that "bitter" seems a curious word for a meteorologist to use, a word that is oddly poetic and imprecise and also endearing. They talk about a recent by-election, a swerve to the right, and about the problem of noise from overhead aircraft.

Today he tells her: "I'm glad you've moved back to your apartment, Fay. Even though you may find it difficult at first, being on your own."

And what about you? she wants to ask. How are you finding it, being alone?

He's explained to her over and over, and to Clyde and Bibbi, too, just why he had to leave home, that his long peaceful marriage had somehow overnourished him. He couldn't breathe. He felt watched, insulated, incapacitated.

Fay finds all this baffling. Love is love. Her mother's only transgression, as far as she can see, is to have loved him deeply.

"*Too* deeply," Bibbi said to her a week ago. "Too richly. Too much." Her words had the force of an announcement. "You remember, Fay, when I was nineteen and ran away from home. It wasn't freedom I wanted—that's what everyone thought. Or drugs or sex or craziness or any of those things. I had to get away from all that love. That storm of love, it never let up. You and Clyde had left home by then, and I was in the middle of it. It was like a terrifying magnetic field, it kept pulling me in closer and closer. I knew I was hurting everyone by running away, but I had to. I would have died otherwise."

IT TOOK MORE than an hour for Fay to open her accumulated mail. There were the usual bills: telephone, electricity, Visa, and also a handful of invoices for such items as wedding invitations and for the gold wedding band she had picked out for Tom, a ring which had been sent away for engraving and was now ready to be picked up from the jeweler's. There was an invitation from the Salvation Army to contribute to their Christmas drive. And a reminder from the Handel Chorale about the final rehearsal schedule and the Christmas concert itself. There was a painful clutch of little notes from friends, notes meant to console, to offer hope for the future, to pledge assurance of friendship and understanding, and especially, *especially*, to bridge the awkwardness that accrues around arrangements that have been mysteriously capsized.

Finally, there was a brisk announcement on a red printed card.

> *Fritzi Sweet and Peter Knightly*
> *are Pleased to Announce*
> *their Marriage*
> *which Took Place*
> *at a Family Ceremony*
> *on November Twenty-Third*
> NO GIFTS PLEASE

ON TUESDAY, when Fay finally goes back to the folklore center after an absence of one month, Peter Knightly is the first person she runs into. "Congratulations," she says. The brightness of her voice seems to strike shock waves off the corridor walls.

He looks embarrassed. "I'm so sorry, Fay. About you and Avery calling it off."

Avery!

Shut up, shut up, why don't you.

She is dismayed by how much she hates Peter Knightly at this moment.

No gifts please.

The arrogance.

She has a sheaf of papers in one hand, and in the other her key ring. She wonders what would happen if she raked the keys across his face, how much damage she could do.

She manages a faint smile and gestures vaguely, desperately, in the direction of her office, where a thousand pressing details await her attention: reports, offprints, another enormous pile of mail to open. "I think I'd better . . ."

"Of course," he nods.

A grotesque nod. Almost—she can hardly believe this—almost a *bow*. An absurd, pitying, gentleman's bow. *Oh, God, God.*

She sits at her desk for a minute, panting. What next, what will she do next?

She picks up a thin envelope and slices it open with a paper knife.

Dear Ms. McLeod:

    We are happy to inform you that your interesting and highly original paper, "Mermaids and Meaning," is one of six selected for discussion in the opening session at the June meeting of the NAFA in Chicago. The committee sends you warm congratulations and looks forward to your presentation.

    Program details will follow.

So! She will be going to Chicago, taking her slides along and attempting to persuade a roomful of people that the mermaid myth is at once private and collective, born of sexual longing and a need for solace, or possibly hatched from the residue of racial memory. *Think of it!* In the mythic system the mermaid has specific gravity, even though its legends wobble with beguiling ambiguity.

She will actually do this. (Six months is not far off.) She can already picture herself (new dress? dark green? summer jewelry?) ascending the three or four steps to the platform, arranging her notes on the lectern, clearing her throat, glancing at her watch. A serious professional woman, a little thin, perhaps, but with such a disarming smile, delightful presentation, really, though she's maybe a little defensive during the question period, almost sharp, you might say. A woman who's made her choices, quite possibly one of those women who avoid love out of a fear of its reversals . . . or perhaps . . . perhaps . . .

This is what she'll become. A tourist in her own life. Well, she's going to have to learn a few things—such as how to blow with calm ordinary breath on the happiness of others or else risk being thought ungenerous. Possibly she'll decide to cultivate a leaner and lighter set of responses, nursing at the same time (but slyly) a delectation in the brokenness of friends, collecting stories of divorce and breakdown and deformity and illness. Probably she'll begin to think of her body as a betrayer and resolutely refuse to imagine the shape of the future.

Day by day, that's the way to go. Keeping herself alive on the air of conjecture, scornful of the happy/sad balance sheet of the young, eating off the edge of a table and lying down in her bed at night, rehearsing her anger, counting up her enemies, waiting for the blessing of recovery, knowing it will come.

THE WORST MOMENT of the day is this moment, six o'clock, when she puts her key in her own front door and thinks about what lies on the other side.

What lies on the other side is about to jump out at her. Her feet hurt, she's exhausted. All the way home on the bus she's comforted herself with the thought of a peaceful evening, how pleasant, how agreeable—her pretty living room, her refrigerator full of food. But now, turning the key, comes the moment of terror.

She has strategies, of course. Enter humming. Then switch on the radio fast and fill up the air with electronic hubbub. Tell yourself you'll get used to this, you'll get so you prefer it this way. Pour a glass of cold white wine. Drink it slowly, thinking: I deserve this after a hard day, this little cushion against stillness.

After ten, twenty minutes she really will feel better. She'll find something to eat, something quick, and then she'll go out again—there are all kinds of things to do in the evenings. For one thing, she can't afford to miss any more rehearsals for the Christmas concert. She might sign up for an aerobics class in the new year. Or possibly a course in conversational Russian. The world is full of possibilities, satisfactions.

It's only this one agonizing moment in the day—when she turns her key in the lock and pushes open the door.

It's coming at her, it's about to pounce. The emptiness flowing toward her like a cloud of gas.

"I'm home," she announces to the silent walls.

SHE WENT TO BED with a new book, but she must have drifted off early.

She dreamed she was walking through shallow water in her bare feet. The water was warm, it was lake water, and she could feel her toes gripping the ribbed sand of a lake bottom. She took a step. The sun fell around her shoulders—it was such a surprise, this sunlight—and she moved out a little deeper. But then something called her back. A loud ringing, scolding voice. It went on and on.

She woke slowly, as though she were rising up through a bubble of air. What was this?

Her doorbell was ringing. She opened her eyes, confused by the blaze of light from the bedside lamp and the digits of the clock radio—Tom's clock radio. It was 2:45 in the morning.

There must be some mistake, someone looking for another apartment, someone drunk. She pulled on her robe, shivering. She knew better than to open the door at this hour. "Who is it?" she called out loudly, a hoarse squawk.

"It's Onion," she heard.

"Onion?"

She slipped back the bolt and opened the door.

Onion was wearing her ancient mink coat. Fay couldn't remember a time when she hadn't owned this old, bulky coat, though nowadays she wore it only in the most extreme weather. A plaid woolen muffler was wrapped around her head and knotted beneath her chin. Her face was creased, thin, terrifying, and cold. "He's gone," she said.

Fay blinked.

"Strom. He's gone. Just after midnight. He slipped away."

"Oh, Onion." Fay put her arms around her and drew her inside; she could feel, under the matted fur, the stiff cracked animal skins that had hardened and dried, and beneath that On-ion's trembling body.

"I saw your light was on. I couldn't bear to go home."

"Of course not."

"There's nothing there. Not one thing."

"I know, I know," Fay said, rocking her.

"I was holding on to his arm when he died, rubbing it and rubbing it, trying to keep the pulse alive, but of course he didn't know I was there, he didn't know anything at the end."

"Come in and get warm. Let me get you something hot to drink."

"It was dark, I couldn't bear—"

"Onion, you can stay here. I'll make up a bed—"

"I couldn't bear thinking I didn't belong anywhere, not to anyone."

"You loved each other." Fay said this consolingly, letting it roll out of her mouth.

Onion abruptly drew away from her and gave her head a violent shake, in anger or grief, Fay wasn't sure which. "You've made a mistake, Fay," she said. "I don't know what's got into you, why you've gone and done what you've done, but you've made a terrible mistake, and you've got to stop it right now. You've got to do something. You've got to admit it to yourself. You've got to listen to me for once in your life."

CHAPTER 36

Out of the Blue

THE LANDING WHEEL OF AN AIRPLANE CAME FALLING OUT OF A CLEAR
blue December sky.

The plane was a DC-4, carrying a light load of drilling equipment up from Grand Forks, and coming in at three degrees for
a landing at the municipal airport. It was flying at about seven
hundred and fifty feet when the wheel detached itself. The crew—
pilot, copilot, and flight engineer, all of whom were interviewed
later—claimed they had been unaware that anything was amiss;
their instrument panel had registered only that the wheel assembly
had been successfully lowered.

A number of witnesses, mostly motorists and midday shoppers, watched the wheel as it fell through the air. This fact Tom
Avery found surprising; he would have guessed city dwellers were
too habituated to aircraft noise to stop and look up at a passing
plane.

One of the witnesses was a nineteen-year-old bank employee
named Kimberley Kozak who had just returned from a fast-food

outlet (next door to the bank) with a tray of coffee and sandwiches ordered by her coworkers; it happened to be a few minutes before noon, lunch time. She set the cardboard tray on her desk and dialed the police emergency number, 911. "A wheel just fell off an airplane," she reported in a calm voice. "Just east of Kenaston Avenue, and south of Portage. I don't know what kind of plane it is, just a plane, and it looks like it's about to land." This, too, Tom found surprising: this cool-headed girl, her quickness, and her instinctive notions of responsibility.

It had been observed at the control tower that *something* had fallen from the plane, but what? Luckily, Ms. Kozak's call was relayed in the nick of time.

The pilot was radioed: "You've lost a wheel." The runway was quickly foamed, and the plane came down, a little jittery with one side wheel missing, but a decent landing nonetheless. A structural problem in the landing-gear assembly was the reason put forward for the malfunction. Poor maintenance or a design fault? There would undoubtedly be an official investigation.

The falling wheel itself, a rubber tire just a little larger and fatter than an ordinary automobile tire, achieved enormous velocity during its brief descent; the *plummeting* wheel (in the words of the six-o'clock newscaster) fell like a *speeding bullet* through the roof of a west-side apartment building, punching its way through asphalt roofing, layers of vapor barrier, wooden supports, insulation, ceiling plaster—and into the kitchen of a fifth-floor apartment, where it wedged between a small apartment-sized refrigerator and a cupboard.

The tenant (Richard McLeod, sixty-six, retired) was standing four feet away in a small hallway, removing his overcoat, having just returned from the funeral of an old friend. He was shaken by the incident but uninjured. His photograph, which appeared in the evening paper, showed the dazed, childlike face of an earthquake survivor.

"What was your first thought, Mr. McLeod, when you saw the wheel coming through your ceiling?" This was the question put to him by the six-o'clock-news team.

There was a pause. He blinked twice. A microphone was pushed directly in front of his mouth, ready to catch whatever might spill out. "What did I think?" he said quietly. "Nothing, and everything. I suppose I thought that the world had come to an end. And I had no one to tell."

SOMETIME LATER that same evening, about nine or ten o'clock, Richard McLeod phoned his wife, Peggy, out of the blue and asked if he might come home.

Tom, when he was told of this phone call, couldn't imagine what words Richard McLeod had found or how they were strung together. Even harder to imagine was his tone of voice. Was it stricken? Remorseful? Resigned? Frightened?

"Yes," said Peggy McLeod, who by this time had seen the television report and read the newspaper coverage, "come home." Or words to that effect.

"I'm sure she didn't hesitate for a minute," Fay said to Tom.

He watched her closely. "How can you be so sure?"

"I just know her," Fay said.

"It seems impossible that they can—that they can live together again, after all that's happened."

"I know," Fay said, and looked directly into Tom's face.

The airplane incident took place on a Monday. By that time he and Fay had been married for three days. Seventy-two hours. Wedded. Husband and wife.

HE'D COME HOME from the station the previous Friday at six o'clock on a cold, dark winter's morning. He'd climbed the three flights of stairs wearily and found her curled on the floor in front of his apartment door, sleeping.

Driving home, his gas line had frozen. He sat for a few minutes in the stalled car, staring through the fogged windshield, listening to the wind hammering the side of the car, too tired even to curse. The temperature was thirty-five degrees below zero and dropping; Pembina Highway, deserted in the early-morning hours, was streaked by bluish sodium lamps. He felt immobilized with dread and exhaustion but managed, finally, to shake off his inertia, phone a tow truck, and get a taxi to drive him home.

He almost fell over her, this shapeless thing blocking his way— the light on the landing was nothing more than a dim red exit sign. He'd reached down and encountered the surprise of hummocky fur—old, musty-smelling fur. Some instinct made him draw back. A creature who'd wandered in from the cold. A large rumpled warmly breathing creature, asleep in his doorway. He knelt to investigate.

Fay.

"Tom," she said, opening her eyes. "It's me. I've been waiting for you."

"THE STATE OF matrimony is a state ennobled and enriched by a long and honorable tradition of love and devotion."

Tom and Fay stood in a downtown courtroom not much larger than Fay's living room. The ceiling, though, was exceptionally high, so that the room formed a kind of square box, whose walls were painted a sobering legal green. The Marriage Commissioner— hurriedly called in—was a woman of about sixty (Tom guessed) whose crisp permed hair and beige wool cardigan put him in mind of his mother.

"There is a desire for a lifelong companionship," she pronounced, reading from a rather worn photocopied sheet and shifting her weight from one hip to the other, "and a generous sharing of the help and comfort that husband and wife ought to have for one another through whatever circumstances."

Tom caught Fay's eye and held it.

"Marriage is not to be entered into lightly, but with certainty, mutual respect, and a sense of reverence."

It was Friday afternoon. They had come alone, just the two of them. This was the way they wanted it. Two women from the secretarial staff had volunteered to serve as witnesses for the brief ceremony.

"Marriage symbolizes the ultimate intimacy between man and

woman, and is based on love, which is the most elusive of human bonds."

A civil ceremony, this was called, yet it was emblazoned with hope-filled poetry—and mystery: *the most elusive of human bonds.*

"Do you undertake to afford to this woman the love of your person, the comfort of your companionship, and the patience of your understanding?"

"I do," he said.

Then turning to Fay, "And do you undertake to afford to this man the love of your person, the comfort of your companionship, and the patience of your understanding?"

"I do," Fay said, her eyes stern.

Fumblingly, they exchanged rings.

These rings they had picked up at the last minute from Greening's Jewelers on Graham Avenue. ("I tried to phone you a couple of weeks ago," the jeweler said rather crossly, "to tell you they were ready.") The date engraved on the inside of the two rings could be changed later, but there would be a small charge, of course.

"And thereto I pledge you my troth," Fay said. He could tell she loved that word "troth," she said it so lingeringly, its long *o* sound.

"That's it," the Marriage Commissioner announced, folding her creased text in quarters and slipping it into her zippered bag.

Tom turned and looked at the two witnesses, who were now bent over, signing the marriage record; their expressions were placid but unreadable, and the thought came to him that they must have seen hundreds of such ceremonies and that for them there could be scarcely a flicker of meaning left behind the ritualized phrases.

Homilies. Questions and answers. Promises. And a groping after definition—mere words, elusive words. He had pronounced them before, but today they came toward him newly minted.

Fay was signing the record now, her large, careful script unrolling. He watched her wrist move across the paper and wondered if the moment had filled up for her as it had for him.

"We did it," he said, taking her arm.

"Yes," she answered.

"HONEYMOON" IS A WORD that's been out of favor for a long time, too honeyed or too moony, Tom supposes, and too weighted with old-fashioned notions of innocence. And yet, it is a word he loves.

"And where did you and your wife go on your honeymoon?" he imagines some improbable stranger asking in the course of an improbable, fast-forwarded future.

Well now, that's a long story. No, not a long story, hardly a story at all—at least, not a story worth telling. They stayed in Tom's apartment. The wind raged around them for two long days and nights. The Saturday following their wedding was the coldest twenty-four-hour period ever recorded in the region, and the gas furnace in the Grosvenor Avenue building never shut off once, not for one second; it burned and burned, trying to keep pace with the unprecedented cold. (More fuel was consumed in the city on that day than ever before. They heard this later.)

They made a few necessary telephone calls announcing their new state and then unplugged the phone. In the cupboards Tom found cans of soup, also tomato sauce, salmon, sardines, some rice, macaroni, a box of crackers, a packet of dry-roasted peanuts, corn oil, salt and pepper, a box of cornflakes which he roasted back to freshness in a hot oven, instant coffee, tea bags, a jar of raspberry jam, a plastic tub of honey. These discoveries brought him little jolts of happiness. There was no need to venture out-of-doors. The windows were completely frosted over. He and Fay were survivors on an opaque island, their own earth and sky, shut off from the noise of the world, warm and fed, sufficient unto themselves.

And that, Tom would say, if asked—that was our honeymoon.

DURING THOSE PERIODS when his life was going badly, he'd sometimes felt himself elected to undergo a series of disappointments. It seemed he was helpless to contravene the approach of difficulty, and he'd found it painful to reconcile himself to this idea—that a quirky fate had penciled him in for failure. It was unfair, it was undeserved—he knew this—and it was frightening.

He imagines that Richard McLeod's near-collision with the wheel of an aircraft carried the same overwhelming incomprehension. There were, after all, hundreds of other rooftops where the wheel might have fallen, thousands of back yards, parking lots, and roadways. But it was one particular roof that was pierced— his; his refuge that was invaded.

Even those who have been wedded all their lives to a rational stance and who are daily witnesses to the randomness of events, even they are required to respond to damage as accurately aimed as this. Why me? is the traditional cry. A weak, lonely sound.

And in the silence that follows there is an instinct that sends the victims scurrying blindly toward safety, toward home, toward an innocence of vision they thought they'd left behind.

Home. That's where Tom feels himself to be. He's been away for a long time, and now at last he's home.

IT'S CALL-IN TIME down at CHOL, the last call-in show Tom will ever do.

Out of the blue, Big Bruce has offered him the driving-home show (4:00 to 6:00 p.m., five days a week). Siggy Thorvaldson, who's hosted the show all these years, is up for retirement, and anyway, the slot needs some brightening up (that certain Avery touch, is how Big Bruce put it). Tom's thought it over and he's decided to go with it; he'll start next week. There's no doubt about it, he'll miss "Niteline," but it's time for a change, he's decided— time to see what the world looks like in the mellow late afternoon.

Tonight's question: What can you do to help keep the earth green?

The first caller speaks in a sweetly cracked, no-nonsense contralto: "Baking soda. Get your listeners going on baking soda, Tom. Bicarbonate of soda. Sprinkle a little on your kitchen sink, on your bathroom fixtures, whatever, and just wipe clean. It's natural, it's pure, it runs straight down the drain and back into the earth."

"Hey," the second caller says, "Wally Badarou's the man to keep us green. How about playing a little Badarou tonight instead of all that folky goop you've been dishing up lately. My favorite's a piece called 'Rain.' "

A man calls in and says: "Ban snow blowers. They're noisy and they use up precious fuel, and they blow snow all over your neighbor's driveway. I got a fella next door that I sure hope is listening in tonight."

A woman says: "I plan to cut the shoulder pads out of all my blouses and dresses and load them on a barge and dump them in Lake Winnipeg, creating a tidal wave which I'm told can be harnessed to provide electric power to the entire region."

"I like to chant a couple of lines of poetry into the ozone layer every day or so," another caller says. "That's my contribution."

"You know what?" the final caller says. "We've got to get back to neighborliness. We've lost it. Saying good morning to each other? Saying how do you do, how are you feeling, how's the world treating you? Recycling plastic bags is peanuts, ditto with phosphate-free detergent. We're always hollering these days about the infrastructure of our cities, but love's got an infrastructure, too. Love your neighbor, let him love you back a little. Love's the greenest stuff going. Let's hear it for love."

Fay

RATIONALISTS WHO SEEK TO DISABUSE THE WORLD OF ITS MYTHOLOGY have suggested that mermaids sighted by seamen in the days of yore were, in reality, small aquatic mammals known as manatees, or their cousins, the dugongs. These curious, rather ugly creatures have no hind limbs but possess forelimbs which are small fingerless flippers. The female occasionally uses these flippers to clasp her young to her breast. Manatees and dugongs (both of which belong to the order Sirenia) are able to remain submerged for about a quarter of an hour at a time. They are covered with short bristly hair and frequently live in small family groups. Fay has examined photographs of these animals and finds that, in fact, there is little resemblance between them and the mermaids of legend and art. She is much more willing to put mermaid sightings down to a three-cornered mixture of ocean mist, sailor's rum, and profound spiritual hunger—a combination capable of producing a vivid optical illusion. Allurements. Immensities.

She knows how persuasive optical illusions can be, recalling how witnesses, observing the airplane wheel that hurtled toward the building where her father was living, swore that the object appeared to "float" in the sky, drifting in an almost leisurely manner toward its destination. ("A deus ex machina," she remembers saying to Tom at the time, and then, reading his baffled face, waved her hands, mumbling, "An act of God, something like that." Whatever it was, it brought her father to his senses—or so she believes— a violent electric shock, a jolt to his mortality.)

In the days before she married Tom Avery there came to her a vision (a vision whose colors kept fading and threatening to disappear) of how it might feel actually to be a mermaid, adrift in cold sea foam and endlessly circling the confused wreckage of floating timbers and drowned, scattered human bodies, her pale hair painted the same translucent blue as her element.

It seemed to Fay, who judged herself harshly during that disordered period, that the traditional mermaid was her spiritual sister—plaintive, coy, and greedy. Her shimmering frontality, taunting mouth, phosphorescent torso, and thrusting tail—these bodily parts gave off the fishy perfume of ambiguity. Above this salty scene rose a wan yellow moon whose paleness announced a troubling imbalance: the conjoined life and its unscrolled intimacies were weighed against a singular satisfaction, and found wanting—too full of domestic spoilage and cluttered history, too burdened with risk and danger. To love or not to love; it was not a proposition but a subtle threat, although the yield in terms of happiness or sorrow came to the same thing. (She hadn't counted on the particularity of desire—on Tom's midnight voice, the remembered covering of flesh across his back—or on how the blessings and admonitions of the bereft—Onion in particular—would drive her beyond her stumbling abstractions.)

"We've rethought the situation," Tom told friends and family in the weeks that followed, and before long this became the official version, as opposed to the unspoken account, based on the careful apportioning of pain. (Love renewed is not precisely love redeemed, and Fay seems less able than Tom to chase that thought away; she is, after all, a woman who sees life in symbolic images, and the image she will never be able to absorb completely is that of herself, an exhausted, desperate, aberrant creature, slumped in Tom's doorway, pleading for admission.)

The suddenness of the married state, so dense and layered with detail, so thick with contingency, so open to intrusion and minor vibrations, so different from the finished and mannered and well-rehearsed marriages of others, drove her at times, especially in the early years, back to her old habits of solitary Saturday-afternoon walks, and also to lingering on weekdays an extra quarter-hour in her office before turning out the lights for the day. She still has the Leonardo da Vinci quote taped over her desk, "Art lives from constraints and dies from freedom," and she wonders if these words might apply equally to love.

She loves driving home (she's bought herself a little Toyota, bright green), and as she moves along in traffic she tunes in to CHOL, and is unfailingly surprised at the buzz of heat that Tom's voice brings on. She prizes his on-air self, his else and his other—his absence, in fact—and wonders if other people come to depend on this currency of separation.

She observes her parents, who appear to have aligned themselves around something edgy and uncomfortable—she's not sure what that something is but believes it is more than a fear of being alone. Her father refers (very occasionally) to his "spell of madness," and her mother, speaking ironically of the same period, uses the word "vacation." Neither of them has changed noticeably, except that they are getting older, more forgetful, more easily rattled.

They both arrive, a little late and out of breath, for the launching of Fay's book, *Mermaids of the Inner Mind*. Tom is there, too, beaming, but with a look of bafflement clouding his face (Fay has come to understand, and to accept, more or less, that he will always be a man who is puzzled by life's offerings). And Muriel Brewmaster is there, and Clyde and Sonya McLeod, also Bibbi and Jake Greary (whose post-Lithuanian posture is kinder and gentler) and their infant son, Tyler, in a sling around Bibbi's neck, and Iris and Mac Jaffe, and a rather frail-looking Onion Boyle (to whom Fay's book is dedicated). About a hundred and fifty others crowd into the brightly lit reception room at the folklore center, where they drink champagne and nibble a variety of small sandwiches and cakes and listen to Fay read a brief passage from Chapter One.

She is on the whole happy with the book, which has followed a surprisingly straightforward Jungian path. The rising of the female figure from the sea, she has concluded, represents the emergence of the anima from the unconscious. This anima is imprinted on the brain, and thus, those who claim to have seen mermaids have indeed done so, since the brain will, when the psyche is in upheaval and poised for change, project the images of the unconscious.

There are twenty chapters of explication, some glorious photographs, and thick, rich webs of footnotes and appendices. The cover (in shiny reds, blues, and greens) shows a mermaid surfacing from a wavy stretch of sea water. Her face is blurred. Her abundant hair gestures toward sexual potential. In one of her hands is a comb, representing love and entanglement.

The other hand, which is uplifted (waving or perhaps beckoning), symbolizes a deep longing for completion, the wish for rapturous union, a hunger for the food of love.

Carol Shields

Mary Swann

'A brilliant literary mystery. Read it'   *Independent on Sunday*

'One of the best novels I have read this year. It's deft, funny, poignant, surprising, and beautifully shaped'   Margaret Atwood

Mary Swann, a latter-day Emily Dickinson, submitted a paper bag full of poems to newspaper editor Frederic Cruzzi mere hours before her husband hacked her to pieces. How could someone who led such a dull, sheltered life produce these works of genius? Four very different people search for the elusive answer in this teasing, inventive and beautiful narrative . . .

'A very good novel , alive in every sense: formally ingenious and inventive, strikingly evocative of place, of character, of the world of things, capable of both comedy and tenderness, and above all beautifully written'   *London Review of Books*

'Clearly the work of an experienced and skilful writer . . . This is not only a first rate read, it is also sophisticated and ingeniously crafted'   *Listener*

flamingo

Carol Shields

Happenstance

'The biggest pleasure remains Shields' prose, at once dense and delicate. Her great strength is her ability to capture small moments and make them important . . . Shields displays in her careful delineation of her characters a tenderness for the ordinary which shines through the sheer cleverness of her work.' *Literary Review*

'A celebration of marriage as historical accident, *Happenstance* makes a delightful portrait of a partnership, full of quirky humour.' *The Times*

'The beautiful irony of *Happenstance* is that its novels are both bound together and held apart by the strength of the marriage they describe.' *Harpers & Queen*

'I highly recommend *Happenstance*. Both stories are funny – but compassionately so. Crucially, Carol Shields allows all the characters dignity. This is a tender, lovely book, about people who need each other. It is also superbly told.' *Marie Claire*

'With dazzling deftness Shields demonstrates the alienation innate in the most loving relationships . . . *Happenstance* is a remarkable, perceptive and painfully accurate work that yields more with each reading.' *Sunday Times*

flamingo

E. Annie Proulx

Postcards

'The richness of America is portrayed with memorable effect in this remarkable first novel – Faulkner springs to mind. *Postcards* is written from the heart and – for its raspy dialogue, laconic humour and beautiful description of the natural world – deserves to be widely read.'
Independent on Sunday

Postcards is the story of Loyal Blood, a man who spends a lifetime on the run from a crime so terrible that it renders him forever incapable of touching a woman. The odyssey begins on a freezing Vermont hillside in 1944 and propels Blood across the American West for forty years. Denied love and unable to settle, he lives a hundred different lives: mining gold, growing beans, hunting fossils, trapping, prospecting for uranium and ranching. His only contact with his past is through a series of postcards he sends home – not realising that in his absence disaster has befallen his family, and their deep-rooted connection with the land has been severed with devastating consequences . . .

'*Postcards* is a remarkable novel: poetic and yet driven by a strong narrative, tragic and yet scored with deep veins of humour. Loyal Blood is one of those rare, haunted characters who continue to live in the mind after you finish the book. *Postcards* is told in a fulsome and resonant prose that both soars and gets down in the dirt – a début which should be read by anyone who values fine, honest writing.'
Literary Review

■ *flamingo*

Amy Tan

The Hundred Secret Senses

Olivia Yee is only five years old when Kwan, her older sister from China, comes to live with the family and turns her life upside down, bombarding her day and night with ghostly stories of strange ancestors from the world of Yin. Olivia just wants to lead a normal American life.

For the next thirty years, Olivia endures visits from Kwan and her ghosts, who appear in the living world to offer advice on everything from restaurants to Olivia's failed marriage. But just when she cannot bear it any more, the revelations of a tragic family secret finally open her mind to the startling truths hidden in Kwan's unorthodox vision of the world.

'Kwan emerges as a splendidly vital comic character...and her sensibility – call it superstitious and crazy, or call it colourfully imaginative and indicative of a proper respect for the past – pervades every part of this highly enjoyable novel.'
LUCY HUGHES HALLETT, *Sunday Times*

'The story works like a dream...and the novel is most compelling and alive when the two sisters are sparring and squabbling. Tan has a great ear for feminine chitchat, its spikiness and hilarity, its mockery and teasing.'
MICHELE ROBERTS, *Independent*

'Resist the temptation to feast on this latest offering from Amy Tan in one voracious sitting – instead, savour it, slow time. Tan's writing rolls along effortlessly, like the best-told folklore – it's simply mesmerising.' *Elle*

Available in paperback £6.99

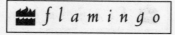

Jane Smiley

A Thousand Acres

Winner of the Pulitzer Prize for Fiction
and the
US National Book Critics' Circle Award

Larry Cook's farm is the largest in Zebulon County, Iowa, and a tribute to his hard work and single-mindedness. Proud and possessive, his sudden decision to retire and hand over the farm to his three daughters, is disarmingly uncharacteristic. Ginny and Rose, the two eldest, are startled yet eager to accept, but Caroline, the youngest daughter, has misgivings. Immediately, her father cuts her out.

In *A Thousand Acres* Jane Smiley transposes the *King Lear* story to the modern day, and in so doing at once illuminates Shakespeare's original and subtly transforms it.

'*A Thousand Acres* is a strong, gnarled shocker of a novel . . . superb. Its success is down to Smiley's ambitious gusto, her intuitive handling of the relationship between character and landscape, and her willingness to haul genuine moral freight across the panorama she has so expertly painted.'   *Sunday Times*

'*A Thousand Acres* is a superlative, extraordinary, amazing new novel . . . a great American tragedy about the failure of a family's land and the failure of its love. There may have been better novels than *A Thousand Acres*, but I fear I didn't read them . . . a haunting inquisition into the decline and fall of a family.'   Anthony Quinn, *Observer*

'Her singular gift is the grace with which she can move up through the literary gears to imbue her long, gripping, multi-layered narrative with real grandeur and moral seriousness. The novel's emotional power comes from the accretion of piercingly good small things.'   *Independent on Sunday*

flamingo

Suzannah Dunn

Venus Flaring

'Suzannah Dunn is a gifted writer'   *The Times*

Ornella and Veronica are the very best of friends, inseparable throughout the trials and minute details of their lives, sharing everything, hiding nothing. They grow up and find their way into the world together – Ornella, flamboyant and domineering, becomes a doctor, Veronica, observant and self-possessed, a journalist. But then something goes horribly wrong between them, and what was once the truest of friendships disintegrates into an obsessive nightmare of smouldering resentment that can barely be controlled. As Ornella's loyalty fades, Veronica's desperate need for reconciliation becomes a matter of life and death – and if you can't trust your best friend with your life, then who can you trust?

In prose that soars and fizzes with startling truths, Suzannah Dunn has created a deliciously disturbing and stylishly compelling tale of loyalty, love, memory, obsession and ultimate betrayal.

'Dunn writes with a warm attentive style which makes her characters compellingly real.'   *Time Out*

'Suzannah Dunn writes in loaded and knowing prose, like a hip Edna O'Brien or Muriel Spark in a gymslip.'
                                               Glasgow Herald

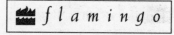

Dorothy Allison

Bastard Out of Carolina

'Resonant, emotionally complex and strong as hell'
Mary Gaitskill, author of *Bad Behaviour*

'Compulsively readable, *Bastard Out of Carolina* is filled with juicy writing and full-blooded characters. Alison can make an ordinary moment transcendent with her sensuous mix of kitchen-sink realism and down-home drawl'   *San Francisco Chronicle*

This astonishing first novel tells the story of the Boatwrights of Greenville County, South Carolina, a 'white-trash' family of hard-drinking men and indomitable women. Proudest of them all is Anney's illegitimate daughter, Ruth Anne, known as Bone. With little hope of employment beyond the textile mills and roadside diners, Bone dreams of a life not only away from Greenville but also far away from Daddy Glen, her stepfather, whose sly coldness and dangerous fury will test the love of them all.

Written in a mesmerizing voice that mingles the languid rhythms of country music with raw, unsparing descriptions of emotional and physical violence, *Bastard Out of Carolina* marks the emergence of an extraordinarily gifted writer.

'*Bastard*'s success is in its emotional precision and irrepressible lyricism, forcefully combined. Allison relates the difficulty of Bone's struggles with intensity and humour . . . An irresistible cast of characters, Allison renders their every look and touch with absolute precision and discernment'
San Francisco Review of Books

Penelope Fitzgerald

The Blue Flower

'A novel in which the unsaid speaks; it is a masterpiece.'

CANDIA MCWILLIAM

'A masterpiece. How does she do it?'

A.S. BYATT

'A magical little book.'

DORIS LESSING

The Blue Flower is set in the small provincial and university towns between Leipzig and Berlin at the very end of the eighteenth century. It tells the story of the young and brilliant Fritz von Hardenberg, a graduate of the Universities of Jena, Leipzig and Wittenberg, learned in Dialectics and Mathematics, who later became the great romantic poet and philosopher Novalis. The passionate and idealistic Fritz needs his father's permission to announce his engagement to his 'heart's heart', his 'true Philosophy', the embodiment of all his yearnings, twelve-year-old Sophie von Kühn. It is a betrothal which amuses, astounds and disturbs his family and friends. How can it be so?

'*The Blue Flower* is an enchanting novel about heart, body and mind. The writing is elliptical and witty. . . so what could be a sad little love story is constantly funny and always absorbing with a cast of characters both endearing and amusing. This novel is a jewel.'

CARMEN CALLIL, *Daily Telegraph*

'Her sense of time and place is marvellously deft, done in a few words. She knows how they all walked, eased their old joints, she knows the damp smell of decay of the ancient schlosses. In a bare little book she reveals a country and an age as lost as Tolstoy's Russia and which we seem always to have known.'

JANE GARDAM, *Spectator*

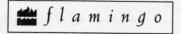